Lynne Graham was born in Northern Ireland and has been a keen romance reader since her teens. She is very happily married, to an understanding husband who has learned to cook since she started to write! Her five children keep her on her toes. She has a very larr, a very small . When time al

Lorraine Hal writer. She wa head in the cl out, is the perfect combination for spending her days creating thunderous alpha heroes and the fierce, determined heroines who win their hearts. She lives in a potentially haunted house with her soulmate and a rumbustious band of hermits in training. When she's not writing romance, she's reading it.

CONVENIENTLY ARRANGED

LYNNE GRAHAM

LORRAINE HALL

MILLS & BOON

First published in Great Britain 2025
by Mills & Boon, an imprint of HarperCollins*Publishers* Ltd,
1 London Bridge Street, London, SE1 9GF

www.harpercollins.co.uk

HarperCollins*Publishers*, Macken House, 39/40 Mayor Street Upper,
Dublin 1, D01 C9W8, Ireland

Conveniently Arranged © 2025 Harlequin Enterprises ULC

His Royal Bride Replacement © 2025 Lynne Graham

A Wedding Between Enemies © 2025 Lorraine Hall

ISBN: 978-0-263-34462-2

05/25

MIX
Paper | Supporting
responsible forestry
FSC™ C007454

This book contains FSC™ certified paper
and other controlled sources to ensure responsible forest management.

For more information visit www.harpercollins.co.uk/green.

Printed and Bound in the UK using 100% Renewable Electricity
at CPI Group (UK) Ltd, Croydon, CR0 4YY

HIS ROYAL BRIDE REPLACEMENT

LYNNE GRAHAM

MILLS & BOON

CHAPTER ONE

PRINCE ALESSIO MARCHETTI strode out of his private apartments in the Sedovian palace. Six feet four inches tall, he had a shock of unruly long black hair that brushed his shoulders and bright green eyes set into a lean, sculpted face. A tiny gold hoop gleamed in one ear while the hint of a tattoo showed below the edge of a pristine shirt cuff. Impeccably dressed though he was, in a Brioni suit complete with monogrammed cufflinks, there were hints that he was not as conservative as he might appear at first glance.

Alessio slid fluidly into the luxury car awaiting him in the courtyard. His security team, all of them in a dour mood at the prospect of policing him in a public place, where anything might happen, swung into two far less noticeable vehicles to follow him down the hill into the city of Severino.

It was a sunny, early summer day and the air was crisp and clean. Alessio braked to avoid the morning parade ground activities of the household guard out front before angling the car deftly over the bridge that led down into the town. Picturesque as any postcard with colourful window boxes and quaint, narrow buildings with steep roofs, the streets were busy.

Tourist numbers were down though, because many of their country's visitors had picked their holiday dates to coincide with Alessio's wedding and its accompanying festivities, which were due to take place in two weeks' time. The wedding would soon be followed by an equally grand coronation at which Alessio would ascend the throne, alongside his future consort, Princess Graziana of Eboltz, an island nation off the coast of Sedovia.

Alessio, meanwhile, was dreading the wedding with every fibre of his being. He was almost twenty-eight years old and he had always known he would have to marry young. He could not become king until he was married and in a position to provide an heir. It was just Graziana…a perfectly nice woman, he reminded himself, who he had known since he was ten, although they had not met that often during their childhood and neither of them had sought each other out as adults.

Sadly, Graziana had no sense of humour, he reflected uneasily. She was also short-tempered with the staff and given to childish tantrums if challenged, but he could handle that, he hastily assured himself. It would be a modern-day marriage of convenience. Just like his parents, they would marry, eventually produce a royal heir and then discreetly go their separate ways, duty done. It had worked for his parents, although they had pretty much hated each other and had not been much keener on their single offspring, no matter how hard Alessio had tried to impress and please.

A vague memory of gathering flowers for his mother assailed him. She had thrust them away in absolute horror lest the pollen from the stamens stain her dress. He had been punished for that gift, just as he had been punished for sneaking into his father's study to tell him that he had won a prize in mathematics only to discover that his parent was entertaining a half-naked woman in there.

No, neither of his parents had liked him much. He had been both a necessity and an inconvenience to them. Neither of them had enjoyed the intrusion of a noisy little boy in their sophisticated, separate households. And they hadn't warmed to him any better when he'd tried to be quiet and studious instead. That he had gone off the rails as a teenager had been almost inevitable. Hence the long hair, the tattoos, the earring, the ultra-defiance of the adolescent years. His reputation as an international playboy had, for a handful of years, been equally stellar. His mother had rolled her eyes in bored disgust, his father had laughed and advised him to visit exclusive brothels where the women were rather more discreet.

Alessio had learned the hard way that he wasn't and never would be a loved son. And that was why he wanted a family of his own—because he had never had a family as such. He would create a family with Graziana and love them and *her*. He had to learn *how* to love her to make the family unit secure and happy. It had disappointed him when Graziana had laughed at the idea that love could eventually grow between them.

'Don't be naïve,' she had quipped with sneering amusement. 'People *like us* aren't expected to experience feelings like that.'

He drove down the street and double-parked under the combined gaze of a flock of tourists and the whirring, clicking cameras of the waiting paparazzi. Before he could climb out of the car, his newspaper arrived courtesy of a curvaceous blonde. Accepting it, he thanked her, deftly ignoring the card she gave him with the paper. At his final stop, he just about made it out of the car to collect his coffee from the beautiful brunette already awaiting him on the pavement. He had only once made it into the café to buy his own but that had been embarrassing because in spite of his protests everyone in the queue had been neglected while he'd been served ahead of them.

Unfortunately, Alessio's PR team ruled his schedule. Despite his regular participation in red-carpet ceremonial and charitable events, the team had decided that he was not being sufficiently visible to the general populace, hence his now well-known coffee and paper trips into town once a week. He hoped that they had already worked out that his future consort would never agree to do something so beneath her dignity. Graziana was very conscious of her lofty royal birthright and status. Even so, she would have to learn to take a genuine interest in their people. Above all, the small country of Sedovia on the edge of the Mediterranean was known as a friendly, relaxed place and Alessio was proud of that reputation.

'Catch you later!' Rosy told her sister, Vittoria, who was freshening up the floral arrangements on the veranda that fronted the hotel. Vittoria's husband, Patrick, was up a ladder repairing a shutter. With the royal wedding approaching and a bunch of guests due to arrive, it was all hands on deck to ensure that the hotel was spruced up to perfection.

'Have a good day,' her sibling shouted cheerfully as Rosy set off on her ancient bike to work.

As Rosy filtered into the busy traffic, she was thinking of how very gutsy Vittoria and Patrick were. They had dealt with their financial problems and now, relieved that their finances appeared to finally be on the road to recovery, they were working round the clock and making the best of every moment of their move to Sedovia. The Cathedral View Hotel—Vista Cattedrale in Italian—was unsurprisingly an eighteenth-century building directly opposite the cathedral where the royal wedding was to take place in a couple of weeks. The previous year, Vittoria and Patrick had bought the aging hotel at a knockdown price online and had spent a small fortune renovating it to a very high level of comfort.

Unfortunately, Vittoria and Patrick had required a big bank loan to finance the improvements and, over the winter, when they had fallen behind on the payments, the bank had threatened to repossess the hotel. Only the truth that the hotel had been fully booked since the spring had staved the bank off and had ensured that the regular repayments continued without any further problems. But it was still a precarious way to live, Rosy reflected ruefully, and wholly dependent on the number of guests keen to have a bird's-eye view of the stupid royal wedding from the balconies attached to their rooms. Heavens, right now the wedding was all *anyone* could talk about and it had been like that for *months*!

Perhaps the problem was that Rosy wasn't quite as patriotic and royalist about Sedovia as the locals. She had grown up in London with her Sedovian father, Franco Castelli, and her half-sister, Vittoria. Italian had been her first language and, while she had always hoped to visit Sedovia, she hadn't ever planned to actually make her home there. No, that had long been her sister's dream, not Rosy's.

Even so, there was nothing that Rosy wouldn't do to make Vittoria happy. Over twenty years her senior, Vittoria had virtually raised Rosy from birth. Poor Vittoria hadn't had much choice about that with a workshy drunk of a father and a stepmother, Heather, who, having decided that motherhood and possibly Franco Castelli were not for her, had abandoned Rosy at the hospital.

Vittoria had stepped into the breach like the trooper she was and to all intents and purposes, as she'd taken on the role of a single parent, she had become the only mother that Rosy had ever known. And she was a terrific mum, not just to Rosy but to her own twin teenaged sons, Matteo and Elio. Rosy had been loved and supported through every year of her childhood, by both Vittoria and her brother-in-law, Patrick, who called her the daughter that he would never have, she recalled fondly, for the couple had recently given up hope of ever having another child of their own.

As the traffic ground to a halt, Rosy looked ahead

and groaned out loud before uttering a very rude word below her breath. It was that idiot prince snarling up the morning traffic again, utterly ignoring the fact that most people were trying to get to work. Why on earth did His Royal Highness Prince Alessio Marchetti insist on causing a traffic jam at least once a week by fetching himself a coffee and a newspaper from town? As if he couldn't have both brought to him at his palace on the hill by one of his many minions! Good heavens, the guy had a staff of hundreds who would go to any lengths to ensure his comfort. The palace staff adored their prince and the entire palace revolved around him. Rosy knew all about it because she worked at the palace too.

Aware her tetchy boss, Lucy Ragusa, would be hugely irritated if she was late, Rosy broke the Sedovian traffic rules and began to cut through the lanes of cars on her bike. She did so well that she managed to steer along the back of the locals and tourists vying to get a better view of their prince. Then, out of the crush and free, she stood up on her pedals and began to push up the steep hill to the palace, perspiration beading her brow below her sun hat because it demanded considerable physical effort.

Alessio swung onto the bridge and saw *her* and immediately hit the brakes. An irreverent grin slashed his lean, darkly handsome features. The best legs in the kingdom of Sedovia, potentially even the best female rear view in history, he reflected with wry amusement. She was clad in her usual denim shorts and vest top, standing up to steer her bone-rattler of a bike uphill. Sometimes she ducked the challenge and walked up the narrow footway wheeling the bike. He admired her persistence though, even if her efforts and slow progress slowed the Bugatti to a complete crawl. But then she never ever got out of his way and he liked that too; loved that she never looked back, never noticed him.

He had first noticed her about three months earlier and she seemed to arrive at the palace every morning around the same time. Obviously, she was a member of staff but he didn't know who she was or what she did and he wouldn't enquire because it would be inappropriate. She could be a gardener, a kitchen helper or a maid. Or an electrician, a mechanic or a plumber. The palace staff was gargantuan and covered every eventuality. Her job, however, was none of his business. He only knew that she wasn't one of his administrative staff or a member of the PR department.

And then even as he was watching a delivery van rounded the corner too fast and swung out, catching her bike with its bumper, and both bike and woman went flying, before landing in a sudden heap. Alessio swore and braked so hard that only his seat belt saved him from hitting the windscreen. He vaulted out of the car to go to her assistance without even thinking about it. Behind him a police siren went off, signifying an incident and only because *he* was present. Ignoring it and the security men hastening to his side, Alessio approached the fallen woman.

She sat up in the roadway, groaning in pain and swearing in English with admirable ferocity. *Eng-*

lish? Blood streaked her legs and one arm. Hair like a gorgeous crimson and copper sunset tumbled in pre-Raphaelite curling locks in a mass around her delicate, pointed face. He was staring, he knew he was staring, but he had never seen her face before or her hair and, stooping, he retrieved her sun hat and extended it to her.

'Let me get you out of here,' Alessio urged, aware that the paparazzi would be on them within minutes. A television helicopter was already circling noisily overhead. He turned to the security man next to him and said, 'Retrieve her bike so that the traffic can get moving again.'

A police officer was already interviewing the shaken van driver.

'Did you hit your head?'

'No,' she mumbled, scrubbing at the blood on one knee and wincing when it hurt before looking up at him, squinting in the sun.

Alessio saw the sunglasses that had fallen off her nose and lifted them to offer them back to her. *Madonna mia*, she was gorgeous, he thought abstractedly. Eyes with the depth and colour of amethysts set in a heart-shaped face, a soft pillowy pink mouth and skin as velvety smooth as a creamy lily petal.

Rosy was staring and she just kept on staring because she couldn't believe her eyes. She accepted the sunglasses even though one of the lenses had smashed. She could hardly put them on again like that and crammed them into a pocket instead. She breathed in slow and deep, striving to steady herself and accept that Ales-

sio Marchetti, the Crown Prince, well, the *only* Prince
of Sedovia, was crouching down beside her acting like
a good Samaritan. The intensity of the emerald-green
eyes locked to hers left her feeling oddly dizzy.

'Can you walk?' he asked as the hubbub around them
grew and cameras began to show in a sea of surrounding obtrusiveness.

'Of course, I can,' Rosy told him, grudgingly accepting the hand he extended and beginning to rise with his
help, only to stiffen and flinch as her ankle sent a jolt
of pain running up her leg. 'I think I must've turned
my ankle when I fell.'

Alessio stooped to lift her into his arms and slotted
her with care into the passenger seat of his car while
phone cameras operated and questions were hurled by
breathless journalists, who had raced up from around
the corner. He dropped her sun hat back onto her head
and she crammed it low, not wanting to look at anyone,
not wanting to be identified in such company. She was
too well aware that everything Alessio did and everyone he interacted with was of interest to his loyal public and of even greater interest to the media.

The policeman approached the car and spoke to
Alessio, who said that he would give a witness statement to the police later in the day, and at that news the
policeman retreated and stopped the traffic, making
some vehicles reverse while his companion cleared
the road so that Alessio could drive across the bridge
into the palace.

'What on earth are you doing?' she demanded.
'Where are you taking me?'

'Into the palace for treatment.'

'I use the employees' entrance.'

'Right now you can't walk and my office is within easier reach,' Alessio countered.

Rosy compressed her lips and gritted her teeth at having to respect that tone of authority. Ultimately, he was her employer, she reminded herself in exasperation. She might never have met him before but arguing wasn't a good idea.

'What's your name?' he enquired smoothly.

'Rosy... Rosy Castelli,' she said. 'Rosy short for Rosalia.'

He drew the powerful sports car to a halt on the cobbles and left the car as she struggled frantically to get the heavy passenger door open. 'Chill, Miss Castelli,' the Prince urged. 'The only cameras here are of the security variety.'

A little of her panic dissipating, Rosy winced as she clambered out, balancing on one foot and the door.

With a muttered imprecation, her companion swept her off her feet again and she trembled and gasped.

'Nervous little creature, aren't you?' he quipped. 'What do you think could happen to you here where we are surrounded by so many other people?'

Face as red as a tomato, Rosy glanced at his security team hovering, the faces under the portico of the staff all wide-eyed with wonderment at the scene that met their eyes. 'I don't like being the centre of so much attention,' she said truthfully.

Alessio sighed. 'Clearly there isn't much excitement round here if we're attracting this much interest,' he muttered, brushing past the bowing minions on the doorstep while ordering an ice pack and requesting that Dr Rossi be called to his office.

'There's a doctor on staff?' Rosy exclaimed in astonishment.

'Dr Rossi is the head librarian and also a doctor. He prefers books to doctoring but he's happy to help out in an emergency.'

'I'm *hardly* an emergency,' Rosy quibbled as he elbowed open a door off the giant echoing marble hall while the heat of him scorched the side of her body and the scent of him—ocean-fresh and clean with the merest hint of some woodsy cologne—flared her nostrils. 'A few bumps and scrapes.'

'*And* you'll be on crutches for at least a few days,' Alessio interposed drily as he laid her down with care on an opulent leather lounger.

'Nonsense!' Rosy protested as he dropped down into an athletic crouch beside her.

He was too close, way too close for comfort, those shimmering green eyes squarely locked onto her. Her breath was trapped in her throat, her heart speeding up and she felt, with a sinking heart, her breasts swell inside her top. 'Your ankle is already puffing up,' he pointed out, standing back as an ice pack complete with protective cloth was laid down beside her and he asked for a first-aid kit.

'I can do all this for myself,' Rosy objected shakily, shattered by the effect his proximity had had on her because she didn't ever react that way to men. Sure, he was good-looking, sure, he was the pin-up of Sedovia, indeed of Europe itself, but she wasn't the sort of woman who reacted physically to such a man…*was* she?

'Tea or coffee? What's your preference?' Alessio shot at her as she roasted like a pepper on a grill, mortification claiming her entirely. *Not* such a woman, she reminded herself, not the sort of woman who would compare his luminous eyes to jewels, who would notice the lush black lashes framing that stunning gaze and the warm intelligence etched there.

'Tea…' another voice interposed quietly. 'Sweet. Miss Castelli is in shock.'

Yes, she was in shock, Rosy conceded ruefully. The boss got too close and she got way too embarrassed. 'You know her, Aldo?' the Prince remarked in surprise, standing up with a friendly smile to greet the older man.

'Dr Rossi,' Rosy said awkwardly.

'Yes, she works with Lucy Ragusa.'

'Lucy's *still* around?' Alessio commented in surprise. 'I thought she would've been retired from the conservation department by now.'

'Lucy's job is her life,' the small, bespectacled doctor responded as he bent down to examine Rosy's ankle and asked her to perform a series of small movements, some of which caused her considerable pain. 'Clear the room, Alessio. Our patient doesn't need an audience.'

Rosy breathed a sigh of relief as some of the faces disappeared. Silence fell as the older man tended to her wounds and she closed her eyes tight against the discomfort of gravel being removed from her legs and arm while the icebag was wrapped round her ankle and the chill soothed some of the hot, throbbing discomfort.

'A sprain. Get the swelling down, prop it up and rest it for a few days and you'll be fine. There's bound to be a pair of crutches somewhere in the household. I'll take my leave, then,' the doctor announced and a door closed.

A cup of tea was eased into Rosy's hand. Involuntarily, her hand trembled and the cup was swiftly withdrawn again. As she opened her eyes, she could feel the hateful prickle of tears burning behind them and she sucked in a steadying breath.

Alessio towered over her, looking anxious, and then he sank down on the lounger beside her but still at least a foot away from her. 'It's normal to be upset. You almost had a very nasty accident and naturally you're in shock.'

Rosy snatched in a shuddering breath. If she cried in front of him, she would die.

'Breathe in, breathe out, slowly,' he advised stiffly.

Gently, carefully, she followed his advice, one breath in, one breath out.

'Shall I fetch Lucy?'

'Oh, heavens, no!' Rosy gasped in dismay, her tension reclaiming her at that prospect. 'She would think I'm making such a fuss and I'm late—'

'I'll ensure that Lucy is informed of the accident,' he hastened to assure her as he tugged a phone from his pocket. 'You are not physically capable of working today.'

'That's not true,' she protested.

'You won't be capable until you are off the crutches and able to walk again,' Alessio pointed out.

Rosy's pink lips down-curved at that reminder. It was horribly true. Her boss depended on her being able-bodied because Lucy Ragusa was *not*. Lucy got breathless just climbing the stairs and suffered from several health conditions. Unable to stand up easily, her arm bruised from smashing against the road surface and her whole body aching, Rosy knew that she herself would be incapable of even painting. A solitary tear escaped and rolled down her cheek.

'It's not the end of the world,' Alessio chided.

'It *is* to Lucy,' she contradicted ruefully. 'We're trying to finish the restoration of your great-grandfather's portrait for the tours that have been organised.'

Steeling himself against his innately sensitive nature, Alessio held himself back and pressed a tissue into her hand. 'Imagine a hug,' he murmured huskily. 'If I could give you one, I would. None of these things matter right now. What matters is that you are safe and you need to go home and rest... Where is home?'

Thoroughly disconcerted by the very concept of the future king of Sedovia giving her a hug, Rosy flushed and the desire to cry ebbed. She mentioned the hotel. 'I live there with my sister and her family,' she told him.

'My driver will convey you home.'

'Oh, but—'

'No buts. You go home and rest until you can walk again,' Alessio cut in.

With difficulty, Rosy snatched her gaze from the

black-lashed brilliance of his, her complexion warming again. 'Lucy will be *so*—'

'Ticked off but she'll get over it,' the Prince interposed as a knock sounded on the door.

A maid appeared carrying a set of crutches.

Alessio vaulted upright to collect them, relieved that the unchaperoned meeting was at an end. She was too beautiful. *Piccola volpe,* he had almost called her when she cried. Little fox, utterly inappropriate. He had wanted to comfort her but that would have been an even more questionable move. He wasn't married as yet but he might as well have been, he reflected wryly. 'My driver will take you home and I don't want to see you back at work until you're fully recovered,' he told her succinctly.

With his assistance, Rosy stood upright and anchored the crutches to use as support. The Prince escorted her back out to the echoing foyer of the palace and signalled a young man, who came running, and instructed him to take Rosy back to her home.

Alessio strode back into his office, got on his phone to their resident tech expert and asked for a full background report to be done on Rosalia Castelli. He had no intention of making enquiries through the palace's HR manager because that would ignite speculation. But there was no harm in satisfying his curiosity, he reasoned, and she was a mystery with her perfectly spoken Italian and her unexpectedly rich store of English curses, both accompanied by that edgy English accent catching on certain syllables.

Coffee was brought. He sipped, unwillingly reliving the accident. It had been a dangerous near miss. Rosy could've been badly hurt, could've ended up beneath *his* wheels. He breathed in deep. She might be supple, slender and strong in appearance, but her actual build was slight, petite and fragile. Luckily, she was bashed and bruised and nothing worse. And why was he still worrying about her? She would be fine. She lived with her family. They would look after her. His family had *never* looked after him, however…but the staff *had*. Only she didn't have staff. In a hotel though? Alessio stamped down hard on that inner flood of thoughts. He only knew that he had never wanted to give anyone a hug so badly…

'Are you sure that you can manage?' Vittoria checked.

'Yes, go away while I check these accounts,' Rosy urged, sitting back behind the desk, one ankle propped up on a stool. 'I'll be running around again by tomorrow. I'm feeling much better.'

'Don't overdo it,' her sister warned her anxiously.

But Rosy was coping, and she liked to keep a close eye on the account books. Vittoria was an experienced hotel manager, well, she had done two years in a tiny London hotel, and Patrick was a chef. Neither one of them was any good at maths and neither one of them was much good at sticking to a budget. It was Rosy's calculations that kept them on the straight and narrow. And in truth, the deeper she got into the books, the more she realised that those winter debts were still in there merely waiting to catch up with her sister and brother-in-law again. Only a fabulous summer season with a hotel crammed with high-spending guests would correct that before winter arrived along with the natural downturn in tourism.

Would she have agreed to throw her lot in with theirs had she known how challenging it would be? When their father had died and the house was left equally between the two sisters, Rosy had allowed her share to go in with her half-sister's share to enable the purchase of the hotel in Sedovia. Why? Well, she hadn't felt entitled to her share at all because that house had originally belonged to Vittoria's mother, only her sister had insisted. Of course that was pure Vittoria, always generous, but no sense with money whatsoever. And here was Patrick spending on extravagant stuff like truffles and lobster because he was determined to make the restaurant super successful to bring in extra customers.

Rosy sighed and laid down her calculator, her head aching. It had been a tough week but her ankle was almost better. She had helped on Reception and prepared vegetables in the kitchen for Patrick, but she hadn't been able-bodied enough to help with the bed changes or the laundry or the serving of meals and snacks. Vittoria was looking pale and stressed this week and she had been ill as well, even if, for some reason, she was keeping her apparently upset stomach a secret.

'You didn't get his autograph!' Vittoria had exclaimed in disappointment when she'd heard about her sister's actual face-to-face meeting with Prince Alessio. The Prince who was literally her sister's idol, the perfect guy. And lifting Rosy off her feet into his sports car when she was injured had only gilded his reputation.

'I don't think he gives those.'

'You don't seem impressed,' Vittoria had said in surprise.

'No, he *is* gorgeous,' Rosy had conceded, 'no doubts about that. His photos don't lie. And truthfully, he was much nicer and a lot less arrogant than I expected. He was kind and considerate but very polite and royally distant.'

'Naturally.' Vittoria had sighed. 'He's on the brink of marrying his princess...his childhood sweetheart.'

'I don't think I believe in that,' Rosy had admitted with cynicism. 'It's much more likely that their parents looked at them—Eboltz with a daughter and Sedovia with a son—and decided it would be perfect if they married and united the two countries. I mean, Eboltz is the size of a postage stamp, so why not?'

Vittoria had frowned. 'What about romance?'

Rosy had wrinkled her small, snub nose. 'It's my bet they're making the best of things. Both rich as sin, both very attractive, both royal heirs. And he's sown all his wild oats and presumably she has too.'

'There's never been an ounce of scandal about Princess Graziana. You're such a sceptic, Rosy,' her sibling had complained.

Rosy marvelled that she could even *be* cynical, growing up as she had on a diet of sweet cartoons and romantic movies and novels. But then, actual romance had never come her way. At school she had stayed flat as a board, skinny and undeveloped and unsought-after by boys. University, when she had been studying for her fine art degree in London, had not been much more promising. She had male friends but more of the 'good mates' variety.

She had yet to pin down what it took for a man to attract her. Men who had demonstrated interest in her had withered in receipt of her lack of interest. Yet the Prince had what it took to attract her in spades, which mortified her. She wasn't about to fangirl over him. That was only a physical thing, she reasoned uncomfortably, based on that long luxuriant hair, those stunning eyes of his and that very hot and seriously great physique he sported. If she hadn't found him attractive, she wouldn't be normal.

Alessio woke up the following morning to an unexpected text from Graziana, who was not in the habit of regular communication with him. Furthermore, the text had been sent in the middle of the night.

I'm sorry. I am so very sorry about this.

Alessio couldn't even imagine Graziana voicing such an apologetic sentiment. As a rule, she was self-contained and never ever humble. What on earth did she mean?

CHAPTER TWO

ROSY WALKED OUT onto the portrait gallery to double-check the state of the wall to which the now restored portrait of the Prince's great-grandfather would be returned when Lucy returned to work the next day.

Lucy Ragusa, her immediate boss, was a world-renowned art expert and restorer and, six months earlier, Rosy had been hired as her full-time assistant because the older woman had been unwell. Her failing eyesight was a not-so-secret secret within the small conservation department of the royal household. The job had been a golden opportunity for Rosy with the added benefit of receiving skilled training in her chosen field. She had learned so much in the past six months of working at the palace.

As she moved back towards the office she heard Prince Alessio's distinctive dark, deep drawl carrying up from the museum on the floor below and she came to a sudden halt. Without hesitation, she leant over the gallery balustrade and stole a look. She needed to thank him for having her bike repaired and returned to her, but she didn't want an audience. In truth her bike had had so much replaced and so much added it was like an entirely new bike.

Alessio stood below, black hair tousled, big wide shoulders encased in a khaki tee, faded fitted jeans sheathing his long strong legs. As he lounged back against a display table, soft fabric stretched across his taut abdominal muscles, her mouth ran suddenly dry. He shifted position, his powerful thighs flexing as someone unseen offered to fetch coffee and Rosy discovered that her eyes were locked to the Prince like superglue. With difficulty she shook her head and frowned at her distraction and headed straight for the stairs. He was within reach and alone and, according to his casual clothing, off duty. She would never get a better chance to thank him.

As she reached the museum doorway, she heard a raised voice and stepped back, staying out of sight.

'But this can't happen!' Alessio was ranting. 'It's not possible. The wedding *has* to go ahead. It can't be postponed or cancelled. Get her back, she's your daughter—

'What do you mean she's *already* married?' Alessio growled in audible disbelief.

Eyes wide with astonishment, Rosy grimaced on his behalf.

'No, there's nothing more you can do. But she could have told me herself. I apologise for raising my voice.' Moments afterwards, he tossed something down on the display case surface, probably, she surmised, his phone, the call clearly finished.

Silence fell and Rosy appeared in the doorway. In the act of raking long brown fingers through his black luxuriant hair, Alessio stilled to stare at her.

'How long have you been standing there?' he demanded curtly.

'I heard you on the phone and stepped back out of view,' Rosy admitted honestly. 'It didn't seem like the right moment to interrupt.'

'Then I must ask you not to repeat a word of what you may have overheard. In case you haven't guessed, the wedding of the century has tanked,' he murmured with sardonic bite.

'I couldn't repeat anything even if I wanted to. I had to sign an NDA my first day here,' Rosy pointed out. 'And I'm only here now because I wanted to thank you for having my bike picked up and repaired.'

'Your...bike?' Alessio repeated blankly.

'Yes, you had it repaired for me and I am grateful. You were kind to me that day.'

'I'm sorry. I'm not quite with you,' Alessio breathed in a raw undertone. 'I'm in shock.'

'Understandably, if the wedding's not going ahead.'

'It can't. My bride married her bodyguard last night and took off to New York with him,' Alessio spelt out flatly, studying her in the workmanlike overalls that only enhanced her tiny, slender frame, her bubbling vibrant curls restrained in a topknot arrangement. Not a scrap of make-up and still exquisite. Rosy, that was her name and it suited her. He still hadn't checked through that file on her background, had deliberately ignored it after his PA had asked him why he had asked for it in the first place. In fact, he had felt rather guilty and a little embarrassed for requesting that unnecessarily intrusive check.

'It sounds like you dodged a bullet,' Rosy whispered awkwardly.

'No, it's more like Graziana has exploded a bomb in my life...in this country...*and* in her own.'

'I'm so sorry.' Rosy began to back away as she heard the sound of steps approaching and reckoned his coffee was about to arrive.

Trying not to think about the shock news she had overheard, Rosy went back to work. Lucy was a perfectionist and had left a list of tasks to be accomplished during her absence, more than could be easily accomplished in the hours available. Of course, Rosy had had a week at home while her ankle recovered and undoubtedly her boss felt that she had to compensate for that time off. After all, everything and everybody within the Sedovian palace was gearing up towards the royal wedding. The wedding that wasn't going to happen now, she reflected, and then quickly suppressed the thought. Would the special tours of the palace, the museum and the art gallery even still go ahead? Right now, it felt as though the whole of Sedovia was preparing for the wedding. And now it wasn't going to happen...

Before she suppressed the feeling, a current of sympathy for the Prince filtered through her. He was being jilted and with minimal warning. He had been very much in shock. Rosy reckoned that the whole populace would go into shock when the news broke, as break it must very soon. Princess Graziana had seemed demure and dignified, not the type to throw her cap over a rainbow and run off with an employee, although Rosy had heard other rumours about Alessio's bride-to-be following her brief stays in the household. That she was very demanding and spoilt, prone to angry outbursts and definitely not a fan of Alessio's more casual approach to formality.

By the time Rosy was riding home on her bike, her mood was sombre. She was thinking of how a wedding cancellation would impact the family hotel and her heart sank. A lot of people had booked on a special royal wedding package that had chosen the Cathedral View Hotel as one of a small, exclusive selection for discerning guests. All those guests might well cancel now and Vittoria and Patrick's finances would sink without trace. There was nothing left in the kitty for rainy days. The rainy days fund had been used up last winter when guests had been few and the final renovation bills had come in even higher than expected. Rosy broke out in perspiration. The truth was that if the wedding failed to happen, her family's business would probably go bankrupt sooner rather than later.

Alessio didn't pause to speak to anyone on his impatient walk back to his private apartments. As he poured himself a whiskey, he told himself that nobody had foreseen the likelihood of Graziana's defection, he least of all. Graziana had never struck him as the impulsive, passionate type. Indeed, Alessio had found her quite averse to any sort of physical intimacy, which he could now better understand if she had been involved in a secret affair all along. Even so, the wedding arrangements had begun only six months earlier and she had insisted then that a marriage of convenience would be a perfect fit for her. In fact, *she* had been the one to float the idea of their marrying first.

'I'm not getting any younger,' she had said briskly. 'You need a wife and a child and you're only a couple of years younger than I am. It could work.'

And at the time, if Alessio was honest with himself, it had felt like the end of the world on his terms, because he hadn't felt ready for marriage, but he had also known that Graziana would probably be a very popular candidate. Everyone had been ecstatic when they'd announced their engagement. Graziana had also appeared fully involved in every tiny wedding detail. There had been no hint that there was anything amiss, except perhaps when she'd stepped back from him when he'd attempted once to close his arms round her and said, 'I'd prefer to wait for all that until we're married.' Not a problem, he had decided at the time, concluding that his future bride was just not a very physical person, refusing to allow his reflections to linger on what that disappointing discovery meant for him.

With the few facts he knew chasing revolving circles inside his brain, Alessio groaned out loud. Well, if Graziana had found true love, he wished her well. He felt a little foolish now for having practised celibacy on her behalf for so many months. But had she the smallest idea of what a nightmare she had unleashed on her widowed father and the economy? So very many business ventures were invested in the wedding occurring. But what could he do about any of it without a bride? Find another one? Pull some magical woman out of a hat like a white rabbit? *Impossible!* Stop dwelling on it, he urged himself.

In an effort to distract himself, he lifted Rosy Castelli's file off his desk. She had impressed him even before she had overheard that ghastly exchange with Graziana's unfortunate father. She had not made a fuss over her accident either, had been stoic, practical and controlled. And then, after hearing that bombshell phone call, she had not lied and faked ignorance, she had been honest about having overheard and had apologised, even offered a little sympathy. And now that he was single again, he didn't have to feel guilty for thinking that Rosy looked exquisite even clad in paint-stained workmen's overalls. But she was *still* a member of staff, he reminded himself circumspectly before he travelled further down that dangerous road.

He glanced at the file he had opened, and it was the figures that grabbed his attention first because he had worked as an investment banker for several years. Rosy's family were trying to run a business on a shoe-string and sailing very close to the wind in their indebtedness. They would likely be ruined by the collapse of the wedding-based celebrations.

And there his mind was, right back where he didn't *want* it to be, hammering away at Graziana's betrayal and what a disappointment his supposedly perfect bride had turned out to be.

When Rosy got back to the hotel she had to seek out Vittoria and she found her sister in their spacious rear apartment off the courtyard, sitting at the kitchen table with tears streaming down her quivering face.

'What on earth?' She gasped, for her sister had never been a crier.

Vittoria nudged a creased letter across the table to her sister. 'The roofer, Mr Calabrese, who sorted us out after that flood in the winter. He said he was willing to wait for payment but he can't wait any more… and why *should* he?' she cried, stricken. 'But now he's taking legal action to get what he's owed!'

'Oh, my goodness,' Rosy framed in dismay as she studied the letter. 'You didn't tell me about this bill. It's not on the books.'

'No. I didn't want to worry you and it was an emergency…you know it was.'

'Yes, but Mr Calabrese needed it paid and there are other things that could have taken a back seat while we worked to meet his bill,' Rosy reasoned unhappily, thinking of things like the purchase of truffles and the very best linen available.

'He did a great job. He deserves his money,' Vittoria agreed. 'But this is the worst possible time for this to happen with the wedding coming up…and me.' Her sister grimaced and looked guilty. 'I'm pregnant again.'

'I beg your pardon…' Rosy was shattered by that announcement when the last she had heard, after Vittoria had spent years trying without success to have a third child, was that her sibling was going through an early menopause.

'Even the doctor thought it was the menopause.' Vittoria sighed. 'But he did a test and then an ultrasound.

I'm three months along already…and could you think of a worse time for such a development?'

'It's wonderful news, news you and Patrick have wanted for a long time,' Rosy responded tautly. 'OK, so the timing is not what you would have chosen but you're better concentrating on the positive right now.'

'This giant bill we can't pay,' Vittoria exclaimed tearfully. 'And the twins are going to be so embarrassed that I'm pregnant!'

It took time for Rosy to bolster up her sibling's flagging spirits, sticking to the few positives she could grasp after that conversation. There was no way on earth that they could cover that bill and it looked as if bankruptcy was on the horizon because, without the wedding, there was no promise of future prosperity to take to the bank and persuade them to extend the bank loan.

Her tummy churned sickly at what now lay ahead of her family. They would lose the hotel and she would have to give up her job as presumably they would have to return to the UK. Or would they? That would be such a shame when her nephews had already settled so well into their schools and made friends. Patrick could get work as a chef somewhere else. That would be two wages coming in, hers and Patrick's, she reasoned in desperation, knowing she was being foolish in trying to second-guess an unknown future. Would the bank repossess and sell the hotel immediately, throwing them out on the street? How long would that procedure take? Months? *Weeks?*

It was hardly surprising that Rosy got very little

sleep that night. The prospect of losing everything, even the roof over their heads, was terrifying, particularly with Vittoria going through what might yet prove to be a difficult pregnancy. Certainly, her sister looked pretty sickly right now. The situation was horrific and she felt guilty that she hadn't broken that non-disclosure agreement and warned her sister that the royal wedding had fallen through. In reality, she decided, she hadn't been able to *face* telling Vittoria what she had accidentally discovered. Presumably, however, that news would soon be on TV and in every newspaper because the Prince could hardly keep that announcement to himself.

Alessio didn't sleep that night either. He tossed and turned. He hated disappointing people and that, first and foremost, all practicalities aside, was what he was about to do when he announced that the big wedding was off. He hated failure and Graziana was a failure of elephantine proportions. Whose fault was that but *his*? He should've questioned her more about her values and then possibly he might have suspected that she was utterly ruthless, if not cruel, when it came to putting her wishes above everyone else's. Her country, her father, her own people, not to mention Sedovia and its unlucky prince.

Now if there were a practical solution to his lack of a bride, he could have handled it. It crossed his mind that he handled most problems with the liberal application of business opportunities or cash. And if he took that road with this crisis? Would he choose one of the calculating socialites he had met over the years who would do virtually anything for money or enhanced status? Or a young Sedovian woman who worked for a living and who might just want to save her flesh and blood from the consequences of their financial mistakes? A beauty with sterling qualities he had already noticed. There was nothing spoilt, selfish or snobbish about Rosy and she was a beauty. Not a classic tall, blonde beauty like Graziana. No, much more of a slender, delicately curved and exquisite package of the more unusual and colourful variety. She attracted him.

Madonna mia, he hadn't thought of hugging a woman since his mother's rejection!

'I thought I was to help you with the rehanging of the portrait this morning,' Rosy murmured in surprise when Lucy Ragusa showed her into one of the attic workrooms and indicated a small broken ornament that required fixing.

'The workmen will do the hanging with my supervision,' her boss announced. 'I mustn't get into the habit of expecting you to always work by my side.'

But that was what I was hired to do! Rosy almost countered because the older woman was looking her over in the strangest way, as if she had never quite seen her before, and then nodding thoughtfully as she departed again. With a suppressed sigh of confusion, Rosy gathered the tools to make the repair, deciding that she didn't have to don her overalls for such a task. It would be painstaking, fiddly work, rather than messy, although she might well have to touch up the paint after she had it put back together. Carefully gathering the pieces, she studied them one by one below a magnifying device.

A knock sounded on the door and she flinched in surprise just as it opened and the very last person she had expected to see appeared in the doorway for a split second and then strode in, carefully shutting the door behind him.

Rosy stepped back from her worktable, her cheeks warming. 'Your Highness,' she said in a slightly strangled undertone, wondering what on earth could bring him to a workroom.

'I'm sorry to disturb you while you're working but I needed a discreet place in which to meet with you, and Lucy was kind enough to help me,' he proffered, bewildering her even more with that mystifying speech.

Frozen to the spot, Rosy simply stared back at him, one hand braced against the table as though to keep her upright. Holy moly, he was so hot he sizzled in her mind's eye, effortlessly elegant and gorgeous in a designer navy pinstripe suit. He was so tall, so sophisticated, so everything, from his thick blue-black hair that she wanted to plunge her hands into to his probably handmade shoes and everything that lay in between. Brilliant green eyes held hers and she paled as though she had been cornered by a lion and was too afraid to make a run for it.

'You needed a discreet place in which to meet *me*?' she queried unevenly, gazing back at those extraordinarily intense green eyes of his with difficulty. *So* intense, so powerful; she felt frozen to the spot.

Prince Alessio swung out a chair by one of the tables and set it beside her. 'Please sit down and please *try* to relax because I have an offer...a proposal to make and you must feel able to speak freely to me without fear of causing offence.'

Rosy blinked rapidly, her agile brain skipping over that phrase as she tried to imagine in what possible reality he might have an offer of any kind to make to her. She snatched in a jerky breath to keep her lungs working and dropped down into the chair. *Not* surely an indecent proposition of any kind? He emanated no sleazy vibes and yet why would he wish to see her alone where they would remain unseen?

'I have to announce Graziana's marriage to another man today. I cannot keep such news from all those who need to know, but I have an idea and I urge you not to become angry with me until you have heard me out. I have no wish to insult or offend you.'

'Right...' Rosy nodded very slowly, none the wiser as to what was coming her way.

'Your family are deep in debt.'

Rosy gritted her teeth on the wish to ask him how he knew that and then she wondered if the court action the roofer was taking against her sister and brother-in-law was already common knowledge within the higher palace echelons. With care, she compressed her lips and slowly nodded again.

'So deep in debt that the cancellation of the wedding will likely put them out of business,' Alessio continued as the cheeks that had flushed paled at that forecast.

'That is true,' Rosy conceded heavily.

'What I need at this moment is another bride, a replacement for Graziana so that the wedding can go ahead. That would, at least, alleviate the serious damage that will be done to the Sedovian economy if the wedding were to be cancelled altogether at short notice. Thousands of business people have made expensive plans and hired employees, pledging their fortunes to invest in the boost to the tourist season that the wedding will deliver.'

'But where the heck are you to find another bride with only nine days to go?' Rosy asked helplessly.

'I'm looking at her and hoping she will give me a shot,' Prince Alessio murmured with the most extravagant smile. 'I'm willing to settle your family's debts and ensure that their hotel is a success in any way that I can if you will marry me and try to pretend that we're in love…that this is *not* some last-minute face-saving move to shield me from the fallout of Graziana's insane flight.'

That smile unleashed butterflies in her tummy. She blinked again.

I'm looking at her and hoping she will give me a shot.

The future King of Sedovia was asking her to become his bride in Graziana's stead.

'This is crazy,' she whispered shakily, plunged deeper still into shock by his words.

'No, it's not. The PR team could spin it. We have photographic evidence of our first meeting on the bridge or we pretend I'd already met you here where you work. You're a Sedovian citizen. There is nothing shady about your past. If I pose as a man in love with another woman rather than a jilted bridegroom it will make the sting of Graziana's betrayal annoy people less. I'm angry with Graziana but I have no desire to punish her and she's in my past now. If she has chosen love over a royal marriage of convenience, who am I to criticise when I would have done the same thing?' he declared, lean brown hands moving in a series of eloquent gestures to express his emotions.

And the fluid hand movements were very expressive of a *lot* of emotions, many more emotions than she would have believed he possessed. 'Only I was not fortunate enough to meet a woman I could love,' he completed grimly.

'But you can't want to marry me...a complete stranger.'

'I believed that I knew Graziana well enough and where did that get me?' Alessio enquired. 'I would never have dreamt that she would do what she has just done. I thought she was conventional, loyal and dutiful, as we were both raised to be. I assumed I was the more volatile of the two of us and I was wrong because I would *never* have done this to her on the brink of our wedding.'

For a dangerous moment, Rosy let herself picture how much happier her family would be if she agreed and how well the hotel would thrive without the burden of that bank loan and without the constant striving to make ends meet and settle bills. Without a doubt it would transform her family's lives in very positive ways, particularly now that Vittoria was pregnant with a much-desired child and needed to be protected from stress. It was a wonderful idea, but she just could not imagine herself marrying Prince Alessio Marchetti... That was where her imagination went flat and utterly refused to co-operate.

'I can't believe you're serious with this...er...suggestion.'

'I never expected to marry for love. No doubt, you do. We have different goals and have probably always had different expectations of life. I don't have the space to give you a decent amount of time in which to consider my proposal either. I need to know right now if you could *consider* marrying me in nine days' time.'

Rosy sat there in a daze. She was thinking of all the sacrifices her sister had made on her behalf from when she was a baby, Patrick's acceptance of a pseudo-daughter into their newly married world when they had both been only in their twenties. She owed them everything she was and had become and it was a debt she could never repay. If she could finally bring them some good fortune in return for their sacrifices, if she could save them from bankruptcy, homelessness and all the attendant horrors that would assail them, they deserved that she put their needs first *just once*, rather than her own.

'I can't imagine marrying you... It's not like we're equals,' she said awkwardly. 'You inhabit a world very far removed from mine.'

'It will become your world too,' Alessio asserted. 'I will do everything within my power to help you to adapt and be happy. I do not want you to feel as though I'm trying to buy you.'

'But whichever way you look at it, you *are*.'

A wheezy little giggle was wrenched from Rosy and he looked at her with a frown of incomprehension. She crammed her hand guiltily to her mouth.

'I laugh when I'm nervous. Me…a princess? It would be unreal and impossible.'

'It *will* be possible, Rosy, should you agree.'

Rosy breathed in slow and deep to evade that questioning tone. 'Do you know how much in debt my family is?'

'I do, but I inherited enormous wealth when my parents died and have since made a great deal more on my own behalf. Your family's debts are a drop in the ocean to me. I know you're not a mercenary woman but your life will become much more comfortable if you marry me,' he pointed out.

A tremulous smile formed on Rosy's tense lips. 'I can't picture that either but you're incredibly persuasive.'

To her shock, Alessio dropped down lithely on one knee in front of her and he was so tall they were almost level. 'Will you marry me, *piccola volpe*?'

Her throat closed over so tightly she couldn't breathe. She wanted to tell him that he couldn't railroad her into marrying a stranger and becoming a princess. She wanted to tell him that he was a shockingly beautiful guy and too much altogether for her to withstand when she had never before been exposed to a man of his calibre. And then he called her little fox and even though she had a million questions, she couldn't concentrate enough to ask them because he was actually taking her hand in his. She swore an electric charge raced right up her arm when skin-to-skin contact was finally made by his light, warm hold.

'Yes, but it's for my family and a little…because I have sympathy for your predicament right now,' she admitted in a rush, determined not to show an ounce of her susceptibility because he was too smooth by half.

'This was my grandmother's ring.' Rosy watched wide-eyed as a glittering oval pink diamond ring was eased onto her ring finger. 'She had tiny hands like you and here…it fits,' he pronounced with satisfaction. 'Do you think that's a good sign?'

'I'm not thinking anything right now,' she lied as she noticed that unexpectedly happy sparkle in his green eyes that suggested that she had just made his day. And she supposed she *had* because he had found his replacement bride at very short notice and she was conveniently right on his doorstep in the palace. An ordinary young woman, so shocked and impressed by who and what he was that she wasn't demanding answers to any of the questions she still had tccming on her tongue. But, of course, he couldn't mean a *real* marriage with sex and all that and he couldn't be talking for ever either. Right now Prince Alessio was choosing a temporary bride to take him and Sedovia through the crisis that Graziana had left in her wake. In a year's time or so, or possibly even sooner, he would be urgently requesting a divorce.

He vaulted upright again. 'I'll make my announcement. I will always be grateful for your trust and generosity and you won't have to worry about anything ever again,' he intoned fervently. 'My staff will sweep every obstacle from our path to enable us to marry. You need to give me your phone number. A rather prosaic request, which underlines how little we know each other.'

'Yes.' Rosy dug out her phone and they exchanged numbers. It brought her down to earth but she was still in shock. She had agreed to marry a ruling prince. But it still didn't feel real.

CHAPTER THREE

'SIT DOWN,' VITTORIA urged the bride, because Rosy was white as milk and visibly trembling and, in the background, they could both hear the festive roars of the crowds in the streets below, already gathering for the wedding day celebrations.

The older woman leant down to whisper in her sister's ear, from which a priceless pearl and diamond drop earring was suspended. 'You don't have to do this. I may think Prince Alessio's the most fanciable thing since Patrick first made sour dough but if the prospect of Alessio is truly what is making you look sick, you can *still* walk away.'

'What, and get murdered by the mobs out there?' Rosy whispered shakily but a loving smile softened her lips at her sister's generosity.

'I'm not saying that escape would be easy but it's possible right up until you say "I do" at the altar,' Vittoria insisted briskly. 'Alessio's not been doing what he should've been doing this past week.'

'He's been working, selling the story, if you want to call it that. He's got the media skills… I haven't. No, it's just the crowds and the excitement getting to me. It freaks me out a bit.'

'He should've been spending more time with you, helping you shape up, getting to *know* you,' Vittoria spelt out in a punitive hiss. 'And so I told him at that stupid dinner.'

Rosy nodded, trying not to imagine how Alessio would have responded to such blunt interference, and a flush of mortified colour finally warmed her pallor. The 'stupid' dinner, which they had both attended at the palace a couple of nights earlier, had been a mere photo opportunity to capture the Sedovian prince meeting his lady love's family. Vittoria and Patrick had weathered it well. Patrick had predictably hived off to meet the palace head chef and discuss some new kind of ravioli that had appeared on the dinner menu. Her nephews had disappeared into a games room that was stacked with options to entertain teenagers.

And Vittoria had basked in Alessio's attention, trying to sum him up and get a good read on him because that was what Rosy's sister did with anyone getting close to her family. Only possibly Vittoria was working out what Rosy had already learned about Alessio—he didn't *let* people in. He was always courteous, charming and a hell of a polished communicator, but he didn't allow people to get close.

Rosy had had a rare glimpse of the *real* Alessio the day he'd proposed to her when he had told her stuff, more personal stuff because she'd already known about Graziana, and he had seen no need to prevaricate on that topic. She had been shaken when he had said very, very convincingly, 'I was not fortunate enough to meet a woman I could love,' and a little piece of her soft heart had broken off and gone in his direction because he had been sincere. She had truly believed that *had* he met a woman he loved there would never have been a marriage of convenience with Graziana arranged in the first place.

But Rosy had not seen a glimpse of the real Alessio since then, in spirit or in the flesh. Once Prince Alessio had made his shocking announcement about the change of brides and Graziana's elopement, the Cathedral View Hotel had been mobbed by the media and Rosy had had to move into a guest room at the palace to give her family the peace to continue running their hotel. She had been handed over bag and baggage to the household staff to be packaged as *the bride* and that had proved to be serious business.

Little capsule etiquette lessons on how to address the other royals and VIPs attending the wedding. They had discovered that she didn't need coaching on the cutlery or art or in various other fields because she had been educated well and sensibly brought up. Good manners, patience and tolerance were innate in her but Alessio's vanishing act—to work or otherwise—had left her feeling abandoned by the guy who had promised to help her adapt while he still remained, by his own choice, a virtual stranger.

And she now assumed that that was how he expected their supposed marriage to work: as a romantic pretence in public and nothing whatsoever in private. Certainly, the palace had to realise that they were fake because Alessio had kept his distance. And he had not given Rosy any material with which to fashion romantic fibs for her own family's benefit. She had had to tell Vittoria the truth. She was the replacement bride and Alessio would very generously reward them all by taking care of that bank loan and any outstanding debts. What she had not foreseen, however, was that her connection to the hotel would cause business to boom there, with the restaurant packed every night, or that would-be guests for rooms that were already fully booked were still phoning and arriving at all hours pleading for a space.

'Are you sure that you want to do this?' her sister had asked her doubtfully. 'Are you attracted to him? Is that why?'

'Yes, I do find him attractive,' Rosy had admitted ruefully. 'But I'm not going to be doing anything about it. This is a business arrangement and it'll stay that way until we part. I'm convinced that he's only willing to marry me because he thinks the Sedovian economy will suffer without this wedding. So, think of me like a wedding doll, not a future wife. I'm a symbol, nothing more.'

Vittoria departed to collect her sons downstairs and head to the cathedral while Patrick remained in the palace to escort Rosy on the strictly timed schedule. Only her wedding gown was Rosy's own personal choice. Her magnificent pearl and diamond tiara, earrings and necklace were Maretti heirlooms. Her bouquet had been chosen by the staff. But the dress? That was very much Rosy's dream. She had been shocked by the number of top designers who'd stepped forward when it had become known that a royal wedding gown was required within the space of a week.

It was classic with a slender silhouette, long tight lace

sleeves and a sweetheart neckline. The silk bodice was adorned with crystals that glittered and the skirt and the train were exquisitely white, embroidered with Sedovian wildflowers. In her opinion, she looked exactly like a fairy princess from a cartoon, particularly with her mad mop of curls left long and loose…hugely persuaded by the stylist, who had told her that Alessio had verbally admired Rosy's amazing curls. She wrinkled her nose, wondering why he had even noticed her curls.

She wasn't wearing anything borrowed or blue. She might be stepping into Graziana's shoes and have inherited most of her bridesmaids—the Sedovian ones at least—but at no stage had Rosy ever viewed herself as a genuine bride. She was too practical to see herself as anything other than Cinderella, but the Prince wasn't hers and there was no fairy godmother hovering in the wings to make her secret fantasies come true.

Did she have secret fantasies? Yes, of course she did, and Alessio could have played a starring role in them had he not been quite so careful to ensure that she didn't get any ideas above her station or any notion that he had any kind of a personal stake in marrying her. She was the convenient stand-in bride, nothing more important, and she was way too sensible to base any dreams on Alessio Maretti. He was as gorgeous as a sunset but as unobtainable as the moon. No, Rosy wanted a normal, hard-working guy, who thought she was as special as the stars in the sky.

Abstractedly, she wondered where he was taking her on their two-week honeymoon. He had been planning to take Graziana to Barbados, but a staff member had remarked that it would be bad taste to take Rosy to the same place, so where was *she* getting to go? Her eyes sparkled with anticipation.

Patrick, closely shaven and unusually immaculate in his fancy wedding apparel, was even more nervous than Rosy was when they climbed into the waiting be-ribboned limousine.

'I'll be glad to get out of this monkey suit,' he lamented, running an uneasy finger round his silk cravat.

'I'll just be grateful when the cathedral and all the fuss is over,' Rosy confided anxiously.

The car moved at a stately pace through the flag-waving, cheering crowds to the cathedral where a line of attendants and security men awaited the bride's arrival. Breathing in deep, her train caught up immediately by an attendant to aid her exit, Rosy emerged to a burst of cameras, mercifully kept back by the protective barriers. She kept her back straight and her head high and forced a smile. Bride, wedding day, look happy. It was a pretty simple role, she told herself as she was escorted into the church and the splendid music started up, along with the soaring voices of the choir. There had been no time for a rehearsal but the aisle was a straight passage, if a very long one, and she walked down it, her hand braced on Patrick's arm, the bridesmaids flocking in behind her.

Alessio watched his bride and he couldn't take his eyes off her.

'*Madonna mia*, she's tiny!' his best friend and legal counsel, Eduardo Conti, hissed. 'And beautiful. You're doing better than you deserve with this one.'

Rosy was doing *so* well, Alessio decided. He knew she was extremely nervous because he could see the tension etched into the delicate lines of her face, but she wasn't showing it otherwise, walking erect and dignified with her head high, the tiara lodged in her magnificent fiery fall of hair. She had worn it down for *him*. Although he had not asked specifically, only hinting to the stylist, he was pleased.

She looked absolutely spectacular, and the thought shook him because Alessio had never thought of a woman in such exaggerated terms before. He drew in a slow, ragged breath and realised that, while he had dreaded marrying Graziana, there wasn't any dread in him now, only a sort of hopeful expectancy that *they* would work as a couple. It didn't hurt that she turned him on hard and fast, even with a cardinal standing over him in all his church regalia, and for Alessio, who prided himself on his self-discipline, that was a revelation. Something about Rosy Castelli fired him up like dynamite.

'You look incredible,' he murmured when she finally looked at him, something she had appeared determined *not* to do on her passage down that long aisle in the full glare of the television cameras.

Her polite smile barely moved. The cardinal began to speak. Alessio's mind wandered but Rosy listened. She was more serious in the religious stakes than he was, he decided.

Holy cow, he was so breathtakingly beautiful, Rosy could barely believe that Alessio was real flesh and blood. The lean angles and hollows of his perfect face, the high cheekbones, the proud jut of his nose, the moulded sensuality of his full mouth but, above all, it was always his eyes that she carefully avoided, lest in some mysterious way he guessed that she found him impossibly attractive. That lustrous vibrant green surrounded by a layer of thick inky lashes? Her heart stuttered to a stop before ramping up in pace. Her muscles all tightened in defence, that ache stirring low in her pelvis again, her breasts swelling and tightening inside her dress; all the embarrassing hallmarks of what was wrong with her, she reflected in pained discomfiture.

Rosy had never been so drawn to anyone in her whole life and when it was Alessio, it embarrassed her to death at the same time as it terrified her because that magnetism of his made her feel out of her depth and out of control. She refused to be silly about him, however, totally refused to be that stupid. She was an adult and she knew they had no relationship and that they were enacting a deception on the real world. She had been in the same room when his PR team had discussed how popular a choice she would be in comparison to someone like Graziana, who had apparently insulted the entire country of Sedovia by letting Alessio down. Rosy might have her role in the Cinderella story but she wasn't in line for Cinderella's happy ending.

Alessio slid the wedding ring onto her finger and she surfaced again to the ceremony, colour burning her cheeks as she realised how she had mentally drifted away. A ring was passed to her and she tried to slot it onto Alessio's finger but by that stage her hand was shaking and he had to take care of it. It was done, it was done, she thought in relief, the main event accomplished and complete: they were married.

'You were very brave,' Alessio murmured soothingly as they signed the register. 'For someone unaccustomed to crowds, you're managing very well.'

'Thank you,' she said stiffly and braced herself to walk back down the aisle.

Alessio banded an arm round her as they reached the cathedral's main entrance. 'One kiss for the cameras?' he whispered.

'Of course,' she agreed because it was part and parcel of the whole performance of a couple supposedly in love, she thought ruefully.

His hand eased down her spine to catch her to him, while his other hand tipped up her chin. 'You're a very long way down,' he complained teasingly as he bent his dark, arrogant head.

Rosie braced as though she were in a queue for the guillotine. And then his sensual mouth engulfed hers and not in the fleeting salute she had innocently prepared for. The tip of his tongue parted her lips and he nibbled the lower one as though they had all the time in the world and no audience, and only then did he kiss her. The whole world fell away from her. Her head spun at the intoxicating taste of him and a flush of raw heat flamed through her every nerve ending as he welded her against him with big hands. She felt the unyielding hardness of his broad chest, the solid strength of him, and she was dizzy with the multitude of sensations striking all at once.

The best man gave Alessio a covert nudge. 'You're shocking the press...'

Alessio started to free his bride, discovering only then that he had lifted her right off her feet and she had dropped her bouquet. He stooped to retrieve it and returned it to her. 'I forgot where we were,' he said apologetically.

On the drive back to the palace, Alessio talked smoothly about some of their most important guests, educating her for the reception party, Rosy gathered. It was as if the kiss hadn't happened. Although she felt relieved, in the sense that she felt she had responded with too much enthusiasm, she was also tempted to ask him what he thought he had been playing at with such a kiss in a non-existent relationship. It wasn't as if they had even dated. In any case, nobody had ever kissed her so intimately before and she didn't really want to openly complain about that because the fact that she had never had a lover was her business and not his. But he was a guy, an international playboy, and maybe he thought nothing of such a kiss. If she complained, she would come across as ridiculously strait-laced and out-dated in her ideas.

Once they arrived at the palace, the regimented reception schedule kicked off. There were greetings and drinks with arriving guests, followed by entertainment by Sedovia's most famous artistes. Rosy spent a little time with her former work colleagues and realised only then that she was out of a job she had loved for good at the palace. Nobody was likely to put Alessio's ex-wife back on the staff. Of course, she would have the divorce settlement mentioned in one of the many documents she had had to sign prior to their wedding, and she wouldn't be poor, so possibly she would look for a conservation job elsewhere in Sedovia.

The reception drifted on, seemingly endless with the speeches, the polite socialising with strangers, the cutting of the cake, even the tossing of the bouquet because it was a very traditional wedding. By the time she had to move out onto the dance floor to do that first couple's dance thing, Rosy had had more than enough of the pomp and ceremony and, even worse, the having to dance in front of the guests when she couldn't dance. Predictably Alessio compensated for that lack by letting her simply shuffle in time with him.

'We can leave now,' he murmured into her hair. 'You've had enough.'

'Thank goodness,' she muttered, letting him tug her through the crush and urge her across the giant foyer towards the lift in the corner. 'Where are we going?'

'It's a surprise. I think you'll like it. It's private and not too intimidating.'

On the floor above, he ushered her into a bedroom and paused in the doorway of a connecting room. 'This is your room. I'm next door. Your maid will help you change.'

And then he was gone, the stranger she had married. A young woman arrived, dressed in the household uniform, and told Rosy that her name was Maria. Rosy could never have got out of her gown without help and she was relieved to have someone untangle the laces and unhook the hooks and undo the buttons.

'Will I leave you to get dressed? Or should I stay?' Maria asked her uncertainly. 'I'm very good with hair. Your luggage is already packed and ready for your departure.'

'You can leave. Thanks for your help,' Rosy said warmly. 'I'm not going to need anything more done to my hair today.'

An array of unfamiliar clothes was laid across the bed. The new wardrobe that Alessio had briefly mentioned during one of his fleeting phone calls? She had been kitted out like a new army recruit, she thought with amusement, selecting black linen trousers and a shimmering but light silky top for the journey, deeming comfort most important while travelling. She removed the jewellery, glad to see the back of the heavy necklace and tiara, rubbing her sore neck as she removed the earrings. She didn't think she had ever been so tired in her entire life.

As she was emerging from the bedroom, one of the household stewards was hovering. 'The Prince is waiting downstairs, Your Highness.'

It was the first time she had actually registered being addressed as a princess and she reddened and nodded, too weary to point out that it wouldn't do any harm for Alessio to wait on his bride for a few minutes. Unfortunately, the entire household revolved around him, but the needs of others had to be considered as well, she reasoned ruefully, determined not to become one of the 'adulation of Alessio' clique. He was human and flawed like everybody else, hence that utterly inappropriate kiss at the cathedral. She had let him get away with that but he wasn't getting off with much more around her.

Alessio was already at the wheel of a large SUV. Rosy climbed into the vehicle with difficulty because it was so tall, and she slumped in the front passenger seat while smothering a polite yawn. It wasn't too far to the airport, she reflected sleepily, struggling to stay awake.

A hand shook her shoulder and she moaned and sighed. 'Don't make me get up...'

'I have to. We've arrived,' Alessio informed her gently, all too aware that he had not appreciated how exhausted she was until she fell into a solid five-hour nap beside him. And she'd looked so cute asleep, all ruffled foxy curls and that delicate little upturned nose with its handful of freckles above that pink luscious mouth.

Rosy shook herself like a dog coming out of water and sat up, eyes squinting into the darkness lit only by the glaring headlights. She couldn't see anything but big dark trees and driving rain thumping down on the bonnet. 'Weather's not the best,' she mumbled helplessly. 'I don't even remember getting on a plane... how is that possible?'

'We drove here. We didn't fly, although if we ever return, we will fly. The time it would take to get here was seriously underestimated and the mountain roads are bad.'

Mountain roads? They had *driven* here? It didn't sound like any honeymoon Rosy wanted to be on. Alessio virtually bullied her out of the car and, by virtue of a torch, she saw their luggage already stacked on the front porch of a...giant mountain cabin surrounded by overhanging trees. Graziana had been deemed worthy of Barbados and Rosy got…? A mountain cabin. With resolve she lifted her chin, not wanting to be difficult. Maybe Alessio fished or climbed or hiked or some such thing and this was *his* dream destination. Yes, that made sense.

Although Rosy was determined not to make endless excuses for his omissions, she knew that she had to make allowances for his background, which she had heard all about just working within the palace. Alessio had always been alone, no siblings, not even cousins, and with detached and indifferent parents. He had existed in a cocoon of *one* from birth. Clearly it didn't come naturally to him to consult others about *their* preferences, needs or wishes. Nor did it help that he was surrounded by fiercely loyal and sycophantic staff, who believed that he could do no wrong.

The front door was unlocked and they stepped into gloom until she found a light switch that illuminated the huge and very ugly antler chandelier above them.

'I don't understand,' Alessio breathed. 'Where are the staff?'

'How many of them are there?'

'I haven't a clue. This was my grandparents' holiday home and I haven't been here in over twenty years,' Alessio startled her by admitting. 'But the same family have been paid to maintain and look after the place for generations.'

'It looks like they dropped the maintenance, certainly the cleaning,' Rosy remarked, noting the layer of dust on everything and already moving further to explore, walking through a door to the rear of the hall to find herself in a country-style kitchen that had much more appeal than the dusty hall with its old-fashioned furniture. She investigated the fridge and found it packed with food.

'Somebody *tried* to prepare for us coming.' She pointed out all the food to Alessio.

'This place is a dump. We can't possibly stay here.'

'It's too late at night to move anywhere else,' Rosy said with common sense. 'The roads are bad, it's dark and it's pouring with rain. I'll check out the rest of this place.'

She went across the hall, illuminated a giant reception room ornamented with horrid hunting trophies and an array of sofas. There was a small library, a formal dining room, a games room and a study with an ancient desk. She padded upstairs and heard a sound that she had unhappily become familiar with during her first months with her family at the hotel: the sound of water dripping in more than one place. She began opening doors, switching on every light she came across and discovered bedrooms too damp to occupy until she reached the double doors at the end of the landing and walked into a large room that was obviously a later addition to the cabin because even the furniture was more modern.

And someone had prepared the final room. The faded rugs and the floor were spotlessly clean and the giant four-poster bed was freshly made up in clean linen. There was even a bunch of wildflowers on a table by the window and she smiled. Someone had done their best with a giant neglected house left to go to rack and

ruin and she appreciated it. A relatively modern bathroom with working plumbing also lay through a door,
which took care of her last concern.

Alessio was still pacing along the cavernous porch
and totally unable to get reception on his phone, rage
and frustration emanating from him in perceptible
waves.

'Forget it. We've got food and accommodation. We'll
manage. I'm going to make some food. I don't know if
you're hungry but I'm starving,' she told him and simply left him to pace.

'This is *not* accommodation,' Alessio objected from
the kitchen doorway as she slammed through drawers
and cupboards to find pans.

'It may not be what you're used to, but it will do.'

'Not for our wedding night.'

'Yes, but it's not a real wedding night. We're a fake
couple, remember?'

Silence fell for a beat and then another. She tensed
and turned to look at him. He was frowning at her,
perfect ebony brows drawing together in apparent surprise. Vibrant green eyes suddenly struck hers like la-
sers. 'Is that your way of saying that you're not sharing
a bed with me?'

CHAPTER FOUR

IT WAS ROSY'S turn to frown. 'You mean, you actually assumed that I *would*?'

'Of course, I did,' Alessio proclaimed without a shade of discomfiture.

'Well, I'm not doing that with you and I can't think why you'd expect it anyway with us barely knowing each other,' she began, talking faster and faster as embarrassment threatened to consume her. 'I couldn't do *that* with a stranger!'

'I haven't felt as though you were a stranger from the first moment I met you,' Alessio told her truthfully. 'But that's not a reproach or an argument. We should've had this conversation *before* the wedding but I was in too much of a rush to win your agreement.'

'To be fair, you didn't have the luxury of time or space with that announcement about Graziana to make.' Rosy shook her head and turned away, still scarcely able to credit that he had simply assumed sex would be included in their agreement.

But were his expectations so far removed from reality? a little voice chimed inside her head. In a world where men and women could meet once and have sex and never meet again? Suddenly she was quite sure that she had come across as a terrible prude but she wasn't about to apologise for it. There were limits to what she was prepared to do on her family's behalf and casual sex was a hard limit for her.

She had stayed a virgin to the age of twenty-two not because she was a moralist, not by any specific choice but mostly by an awareness of her own nature. She was a romantic, she was cautious, and she was cynical about attachments based on sex because she had seen so many of those fail around her. She didn't want to risk falling for some loser who wanted her only for the fleeting release her body could give him. She valued herself a little higher than that. Undoubtedly, she had been helped by the simple fact that she had never met anyone she truly craved a closer physical connection with.

And then Alessio had appeared on that bridge and raw, visceral attraction had flared through every inch of her being the instant she'd met his stunning eyes. Ever since then she had been determined to protect herself and not yield to that shocking physical chemistry. Alessio would forget her existence the day the ink was dry on their divorce papers. He would remarry some lofty, titled lady similar to Graziana, have children and probably never think about the Cinderella who had briefly dug him out of a difficult predicament ever again. That was just a hard fact of life.

'We'll discuss it…some other time. Not while I'm wondering where I can sleep tonight,' Alessio murmured with wry humour.

So, he wasn't about to dispute her stance. Relief filled Rosy. 'I'll look for bed linen and you can pick a sofa in that nightmare-inducing drawing room. When was this house last checked by the palace?'

'I have no idea.'

'It must've been years ago. The roof is leaking like a sieve upstairs. You can't leave a property like this untended for so long. Whoever is responsible for property on your staff dropped the ball, and, if I were you, that would make me ask for a check on any other properties you have in your portfolio.'

'You're cooking... I am so grateful that you *can* cook,' Alessio groaned, appreciating her point. 'I'll check out the bed linen, take a look upstairs. I'm *not* helpless.'

He strode out, leaving her at the stove, engaged in making one of Patrick's signature quick pasta dishes. She listened to him hefting cases up from the hall and she smiled, deciding that she might even be kind enough to make up the chosen sofa for his benefit.

Alessio wandered round the upper floor in a daze. It was a dump on the brink of extinction, and he was inclined to let it self-destruct. He walked into the single habitable bedroom and immediately recognised his mother's signature colour scheme of white with touches of blue. His stomach churned and he no longer wanted to argue about sleeping downstairs on a sofa. But the sharing of the single *dry* full-functioning bathroom in the house still had to be negotiated. He might be willing to sleep on a sofa but he wasn't willing to do it unwashed.

And what about that? A wife who wasn't a wife?

He had made an unbelievably naïve assumption. He had imagined that Rosy understood what he intended with their marriage. He had never, not for one moment, planned on *fake*. She believed that he had married her to be a figurehead, presumably, a last-minute replacement and no more for Graziana. It hadn't occurred to Rosy that he found her far more attractive and appealing than his former fiancée, that he wasn't a man who had ever expected to have much say in who he married or much genuine liking or desire for his bride. But Rosy had broken the mould of his expectations, giving him a glimpse of brighter possibilities in his future...and he had simply reached for her and grabbed.

Without explanation.

That was where he had gone wrong. He was a man who from adolescence had been surrounded by women who would give him anything he wanted without question. He had never ever had to explain his wants, needs or wishes. Everything had come to him without him even asking for it. All those women had wanted one or more of three things from him. Sex. Luxury. Status. Only it seemed Rosy didn't crave any of those benefits. And yet when he had kissed her, he had fully believed she desired him as much as he desired her. So, what else had *he* got wrong aside from the horror-movie wedding night in a hopefully un-haunted house?

He located a linen cupboard for the first time in his life, ridiculously relieved that the dripping water hadn't accessed its contents. He yanked out musty sheets and a pillow and returned to the drawing room. It creeped him out too, all those moth-eaten trophies with their glassy eyes staring down. He shook out a sheet and draped it over a sofa, dropped the pillow into place.

'Alessio!' Rosy called.

He appeared in the kitchen doorway. 'Is there time for me to take a shower before we eat?'

'If you can accomplish it within twenty minutes,' she warned him. 'Is there any wine here that you know of?'

'I'll check the drawing room.'

He returned with a dusty bottle and two glasses. 'There's a fully stocked wine cellar under the house. I remember that.'

'You're not going down into a basement in this place,' Rosy told him firmly. 'Not on my watch. There could be rotten wooden steps, *rats*...who knows?'

Alessio laughed, green eyes glimmering with appreciation. 'I hear you.'

'Do you mind if we eat in here? I know it's a kitchen but it's clean and the dining room isn't.'

'That's fine with me.'

As he departed, Rosy sighed and set the farmhouse table. He had cooled off quickly, travelling from angry frustration to laid-back acceptance, and that relieved her. Her father had been an angry, offensive drunk whom they had all carefully avoided to the best of their ability when he'd been under the weather.

Alessio returned just as she was putting out the meal. She took a single glance at him, sheathed in jeans and a white tee, and her tongue cleaved to the roof of her suddenly dry mouth. Black hair still damp from the shower and tousled, falling round his lean, sculpted features, green eyes crystalline with clarity and vigour.

She snatched a sudden breath and turned away quickly. He had gone through the same day she had and he had not had the chance to sleep and yet he was *still* buzzing with energy. How could that be?

'I laid out fresh towels for you from the linen press.'

'My goodness, you're very well house-trained,' Rosy quipped as she set the plates down on the table and he opened the wine. 'Where are your security team staying?'

'They have a bunkhouse at a local farm and here they work in two teams, four off and resting and then four on for every shift.' Alessio speared a piece of pasta and savoured it. 'You're a hell of a good cook.'

'Can't be anything else growing up with a chef in the house. Patrick imbued me with his love of food. I used to cook with him after school when Vittoria was at work. He usually worked evenings and we'd all have dinner together before he left the house.'

'Sounds very family orientated.' Alessio paused. 'I never had that. Where was your father in all of this?'

Rosy stiffened. 'How detailed was your background check on me? Dad was an alcoholic but he didn't want to deal with it. Plenty of people tried to help him and failed. Life was better after Patrick moved in because Dad was scared of him, so the shoving me and Vittoria out of his way and the verbal abuse pretty much stopped then. Mostly, Dad spent half the day in bed and the other half out drinking. He was never there for me or my sister and she had a tough time with him after her mother died.' Rosy grimaced. 'Just think, she went through all that and still had enough room in her heart for me ten years later. But then that's Vittoria, she just puts her head down and gets on with it the best she can.'

'And that's why you couldn't stand back and let your sister and her husband lose their dream with the hotel,' Alessio slotted in. 'Evidently you have the same big, soft heart.'

'Except where you're concerned!' Rosy flipped back teasingly. 'Not about to share a bed with you because you put a ring on my finger!'

'Wait until I ask,' Alessio advised, having cleared his plate. 'And please note, I haven't *asked*.'

'Noted,' she said, a little breathless, rising from the table to deal with their plates, grateful that there appeared to be a working dishwasher because tiredness was beginning to build on her again with an ache in her back and a heaviness in her eyes. She didn't even know why she had mentioned the 'sharing a bed' angle again, most probably because she felt awkward and a little bad at subjecting him to a sofa.

'Do you mind if I ask you a question?' she added abruptly.

Sipping his wine, Alessio leant back in his chair and surveyed her. 'Anything.'

'Why did you decide to bring me here to the mountains, and not to a more conventional honeymoon getaway?'

Alessio winced. 'I assumed that you wouldn't welcome the attention. Graziana revelled in media interest and in one of the more conventional places there would be a great deal of it for the newly-wed Prince and Princess of Sedovia. Our every expression interpreted, our every outing and gesture and choice of clothing commented on. I didn't want you to feel that you had to tolerate that level of curiosity. I also believed we could get to know each other here without other distractions. I assumed—possibly wrongly—that peace and quiet would be more your style.'

'It *is*,' she agreed, disconcerted by his explanation because on some level she had assumed the worst about him: that being seen with her ordinary self in public might embarrass him or that someone like her didn't need or require an opulent break. But all those kinds of feelings only magnified the insecurity that she had struggled to hide from him, and she didn't want to admit that out loud. That he had been thinking of her needs, that he had been considering what was best for her instead of what he might want just blew her away. Her conscience twanged and her heart softened.

'Look, I'm going to head to bed,' she murmured, having loaded the dishwasher and put it on. 'I'll probably be better company in the morning.'

'Goodnight,' Alessio said lazily. 'We'll find out what happened to this place tomorrow and then head down to the beach for a break.'

Rosy paused and turned her head back with a frown. 'What beach?'

'There's a private cove below the woods. I remember it from childhood. That's why there's no pool here and we can probably be grateful for that because that would have been left to go to rack and ruin as well.'

'I'll look forward to that,' Rosy muttered before heading for the stairs while thinking abstractedly of

Alessio as a little boy who had once enjoyed bucket and spade holidays at his grandparents' summer home.

She went for a shower, used the towels he had replaced for her, and avoided washing her hair because she always let it dry naturally. She climbed into the giant bed and felt guilty. It was so big that she could've let him share it. It wasn't as though she were afraid that he might assault her. And there would surely be occasions while they remained married that they would have to share a bedroom, particularly if they were away from the palace, so, really, what had she been whinging about? The fact that he had dared to assume that she might have sex with him? Was she punishing him for that?

Of course, she hadn't expected to share a bed with him when their marriage wasn't real. But, at the same time, any sort of intimacy with Alessio would expose her to experiencing the sort of possessive feelings about him that she really couldn't afford to have in her situation.

Still tired though she was, she shifted, sleepless in the surprisingly comfortable bed. About an hour later, her every joint snapped taut when she heard a soft knock on the door. She sat up and switched on the bedside lamp. 'Yes?' she called.

Alessio stepped through the door, bare-chested, a pair of black pyjama pants anchored to his lean hips and a clutch of bedding clamped below one arm. 'May I sleep on your floor? The sofa is damp and feels like a rock. It's in here or the kitchen,' he told her flatly. 'They're the only dry places in this house.'

Rosy clutched the sheet to her pink-flamingo-clad breasts, her favourite pyjamas chosen for comfort. She couldn't take her eyes off him. Stripped, he was pretty intimidating. So tall, so bronzed, so built from his powerful shoulders to the lean, honed musculature of a torso worthy of a centrefold. 'OK,' she breathed, and before she could change her mind added jerkily, 'But I think you'd be more comfortable in the bed. Goodness knows, it's big enough.'

Green eyes glimmered with surprise. 'But *I* thought—'

'I was being unreasonable,' Rosy interrupted ruefully and she lay back down again. After all, there was no point in making an enemy of the man she'd married, was there? To a certain extent, their arrangement would be much easier if they fashioned, at the very least, a friendlier bond.

Unfortunately, she had the best view of Alessio climbing into bed and she shut her eyes fast. All those muscles flexing, not to mention the tattoos that she craved a closer look at. A shuddering breath filled her lungs because she was remembering that kiss and those sensations were stealing back into her treacherous body, filling her with a different kind of tension altogether.

'Mind if I switch off the light?' he murmured, his dark deep voice sibilant and somehow unbearably sexy that close.

'No.'

And she should have done it herself because he rolled closer and stretched up over her, enveloping her in a tormentingly intimate scent trail that was purely him:

outdoorsy, earthy, clean, warm masculinity. Her nostrils flared and she breathed in deep again as the light went out.

'Thanks,' he said wearily in the darkness. 'I was freezing cold down there. We need wood for the fire in there. I'll get everything sorted out tomorrow. I appreciate you bearing with me and cooking and dealing with it all without complaint.'

A sudden giggle escaped Rosy. 'I'm sorry. I was just trying to imagine what would have happened if you'd brought Graziana here…but, of course, you weren't bringing her here, you were taking her to Barbados. I think I was a little jealous of that, but I wouldn't have enjoyed the media fascination or the idea that I was on show all the time.'

'I'll make up for my oversights in the future,' he promised drowsily. 'Go to sleep—you've got breakfast to make in the morning… I *hope*.'

'Hmm,' she mumbled and slid into slumber between one moment and the next.

Rosy wakened sprawled across a living, breathing furnace. She gazed down at Alessio and slumbrous green eyes assailed hers. 'You're a real snuggler,' he told her. 'Every time I moved away, you found me again and hooked a leg or an arm around me.'

Rosy leapt off him as though she had been burned. 'I'm so sorry!' she framed before scrambling out of the bed and disappearing into the bathroom, where she was relieved to see the sunlight drenching the woods behind the cabin.

But even inside the shower she was reliving the feel of Alessio's hot, urgent body under hers, the bold press of his arousal, and her face flamed. She wasn't so naïve that she didn't know that it was normal for a man to wake up that way but there was nothing normal about the way that intimacy had made her feel. All on edge and jumpy, parts of her heated up in dangerous response. Hair washed and patted dry, she returned to the empty bedroom to ferret out something suitable to wear. She yanked a blue swimsuit out and donned it, wrinkling her nose at her reflection before tugging out shorts, a loose top and a pair of canvas shoes.

Alessio was already downstairs and opening a cool box in the kitchen. Lightly clad in swim shorts and a tee, he was a vision of lean, powerful masculinity as he bent down, cotton fabric outlining sleek, flexing back muscles and a strip of bronzed flesh and she sucked in a sharp breath.

'Where did that come from?' she asked stiffly.

'At least one maintenance system hasn't broken down since I was last here. When we're in residence, fresh baked goods, fruit, eggs, cream et cetera are delivered every day from the farm where my bodyguards are staying.'

'Convenient,' Rosy commented as she set about making a lavish breakfast while considering snacks and drinks for the beach, a much easier task with the amount of food that had been delivered.

They were having coffee when a knock sounded on the back door and one of Alessio's security team stepped in, escorting a teenaged girl who introduced herself with timid hesitance as Bianca Marino, whose family were caretakers for the cabin. Alessio frowned, black brows drawing together, and it was Rosy who stepped in to offer the teenager a cool drink and offer her a seat.

When she admitted under Rosy's encouragement that she was only sixteen, Rosy gave Alessio a speaking, expectant glance, remarking on how well prepared the kitchen and the main bedroom had been.

As the trembling, anxious girl relaxed a little, Rosy drew out her story. Bianca's mother had died almost fifteen years earlier, a woman Alessio fondly recalled as Sofia, who had made cakes for him as a child. Sofia had been responsible for cleaning the cabin, her husband for the maintenance. Bianca's father, however, had suffered a serious back injury the year after he was widowed and her brother, who had initially taken on his father's job, had left home to find a better-paying position.

'I will see your father before we leave,' Alessio pronounced calmly.

'Nobody ever came here. It didn't seem to matter what state it was in when it was never used. We didn't mean any harm,' the girl muttered in awkward completion.

Alessio saw her out again, his firm mouth taut.

'Let's go to the beach,' Rosy urged brightly, keen to take his mind off what they had just learned.

'You think I'm being too judgemental?'

'No, I think first you need to discover how Bianca's father was injured, because he was maintaining this house at the time and he may not have notified the palace because he was afraid of losing his job. I also think there should be an annual check on every property you own. If the supervision has been this lackadaisical, when was the level of pay for the job last updated? Three of the family were working here at one stage.'

'Fair point,' Alessio conceded, the squared set of his broad shoulders easing, while he attempted to prevent his gaze from wandering in the direction of his bride's truly spectacular long shapely legs. He was still aching from waking up with her lithe body draped over him earlier. Nothing wrong with that, he told himself. Only, unfortunately, there was no outlet for his very healthy libido, he reflected wryly.

Rosy slung cold drinks and some snacks into a rucksack and Alessio swung open the back door with alacrity.

'You know the way?' she prompted.

'There should be a path, probably overgrown by now, and a bridge over the stream and then it's all downhill from there,' he promised, taking the rucksack from her shoulder to put it on his own.

They headed into the darkness of the woods, towering trees providing a canopy far above them and shading them from the worst of the summer heat but, still, perspiration broke out on Rosy's skin. 'It's hot.'

'Yes…let me check this first,' Alessio urged, stepping onto a roughly built concrete bridge spanning a rushing stream and gripping the wooden guard rail, which fell away from his grasp into the water below.

He strode back, clasping her hand. 'Let me go first. It's dangerous.'

'I'm not one of your little ditsy women, Alessio. I'm a good swimmer and that stream doesn't look deep,' Rosy argued with spirit.

'But if you fell, you could hurt yourself and it's my responsibility to keep you safe.'

Rosy heaved a sigh and grasped his hand, colliding with glimmering crystalline green eyes that sapped her resistance as easily as a vacuum extractor. He guided her over to the opposite bank and moved her on. They were travelling downhill then and the walking, even though it meant threading a passage through light undergrowth on somewhat slippery ground, was less taxing. They were reaching the edge of the woodland when she saw a blue shimmering glimmer below them. 'The sea,' she murmured.

'The cabin should have been built on this side of the mountain,' Alessio opined. 'The views would've been spectacular, but my grandmother chose the land side because she was a gardener and the site she chose was more protected from the wind.'

'There was a garden?' Rosy asked in surprise.

'Once upon a time at the front. It's now run wild.'

As they stepped into full sunshine, Rosy found herself at the edge of a small cliff looking down into a sunlit rocky cove composed of white sand and glimmering blue water.

'It's magical,' she whispered in wonderment.

CHAPTER FIVE

IN ADVANCE OF HER, Alessio moved down the worn, steep, twisting steps to the beach, one hand on hers to guide her every step of the way.

Rosy heaved a sigh but made no complaint. If he wanted to behave as though she would trip over her own feet, she would let him. Even so, it was rather uplifting to be the source of that much care and attention from a guy. Alessio, in fact, bent his entire concentration on her and it was a new and rather intoxicating experience for Rosy, who was much more accustomed to men who elbowed her in the ribs and treated her with hearty sexlessness as though she were a mate. But Alessio, it only slowly dawned on her, was her *husband*, which presumably explained why he was so over-the-top protective of her.

They arrived on the sand and she immediately kicked off her shoes, letting her toes flex as they walked towards the blankets already spread across the sand in the shelter of the cliff. He took her hand and guided her over to a rocky outcrop that jutted out to point out the shallow cave behind it. 'You can change in there if you need to.'

A heap of towels sat beside the blankets. 'How did these get here?' she asked.

'Security put them down for us and delivered lunch and drinks for us.'

'I brought snacks for lunch.'

'But this is supposed to be a honeymoon and I don't want you feeling that you have to do all the catering,' Alessio responded smoothly, watching as she whipped off her tee shirt and dropped her shorts with a remarkable lack of self-consciousness before racing down to the shoreline, a lithe, slender silhouette captured against the bright sunlight.

He watched her walking through the surf and then dancing into the waves like a water sprite, her glorious hair fanning round her and glinting in every shade from red to copper to gold. Absolutely gorgeous. No supermodel could have held his attention more closely. He breathed in deep and slow and shed his tee, watching her wade deeper into the water with an obvious sense of freedom and assurance. He wanted her, no doubt about that, but he wasn't an idiot with women either. He assumed that they had to learn how to function as a couple before he let his libido control him.

He joined her to wash away the heat of the day and waved her away from the rocks where the currents were strong until she finally turned back towards the shore. Clambering upright, she stumbled as a wave hit her legs and Alessio laughed and closed his hand over hers to raise her up and steady her.

'I forgot how much I loved it here,' he admitted, disconcerting her.

'Then why did you wait over twenty years to come back?' she asked, watching water stream down his lean, broad, bronzed chest, trickling through the smattering haze of black hair, noting almost involuntarily the intriguing arrow of dark hair heading down from below his navel to disappear beneath his waistband. Cheeks burning, she raised her gaze guiltily to collide with glittering green eyes.

'Firstly, my parents only came here to please my grandparents. They didn't do rustic and the simple pleasures. And secondly...' Alessio's expressive mouth tightened as he changed tack on a raw note. '*Don't* look at me like that if you don't want me to touch you.'

Flames of mortification and a stricken conscience forced Rosy to drop her gaze again. Inwardly she squirmed because she knew she was sending out confusing signals and naturally he could read her much better than she could read him. Alessio, after all, had the reputation of a heartless womaniser. He had quietened down as he'd moved into his late twenties but he hadn't acquired his rakish image by accident. Before their wedding, she had done her share of online snooping over that phase of his life and she had seen the pictures of him at parties, on yachts and in exclusive clubs filled with celebrities and socialites. Accompanied by a parade of gorgeous women and often more than one.

'It's not that I don't want you to touch me,' she said clumsily. 'It's just that I wasn't expecting it at first and I can be a bit awkward with...er...men. Not a lot of experience. So, you were saying about why you haven't been back here?' she encouraged, forcing herself to stand her ground in the surf and lift her eyes to his again, pride and determination straightening her spine.

His glorious green eyes glinted in the sunshine and he bent down suddenly to drop a teasing kiss on the tip of her pert nose. 'You're not awkward with me, possibly a little shy. Nothing wrong with that except I'm not used to it. But I think I'm beginning to like it,' he said, directing her back towards their picnic spot and tossing her a towel.

With hands that trembled a little, Rosy towelled herself and gulped down cool water. He liked it? What was she supposed to make of that comment? Deeply self-conscious again, she breathed in deep and slow.

'I didn't return because my grandmother had a stroke and passed away here on that last holiday,' Alessio explained grittily, his lean strong features taut. 'I was heartbroken. She was the only softness in my life and I still remember my grandfather crying. They were a sincerely happy couple…and then I went upstairs and my parents were having a screaming row.'

'A…row?' Rosy queried in surprise.

'Yes. The Queen's death put the whole family into official mourning and it meant that my mother couldn't go to her fashion shows and my father wouldn't be able to race his yacht that season.'

'*Oh.*' There was a wealth of comprehension in Rosy's shaken response to those admissions and she reached out and squeezed his hand. 'That's very sad.'

Thinking fondly back to his grandparents' happy marriage, Alessio closed his much larger hand round hers. 'I think it was the first time I saw my parents as they really were. Two very selfish, shallow people. My father didn't even attempt to comfort his distraught father. I suspect he saw my grandfather as being in his way by then. He was forty-five and he wanted the throne.'

Rosy winced.

Alessio frowned. 'But when he took his place a few years later, he was very reluctant to allow his official duties to get in the way of his playboy lifestyle. I don't intend to follow his example.'

Rosy lay back to enjoy the sunshine, slathered on a little more sunscreen and eventually drifted off into a doze, only to wake up to find Alessio unfurling a parasol over her. 'Are you ready for some lunch?' he asked.

'Maybe.'

Alessio dropped down beside her. 'And it's getting late. You've been asleep for a while.'

Rosy blinked, realising that the sun had moved and she checked her watch, startled to appreciate that the afternoon was well advanced. 'You're right. It's past lunchtime. You should've woken me up.'

'It's not a problem. I want us to spend another couple of hours down here. We have people doing stuff back at the cabin.'

'*Stuff?*' Rosy teased with a frown of incomprehension, half sitting up.

'So, we'll have lunch now,' he announced, dragging forward a cool box.

'Stuff?' she questioned with amusement again, blue-amethyst eyes dancing.

'You deserve a surprise, at least a surprise that doesn't send you running screaming for the hills like this place did when we arrived.' Alessio grinned. 'You should've seen your face when you saw the rain and the cabin. You were horrified.'

Rosy reddened. 'Maybe a little.'

'A little?' He laced a hand through the still damp and tangled fall of her hair and cupped her neck. 'May I kiss you, *piccola volpe*?'

Rosy nodded nervously.

And their mouths collided, one of her hands rising, fingers splayed to spear into his luxuriant black hair as he caught her to him, his hand curving closely to the nape of her neck. She shivered as the tip of his tongue dallied with hers. As his tongue plunged, it was like a ride up to the heights on a roller coaster and then a sudden steep fall into the kind of passion that was new to her. A piercing ache travelled through her lower body and she felt her nipples tightening, a faint gasp escaping low in her throat.

'We can't do this here. I need to work at going slow with you,' Alessio quipped as he freed her and turned back to the cool box to emerge with an array of elaborate light bites, which he set out before her.

'You've been in touch with the palace!' Rosy accused in astonishment as she studied the sophisticated selection of tapas.

Evidently, the night before and prior to waking her up, Alessio had driven down the mountain until he got reception on his phone and he had put plans in place then and there. She was impressed because he hadn't mentioned it and had just got on with it, not that she thought even the Sedovian palace staff could do much in a few hours with a cabin left to go to rack and ruin for years. Hopefully they would at least deliver more food of the same calibre.

'If the place can be made more comfortable, we can stay a few days before we move on. I did think of shifting us onto my yacht but, unless we stayed out at sea, we wouldn't get much peace from the paps.'

'I can manage,' she declared, content to eat and enjoy the view of the sunlight sparkling off the sea and listen to the soft rush of the surf.

'Wine?'

'No, thanks. It's too warm.' Rosy paused and then pressed on. 'I gather your parents weren't a happy couple.'

'Well, that's scarcely a secret. My mother had a habit of making very acid comments to my father in public, which enraged him. She married him for wealth and he married her to have a child.'

'So, you must've been a very much wanted baby.' She sighed enviously as they ate.

'*Dio mio*, are you kidding? I was wanted in the sense that my father needed an heir, but neither of them had the smallest interest in children. After I was born, they moved into separate wings of the palace and only appeared as a couple after that at official functions and, even then, only when it was necessary. Bearing in mind that they couldn't stand each other, it was especially ironic that they died together when their plane crashed.'

'You must've been very shocked by that disaster,' Rosy murmured heavily.

'I was…but, although they were still officially based at the palace, they hadn't been part of my life in a long time and I generally only saw them in public. I was given my own household at the age of eight to get me out from under their feet,' he admitted tautly. 'We didn't have close ties.'

'Eight?' Rosy stressed. 'Your *own* household? What did that mean?'

'Essentially that I lived apart from my parents with staff who looked after me, and they did. The staff looked after me *very* well,' Alessio asserted with appreciation. 'But, of course, they didn't act like parents, so I never really knew what that would've been like.'

'You didn't have a proper family,' Rosy said wryly. 'I was much luckier than you with Vittoria and Patrick.'

'After my parents died, my freedom was at an end. I had to clean my act up because I was under too much scrutiny. I never ever expected to come this close to the throne so young. And it was painfully obvious that everyone was keen for me to find a wife to marry. That's how I walked blindly into the arrangement with Graziana. It was expected of me, so when she suggested it, I thought, why not? She's royal, she's popular, she knows what she's signing up for.'

'But there should be much more to a marriage.'

Alessio dealt her an amused glance, sunshine gleaming off the clean lines of his high cheekbones and strong jawline. 'Do you think I don't know that? But at the time, she seemed the best option available and I was willing to commit.'

'So, there was no romantic connection at all?'

'Romantic isn't in Graziana's toolbox.'

'But it must be if she ran off with her bodyguard.'

'I still find that hard to believe. She enjoyed her life the way it was. Something I don't know about must've happened,' he said grimly. 'And why are we talking about all this? Graziana is old history now. You're my wife...'

Rosy winced. 'Well, more sort of...your wife for *now.*'

'Or my wife for as long as you are happy being my wife. *Madonna mia*, I never looked on you as some temporary solution on my path towards some ideal marital candidate!'

'You...*didn't*?' Rosy frowned at him, all at sea, unsure how to interpret that statement or its exact meaning, even though everything it covered was fundamental to their marriage. She scrambled upright, suddenly ill at ease beneath that gleaming green intense gaze of his, which made her feel hot all over. 'I'm going to take a dip and cool off again!'

And she ran down the beach, struggling to work out what he had meant by what he had said.

Following her, Alessio caught her hand to tug her back towards him. 'Rosy...do you really think I could have you crowned by my side in a couple of weeks and then dispense with you a few months later without causing a huge scandal?'

Rosy went pink. 'I hadn't thought about it quite like that.'

'It would make both of us look like idiots for getting married in the first place!'

Rosy flinched. 'Probably...but even so, that's what I assumed you intended.'

'Obviously not. I'm a little more practical and realistic than that. I find you attractive. I respect you. I
think you can do the job. So, why shouldn't we give it
a go?' Alessio demanded forcefully.

Rosy wanted to slap him but she resisted that temptation. Instead, she pulled her hand free of his and darted
into the water to escape the conversation and snatch a
moment alone to think.

Why shouldn't we give it a go?

As if a marriage, a serious relationship, were just
one more novelty to try and she had nothing better to
do with her life than try it with him! And possibly, to
Prince Alessio Maretti, it *was*. She was shocked and
increasingly angry with him.

Matters she should've understood before their wedding were only now falling into place to form a totally different picture of his attitude in comparison to
her own. But whose fault was it that she had got totally the wrong idea about their marriage? He hadn't
spent any time with her before the ceremony, hadn't
discussed any important details or his own expectations, never mind hers. No, he had just dumped those
on her unforewarned the night before when she had
realised that he had simply assumed that she would
share a bed with him.

Alessio took a lot for granted with women, she reflected angrily, breaking into a fast crawl and plough-
ing back and forth through the water in the mouth of
the cove. That wasn't a surprise. How many women
had ever said no to Alessio? He rejoiced in a level of
male beauty that was surpassingly rare and he was in-

credibly sexy. He was drop-dead gorgeous, wealthy beyond avarice and charming even with the staff. He was accustomed to being the centre of attention. He was royal, and that explained a lot. A kind of unconscious arrogance and very high expectations. He assumed that people would go out of their way for him. He assumed his attentions would invariably be welcome. He assumed that most women would be attracted to him. He assumed that the ordinary Sedovian citizen he had married at the last minute would naturally go that extra mile for him.

But no blasted way on earth was Alessio Maretti going to give marriage *a go* with her! He hadn't asked her to marry him and *stay* married to him. He hadn't *asked* her to share a bed with him as his wife. No, he had left her to assume that their marriage would be as fake as plastic flowers and as short as *he* chose. As for the prenup, there had been more about the terms of them breaking up than staying together. Yes, it had said that for every year she remained married to him her eventual settlement on their separation would increase. Yes, it had said that any children born of the marriage would have to remain in Sedovia with him as royal progeny.

Obviously, none of those terms had surprised her because Rosy had not at any stage expected Alessio to tell his legal eagles that their marriage was a big fat fake in which no marital bed would ever be shared. She had naturally believed that those specifications belonged to his desire to be discreet about their secret arrangement. On the strength of that conviction she had signed the prenup, sincerely crediting that none of those terms would ever come back to haunt her. And *now* that they were well and truly married, Alessio had not only moved the goalposts, he had blown them sky-high!

Rosy stalked back up the beach in a temper such as she hadn't experienced in years. She snatched up her clothes and a towel and headed for the cave to get changed without looking at Alessio once. It would be rude and inexcusable to slap him and probably juvenile to scream at him for misleading her, and Rosy did not like to be rude, aggressive or juvenile. Staying out of Alessio's way until she simmered down was definitely a necessity. And then later, she would sit down with him and talk like an adult, she promised herself. She would admit that she felt deceived, insulted and angry.

Give it a go?

He could forget that idea! Her teeth gritted as she stripped off her swimsuit and wrung the sea water out of it.

It was cool in the shade of the cave. She shivered as she dried herself and wriggled back into her shorts and her halter top, wishing she had thought to pack under garments. Her toe nudged something slimy and she fell back with a stifled shriek, looking down to see that she had got her foot entangled with a strand of seaweed. Rolling her eyes at her own foolishness, she kicked it away.

'Rosy? I heard you cry out. Are you all right?' Alessio called urgently from out of view.

'A stupid piece of seaweed gave me a fright. I'm fine,' she said thinly.

'But very angry with me,' Alessio commented, stepping into her line of sight and lounging back against the rocky outcrop that guarded the cave's entrance from sight. 'You don't hide it well.'

'So sorry about that. Does your security team have binoculars on us? I will try to do better in the future,' she said stiltedly, dark blue eyes flaring like flames. 'But maybe you could try *not* making me angry the next time.'

'I don't know what I said or did to make you this angry,' Alessio informed her without hesitation.

Rosy sent his lean, powerful figure a stabbing glance of resentment. 'You're not that stupid. You didn't spell out what I was getting into *before* the wedding. Now you're trying to change our agreement altogether. I didn't sign my entire life over to you, Alessio! I believed this marriage would last eighteen months or two years at most, now what are you talking about? I also don't want anyone giving me a *go* like I'm a new shoe to try on—I deserve better than that!'

'Of course you do,' Alessio agreed. 'I'm sorry that my words offended you but it was not meant that way. I only meant that this marriage could become a normal marriage if we both wanted it to.'

'Well, I didn't sign up for that! A *normal* marriage!' she gasped accusingly. 'I was a substitute bride, nothing more. You talked more about the wedding saving the Sedovian economy from a slump than about what being married to you would entail, so if I misunderstood what was intended, it is entirely your fault for not taking the time to spell out your agenda!'

'I don't have an agenda, Rosy,' Alessio breathed curtly, wide sensual mouth compressed, a suspicion of angry pallor beginning to circle his jawline. 'I concede that we should've had this discussion before we married. I will even agree that the fact that we didn't is my fault because I was too busy trying to make us seem like an acceptable couple for the benefit of the public. But this is not a game for me or for you, Rosy. This is a marriage like any other.'

Rosy threw her hands up in the air in an almost violent gesture. 'But *I* didn't know that! You weren't honest with me. I didn't even know you found me attractive. I certainly never dreamt that you might believe I would share a bed with you.'

'I've been attracted to you from the first moment I saw you and, unless you're a liar, you will admit that that attraction is mutual.'

Rosy almost ground her teeth together in rage at that direct attack. '*Somewhat* mutual,' she qualified stiffly.

'Want to test it out? Resist a kiss and I'll back off,' Alessio traded.

One kiss? Was this a prince who thought he was about to magically awaken Sleeping Beauty? An angry laugh was wrenched from Rosy as she pinned her lips firmly together. 'Oh, *please*, test me in the mood I'm in now,' she encouraged.

'You look like a very cross, pouting toddler when you do that.' Alessio sighed heavily.

Rosy relaxed her face in shock at that retaliation, determined to feel absolutely nothing as he backed her up against the wall. But the heat of him at least drove out the chill still clinging to her damp skin below her light garments.

Alessio stalked closer, suddenly immeasurably tall and broad in the confined space. Rosy snatched in a sudden breath and closed her eyes the better to block him from her awareness. It occurred to her that she *wanted* him to kiss her, that in the act of denying that truth, she was, in fact, playing a game. Her eyes flew open again. 'Alessio,' she began as his hands came down on her shoulders and flexed.

'Rosy…' he said gruffly, tilting her head to one side to expose her slender neck and burying his mouth there, sending a flash fire of unexpected reactions rippling through her. She squirmed closer to his lean, powerful body, needing, craving more physical contact. Her whole body thrummed with sensitivity, her breasts swelling, her nipples pricking up against the cotton of her top.

Alessio swung her round so that she no longer had her back to the wall and lowered his head to find her parted lips and claim them. Her heart hammered madly inside her. Her hands lifted to lace into his hair. As he traced her mouth with his, plucking at her full lower lip and then exploring, she felt as though the liquid fire of impatience was pulsing through her veins. Heated warmth and dampness were pooling at her feminine core and she strained against him, instinctively seeking greater contact. Just a kiss, just a kiss, she reasoned with herself, even though just a kiss didn't explain the insane hunger building inside her.

Alessio slid down the wall, carrying her with him

and pulling her across his lap. 'Easier,' he muttered as she looked up at him with disconcerted eyes. 'You're way too small.'

'Sizeist comment,' she scoffed shakily. 'Maybe you're too tall.'

'Nothing we can't work around,' Alessio countered with assurance, long fingers smoothing down her bare thigh and making her shiver before his hand travelled back again and his fingertips flirted with the frayed hem of her shorts. 'And what are you worrying about? You have a beautiful face, fantastic hair, fabulous legs and an even more spectacular bottom. Haven't I been admiring them for months every time I saw you on your bike heading into work?'

Rosy looked up at him in astonishment. 'You... have?'

'Yes, I have been...quietly appreciating you from my car whenever I saw you on the road.'

It was odd, she thought later, how much that admission pleased her. That Alessio had noticed her before Graziana ran away and that it wasn't only her accident on the bridge that day that had attracted his attention to her.

'What are we doing?' she mumbled as he kissed her again.

'Well, we're not fighting any longer,' Alessio pointed out with dancing eyes and a wickedly sexy grin, long brown fingers stroking her taut ribcage. 'I think that's a win, don't you?'

His sensual mouth caressed hers open again and he ravished the tender interior, sending a new tension into

her splayed limbs and a wild anticipation. His hand
eased below her top and rose to cup her breast and a
moment later the hot damp heat of his lips closed round
the straining peak, alternating between the prominent
buds, dallying and teasing until the coil of heat in her
belly was at boiling point. And she wanted more, her
body twisting and rising over his, she wanted more
from him than her next breath. She needed the satisfaction that he had taught her responsive body to crave
to an unbearable degree.

With a clumsy hand she reached down to unbut-
ton her shorts and he kissed her again and wrenched
them out of his path while he was doing it. And then,
at last, he was touching her where she most needed to
be touched. He pressed his thumb against her throbbing
clit, stroked a finger through her damp folds, toyed with
her damp entrance where she was ultra-sensitive. Her
heartbeat pounded and her spine arched at the sweet
pleasure. And the strengthening band of tension in her
pelvis tightened another agonising notch until he delved
inside her, easing the terrible hollow ache assailing her,
and then brushed her swollen bud. It was as if he had
set a chain of fireworks off inside her body. She ignited
beneath that blissful surge of release, sensation pound-
ing through her in wave after delightful wave. As she
cried out and arched, he caught her mouth under his
again to smother the sounds she made.

And when Rosy finally surfaced from that climax,
he was already tugging her clothing back into place,
tugging her gently to her feet while she struggled, all
fingers and thumbs, to do up the button on her waist-

band. Even as she did so, she was hugely aware that their intimacy had been strictly one-sided and embarrassment claimed her because she hadn't touched him, hadn't even tried to do so. There was some excuse for the fact that she wouldn't really have known what she was doing, but she was painfully aware of his visible arousal.

'I'm going for another swim,' Alessio breathed thickly, not trusting himself to linger when he was so aroused and not really knowing what to say to her at such a moment because he knew that she had to make a decision as well as to what happened next. 'And then we'll head back to the cabin. Bearing in mind what you said earlier, you need to decide what you want in this marriage before we go any further, *piccola volpe.*'

He dropped a careless kiss on the top of her bent and swimming head and strode out of the cave. Rosy blinked rapidly, still all shaken up by what had happened between them. How they had travelled from fighting to kissing escaped her just at that moment. But she perfectly understood what he had said. If she wasn't prepared to stay in their marriage for longer than she had originally expected to stay, intimacy was a bad idea. If she was prepared to stay, for how long would she stay? What was her timeline, not to mention *his*?

And what would such a relationship do to her? How could what started out as fake *ever* become real? Alessio, she thought almost vengefully, had made his point. She wanted him. She hoped he didn't know it but she found him irresistible and that wasn't a good thing either, was it? What if she fell in love with him? What if she had a child with him? Would she always feel as if he had only married her as Graziana's conveniently available replacement? As the substitute, there to play a good walk-on part?

CHAPTER SIX

ROSY WALKED BACK through the woods, lost in the turmoil of her whirling thoughts. As the cabin came into view, she saw the workmen scattered across the roof.

'Temporary repairs. A proper fix will have to wait until we leave in a few days,' Alessio explained. 'I also asked for the damp rooms upstairs and the drawing room to be cleared and the furniture disposed of. The linen should all be replaced as well—'

'So, does all that mean that you're planning to keep this place?' Rosy pressed in surprise.

'Yes. Coming back here with you has somehow dispersed the unhappy memories,' Alessio admitted quietly as they walked into the kitchen where she immediately saw the changes. A large fridge freezer had replaced the old fridge, and the freezer compartment was packed with ready-made gourmet meals. A microwave had appeared and a sophisticated coffee machine sat in another corner. The fridge was stuffed with fresh food and a prepared meal for that very evening.

'I was quite happy cooking for us,' she said ruefully.

'But now you won't *have* to work so hard at it and we can relax,' Alessio pointed out as she moved out into the hall and then crossed to the drawing room to stare at the new contemporary sofas and note that the moth-eaten hunting trophies had been removed.

'Did you have furniture brought all this way from the palace?' she asked with growing incredulity at the improvements that had been implemented in such a short space of time.

'No, a store in Rifka was happy to step up and supply us with everything. It's only twenty miles from here,' he pointed out, referring to Sedovia's third largest city.

Rosy could only imagine the alacrity with which a store proprietor would have stepped up to provide Sedovia's reigning prince with such purchases. She glanced upwards and wasn't at all surprised to see that the ugly antler chandelier had been replaced as well.

Alessio noted the direction of her gaze, his emerald-green gaze gleaming with wry comprehension. 'I'm head of the Sedovian conservation society. Such relics from the past are better removed and there will have to be some sort of public consultation about what to do with them because the palace still contains problematic items as well. Destruction—denying our past—may not always be the best remedy. Hunting within accepted guidelines is still a popular rural pursuit.'

'I can't see anyone wanting to go to a museum dedicated to old hunting trophies,' she remarked. 'But you could be surprised, if you included the artworks that devolved from them. Add in an antique gun exhibition and old photos and it could work though, particularly if you added a conservation exhibition, showing how much attitudes have changed over the years.'

'I hadn't even considered that possibility.' Alessio dealt her an appreciative and lingering appraisal. 'That's quite a comprehensive plan to come up with so fast. I can see that your museum training will be an asset.'

Rosy flushed, striving not to show how pleased she was by the compliment. 'Let's go upstairs,' she suggested, because she wanted to shower and change.

'We'll have the Internet back now and a booster has been installed for phone reception,' Alessio proffered as she glanced into the study to see one of the palace technicians still at work.

'You really did think of everything.'

'Not really. I had to concentrate on what could be done quickly. Even for a few days we don't want to live inside a building site. The whole place requires extensive work but at least it should be clean and reasonably comfortable now.'

'It's certainly clean,' Rosy conceded as they walked past empty bedrooms now stripped of all evidence of rot and damp and another bathroom that now looked surprisingly functional.

As she opened the door on their bedroom, Alessio was opening the room next door. 'And this will be my room,' he advanced calmly, walking into a neatly furnished room, coloured in pale shades of blue and grey. 'I'll use the other bathroom as well, so we won't be getting under each other's feet...'

Or snuggling or colliding in the same bed, Rosy translated with an inner wince of discomfiture. Without warning the oddest sense of hurt, regret and disappointment was assailing her and, her cheeks burning at that awareness, she hastened on into the bedroom that they had shared the night before. There she stopped dead on the threshold, only to stare at the unexpected new furniture and the fresh contemporary bedding with a green tropical colourway.

'Why did you change this room?' she enquired.

'It was done in my mother's favourite colours and I dislike being reminded of her,' Alessio confessed rather stiltedly, faint colour scoring his hard cheekbones as she swivelled to look at him.

Rosy compressed her lips. 'Oh,' she said, keeping to herself the reality that she had actually quite liked the previous décor. True, it had been a little shabby, a little dated, but she found feminine florals soothing.

'And you required more storage for your clothes. You were living out of your suitcases,' Alessio pointed out, clearly determined to cover his tracks lest she suspect that he was more sensitive to reminders of his mother than was strictly masculine.

'I was living out of my cases because I was too lazy to unpack last night, and now…' she said in open appreciation as she opened a wardrobe door to view hanging garments, neatly folded garments on shelves and filled drawers '…it's all been done for me, which is wonderful!'

'The maids have been very efficient on our behalf but I didn't request any live-in staff because—'

'We don't need them in a place this size when we're not staying long,' Rosy slotted in calmly. 'You thought of everything…thanks. We'll be more comfortable now but you didn't need to have a second bedroom prepared for yourself—'

Alessio gazed down at her with hooded green eyes that smouldered. 'I *did*. You need your privacy while you decide where you stand in this marriage of ours. I chose to give it to you for your sake as much as mine. If you want a quick exit from this marriage, I want to know soon so that I can prepare the way,' he murmured tautly.

It was the scorching intensity of his gaze that flushed heat through her entire body. She knew he was thinking about the cave. Did he think she was a bit on the wanton side? After all, in a temper just before that development she had told him she hadn't signed her whole life over to him and had assumed that their marriage would be relatively brief. And that was true, but she had also made it surpassingly obvious that she found *him* very attractive and in an outrageously short space of time he had charmed her out of most of her clothes. So perhaps, she reflected as she closed the bedroom door, he was right to say that separate bedrooms were a better idea than too much dangerous proximity.

Even if she kind of really, really strongly resented him for enforcing a separation? After all, she had never known what it was to crave a man the way he had made her crave him. That was utterly new, that was exhilarating, and it was perfectly normal for her to wish that that compelling sexual attraction had been allowed to go to its natural conclusion. After all, she might never again meet a man who attracted her as much as Alessio did. Only, Alessio had put himself off-limits.

Alessio, *very* unexpectedly, was acting like a bit of a prude, wasn't he? In the end, whether they consummated their marriage or not didn't really matter even if they did break up a couple of years down the road, she reasoned unhappily.

Uneasy with the conflicting thoughts whizzing through her head, Rosy went for a shower. Was she trying to argue herself into bed with Alessio again? What else was she doing? So, she was curious about what it would be like to be with him *that* way. Nothing wrong with that when that curiosity came solely from her inexperience. A recollection of the physical feelings that had engulfed her in the cave shimmied through her body afresh and she shivered, still shaken by how potent and powerful those responses had been.

Towelling herself dry in the bedroom while she perused her new wardrobe and selected a casual long dress in a pretty fabric, she heard a noise and walked over to the window. She was astonished to realise that Alessio was chopping wood. Even as she watched two workmen she recognised from the palace approached him, clearly offering to do the job for him. Alessio, however, was determined to do the job himself and he reached behind his back to peel off his tee shirt in that distinctively masculine way. Rosy's mouth ran bone dry.

Tearing her attention from all those flexing back and abdominal muscles on the beach had been tough enough and watching him with an axe was an even hotter experience. Perspiration glistened on his bronzed skin as he worked. For goodness' sake, she was practically perving on the guy! Her face burned as she donned her clothing and wondered why he was chopping wood when it was still so warm. As she went back for another look at his truly stunning torso, muscular biceps and lean hips, she smiled. If she chose to perve over her very hot husband, that was her business.

She went downstairs and noted that the dining room table had been laid for their meal, complete with glasses, tablecloth and napkins. She was being shown the correct way and she supposed Alessio wasn't accustomed to casual dining unless he was on the beach. She had worked as a waitress while at university and she would manage.

Alessio strode through the front door and paused in the entrance to the kitchen. Her hair wildly curly and still rather damp round her incredibly delicate triangular face, Rosy was looking particularly appealing in something summery and soft that clung to the sweet pouting curve of her breasts. As she looked up from her task, the fullness of her lush mouth and the brightness of her blue eyes entrapped him.

In a split second, the nagging pulse at his groin raced from zero to sixty and he shifted his lithe hips as if to ease the pressure of arousal. 'Have I got time for a shower?'

'If you're quick. Dinner will be ready in fifteen minutes,' she told him. 'In the dining room. We're going to be formal tonight in honour of all the work that has been done here.'

'The roofers finished while you were upstairs,' he told her. 'They did a great job.'

Punctual to the minute, Alessio reappeared in the dining room clad in the perfect mix of formal and casual, tailored trousers smoothly outlining his long strong legs, a shirt rolled back to his elbows and open at his brown throat, his luxuriant black hair still damp from the shower. Rosy was setting out the cold starters and he was in the act of pouring the wine when his phone rang and he dug into his back pocket to answer it.

A frown line divided his brows. 'How may I help you?' he asked, his dark deep drawl unusually cool and clipped in tone. His attention moved to Rosy and he said in aside to her, 'Excuse me... I'll take this outside.'

Alessio strode out onto the shaded front porch, anger he was striving to contain paling his olive complexion. 'Graziana?' he prompted in an expressionless voice.

'Look, I honestly believed I had no choice,' she declared stridently. 'I know you have to be angry with me but at the time, I thought I was pregnant.'

'Pregnant?' Alessio almost whispered in his astonishment.

'And I knew that I couldn't do that to you.'

'And that, in our circumstances, I couldn't be fooled,' Alessio cut in with lethal bite, wondering if she was also aware that secret DNA tests were now mandatory with royal births.

'That too. But I panicked. I told Marco and the only answer seemed to be for us to run away and face the music at a later date. I persuaded the palace priest to do the marriage honours and then we rushed to the airport.'

'And at no stage could you find five minutes to phone and warn me?' Alessio interposed with scorn.

'I sent you a text!'

'Saying that you were sorry but not what you were sorry for.'

While Graziana argued weakly that she hadn't known what to say, Alessio thanked her for her explanation, keen to end the exchange.

But his former fiancée was far from finished and continued. 'The important point is that I'm *not* pregnant! I found that out before we even arrived in New York. It was all a stupid, crazy comedy of errors,' she lamented, her tone sharpening into angry shrillness. 'So, now Marco and I are applying for an annulment, but my father has cut off my access to my trust fund. I didn't even know that he had the power to do that!'

'I don't understand what all this has to do with me,' Alessio admitted flatly.

'Oh, don't act as if you're dim!' Graziana snapped. 'Or superior, just because you contrived to produce a new bride overnight to replace me. What I'm trying to say is that you could go for an annulment or a divorce now too, and *we* could—'

'No,' Alessio pronounced succinctly. 'There is no "we" now. I'm married. Let's leave this pointless conversation here and agree to continue as former friends for the sake of both our countries.'

He cut off the call against a backdrop of her protests because he had nothing more to say to her. All he knew was that she wasn't the woman he had once believed her to be. She had no sense of honour or loyalty and now that her father had pushed her into a corner by flexing his financial control, she was trying to turn back the clock in the craziest way possible.

While he was still outside, Rosy finished pouring the wine and sipped hers. She spread her napkin and toyed with a lettuce leaf on her plate before defiantly taking a first bite. Several minutes passed and just as she was about to commence her own meal, Alessio came back.

'Sorry about that,' he breathed, folding down into his seat and reaching for his wine.

'It was… Graziana and I needed to hear what she had to say.'

'Graziana?' Rosy parroted in surprise at the admission.

'I had to speak to her. No matter what she's done, I can't ignore the fact that we should remain on reasonable terms with so close a neighbour,' he admitted grimly.

'What did she want?' Rosy asked baldly.

'She ditched me because she believed she'd fallen pregnant by her bodyguard. That's why she married him and took off. Then she realised she had been too hasty and she's now pursuing an annulment,' Alessio advanced.

Rosy had frozen. 'Might it be your child?'

Alessio groaned. 'No, there *is* no baby. It was only a scare and even if it hadn't been, it couldn't have been mine because Graziana and I haven't had sex.'

Rosy's lips rounded in a silent 'oh' because that information took her aback. Like most people, she had assumed that he and Graziana were already lovers, even if they were not 'in love'.

'And now she's chasing an annulment for her marriage to the bodyguard?'

'On the grounds of non-consummation.'

Rosy nodded and stood up as she prepared to go into the kitchen to fetch their food. 'Are you thinking of doing the same thing?' she couldn't help asking, her heart sinking at the prospect.

Alessio slung her an incredulous look. 'Why would I want to do that?'

'Because she was everything you wanted and, by the sounds of it, she'll soon be available again…and you could be too,' Rosy pointed out, lifting her chin as she headed back out to the kitchen. 'It makes me a little superfluous.'

As she set out the main course on the counter, she realised that she felt deeply hurt by the prospect of their unlikely marriage being set aside before it even got a chance to get going. Why did she feel so hurt? She had married him for the money that had settled her family's debts, hadn't she? It had been an impersonal arrangement, so how had her feelings got involved? But if she had only married him for the money, shouldn't she be relieved if their marriage came to a sudden sharp halt? After all, he was unlikely to ask her or her family to return that money and an annulment would leave her free to return to her life.

Only, she registered, she didn't want to set Alessio free when tantalising possibilities were now hovering on the horizon ahead of them. The chance of them settling into a *real* marriage? The chance of them staying together, eventually raising a family? The concept of such developments between them sent her heart racing and soaring with hope and happiness. And why was that? When had her emotions even got involved? When had she begun caring what Alessio might think and feel? And when had she begun stressing about how he might compare her suitability as a royal wife with Graziana's? Graziana, who would naturally slide into a royal role with all the ease of a princess born and bred?

OK, she reasoned with herself, she was fiercely attracted to Alessio…and she liked him, probably much more than she should. He was good company, neither vain, nor arrogant, indeed he was none of the things she had once dimly assumed he would be. Here with her, shorn of his usual opulent surroundings and servants, he wasn't pompous or condescending or selfish or spoilt. When he had opted for a separate bedroom, he'd been thinking of her, hadn't he? Giving her the opportunity to think about what *she* wanted, no matter how little her ultimate decision might match his needs as a public figure.

'Rosy?' Alessio demanded from the doorway and she glanced up, noting the angry glitter of his jewelled eyes and the tight set of his sculpted jawline. 'What on earth makes you think that I would still want to marry a woman who was clearly cheating on me throughout our engagement?'

'I… I—' she stammered.

'I had a lucky escape and I know it,' he breathed with subdued ferocity. 'Her affair might well have continued *after* our marriage! She was obviously very discreet about the relationship because nobody appears to have known about it or suspected anything.'

'I'm sorry I jumped to conclusions,' Rosy said ruefully. 'It's just Graziana wanting you back and hovering and her being so perfect for the royal role makes me feel insecure.'

'That's foolish and your insecurities are without foundation as far as I'm concerned,' Alessio stated, lifting the plates out of her hands to set them aside and closing his hands round hers instead. 'I'm the son of parents, who lied to and cheated on each other. I have no desire to be married to a dishonest woman without loyalty. Nor could I ever want such a woman to become the mother of my children.'

'I see that,' Rosy conceded, pulling her hands free, her face deeply flushed as she reached for the plates again. 'Come on, let's eat.'

Frustration rippled through Alessio as he searched her shuttered face. Maybe he shouldn't have told her about Graziana's phone call or his ex's current plans. But he preferred honesty and had little tolerance for lies and half-truths. In reality, his parents' numerous self-indulgences had made him into their very opposite in character. He had married a sincere, honest woman and he didn't want to risk damaging her faith in him. That was why he was stepping back from the intense sexual chemistry between them, offering her the space to decide what *she* wanted, because, no matter how much he wanted her, he didn't want to take advantage of her. But first she needed to think through whether or not she was prepared to stay with him and give their marriage a chance.

They were finishing the last course and Rosy had been thinking hard when she said rather abruptly, 'I'm not the only one of us who needs to be considering what he's doing.'

Alessio lifted a satiric ebony brow. 'Meaning?'

'You hand out mixed messages all the time, stop, then start, so that I never really know where I stand with you,' Rosy framed tightly. 'First I think we're in a fake marriage, then I realise I'm in a trial marriage—'

'When did I say that you were on trial?' Alessio demanded, tossing down his dessert fork.

'That's the impression you give me. You want me to decide to be all in or all out before you waste your time on me. You let us get…er…*close* in the cave, and then I return here and you've moved yourself into a separate bedroom to keep your distance. So, you're not one hundred per cent committed either, are you?' Rosy shot at him before she snatched up the tray she had left nearby and began to clear the table.

'Leave those!' Alessio ordered in exasperation.

'No, I don't fancy coming back to them in the morning,' Rosy told him steadily and walked out to the kitchen to begin filling the dishwasher.

'Rosy…' Alessio stalked into the kitchen, his lean, strong features taut with annoyance. 'I said leave them,' he reminded her.

'Oh, did you think I didn't hear you the first time?'

Rosy studied him. He was impossibly good-looking and sometimes, like right at that very minute, it infuriated her because her physical awareness of him put her very much on edge. 'I heard you fine but I'm not one of your little minions, eager to do as I'm told and please. What I'm telling you—in case you haven't got the message yet—is *not* to tell me what to do. I'm neither a member of your staff nor a child. Unless I'm doing something wrong or dangerous or offensive in some way that I don't understand, don't shoot orders at me, because I won't listen!'

Averting her eyes from his taken-aback appraisal, Rosy spread her attention to the kitchen clean-up that was still required and decided that she'd had enough for one day. She would take care of it all in the morning when she was fresh and in a better temper. Slinging down the dishrag she was still holding in one hand, she neatly sidestepped Alessio and headed for the hall.

'Goodnight. I'm off to bed.'

Meanwhile, Alessio began to load a dishwasher for the first time in his life. Rosy had made him uncomfortable by showing him the truth of his behaviour. His parents had pretty much ignored him all his life and he had craved a better relationship with them. He *had* promised himself that when he was married, he would do everything differently. There was just one small problem, he acknowledged: he didn't know *how* to have a normal relationship because he had absolutely no experience in that line. Fleeting affairs didn't count, Graziana patently did not count and the one seemingly good relationship he had had with a woman while he was a student had crashed and burned before he'd even told her that he loved her. Possibly that explained why he was handing out mixed messages on his intentions…

CHAPTER SEVEN

WELL, SHE HAD told Alessio, Rosy reminded herself drowsily as she collapsed into a bed that felt deflatingly empty all of a sudden. It was not as though she actually wanted him in the bed with her—oh, dear, no—but it was the way he had withdrawn that intimacy with that bred-in-the-bone pride of his that had outraged her. He had had no right. Either he was her husband, or he was not. She wasn't the only one who wouldn't tolerate half-measures or his habit of moving forward two steps and then stepping back again, leaving *her* alone and uncertain in unknown territory feeling like an idiot, a fool, who should never have allowed such liberties.

The door creaked open, pausing her on the brink of sleep, and she froze, light from the landing highlighting Alessio, clad only in a pair of boxers. Her eyes widened at the large expanse of lean bronzed muscularity on view.

'I am one hundred per cent committed to this marriage,' Alessio gritted.

'Er…right.' Rosy fumbled for something to say because he had taken her by surprise. 'It just seemed rather insulting the way you took yourself off and then oddly coincidental when Graziana phoned and told you

that her marriage hadn't been consummated either...
not, er, that I'm up for *that* tonight,' she muttered awkwardly. 'I'm far too tired and cross with you.'

Alessio dealt her a lazily amused grin and vaulted
onto the other side of the bed. 'It's actually not the
norm for us to share the same bedroom, interconnecting rooms, yes, but not the same bed, and I assumed
that you would *prefer*—'

'Yes, well, stop assuming stuff, just ask,' Rosy said
with a sniff, still reeling from that heartbreaking smile
of his.

'And I didn't want to risk getting you pregnant before you'd decided that you were staying.'

Rosy stiffened. 'You couldn't get me pregnant. I've
been on the pill since university.'

'But accidents still happen and, if I can avoid it, I
will not have any child of mine growing up with divided parents.'

Rosy sighed. 'You're just a little paranoid because
of your background. Nobody knows if they've got for
ever together. One of us could drop dead next year.'

'*Madonna mia...* I seriously hope not,' Alessio in-
cised with amusement.

'Or, eventually, one of us could decide they can't
stand the other...who knows? Nobody knows. That's
the point. There *are* no guarantees,' she countered.

'Go to sleep, *piccola volpe*. It will all look much less
intimidating in the morning.'

Rosy wakened at the crack of dawn and for the first
time felt rested and more like herself. The royal wed-

ding and all the changes and the surprises dealt by Alessio had taken more out of her than she had realised. She crept out of bed, careful not to wake Alessio. Black hair dark against the pale pillow, ridiculously long lashes lying against his cheekbones, he looked younger, less guarded, relaxed. But still utterly gorgeous with that classic bone structure and perfect physique.

Freshening up, she put on shorts and a top and left the room, only to find lights still burning everywhere, and she frowned as she went round switching them off. Alessio wasn't used to being without staff and she supposed that that was why the ordinary tasks of life could irritate him when he saw her doing them. But Rosy, cheerfully clearing the dining room and returning the kitchen to its former spick and span status, was in her element. She liked jobs completed, preferred order in her surroundings and could only relax once that order was restored.

She brought in the basket of pastries and other perishables from the porch and packed it away before deciding to enjoy an early morning walk in the sunshine. The sky was a blissful blue without a cloud in sight but the tree canopy kept the temperature cool. She reached the stream, which was still quite flooded from the storm, and that was when she heard a cry. An animal cry? She wasn't sure and she frowned, scanning the banks, and then the island of flotsam that the storm had sent down the mountain. A tangle of broken branches nudged the bank and there was something made of cloth in it, something...moving.

It was the work of a moment to kick off her shoes on

the bank and she was about to step into the water when
a voice hailed her from the opposite bank.

'Don't go into the water! It's slippery and dangerous, Your Highness.'

Startled, she glanced up and saw one of the palace protection team and then the little cry came again. 'There's
something in that sack... I think,' she said, flinching
only for a second as the cold water froze her bare toes.

There was a splash and she glanced up in dismay as
the security guard jumped down into the water fully
clothed to stop her in her headlong flight to take care
of the matter. 'Oh, I'm so sorry...now you've got your
shoes wet,' she groaned, guilty that she had been stubborn and had not foreseen that he would see it as his
job to go into the water for her.

He waded across the stream towards her, holding
the dripping sack. As he shook it open on the bank, a
snuffly little black and white spotty snout emerged.

'My goodness, it's a puppy...' Sticking her feet back
into her shoes, Rosy knelt down on the bank and carefully lifted the little animal that had crept out of the
sack, shivering and dripping.

'The rest of the litter weren't so lucky,' her companion told her with regret. 'I'll see that they're buried.'

Realising that the pups had been tossed in the stream
to drown, Rosy flinched, but it was a fact of life that
such things still happened to unwanted puppies. She
held the quivering puppy against her.

'This river runs for miles. We'll never trace where
they came from.'

'I'll take her back to the house, warm her up,' Rosy

said with determination. 'And I'm sorry you've got all wet just doing your job and looking after me.'

'I'm off duty now anyway, Your Highness. I'm heading back straight to bed.'

She thanked him again and hurried back to the cabin to grab a towel and strive to warm up the little animal. She was in the midst of that exercise when Alessio joined her.

'Who's this?' he asked, kneeling down beside her.

'I'm going to call her Clover and we're keeping her.' She took a deep breath and rushed into explaining about the stream and the sack, tears stinging her eyes as she mentioned those who had not survived.

'Why Clover?'

'Lucky four-leafed clover,' she said chokily.

'I'll call a vet to take a look at her. She's not a newborn, so it was particularly cruel to try and get rid of them like that,' he breathed, vaulting back upright as she cuddled the puppy to use his phone. 'But unfortunately, people either don't want or can't afford to pay the vet fees.'

Clover snuffled over to the water in a saucer on the floor and promptly fell in it while Rosy hovered over her.

'Did you have any pets when you were growing up?'

'No, my mother wouldn't have any animals in the palace and my grandmother was allergic to pet fur, so it's been many years since there's been a royal pet.'

'We couldn't have one because my father didn't like them and then Vittoria and Patrick were always working, so it would've been difficult.'

Alessio was on the phone talking and Rosy coaxed the

pup to drink the water, wondering what on earth would be safe to feed it. Deciding to wait for the vet's advice, because Alessio appeared to be having a great chat with the person, she busied herself instead making breakfast. The coffee from the machine was a delight and she bit into a fresh pastry with pleasure. As soon as Alessio completed the call, he had to answer another and she nudged a coffee mug into his hand and he smiled, taking a seat at the table and stretching out his long denim-clad legs. Then his smile vanished and he frowned darkly.

'Once the vet has passed the puppy for travel, we'll be leaving. There are drones flying over the cove and a boat out in the bay so we won't get any peace. It was too much to hope that everyone involved in the work yesterday would keep quiet about our location,' Alessio commented. 'On the other hand, the necessary work can be continued as soon as we leave and we can return for a weekend when all this fuss has died down.'

'I'll be sad to leave,' Rosy confided. 'I just hope we can bring Clover with us.'

'If we can't, the vet will look after her until we return,' Alessio pointed out.

'You'll have to replace the shoes the security guy was wearing when he jumped into the stream,' she warned him. 'I was planning to do it myself and he only went in to stop me from doing it. I'll be more careful in future.'

'I'm glad to hear it. You've got a headstrong streak.'

'And you have an extravagant streak,' Rosy was quick to say. 'You left all the lights on when you went to bed!'

His clear green eyes danced with appreciation at the reproof. 'Duly noted, *piccola moglie.*'

'I do sound like a nag, don't I?' she said in embarrassment.

'No, you don't. You sound like someone who regularly forgets who I am and what that means in this country. It's good for me to have an equal shooting me down. It's a breath of fresh air in my world.'

The vet arrived, a tall, shapely woman in her thirties, utterly charmed by Alessio and fascinated by the sight of Rosy making her coffee. Clover was thoroughly examined and identified as a crossbreed with the long floppy ears and rough speckled coat of a Spinone and, probably, some other hunting breed. However, she wasn't healthy enough for travel and would have to remain under veterinary supervision. The vet had brought puppy food and a pet carrier box with her and Clover ate like a champion before subsiding into a doze on Rosy's lap.

'She's landed on her feet here,' the vet joked as she gathered her belongings to leave and Alessio followed her with Clover secured in the carrier box.

Sad that she had had to part with her new pet almost as soon as she had found her, Rosy went upstairs to start packing, dragging out cases and sighing as she piled stuff on the bed.

'Dress up for the airport,' Alessio warned her. 'There'll be cameras there to record our first public appearance since the wedding.'

The crush at the airport and the amount of security, including police, that shepherded them from their car indoors unnerved Rosy. Her spine was rigid while Alessio maintained a light hand at her back to keep her moving. Cameras flashed and the air was thick with shouted questions. She had never in her life felt quite so much on public show and ensuring that nothing other than a polite smile crossed her face was a distinct challenge. Boarding the opulent private jet was a relief and when it shot into the sky, the relief was even stronger.

'Is it always like that?' she asked, lying back in her reclining seat with a pile of new magazines beside her and a long, cold drink clasped in her weak hand.

'Yes, that's our norm,' Alessio confirmed. 'Eventually you just switch off and think nothing of it.'

Rosy was leafing through the magazines only to immediately pause when she saw Graziana's beautiful face obscuring half the front page. Without hesitation, she went straight to that article, given, she noted, when Graziana was in New York. Reading it made her heart sink and her teeth grind. It was sugary sweet right down to the number of times the Princess of Eboltz had to pause to dry her tears and sip her water. Overwhelmed by the pressure of the royal wedding and insecure about the bridegroom's commitment to her, Graziana explained, she had simply panicked and run away with a 'good friend' on her protection team, who had 'insisted' on marrying her before they took that 'unwise' step. She made herself sound like a little girl without agency of her own and only discreetly mentioned her hope of being granted an annulment of her marriage.

Drawing in a deep breath, Rosy tossed the magazine

into Alessio's lap. 'I've already read it,' he admitted, setting the magazine on the seat next him. 'Our PR team is very efficient.'

'She threw you under the bus!' Rosy proclaimed. 'She's hinting that you and I had something going on before she ran off!'

Alessio shrugged a broad shoulder with a maddening air of nonchalance. 'That was to be expected.'

'Expected?' Rosy erupted angrily.

'She's only inferring what others have been too delicate to comment on,' Alessio reasoned with outrageous cool. 'The suggestion that *we* were carrying on some illicit affair during my engagement to her—'

Rosy was so vexed by that news that she jerked upright in her recliner and pressed it down, her blue eyes shaded violet with resentment. 'How *dare* she?' she seethed furiously. 'How dare anyone think that about us?'

Alessio rested glittering green eyes on her, his surprise at her attitude unhidden. 'But surely you realised that people would think that.'

'No, I didn't,' Rosy admitted grittily.

'It makes more sense that prior to the wedding you and I had, at the very least, an attraction to each other and at worst were involved in an affair.'

'But it trashes my reputation!' Rosy interrupted angrily. 'I wouldn't have got involved with a man on the brink of marrying another woman.'

'What does it matter what other people think, Rosy?' Alessio parried with rich cynicism. 'The great majority were simply happy that when Graziana fled, you and

I were able to step in and still deliver the wedding and that elusive promise of happy ever after.'

Rosy pursed her lips and said nothing because she was unwilling to say anything more. She had no control over Graziana, any more than he had, and no way of silencing gossiping tongues. So, her reputation had been destroyed, but what was a reputation as such in this day and age, she reasoned with herself, striving to cool down.

'Let it go,' Alessio urged with assurance. 'Graziana will do and say whatever she feels she has to in an effort to redeem her public image and since, mercifully, I am not the guy who had to marry her, I intend to ignore her. Her father has cut her off from her trust fund and she is desperate to reclaim his approval by any means within her power. I would imagine that as soon as that annulment is granted, Graziana will marry some important power broker to please her father.'

Thinking about all that, Rosy relaxed back into her seat and set the magazines aside, lest they contain any further interviews with the Princess of Eboltz, guaranteed to boil her blood through her veins. It was past time she wised up, a little voice warned her at the back of her mind. Possibly, she was getting too big for her boots. She was the wife Alessio had *bought* with cold, hard cash. What axe did she have to grind with such a background to their royal marriage? The fact that that money had gone to her family, rather than her personally, was not relevant. She needed to remember that she was a humble art restorer and not a genuine wife. She couldn't do anything about the reality that some would believe that she had been sleeping with Alessio while he was engaged.

Life was tough that way, giving with one hand, taking with the other. Would she even want to turn the clock fully back? Return to her old life? Never ever have been a woman whom Alessio Maretti kissed? A little zing scorched through her pelvis as she looked at her husband, the Prince, rejoiced in that perfect profile of his, the fall of his tousled black hair as he worked at his laptop and chatted in Spanish on the phone. No, she fancied the socks off him, she admitted to herself. No, she didn't wish to go back to her single past.

But was it only that sexual chemistry that drew her to Alessio? She didn't want to fall in love with him. There was no love in a marriage of convenience. This was supposed to be a practical partnership in which both parties benefited from an exchange of mutual needs. Liking, respect and consideration were the foundation of that kind of bond and she believed that they had already achieved that happy balance, so she needed to be less temperamental and more accepting of their differences.

Certainly, she was seeing, if not quite accepting, their differences that afternoon when the SUV that had picked them up in Spain wafted them through a wonderful, tall black wrought-iron gateway and on to a thickly wooded estate. El Palacio, it was called, the former home of Alessio's mother, and it had come to him by inheritance.

'Once, I planned to sell it. My mother had no fondness for it and neglected it and by the time it came to me, it required extensive restoration. I only use it when I'm here on diplomatic visits or in need of a relaxing break, but, as I soon discovered, it has a remarkable charm all of its own,' he advanced as the ancient rambling building came into view above them and the car continued up the steep lane. 'It started out as a convent and changed into being a medieval home, but it was most altered in the eighteenth century when the daughter here married a very rich Portuguese duke. It's a Spanish house but it carries an unmistakeable Portuguese flavour. It's open to the public for most of the year.'

Rosy tried to relax her shoulders as the car came to a halt in a paved courtyard. 'That's good.'

In the fierce heat of the sun, she accompanied him up the steps under the shaded portico and on into a simply vast hall, with lines of marble columns marching ahead of them to frame a twin stone staircase at the rear. Before them stood a uniformed rank of household staff awaiting their arrival.

'The duke was apparently inspired by a Roman villa that had recently been unearthed in the grounds,' Alessio quipped as they moved forward into the blessed cool.

Introductions followed but Rosy missed most names after Jorge, the household steward, made himself known. 'The number of staff tells me that we will be waited on hand and foot while we're here,' she murmured half under her breath as they mounted the stairs in Jorge's stately wake. The inside walls of the staircase were lined with blue and white tiled medieval scenes.

'This house runs like a top-flight hotel,' Alessio

agreed with amusement. 'It's the least you deserve after that experience at the cabin.'

'No, that ended up being fun. I wouldn't change that for the world.'

'And you rescued Clover.'

'No, strictly speaking, Giuseppe rescued her.'

'But he wouldn't have noticed the sack had it not been for you,' Alessio corrected as they reached the landing, which was also an upper gallery exposed to the elements on one side. 'To keep the house cool,' he added.

Rosy surged over to the gallery wall to look across at the other wing of the house and then down. 'Is that a medieval cloister?' she asked in wonderment.

'Yes, the cloisters and the chapel from the convent were preserved, although the duke's piety ensured that the chapel was appropriately embellished.' He walked her on down the gallery where Jorge awaited them, clearly keen to throw open the very large and heavily carved double doors at the foot.

'We will sleep in splendour tonight,' Alessio murmured teasingly.

And she discovered that he had not been joking. A giant carved four-poster bed sat on a dais in a chained-off alcove. 'Gosh, we're going to have our own state bed,' Rosy remarked. 'I hope the mattress has been renewed since the duke's days here.'

Two maids were already busily occupied unpacking their luggage in a big dressing room furnished with wall-to-wall closets.

'Have we got a bathroom?' Rosy whispered anxiously to Alessio.

He laughed, humour dancing in his glorious green eyes. 'Yes, we have a plethora, installed before architectural heritage prevented such alterations. Some bedrooms were sacrificed, giving us all the modern necessities, but, as there were so many bedrooms, they aren't missed. Jorge will serve us tea in the cloisters and then we will explore to our hearts' content.'

'Let me change into something more comfortable first,' she urged, nipping into the dressing room to grab shorts and a top and a pair of casual sandals.

'Will you share the bathroom?' Alessio enquired.

Rosy coloured. 'Of course,' she conceded, wondering when the concept of being truly married would sink in so that she was not self-conscious about such unimportant things.

Furthermore, Alessio's was a helpful presence when he unzipped her out of the formal, neat-fitting dress she wore but he was undressing himself as well and that was distracting even in a huge bathroom with both of them stationed at opposite sides.

'You look incredible,' Alessio husked as she stepped free of the dress, clad only in wispy peach-coloured undies, her slim, curvy body stilling beneath his intense scrutiny.

Rosie was convinced that she was reddening like a traffic light from top to toe as he studied her. Her breasts swelled in the cups of her lacy bra and she instinctively pulled her stomach in as a hot liquid feeling pooled at the very centre of her body. Etched in her mind's eye, even as she turned circumspectly away, was a shirtless Alessio, his bronzed torso and tattoos and rippling muscles leading down into long, strong legs. In haste, she dressed, wanting him, not wanting him, still afraid of feeling too much for him while all the time wondering if Alessio had ever been in love.

'I'm serious. You look amazing,' Alessio husked, long fingers touching her shoulder to turn her round again, potent green eyes laser-beam sharp focused on her and smouldering hot in temperature. 'That shower is big enough for both of us.'

Rosy tensed and reached for her shorts instead, for she wasn't quite up to the stage where she might consider stepping stark naked into a shower with Alessio and she didn't know if she would ever be. That level of intimacy stretched way beyond even her imagination. Flushed and taut, she zipped her shorts and pulled on her top, saying merely, 'Jorge has refreshments waiting for us.'

'This is still our honeymoon,' Alessio chided softly, and his hand slid down to enclose hers, turning her back to him again.

'Alessio…' she began anxiously.

His other hand framed her cheekbone and his erotic mouth claimed hers, teasing and parting and delving with only the tip of his tongue until a shudder ran through her, igniting a burst of heat deep down inside her, ensuring that her legs wobbled. He ran his lips down the slope of her neck, pausing to nip and tease and she shivered again. She fell back from him in a sensual daze of tense anticipation as his dark head lifted. He gave her a slow-burning smile and reminded her that Jorge was waiting for them downstairs.

Suspecting that had been one-upmanship on display by a more skilled player than she was herself, she walked slowly down to the charming sunlit cloister where Jorge awaited with a prettily decorated table and a choice of tea or coffee and a selection of sweet treats. She rested back in her comfortable seat and waited for Alessio to reappear.

She was nervous of having sex for the first time; she knew that that was the real problem. She didn't want to be a disappointment. She didn't want to come over all shy and unsure and embarrass herself. She didn't want to think or behave as though the act of sex would actually be important to him. After all, she assumed it wouldn't be to a guy who had once figured in the media as an irrepressible Casanova. Consummating their marriage might well be the only way she prevented Graziana from sneaking back in as a marriage candidate again. How was she to know otherwise when Alessio already seemed to have forgiven his ex and hadn't uttered a single critical word about that interview she had given?

Sipping her favourite Earl Grey tea, she pulled out her phone and called her sister. She hadn't spoken to Vittoria since the wedding, had only contrived to send her a couple of texts. Her sister burst straight into excitable speech, complaining bitterly about Graziana's interview and the implied slur laid on Rosy's behaviour. Firming her slight shoulders, Rosy brushed off the sting of her sister's feelings on that topic and brought Vittoria up to date on the cabin, the Spanish house and Clover. But, of course, what her sister really wanted to know was how Alessio was treating her.

'I've got no complaints whatsoever,' Rosy framed stiltedly because Alessio was currently striding down the gallery to join her. 'It's been really good…look, I have to go for now.

'Vittoria,' she explained. 'She's got herself in a bit of a temper over Graziana's interview.'

'Yes, I've dealt with that,' Alessio startled her by claiming. 'There will be a statement made by the palace that I first met you on the day you were knocked off your bike and that it was only after Graziana's departure that we first got to know each other. I was remiss in not immediately understanding your feelings on the matter. In any case, why should we support Graziana in her attempt to excuse herself by smearing us with a lie?'

Rosy was entirely thrown by that succinct declaration on her behalf. She was finally receiving the support she had unconsciously expected from him and had been disappointed not to receive. Bereft of breath, Rosy stared back at him. His change of heart came as a huge relief. 'That's what I thought. Thank you for that. I was annoyed by it,' she muttered unsteadily, unprepared to admit as yet that she had been more hurt than angered.

'You don't need to thank me for what I should've seen instantly. You're my wife and you should always be able to rely on me to defend and protect you. I've grown more cynical over the years and I won't always see matters in quite the same light as you do,' Alessio warned her tautly. 'But neither of us deserve the rumours that Graziana is happy to use against us. I, after all, was the fool who has not been with a woman since the week of our engagement last year.'

Rosy was so disconcerted by that unexpected revelation that she said doubtingly, 'Even though you and she *weren't*... Are you serious?'

'I believed it would be disrespectful for me to seek solace with anyone else. No matter how discreet I would've tried to be, there was too big a chance of any fling ending up splashed across the tabloids,' he breathed tautly. 'When I realised she'd been involved in an affair throughout, you can imagine how I felt.'

'Proud that you had more loyalty and respect for her than she had for you?' Rosy queried. 'There really is no excuse for what she did or how she's behaving now, trying to pose as the innocent party.'

An almost luminescent glow had lit Alessio's jewelled eyes as he looked at her and listened to her. 'You're on my side,' he said in apparent wonderment.

'Of course, I am...' Rosy frowned. 'You're my husband and you've defended me, so naturally I see the situation from your point of view. Sit down. Do you want tea or coffee?'

'Not right now.' Alessio threw back his dark head and suddenly laughed with wicked amusement before his hand closed over hers to almost lift her out of her seat to stand before him. 'Right now, *piccola volpe*, I want my wife...and I want her more in this moment than I have *ever* wanted a woman before!'

CHAPTER EIGHT

'It's THE MIDDLE of the day!' Rosy gasped as Alessio urged her back upstairs by a narrow staircase she had not even realised acted as a shortcut.

'No, symbolically speaking, it's the first day of our marriage...as it should've been,' Alessio countered levelly. 'We didn't have this understanding then but *now* we do.'

'What understanding?' she queried as she stumbled in the entrance to their bedroom and he swept her off her feet.

'You are here for me and I am here for you. Not to put too fine a point on it, I've been waiting to hear that *all* my life,' Alessio spelt out in a raw undertone as he dropped her down on the bed and then went to work on the zip of her shorts. 'Someone who is with me and only me, even if she doesn't always agree with me, even if she has doubts.'

'That's a pretty tall order, Alessio.'

'But one that you're more than able to meet,' he told her, discarding her shorts on the floor and embarking on her top.

'Even if I'm not quite up to burning the sheets off

the bed?' Rosy pressed a little desperately, her voice strangling in her dry throat at his haste.

Alessio looked down at her and laughed. 'What are you trying to say?'

'I haven't had sex before,' she admitted in a driven undertone. 'And no, I don't want to talk about it.'

Alessio dealt her a stunned appraisal that fully conveyed his astonishment and whipped his hands off her. 'I appreciate you telling me beforehand,' he breathed tautly. 'I am so sorry that I didn't even consider that possibility. I thought you were simply shy.'

Rosy sat up and hugged her knees in the centre of the bed. 'It's okay. Don't make a big deal of it.'

Alessio vaulted off the bed. 'I need a shower,' he told her, disconcerting her because she knew he had showered before he even came downstairs.

'A cold one,' he specified, interpreting her look of bewilderment.

Rosy sat frozen on the bed and then regained her wits. She slid off the bed, removed her remaining garments and scrambled back in again. Alessio returned to her, hair still damp and tousled and, if anything, even more breathtakingly gorgeous. A line divided his ebony brows as he looked at her. 'I forgot to kiss you,' he husked, mounting the steps to the bed to come down beside her. 'Stupid oversight. Write it off as an excess of enthusiasm.'

'I will,' she said breathlessly, his firm hard mouth ravishing hers with the kind of intensity she had only met before in him. As though nothing mattered but that particular moment, as though he would pour all of himself and everything he was into the endeavour. It unleashed a flock of butterflies in her tummy and made her heart race so fast it pounded at the base of her throat.

'It's like unwrapping a present,' Alessio growled as he wrestled her free of the sheet and curved possessive hands over the pouting thrust of her breasts, his thumbs teasing at her swollen nipples.

Her spine arched, delight and anticipation snapping together in a wondrous connection. Glittering green eyes, luminous as jewels in sunlight, gazed down at her searchingly. 'Are you quite sure about this? I can wait—'

'I wouldn't be in this bed if I wasn't sure,' Rosy declared.

And in the end the truth wasn't what she had once assumed it would be in any way. It wasn't because they were married. It wasn't because she had some silly thought of ensuring that the marriage was fully consummated. No, her motivation was much more basic in nature. She wanted *him*, she wanted him more than she had ever believed she could want any man and she craved that closer physical bond.

He caught a ripe pink peak in his mouth and laved it with his tongue and her hips squirmed, red-hot reactions snapping through her lower body and bringing it alive. She felt the surge of damp between her thighs and instinctively rubbed against a hair-roughened thigh to ease the desire he was stoking. He settled her back against the pillows and worked his way down her slender length, kissing, nibbling, touching gently, exploring until all of her skin surface felt as sensitive as if she were perched on a knife edge of expectation. She could already feel the surge of quivering heat building in her pelvis and tightening every muscle.

He slid her thighs apart and concentrated on the most sensitive place of all. Her hips jerked up and her lips parted on a moan, pleasure darting through her in shocking waves. Her fingers speared into his black hair and lodged there, tugging as her hips exercised a rhythm of their own and the growing tightening inside her became almost unbearable. And when that sexual tension broke, her climax roared through her like fireworks shot off inside her. Her whole body jolted and she cried out as the blissful waves of release crashed across her and she slumped.

'That was even better than the cave,' she mumbled in a helpless compliment.

And Alessio lifted his head and gazed down at her with unholy amusement. 'Are you planning to rate me now?'

'Eleven out of ten. I'm impressed to death. You were worth waiting for,' she told him shyly. 'And I only waited because I was convinced that the right guy would eventually show up.'

'And you think I'm the *right* guy?' Alessio asked.

Her blue eyes shimmered. 'I hope so but you're definitely the hottest contender. I've never wanted anyone as much as I wanted you.'

'Nobody would ever have suspected that on our actual wedding night when you called me a stranger,' he reminded her.

'I've got to know you since then and I've liked what I've learned about you. I've moved on…as have you,' she pointed out as he pulled her close and planted a kiss on her lips that turned into a more explosive kiss than she had expected. She wrapped her arms round him as if he were the only stable place in a shifting world. And now, she finally felt free to touch him, to work her fingers through his luxuriant hair, run her hands across his wide muscular shoulders and his smooth back and feather down his lean sides.

As he quivered, she laughed. 'Gosh, you're ticklish!'

He rolled over, gripping her with a sexy growl that curled her toes, and ravaged her parted lips with a slow, erotic intensity, and that curl in her lower body spread wings and fluttered with renewed arousal. He was a fabulous kisser. But when Alessio pinned her under him and she felt his erection hard as an iron bar against her, it sent wild thrills of excitement through her. With other men that awareness of her partner's arousal had turned her off because she had known that she had no plans to go further. With Alessio, however, it turned her on so hard and fast it made her head spin.

He spread her out like a starfish and teased and toyed with every sensitive inch of her squirming body and when the pleasure began to surge up again, only then did he move over her. As he eased into her with a care she could feel, she gasped, 'I'm not breakable!'

'Shush. I'm trying to make this as painless as possible for you,' Alessio ground out thickly. 'We can swing from the chandeliers next week.'

Even in the tense grip of more pleasure than she had

ever dreamt of experiencing, Rosy grinned up at him, enchanted by that promise. He tipped her back and shifted his lithe hips, guiding himself into her slick opening. She felt him, strong, forceful, alien and the strange satisfaction of it, the feeling of rightness, made her close her eyes and seek to lose herself in that very private moment. He pushed and a sting of discomfort pulled a gasp from her and he stilled.

In frustration, Rosy angled her hips up to him and gravity sank him deeper until the feat of possession had been achieved and she smiled, revelling in that sense of fullness, of friction as he lifted and began to move. And then, the warm nucleus of liquid fire coiled up inside her started to heat up and the excitement grew and finally burst free. All of a sudden she couldn't stop her own body from rearing up to join with his. The intensity of it all engulfed her and she discovered that it drove her on.

'I want you so much. I've craved this from the moment I met you,' Alessio groaned, thrusting into her welcoming body with lethal power, igniting little hotspots of response all over her, her body leaping and buzzing with renewed energy.

Response to his intensity bloomed with their every movement. Suddenly she was on a runaway train heading towards the ultimate objective, her body out of her control, flaming and burning with hunger. She was inflamed by the knowledge that Alessio had always hungered for her. That raised her way above the level of being a replacement bride and she loved that idea. He pushed her thighs back even further and rose over her like a conquering god intent on domination, and her excitement rose accordingly, her heart hammering, her pulses racing as she surged to the peak and another orgasm swept her off in its tight grip.

Alessio shuddered and growled his satisfaction above her.

'You are so hot,' he breathed jerkily in her ear while he flattened her with his weight.

Rosy was floating, quite unconcerned by such bodily necessities as having to breathe. 'Only to you.'

'Absolutely to me,' Alessio growled, dropping a kiss on her brow, his arms tightening round her as he rolled over to release her from his weight. 'My bride, my lover...when I first noticed you on your bike months ago and I realised you must work at the palace, I wouldn't let myself find out who you were and what you did. All I had seen then was your incredible legs and behind and then, because of the accident, I saw your face and your hair and I was transfixed.'

'But you were engaged,' she reminded him doggedly. 'You weren't about to do anything about it.'

'Do you judge me for that?' Angry green eyes assailed her sleepy ones.

'No, but it's not something I can forget,' she muttered drowsily.

Alessio climbed out of the bed once she was asleep. He wondered how he had fared. Rosy had been his first and, if he had anything to do with it, his *only* virgin. She had enjoyed herself, hadn't she? But still it worried him that his wife was so inexperienced. At some stage, might she be likely to be curious about what sex would be like with someone else? He would talk to her about that, he decided. But would it be wise to put such an idea in her head? She wasn't a cheater; she wasn't disloyal. She had even listened to him partially excusing Graziana's indefensible behaviour without striking him dead. Fortunately, his intelligence had kicked in. Rather belatedly, he had appreciated that his wife had first call on his allegiance and that Graziana was now pretty much the enemy, particularly if she intended to take any more shots in the direction of his wife.

As he showered, he couldn't get Rosy out of his thoughts. Her passion, her fearless honesty, her tenderness with that dog, her unquestioning loyalty and support. He had played a blinder exchanging Graziana's cold-fish personality for a woman who burned with moral strength and attraction. And if he had anything to do with it, she would burn exclusively for *him*.

Late the following morning, after a lengthy breakfast, Alessio took Rosy outside to show her the extensive grounds. They strolled through shaded walks in the woods behind the ancient house, laid out in the eighteenth century to resemble the then fashionable English country garden. When they reached the waterfall, built to resemble a natural one in a giant stone-edged pond but somewhat undermined by the provision of a shell grotto and shrine nearby, Rosy kicked off her shoes and waded into the crystal-clear basin to cool her hot feet.

'Oh, that's blissful,' she moaned, perching on the edge of a stone outcrop and dipping her toes back into the water.

Alessio copied her because for the first time in recent memory he too had chosen to dress down in shorts. He had become accustomed, he conceded, to the company of constantly groomed and polished women, who would not have yielded an inch in their formal dress code even in a hurricane. Once again, Rosy was a breath of fresh air and, taking in her playful smile, he pulled his phone out and keyed in an agreed code with their protection team. Now they had total privacy.

Shedding his sandals, he joined her in the shallow basin, moving forward to nudge her legs apart and step between them and bend down to claim her ripe, pink lips eagerly with his, prying them apart to delve deep into the moist interior of her mouth. And that fast, Rosy's bones and muscles liquefied beneath the heated surge of molten honey rising in her pelvis. It was as if he had pushed a button and hunger gripped her instantaneously.

Her brain couldn't quite handle that sudden change in her own behaviour. She panicked and all she could think about as he tugged off her shorts and knickers and tossed them onto the dry ground was that they would be seen and that he couldn't be thinking of what he was doing and where they were. 'Alessio... we could be seen. Gardeners...oh, my word, your protection team!'

'All elsewhere. We are, in a very rare event, alone, *totally* alone,' he stressed huskily as he whipped off her top and went for the catch on her bra. 'It is our honeymoon, after all. Let's be young and reckless just this one time.'

'Having sex in daylight was a big enough stretch for me!' Rosy protested but he was smiling that wickedly sexy smile down at her and his glorious green eyes were gleaming and vibrant. Her own body was already humming beneath the exploration of his skilled hands. She fell, abruptly, silent. 'I just can't say no to you right now,' she whispered guiltily.

'And shouldn't we rejoice in that?' Alessio chided as he stripped off in front of her, revealing his lithe, lean, bronzed length already primed for action.

Rosy poked his bare chest with a forefinger. 'And you absolutely swear that nobody's going to see us?' she checked.

'I wouldn't take that risk with you.' Alessio nibbled at that spot below her ear in that place that drove her temperature high while he employed his palms and his fingertips to stoke her desire until she was wriggling off her rocky perch in her need to get closer. Only then did he hoist her up into his arms and then slowly bring her down, jostling her into place until he stretched her slick sheath with his urgent fullness. The sensation was overwhelming.

Indeed, she was only starting to adjust to his effortlessly arousing movements when he stepped beneath the waterfall and she let out a startled shriek. 'You—!'

His mouth clamped over hers for a split second, silencing her objections. Water streamed down over them but the sensations at her hot core drove them out of mind. Arms linked round his neck, she transformed into less the seduced and more of a partner, pushing down on him, moaning with raw excitement as the increasing pressure in her pelvis pushed her onward and upward. And then she was flying high and soaring in ecstasy and Alessio was stifling her cries with his lips on hers.

She sagged against him as they stepped out from below the water. 'I'm never going to move again,' she swore shakily.

'You will. Jorge has a splendid lunch awaiting us at our next stop.'

In the act of gathering her clothes, Rosy fixed accusing blue eyes on him. 'Did you *plan* this?'

Alessio laughed. 'If I'd planned it, I would've had towels stashed in the grotto!'

And she acknowledged the truth of that admission as she clambered, damp, into her clothing again while also appreciating how much her own world view had changed within the space of twenty-four hours. As they walked on, she remarked on the fact that, on this occasion, Alessio had not employed extra contraception on their behalf.

'We can afford to take that very slight risk now that I know you're staying.'

'I haven't actually said that yet in a long-term sense,' Rosy adjusted with care. 'You take a lot for granted sometimes.'

His big hand tightened its hold on hers. 'Losers rarely take all. I have confidence in us as a couple. I believe we'll go the distance.'

'I hope we do as well,' she murmured quietly. 'But I won't be ready to have a child for a while. I'm only twenty-two.'

'In comparison, I can't wait,' Alessio admitted candidly. 'I want my own family. I love children. It's important to me but I can accept that you're not at that stage yet.'

She wondered if she was being selfish and scolded herself for the thought. They strolled through the peaceful canopied green lanes that criss-crossed the woods. By the time they arrived at a glade containing a very imposing but mossy statue of the Portuguese duke with one hand on a sword and the other on the head of a giant lion, Rosy was ready for a drink and something to eat. Food awaited them there in a cool box.

They settled down and ate at the circular stone table and benches in the shadow of the statue and her hair dried in the sunshine while they talked.

'Have you ever been in love?' she asked him.

Alessio looked both amused and thoughtful at that blunt question. 'One and a half times.'

'How can you be half in love?'

'Because I was fifteen and it was a crush. It came to nothing when I realised that she preferred girls to boys,' he told her lightly.

Rosy set down her wine glass. 'And the other time?' she prompted with greater curiosity.

His bright gaze hooded, the memory clearly not a good one. 'I was twenty, still a student. She was the daughter of one of our leading Sedovian families. I brought her back to the palace to a party she was desperate to attend and...' He hesitated, frowning.

'And?' she pressed uncomfortably, somehow feeling as though she was prying.

'She slept with my father,' Alessio told her very quietly. 'And tried to deny it but he boasted about it. He was a vain man, used to choosing whichever woman he wanted, and bedding her reassured him that he was still irresistible.'

Rosy had paled, disgust now clouding her troubled gaze. 'That's horrible. How could she?'

'Oh, that was easy. He was a *king* and, even though he was a married, much older man, that was all it took. Maybe she had a vision of him divorcing my mother and marrying her...who knows? Stop looking so tragic on my behalf, *piccola volpe*. It feels now like it happened a lifetime ago.'

'But how could your father betray you like that?' she muttered.

'He had to share the public stage with his heir and he disliked anyone who took attention away from him. As I grew up, he began to see me as a rival.'

Rosy sighed. 'And I thought I had it rough because my father barely noticed I was alive and had no interest in me.'

'But don't you see that your experience, like mine, will probably make us better parents when the time comes?' Alessio countered calmly.

'Perhaps, but this is the very first week of our marriage and we're not talking about that as yet,' she reminded him lightly. 'I do understand though that you probably feel the pressure of having to try and provide an heir for the throne.'

'No, it's not that. I genuinely want a child, a little being to love and cherish and the stability of feeling part of a family. I know it's not usual for a man to admit that but some of us do feel that way.'

'And how courageous to admit it,' she murmured, sidling along the bench to seek his tempting mouth again for herself.

After a couple of glasses of wine, she was getting sleepy when they returned to the house and she decided to take a nap before dinner in the hope that it would waken her up for the evening.

Alessio promised he would wake her later and went off to do some work. She recalled the light in his gaze when he confessed that he simply wanted a child and his unashamed honesty had touched her. He was like water steadily dripping on stone, she warned herself squarely. Except that he had buckets of charisma and was sexy as all get out. If she wasn't careful, she would find herself agreeing to have a child just to please him. Their relationship needed time and space to develop before they made such a major decision. But her own emotions were getting so tangled up with him and she had been naïve not to realise that that would happen.

The sex was amazing. Foolish of her not to appreciate that she could not get that close to Alessio without feelings becoming involved. *Deeply* involved, she acknowledged. She was falling head over heels in love with the man she had married. He was everything she had ever wanted in a man. Intelligent, loyal, kind, considerate, surprisingly sensitive. His troubled childhood might have damaged him but he had dealt with it, learned the lessons and moved on. Their marriage was no longer a fake. She was something more than a replacement bride now, she reflected with satisfaction before she fell asleep.

It wasn't Alessio who wakened her, it was some internal alarm of her own because she opened her eyes, checked the time in dismay and surged straight into the bathroom to freshen up before dinner. They had skipped dinner the night before and rifled the fridges at long after midnight to feed themselves. This evening, she would do the whole formal thing, she decided, yanking out a long blue dress. Act like a princess for once, she thought ruefully, but, with Alessio around and his penchant for al fresco encounters, that was likely to be a challenge.

She smiled to herself then because his passionate streak of unpredictability thrilled her just as much as his sheer intensity. She reckoned there would be plenty of times they had to act as if they were much older and staider than they were, so it was probably good for both of them to go a little wild occasionally. Although she suspected that making love outdoors in a waterfall did not seem as shocking or daring to Alessio as it had seemed to her.

Dressing, she heard someone giggling and realised that either a member of staff was having fun or Alessio was entertaining, because the room he used as an office was directly below their bedroom. From the landing, she peered down at the gallery below but it was too awkward an angle to show her much. She caught a flash of scarlet just out of view and the sound of Alessio laughing. Returning to the bedroom, she dashed on some lipstick and mascara before cramming her feet into high heels, keen not to look like a wife who might embarrass him. Ready, she started down the staff staircase that acted as a shortcut to the gallery.

Emerging onto the gallery, she caught the merest flash of a gorgeous brunette in a scarlet dress walking into Alessio's office, talking volubly in what sounded like Spanish. A mane of long silky black hair worn loose, a figure-hugging dress with a low neck and towering heels—she was unlikely to be a business connection, she reasoned, stopping in the open doorway to look into the office. Alessio's back was turned to her as the brunette flipped through images on the laptop in front of him while she talked very fast. She was so close to Alessio that her swishy hair was brushing his shoulders and as she bent over, her hands rested on his shoulders for balance. Annoyance flashed through Rosy like a match thrown on a hay bale and her blue eyes blazed.

'Sorry if I'm late…you were supposed to wake me,' she reminded Alessio.

At the sound of her voice, he swung round and stood up, dislodging the brunette, who backed off with a flirtatious smile and purred in Italian, 'And who is this, Your Highness?'

Her familiarity with Alessio turned Rosy's tummy over with a sick lurch. His smile in Rosy's direction was distinctly tense.

'Rosy…allow me to introduce you to Lucia Garcia Perez, the tourist board's manager for this area. El Palacio is to be the focus of a new advertising campaign in the spring. Lucia, allow me to introduce you to my wife, Rosalia.'

'Your *wife*?' Lucia gasped, all wide dark eyes and parted lips. 'You've got married? I had no idea.'

Tempted to ask what rock she had been hiding beneath to avoid the blanket European media coverage of Graziana's defection and Rosy's last-minute substitution as the bride, Rosy forced her lips into a polite smile. 'Pleased to meet you,' she said, extending her hand. 'I've fallen in love with this place. Tell me about the campaign.'

'There's no reason for you to get involved in this,' Alessio sliced in, having raised a staying hand as Rosy made to move towards the laptop he had been studying with the brunette. 'Give me fifteen minutes and I'll be done.'

'I'll ask Jorge to send in some refreshments,' Rosy murmured coolly, returning to the doorway.

'Thank you but there's no need, Your Highness,' Lucia interposed brightly, her dark eyes snapping with enjoyment as if she could sense Rosy's concealed vexation. 'Alessio will look after me. We're old friends.'

With a non-committal nod of acceptance, Rosy departed, her spine stiffening as she heard the door close in her wake. She didn't think he should be in that office alone with so forward a woman. Old friends indeed! She'd heard that expression before in an old sitcom and it should've been left there. Lucia had been touching him, all over him like a rash, fixing his cufflink, for goodness' sake!

Quietly seething, Rosy went into the drawing room, where Jorge served her with a drink. It took almost half an hour for Alessio to join her. By then, he had changed into a dinner jacket and classy narrow black trousers to match her appearance and he looked arrestingly hand-

some. His strong jawline was slightly clenched, however, his lean dark face a little taut.

'I didn't hear your visitor leave,' Rosy heard herself
quip, even though she had not intended to make any
reference to the gorgeous Spanish lady.

'She's always used the side entrance into the library,'
Alessio countered.

'Old friends indeed.'

'Don't be passive aggressive about it. Just say what
you're dying to say.'

Rosy felt the heat of the colour flushing her face at
his intonation. 'I thought that she was far too familiar
with you and that you should've told her to back off,'
she said quietly.

'Madonna mia!' Alessio bit out impatiently. 'If it
only takes the appearance of an old lover to make you
throw a jealous fit, how will you ever cope with my
misspent past?'

CHAPTER NINE

THE GHASTLIEST SILENCE FELL. Into it, Jorge surged to pour Alessio an aperitif and offer her a second, which Rosy refused.

Stiff as a concrete post, Rosy tilted her chin. She hadn't seen Alessio angry before, so it was a new experience, and he was angry with her, angry, tense and uncomfortable and that bothered her and, she discovered, *wounded* her. All of a sudden, she felt like the replacement bride again, guilty of crossing boundaries that she had had no right to cross. Jorge, evidently a good reader of the room, was already striving to usher them across the hall into the dining room and their first formal meal in the rambling house.

Rosy almost winced when she saw the polished table scattered with rose petals and crystals. It was the ultimate honeymoon dining experience with tiny heart-shaped savoury tarts on the plates awaiting them and she was quick to compliment Jorge on the beautiful and elegant setting.

Listening to her gracious comments, Alessio breathed in deep and slow to calm his volatile temper. He was annoyed with himself and with Lucia, *not* with Rosy.

'It's not a matter of petty jealousy,' Rosy murmured with quiet pride as soon as they were alone. 'It's a question of what's appropriate and Lucia was *touching* you.'

'No, she was not,' Alessio contradicted curtly.

'She was fiddling with your cufflink, her hands on your arms and your shoulders, her hair tossing round you,' Rosy specified with pink cheeks. 'Put yourself in my place. If a man was touching me in the same familiar way, would you ignore it? Would you be quite content to watch that happening in front of you?'

Alessio gritted his even white teeth hard enough to chip them because he *knew* that he would not be accepting in any way of such a display. He would not stand still for a second to watch another man touching his wife. His possessive streak ran deep and strong and her logical reaction infuriated him. 'I'm not accustomed to discussing my private life with anyone,' he admitted in a driven undertone. 'I have been an independent operator for too long. But now, I have to appreciate that I can no longer have that autonomy when I have a wife.'

'I understand that,' Rosy murmured, the tension in her shoulders easing as she recognised that he had mastered his anger. 'Your past, however—misspent or otherwise—is none of my business.'

'Up to a point that is true, but not when it intrudes so blatantly into our marriage,' Alessio retorted without hesitation. 'I was embarrassed by Lucia's visit and that made me angry. I had to tell her that what we had would not be continuing.'

'She knew you were now married and I gather it was a longstanding relationship,' Rosy guessed.

'She was trying to save face when she pretended that she was unaware of your existence. I've not visited Spain since my engagement to Graziana. I didn't have a relationship with Lucia, merely a casual friends-with-benefits arrangement when I was here. She didn't want any publicity either because her family would have disapproved. In recent years I have been much more discreet about such matters than I once was,' Alessio explained tautly. 'Lucia suited me because she had no ambition to be splashed over the tabloids with me beside her.'

Embarrassed? She respected him for admitting that to her but could not help wishing that she had not seen the lovely Spaniard at all. It had only created dissension and left her feeling insecure because Lucia had proved to be one of those supermodel perfect beauties like all the predecessors Rosy had viewed in Alessio's company online. And those comparisons simply made Rosy feel so *very* ordinary with her red curls and diminutive height.

'So, if she knew you were now married, she was—'

'Fishing? Testing the water to see if I wished to continue...and naturally, I don't,' Alessio asserted. 'There will be no other women in my life while you are with me.' His brilliant crystalline green eyes assailed hers with a ruthless gleam and he toasted her with his wine glass. 'Where do you think I would get the energy from?'

And Rosy almost choked on her wine as she thought of the number of times they had had sex over the past thirty-six hours. 'I suppose we've been busy,' she framed. 'Like rabbits or whatever.'

Alessio flung back his head and laughed with rich amusement. 'I think they are more famous for producing little rabbits and we're trying not to do that!' he contradicted. 'I can talk to you about anything, and I've never had that before with a woman. It's a valuable advantage for both of us.'

And just like that, Rosy reflected in silent wonder, all the tension and the messy emotions drained away and she found herself smiling back at him, entranced by his breathtakingly handsome lean, dark face. Her heartbeat had kicked up pace, her tummy awash with butterflies, and she knew right then in that moment that it was too late to worry about falling in love with a husband who could still decide to eventually dispense with her as a wife. After all, her surge of pleasure and excitement was warning her that she had already fallen victim to his appeal.

'I'm hardly going to see you after tomorrow.' Rosy sighed, her expression wry because there was no point regretting the reality of Alessio's busy life.

It was the last night of their honeymoon and in the morning, they would be returning to the palace in Severino, the capital of Sedovia. Their little idyll in Spain of total privacy and togetherness would be at an end. They would be plunged straight into the fuss and complexity of the royal coronation, due to be staged in another two weeks' time. There would be multiple meetings with all the many people involved, garment fittings and rehearsals. They would have to fight an often-rigid schedule to find time to be together and she felt guilty because she was already dreading those changes in spite of the fact that she now felt much more secure in her role as Alessio's wife and princess. Two weeks together had changed so much for them as a couple. She was now calmer and more confident in the awareness that Alessio liked her, respected her, understood her and, also…lusted madly after her.

'Why would you think that?' Alessio demanded, breaking off from a lingering and leisurely exploration of her slender, curvy body to sit up and look at her in apparent disbelief.

'Because that's what it was like before the wedding. You didn't have any time for me.'

'Everything's different between us now. Back then, I was still in shock from Graziana's betrayal and I was also afraid that you might panic and retreat from all the demands and responsibility coming your way as a royal,' Alessio admitted, thoroughly disconcerting her, for it had not once occurred to her that he might have feared such a development, although admittedly she had found the days running up to their royal wedding hugely stressful. 'I couldn't afford to take anything for granted until you actually *married* me. I worried about making the wrong move, about saying or doing anything that might upset you.'

Rosy nodded, secretly amused by that explanation. 'So, I should've said, "Alessio I want to spend time with you"?'

'And if I could've seduced you into bed, I would have been even keener, *piccola volpe*. But I know there would have been no chance of that now.' A wicked glitter made Alessio's eyes gleam like jewels in the lamp-light as he stroked an expert fingertip across a tight, straining nipple with sensual intent. 'I know for a fact that you're not the kind of woman who'll sleep with a stranger on her wedding night!'

'But it didn't take you long to change my mind, did it?' she teased back, covering his wide mouth with her own, tipping him back against the pillows with a sensual assurance she could not have utilised just two short weeks before.

Right from the outset, she had realised that Alessio had set a newly discovered part of her nature free and it had empowered rather than diminished her. She revelled in the fact that Alessio couldn't keep his hands off her because it was the same for her. On that level, she conceded, they were equals. It was only when she put in the emotional attachment that she had developed for the man she had married that she felt a little foolish and lacking.

Once the passion had subsided, Alessio rested back with Rosy's limp length still in his arms. He was also in no hurry to return to the palace. He knew that he had allowed too many staff to organise his schedule for too long without question. He had seen it as his duty to the throne and had avoided demanding personal time of his own. There would have to be modifications, he acknowledged grimly, so that he had hours to spend with his very beautiful, very sexy wife.

Rosy made him ridiculously happy in some weird way. Somehow, and he had no idea how, she stopped him worrying, stressing and overworking. He was becoming conscious that he had been too agreeable a royal heir, far too focused on *not* following in his father's self-indulgent footsteps. Unfortunately, that guiding ambition had merely sent him to the other extreme in which he had allowed too many people to demand his time and his appearances. The result was that in the few years since his father's demise, he no longer had anything that could be described as off-duty time. And how could that truth possibly help to build the family life he had long hoped to achieve?

It certainly would not impress Rosy, who set high standards, refused to be rushed into anything and moved steadily at her own pace. Rosy was strong, *but*? There was no way that he would allow the royal staff to take over Rosy's schedule and try to guilt her into working endless hours and late nights for the myriad causes that sought palace support. Firmly resolved to immediately begin the changes that he saw were necessary to protect his wife, Alessio was already making plans.

'Now, this is a question I keep meaning to ask you and forget to,' Alessio admitted during their flight back to Sedovia. 'Is there any chance in the future that you might want to decide to search for your missing mother?'

Dumbfounded by that enquiry coming at her out of the blue, Rosy frowned in bewilderment. 'Definitely not. I spent twenty years living in the same house with the same family she left behind when I was a baby. At any time, she could've visited, phoned or written if she had ever been curious about me…and she never *did* and that tells me all I need to know,' she confided calmly. 'Wherever she went, she didn't look back on abandoning me with regret. I'm just not interested now. Vittoria gave me photos of my mother taken during the eighteen months that she lived with my father and was able to satisfy my curiosity. I look a little like her.'

'But what if she chooses to get in touch with you?'

'Why on earth would she do that?'

'Our marriage has been widely covered in the newspapers and an abandoned child who has become a queen may be a more alluring prospect,' Alessio remarked with unhidden cynicism.

'I would still not want any interaction…or the complications that could come with it. Is it awful to admit that I'm more excited by our coming reunion with Clover?' she muttered uncomfortably. 'Am I heartless?'

Alessio closed a hand round her clenched fingers. 'Not at all. I admire your practicality and backbone. You can't feel an attachment to a stranger who made it obvious that she was not attached to you.'

'Even though I'm aware that there may have been extenuating circumstances?' Rosy winced as she made that intervention. 'I mean, maybe she was suffering postnatal depression and was simply too ashamed when she recovered to check up on me. Possibly my father was abusive towards her as well. There could be a lot of stuff I don't know about her situation back then, so I've always tried not to be judgemental about it,' she confessed ruefully.

'I feel that in *our* circumstances,' he stressed, 'it

may be wise to look into her disappearance in advance
and discover, if we can, what *did* happen. Did she remarry and have more children? Are there other family
members involved? She may not even still be alive…
unhappily, that possibility has to be checked out. But
it's up to you what you choose you do. May we seek
further info…or not?'

Rosy swallowed hard at that fair enquiry. She saw
his point, she more than saw his point because, as the
Queen of Sedovia, she would be very visible, and it
was his job to protect the monarchy. 'You can make
enquiries if you think it's necessary, but I would prefer
not to know the results…unless she has passed away.
That, I would prefer to know,' she specified.

Although that was a partial lie she was giving him,
she acknowledged inwardly. Her mind was already
roaming through other various possibilities that had
not occurred to her before. That she might have half-
siblings? A living mother out there? Things she had
never allowed herself to wonder about before because
they had seemed pointless. Unsettled, she lay back in
her leather recliner and closed her eyes, striving *not*
to wonder.

Alessio's gaze rested on her delicate, taut profile
and he suppressed a sigh. He had suspected that his
question would upset her, and it had. But hopefully, he
reasoned, it would be worth it in the end because he
was less concerned about some silly scandal that might
shadow the throne in the future and rather more concerned with protecting Rosy from the unexpected and
the risk of distress. She had dealt bravely and compas-

sionately with her mother's desertion, and he refused to let that issue come back to haunt her.

They had barely arrived at the palace and, indeed, were waiting in the echoing hall for the lift when a small, rather pompous man in a suit marched up to Rosy and planted a file in her hand. 'Your schedule this week, Your Highness. I thought we should take the first possible opportunity to go over it.'

'And this isn't the *right* opportunity, Antonio,' Alessio sliced in levelly. 'My wife has been travelling and she is now about to move into her new home. She must have time to settle in and choose her own interests from the large number available.'

Disconcerted by that interference, the man went into retreat while Alessio guided Rosy into the waiting lift. 'I could've done it,' she told him anxiously.

'I know you could but there's no necessity for you to leap straight in with both feet into an unfamiliar environment. I want you to take your time and decide which ventures you wish to support. I thought possibly...' he grinned at her as Clover surged out of the sitting room and the puppy hurled herself at Rosy's knees and she knelt down to deal with loads of puppy kisses and licks '...animal rescue. There are several associations to choose from, any of which would be delighted by your support. And possibly...er, children.'

'If that's viable when I've none of my own,' Rosy quibbled. 'Although I'm hopefully going to be an aunt again in a few months.'

Clover bundled in her arms like a wriggling parcel, Alessio proceeded to show her around his wing of the palace. It had everything, absolutely everything, she registered in pleasurable surprise. It was far larger than she had appreciated on her brief visit to change out of her wedding gown in that bedroom two weeks earlier. There was a gym, an entire room to be devoted solely to her wardrobe, their separate offices and Alessio confided that he had had a small kitchen installed while they were in Spain in case she took the notion to cook for him. The smile in his eyes told her that he was very much hoping she succumbed to that temptation.

'You are a fabulous cook,' he pointed out as they traipsed on through innumerable bedrooms and reception rooms.

'So is the palace chef,' she traded. 'But I do enjoy cooking sometimes.'

'And these will be *our* rooms.' Alessio thrust wide a door into the vast crown prince's suite. 'Not just mine but yours as well. We will rewrite historical precedent and *share*.'

Rosy nodded, a singing in her heart that he had thought that out for himself. She had only the haziest concept of his usual schedule, only a vague recollection that he was always coming back and going somewhere else for the fuss made of his returns was memorable for anyone on the palace staff. He was incredibly popular with employees working for him, which was why she had been startled when he had brushed off Antonio's request because Antonio was one of his senior advisers and probably quite unaccustomed to such treatment. If Alessio wasn't careful, he would make *her* unpopular because without a doubt any changes made would be laid at her door.

Over breakfast the next morning, Rosy listened at length to Alessio's elaborate plans to divest them of long day schedules crammed with meetings and appearances and on her second cup of tea finally mustered the gumption to venture her own opinion. 'Yes, but none of that is really practical just at the moment with the coronation so close,' she remarked apologetically. 'We'll have to buckle down and just get on with it for the next couple of weeks and *then* you can begin making changes.'

Comprehension gripped Alessio like a vice. Possibly two heads being better than one was a more useful cliché than he had previously foreseen, he conceded grimly. He nodded. 'Obviously. Possibly you could be free for Antonio's meeting at some time today?'

Rosy read his air of frustration, quite understanding that Alessio had a new broom mentality, full of fire and vigour, but she was a little more realistic than he was because very little could be achieved overnight. 'Of course. We'll get through this stage bit by bit. It's just unlucky that there's only *one* of you,' she commented. 'When your father was at this stage, he had an adult son to stand in for him.'

Alessio laughed at that 'only one of you' and cracked a joke about the unlikelihood of his parents having ever produced a second child. His less than sunny mood had dissipated as he rose from the table and they parted to go separate ways. 'I'll see you tonight.'

But the heavy list of dinner parties leading up to the coronation meant that they didn't really see each other except in parting or across a room over the following ten days and Rosy was so exhausted when she fell into bed every evening, she didn't even stay awake long enough to notice Alessio's arrival. Most mornings she wakened to a mere dent in the pillow beside hers. She was much too busy to fret about his absence and quite saw why he had hoped to change things, even if he had picked the wrong time to try and do it. He was much more aware of such stuff than she was, she censured herself. This royal life had always been his and *she* hadn't really known what she had been talking about.

And then in the space of a moment, the day before the coronation, everything changed for Rosy when a member of the PR team brought her a printout from a website, titled *Gold-Digger Scams Sedovian Royal Family!*

Rosy was horrified as she scanned a disturbingly accurate financial estimate of her family's hotel misfortunes and her family's obvious prosperity since the wedding. White as milk, she read the entire lengthy report, which invited the Sedovian public to make up their own minds about how a 'commoner' like Rosalia had 'forced' herself on Alessio. Had she or her family used some secret blackmail to entrap the Crown Prince over some youthful indiscretion of his? Blatant lies followed in named quotes of people that Rosy had never heard of, vilifying her reputation with men and money. It was all nasty, sordid stuff.

'This website has already been taken down, Your Highness. The lawyers were able to enforce that under threat of a libel suit.'

'But how many people must have *seen* it?' Rosy gasped, upset beyond belief as she thought of her family hearing about such accusations, most especially when there was a tiny kernel of truth in the story.

And that truth was that Alessio *had* bought his royal bride, like an apple off a supermarket tray. How had she ever contrived to forget that horrendous fact? How on earth had she managed to fall in love with her buyer? Those harsh facts suddenly made her feel cheap and unclean. An hour later, necessity having suffocated any chance of giving way to angry, wounded tears, Rosy emerged from a final fitting of her coronation robes and went straight to Alessio's official office on the ground floor to tell him about the website.

Having neglected to knock, she stopped dead on the threshold when she registered that her husband was in the middle of a meeting and every head turned to see her. 'Oh, I'll see you when you're finished,' she said lightly, forcing an apologetic smile onto her tense face and turning on her heel again.

Being forced to wait even longer to vent her feelings did nothing to cool down Rosy's mood. The more she reread that article, the angrier she became, even though a calming voice at the back of her head warned that it was a very bad idea to keep on heavy-duty dwelling on such a negative item. That was why it was unfortunate that it took Alessio quite a long time to finish his meeting and Rosy had showered and clambered into the casual clothing she always wore after what she deemed to be 'work hours' were over. In fact, clad in her shorts and tee, she was pacing the floor in their bedroom when Alessio finally put in an appearance.

'I need a shave,' he complained, striding through

the door, looking darkly handsome but stressed out and rubbing a hand irritably over his shadowed, stubbled jaw line.

'You always need a shave,' Rosy pointed out quite truthfully for he had to shave twice a day.

In silence she watched him strip. There were times when watching that lean, muscular, hair-roughened physique of his emerge from clothing was the highlight of her day, quickening her heartbeat, turning her tummy over with craving. But this wasn't one of those times. Rosy desperately wanted his full attention and it didn't seem the right moment, but frustration was engulfing her at having had to wait so long to speak to him and just as he was about to stride into the en suite for a shower and shave, she crossed the room.

'I have to talk to you,' she told him in a rush as she set down Clover on the rug. 'It's about this website...'

Alessio flipped round and actually smiled at her, she registered in disbelief. 'Oh, that?' he murmured with unbelievable calm and cool. 'That's already been dealt with.'

'I beg your pardon?' she cried with incredulity. 'You already *knew* about that article?'

Twin ebony brows drew together above his gleaming, assessing gaze. 'Of course. Our IT team are very good. They check out stuff like that every day,' he told her conversationally. 'The government informed the palace about that site as well.'

'So...?' Rosy breathed in deep and fast. 'In other words, just about everybody in Sedovia knew that I and my family had been targeted and maligned…everybody *but* me!'

'I saw no reason to upset you with such nonsense,' Alessio admitted levelly, not turning a hair in spite of the fact that Rosy had got very flushed and was standing there rigid with clenched fists by her sides. Clover, though, had shot below the bed when she had raised her voice.

'You saw *no* reason?' she gasped furiously.

Alessio released his breath in a huff. 'Clearly, you believe I should've told you sooner.'

'*Yes!*' she bawled at him angrily. 'At least I could've warned my family.'

Blind to her temper, it seemed, Alessio skimmed his flashing smile at her. 'You don't need to worry about that either. I took care of that for you and Vittoria and Patrick aren't bothered. In their words, "Sticks and stones don't break bones",' he completed cheerfully and the dog dared to peer out from under the bed.

And that was the last straw for Rosy, the absolute last straw that Alessio could have dared to go over her head to *her* family and warn them of that article while continuing to keep her in the dark!

'All *royally* handled, I take it?' Rosy breathed between gritted teeth in a tone of dulcet sweetness.

'Yes. The website was taken down following the threat of legal action. It was only in existence for a couple of hours and the leak at the bank was traced to a junior employee. He has been dismissed for breaking his employment contract and selling confidential information for cash,' Alessio explained with distinct satisfaction. 'Our staff are excellent at dealing with such incidents.'

Rosy wrinkled her nose. 'So, it was just me you left out of all this handling, even though it was *me* who was most libelled!'

'How did you find out about it anyway?' Alessio enquired, poised there so deadly serious now and clad only in a pair of boxers, acres of bronzed male flesh on show.

'Samantha on the PR team.'

'She's new and she wouldn't have been made aware yet that you are not to be informed of any such personal attacks.'

'Who said I wasn't to be informed?' Rosy very nearly shouted at him and Clover retreated further below the bed.

Alessio elevated an ebony brow. 'I did, of course. I don't want you to be upset by something so trivial.'

'Trivial?' she screeched back at him, making him frown in apparent surprise. 'You think it's *trivial* when I'm called a scheming, gold-digging shrew? Or when the financial background to our marriage is leaked to the public?'

'Of course, I don't think it's trivial in *your* estimation,' Alessio countered more thinly, a faint flush rising along his high cheekbones. 'But, at present, we have won what redress we can for this distasteful incident. We are still pursuing proof of who put up the site, although we have a suspect. Beyond that, there is nothing more we can do.'

'I had a right to be told about that article the minute it appeared!' Rosy launched back at him stridently.

His green eyes glinted like diamonds in sunlight, hard and unyielding. '*Not* if this is how you will react. Being trolled is what happens to public figures, and we are public figures, however, we—as a couple—do not take it personally. That is the bottom line here and I will not move it a centimetre. Now you may understand *why* I ordered that you be protected from such scurrilous drivel.'

As Alessio went on into the en suite without another word, Rosy couldn't bear to let him have the *last* word and she yelled, 'I don't feel like part of a couple!'

The bathroom door closed and Rosy just covered her tear-wet face with her hands and swallowed back an angry, wounded sob while striving to maintain control.

Clover emerged from under the giant bed and gambolled round her feet, relieved the noisy drama was over, and Rosy got a grip on herself and went out through the balcony doors in the sitting room, down the handsome stone steps and took the dog out to play in the courtyard below. Well, now she knew where she stood with the guy she loved!

CHAPTER TEN

ALESSIO AND ROSY talked quietly over dinner, excruciatingly polite to each other while the staff were around.

Over coffee, Rosy murmured, 'So, we're not allowed to talk about this.'

Alessio slung a scorching appraisal at her. 'No, we're not. The discussion is closed. I have said all I can say on the subject.'

'We can still exchange views *quietly*.'

'You can't. You made me angry,' Alessio condemned as though that were an actionable offence. 'And as a rule, I do not get angry.'

'You're not accustomed to anyone arguing with you,' Rosy almost whispered. 'But I'm also sure I'm difficult enough to get you into the habit without it being a total disaster.'

'Enough!' Alessio sprang upright and tossed down his napkin. 'I have work to do.'

Tears stung the backs of Rosy's eyes because she had never seen Alessio so upset about anything and it was true that he didn't normally get angry. It disturbed her that she had managed to get him so riled up.

'Please...' she murmured as he was striding out of the room.

Alessio froze as if she had paralysed him with that single word and then he slammed the door shut and spun round to lean back against it, looking very much as though she had trapped him. Tall, dark and trapped against his will. He breathed in deep and slow before focusing shimmering, stormy green eyes on her anxious face. 'This is our world and I can't change it for you. You will be a target every day of your life if you *stay* married to me. Someone will always have a rumour to spread through the media and there is absolutely nothing I can do to prevent it happening,' he framed with savage bitterness, taking a couple of steps away from the door. 'I can't fully protect you from it— how do you think *that* makes me feel?'

And the last piece of the puzzle smoothly fell into place then for Rosy. He blamed himself for that article that had distressed and embarrassed her. He was a future king and people wanted to know everything about him and that truth had made her, as his partner, equally fascinating. When he went to the lengths of warning her that she would be a target every day she stayed married to him, it was an exchange that had gone too far though, she reasoned. Such an extreme sentiment plunged them into an unnecessary drama as helpful as a dark, suffocating cloud.

'The pressure on us will be relentless because we must live in the public eye most of the time. I've been aware of the glare of the cameras from early childhood,' Alessio bit out in raw continuation. '*Everything* is criticised or commented on, every personal choice, every outfit, every tattoo, every piercing, every woman on my arm. It was at its worst in the past until I reached the stage of not caring any more. I didn't care what was said about me and still don't, but that's no comfort now because I *do* care very much about what is said about *you*.'

'I know and I'm very grateful for that!' Rosy crossed the room and tried to haul him into her arms but he was standing there still, rigid with tension and deep emotion. 'I didn't understand how you felt, not properly, because nobody's ever been interested in me in that line before, because I was so *ordinary* until I met you.'

Alessio gazed down at her, stormy green eyes glittering. '*Extra*ordinary,' he corrected thickly. 'You were never ordinary. You've dealt with everything that was thrown at you but this one thing…the adverse publicity is ironically the most dangerous thing in the life we lead. I've known women and men as well who live for the scandalous headlines and the praise. But, if you want to keep your sanity, you have to stay away from it. Sometimes it's nice, just as often it's vicious.'

'I understand better how you feel now.' Rosy ran caressing fingers up below the silk lining of his jacket, smoothing over his taut cotton-clad torso, feeling the slight shudder as he reacted helplessly to her touch. 'And I know what will make you feel even better.'

Alessio bent down and scooped her up in his arms. 'Yes, I hit the perfect word…*extraordinary*.'

And then he was kissing her with the fierce hunger that made her kick off her shoes as he carted her willy-nilly through a series of interconnecting doors into their bedroom and he launched them both down onto the bed.

'I like being wanted,' she gasped.

'I like being wanted too, *piccola volpe*.'

And the pathos of that admission turned her heart inside out. Alessio, who hadn't been wanted as a child by parents who had needed him only as a means to an end. Alessio, hunted like a big-game trophy by calculating women, who sought his wealth or his title or his body, she thought, reflecting on Lucia, who had simply wanted to enjoy him the way Rosy herself did. Yes, that thought was a true leveller of pretention, reminding her that she was far from unique in Alessio's life, maybe just another woman who wanted him, craved him like an addictive drug because, in reality, he was fantastic in bed. It didn't matter that she loved him, she was probably one of a crowd who had loved him but got no further. In fact, she was simply that one lucky woman who had been in the right place at the right time when he'd needed her to become his bride. It was a humbling reflection, grounding her in the midst of the soaring passion that only he could induce in her.

'What are you thinking so hard about?' he demanded in the blissful aftermath of that fury of desire, long fingers stroking soothingly up and down her spine.

'Nothing,' she fibbed, running her fingers through his silky hair, holding him close, secure in appreciating now that he liked affection, liked being snuggled, liked all sorts of stuff that she had once assumed men didn't like. Alessio Maretti was his own unique self, fashioned by his love-deprived background, and she was his exact opposite because, in spite of her mother's desertion, she had rejoiced in endless love and affection from her sister and her husband. And maybe that was why she understood him better now, what drove him, what troubled him…

And it was a huge plus to learn that Alessio only lost his temper when he saw *her* as being under threat and at risk of distress. He *cared* about *her*. Did he even realise what that little scene had told her? She didn't think so. Alessio didn't spend much time agonising over his reactions, he just seemed to react in the heat of the moment. Volatile and intense. He could be snatched by force from his normal, remote calm control setting to a passionate vehemence of emotion that turned her upside down inside herself. The guy she loved, the guy she had married, and she couldn't believe how strongly she felt about him after such a short time.

She was having a cup of tea at some indescribably early hour the next morning when Vittoria phoned. 'You'll never guess who was outside our hotel last night with a cameraman waiting to capture pics of our celebrity customers leaving?' her sister told her in a playful tone.

'So, tell me—'

'Blasted Graziana!' Vittoria gasped, her incredulity now unconcealed. 'I couldn't believe my eyes when I saw her. I mean, what's a princess doing behaving like that?'

'Alessio told me that her father cut off her trust fund, so maybe she's just trying to make a living as a TV presenter or celebrity blogger or something,' Rosy responded, unable to understand the choices of a woman she had never met but heard all too much about. For her just at that moment, Alessio's former fiancée simply felt like yesterday's news.

'Nobody wants to see Graziana on television or anywhere else. She's too disliked,' Vittoria scoffed.

'I just don't think about her.' Rosy hesitated and then pressed on because this *was* her sister, after all. 'Alessio wasn't attached to her.'

'She strikes me as a bit intense, so maybe he dodged a bullet there,' Vittoria commented before moving on to address the coronation events that would start at eight that very same morning with a military parade.

And ever afterwards that whole day would be a simple blur for Rosy, kicking off for her with a formal breakfast attended by religious personnel and followed by a private meeting. It progressed on, hour by exhausting hour, with a procession to the cathedral in a carriage, and then there was ceremony after ceremony. In her long tailored white dress, she was horribly conscious of the cameras, not to mention the stunning moment when a crown was set on her head. It was a decided relief once she was walking back down the aisle on Alessio's arm even though the cameras were going madder than ever.

Only the presence of her own family in the front pew, her sister proudly pregnant now in a smart maternity dress, stabilised Rosy. That was real life, not the massive pomp and consequence of the coronation, which was intended for Alessio's benefit and only tangentially for her as his consort.

Exhausted by the spectacle, they both crashed into recreation for the weekend afterwards, relieved that the royal household believed everyone had acquitted themselves well in their various duties. And then, Alessio informed her that they were going to dine out as a treat. When she asked him where on earth in Sedovia they could accomplish that without becoming the cynosure of all eyes in the restaurant, he explained that they would have a private room for them and their guests. And as their guests were to be her family and Alessio's friend, Eduardo Conti and his chatty Spanish wife, Catalina, she was delighted because none of their guests were VIPs, whom it was impossible to relax with.

They were ushered in through a rear entrance, which Vittoria thought was wonderfully cloak and dagger, and Catalina giggled at their glimpse of the kitchens with all their rushing, immaculately uniformed chefs. Patrick, meanwhile, being a chef too, was busy eying up the competition, for they were visiting the top restaurant in Severino, which had won multiple foodie awards. Not that her sister and brother-in-law had much to worry about, Rosy reflected fondly. Currently, her family's hotel was fully booked well into the colder months and Patrick's own restaurant, though much smaller than the one they were visiting, was doing a ringing trade and popular with celebrities working at the television studios nearby.

There was much discussion about the food on the plates. Pleased to hear that Eduardo and his wife had already eaten at Patrick's restaurant, Rosy looked up from her plate to find Alessio studying her and she smiled, instantly, gloriously happy when she collided with his smouldering green eyes and felt herself turning hot pink in response.

That was the precise moment that the door burst open and framed the very last person Rosy had expected to see grace their precious, private evening out. It was Graziana, groomed to the nth degree, clad in a very glamorous figure-hugging silver dress. Rosy blinked and looked instinctively at Alessio for guidance, but he was too engaged in pressing something on his phone. As she turned her head to frown, Graziana came closer, snatched up a glass of water from the table and threw it over her, the tumbler falling down on the carpet.

'You stole the man I loved!' she shouted like some ghastly playground bully while Rosy sat there dripping in sincere disbelief at the Princess of Eboltz's behaviour.

A split second later, the room was full of Alessio's security men and a bunch of policemen. The most senior policeman lowered his head to hear Alessio's instructions while everyone else at the table sat dumbfounded by the scene. Ever practical, Vittoria handed Rosy her napkin to help dry her off. Only at that point did she notice the man with the camera on his shoulder and he was being handcuffed. Graziana was screaming and struggling but nobody was paying her the slightest attention and she was getting handcuffed very firmly too. As the senior police officer present told her sharply to stop kicking before she was forcibly restrained, she finally fell silent, staring at Alessio expectantly.

'You can't do this to me. I'm royal.'

'You committed an assault on the Queen,' Eduardo Conti, ever the lawyer, pointed out.

'I threw water at her. I didn't touch her!' Graziana

proclaimed, tossing Rosy a sneering smile of superiority.

'It's still an assault. Any infringement of the Queen's personal space is an assault still on the statute books. You can thank the Middle Ages for that,' Eduardo completed with a satisfied gleam in his gaze.

Alessio dismissed most of the men hovering in the room, leaving only the senior policeman and the head of his security with them. The cameraman was removed as well.

'You can't do this to me!' Graziana shrieked at him. 'I'm the Princess of Eboltz and I hold diplomatic status here.'

Alessio expelled his breath slowly. 'Well, you did until yesterday when I received the proof that you were behind that obnoxious website that libelled my wife. Your diplomatic status was immediately revoked.'

'Revoked?' Graziana exclaimed incredulously. 'You can't do that to me!'

'You are currently under a deportation order to Eboltz, which would've been served on you had we had the time to establish where you are staying. As we didn't have the time, I will now give you a choice.'

'My father won't allow me to go home,' Graziana countered with satisfaction.

'I spoke to Prince Sebastien yesterday. He's changed his mind. He prefers you at home rather than here acting like an embarrassment to Eboltz,' Alessio responded with biting contempt. 'So are you going home or you going to a jail cell tonight? That is your choice. If you refuse to leave Sedovia, you will be charged with assault and you will remain in a cell until the charge is answered in court. You may well receive a short sentence and after that is served, you will *still* be deported.'

'I can't believe you're speaking to me like this, treating me like I'm just anybody!' Graziana screeched in outrage. 'I'm royal. I'm a princess.'

'You have to act like a princess to get the royal treatment,' Rosy surprised herself by slicing into that flood of self-justification, temper stirring now in the aftermath of the shock of the other woman's behaviour.

Graziana had been responsible for that dreadful article on that website. Only hanging, drawing and quartering as a punishment would have lessened Rosy's anger.

'Charge her and put her in a cell,' Alessio advised the policeman, weary of the exchange.

Graziana gave him a wounded look, tears shimmering in her bright blue eyes. 'Alessio, *please…*

'All right, I'll go home!' Rosy heard the beautiful blonde shout outside the door as she was bundled out.

'With so many witnesses, this will get out into the media,' Eduardo forecast with a shake of his head. 'And I'm sorry to say it but I've no sympathy.'

Vittoria hissed a five-letter bad word in Rosy's ear. Catalina said it out loud in Italian and her husband frowned at her in disapproval. Alessio merely smiled with satisfaction. Rosy, who was usually more compassionate, was simply grateful that the spiteful princess would be removed from Sedovia and prevented from making further attacks on either her or her reputation.

'How will she get home?' she asked abstractedly

as their servers reappeared with the main course of their meal.

'On the evening ferry. Fortunately for us, she timed her arrival here well.'

Rosy's eyes widened in disconcertion. 'Graziana… on that little ferry? I can't imagine that.'

'I imagine she won't be able to either.' Alessio finally laughed and, as if by silent mutual agreement, nobody even mentioned Graziana's name for the remainder of the excellent meal.

In the limo that was wafting them back to the palace with police outriders, Rosy said, 'When you said there was a suspect for that article online, was it her? And if it was her, why didn't you tell me?'

'To be frank, I couldn't believe it *could* be her, any more than I could credit what she did tonight to you. How could I have been so blind to the craziness she was hiding behind her bland, formal front?' he demanded.

'I don't think she's crazy, I just think she's been very spoiled,' Rosy contended thoughtfully. 'I also think she's an attention seeker and all of a sudden nobody is the slightest bit interested in her any more and she can't bear that. Life as she knew it has ended. But only someone pretty stupid would think she could walk in on us with a cameraman, do something like that to me and get away with it.'

'And is that your final word?' Alessio queried with unconcealed amusement.

'Yes, I've no doubt she'll face a reckoning with her father and have to keep her head down for the foreseeable future. And hopefully, she'll stay out of Sedovia.'

'You're so calm,' Alessio noted with appreciation. 'Any other woman would be screaming at me for exposing her to that scene with Graziana.'

'How could I blame you for it?'

'I should have told my head of security that Graziana was under suspicion with that website because when she insisted that she was an expected guest in the restaurant, the security team were too aware of her status to question it,' he explained. 'That's how she got in. I've never wanted to handle a woman roughly in my life before but when she burst in and threw that water at you, I wanted to kill her!'

'My goodness…' Rosy was disconcerted by that roughened admission.

'She could have hurt you when she threw that glass and if she *had*, I probably would've laid violent hands on her!' he bit out fiercely. 'I will never allow anyone to get that close to you again.'

'Don't be daft,' Rosy soothed. 'Fortunately, there's only *one* Graziana and she's gone now. She won't be a problem for us again. As for her trying to claim that she *ever* loved you, even I was tempted to slap her for that.'

'Really?' Alessio had elevated an ebony brow in surprise.

'Of course I was after the way she treated you!' Rosy responded with defensive heat. 'Her sleeping with another man while she was engaged to you was the lowest of the low. She cheated on you, deceived you, upset you—'

'I'm not upset now. In fact, I'm fairly certain that ninety nine out of a hundred men would come through an insane drama like that tonight and thank their good

fortune at having been ditched *before* the wedding,'
Alessio said with unhidden amusement. 'I can laugh
about it now but I did make a very blessed exchange of
brides…as your sister was quick to point out.'

'Did she?' Rosy winced as they walked back into the
palace. 'Well, that's Vittoria, speaks as she sees and
she'd have no time for Graziana's dramatics.'

Clover raced across the giant hall as they waited for
the lift and Rosy bent down to greet the puppy. 'What
are you doing downstairs?'

Alessio smiled at the apologetic teenager scooping
up the puppy. 'Rosy, this is Antonio's youngest son, Pi-
etro, and he volunteered to be the official dog-keeper
for the summer. He's keeping Clover for us tonight.'

Rosy's brows disappeared beneath her fringe and
she said all that was proper to the boy before stepping
into the lift. As soon as the doors closed on them, she
exclaimed, 'Dog-keeper? Are you serious?'

'He looks after her when we're not around and
she does need a lot of exercise,' Alessio pointed out
straight-faced. 'So, the vet-to-be is the dog-keeper.'

'Fine.' Rosy resisted the urge to inform him that
she had wanted to cuddle her dog and Clover had just
been carried off.

'I wanted you all to myself tonight,' Alessio announced, gazing down at her in a different way altogether. 'No dog, no distractions, nothing but us.'

Rosy reddened, perfectly able to interpret that
scorching heat in Alessio's eloquent scrutiny. 'Right…'
she mumbled, a little quiver of response filtering
through her pelvis.

'I've decided that you're not a very romantic woman, but then I'm not a very romantic guy. You don't notice the flowers...you don't—'

'What flowers?' she asked him blankly.

'I've been sending you flowers every day for a couple of weeks! How could you not notice? You didn't even read my cards,' Alessio complained.

'You sent the flowers that keep on changing in our sitting room?' Rosy paled in dismay. 'I never looked for a card. I just thought it was the staff ensuring fresh flowers in there for us. I'm really sorry I *didn't* notice.'

'Being calm and practical is fabulous for being a queen,' Alessio told her as he herded her into their bedroom, where champagne on ice and chocolate-covered treats appeared to be awaiting them, making her brow furrow. 'But when you're a wife and you have a husband trying to tell you that he's hopelessly in love with you, it's not so good, *piccola volpe...*'

'Hopelessly in love with me?' Rosy parroted in sheer shock at that announcement. 'Since when?'

'I think it started the day you crashed your bike, because I couldn't take my eyes off you. I was enthralled the whole time I was with you but trying to keep my distance because I was supposed to be getting married,' Alessio explained. 'I accept that I'm not great at the frills when it comes to telling you that I love you, but I've never told a woman I love her before and you're so...silent.'

'Because I love you too,' Rosy finally piped up in a belated rush. 'And I was silent because I was shocked. I honestly didn't think you had those kinds of feelings for me. I thought I was just the replacement bride, the substitute for Graziana.'

'In bed as well?' Alessio quipped. 'Surely not?'

'That's sex, that doesn't count,' Rosy argued.

'Don't be naïve. Love and sex are an unbeatable combination in a healthy relationship.' Alessio eased her up against him and kissed her with passionate hunger and she shivered against his lean, muscular body, thought becoming a distant impossibility. 'And we have both because we attract each other like magnets...and you love me. To paraphrase you, when did that happen?'

'Oh, just along the way somewhere. I got attached. I tried not to but the more time I spent with you, the more it crept up on me.'

'You're making falling in love sound like a distinctly disturbing experience.' Alessio laughed. 'But I'm still crazy about you. I got it wrong on our wedding night but I must have got some things right.'

'You got an awful lot of things right,' Rosy whispered, her hands reaching up to frame his high cheekbones so that their eyes met, his bright and unusually vulnerable, hers steady and warm with approbation. 'But I'm not about to tell you them all and swell your ego.'

'That's mean,' Alessio complained, tugging her down on the bed and uncorking the champagne to send it foaming down into the waiting flutes before slotting one into her hand.

Bubbles tickled her nose as she sipped from the glass and reached out to try one of the dainty chocolate-

dipped fruit treats on the silver salver in front of her. 'I
don't think you have a mean bone in your entire body,'
she told him.

Her conscience was twanging because she knew she
was holding back on him and that wasn't fair. He had
told her that he loved her and she had been so astonished at that announcement, she had simply stared at
him. He had had the courage she lacked. 'You're loyal,
protective, kind, thoughtful, entertaining, honest…at
least, when you're not keeping quiet about stuff in the
unnecessary belief that you're protecting me.'

'It's fundamental to me to protect you any way I can
from anything that could harm you,' he objected.

'I'm strong, Alessio. I can handle all kinds of unpleas-
ant truths. I mean, there's really nothing that you don't
have going for you in the lovability stakes. How can I
possibly be the first woman you've told that you loved
her? What about that harpy who slept with your father?'

'I hadn't got around to telling her that I believed that
I loved her. I'm not sure now that I ever did. I didn't
experience any desire to run around taking care of her
as if she were breakable…as I do with you.'

'I bet if she'd known you were thinking it was love,
she'd never have got with your father,' Rosy opined
with newly learned cynicism.

Alessio swiped her champagne flute from her and
the chocolate treats, ignoring her little whimper of disappointment. 'We're not talking about that tonight. Tonight is for us and nothing else. Let's not waste any of
it discussing my youthful mistakes.'

'I can't believe you love me,' she admitted unevenly. 'It feels too good to be true.'

Alessio continued to strip off his suit and hauled his shirt over his head, exposing every mouth-watering inch of his muscular torso. Her heartbeat pounded and she wriggled out of her dress, cast it aside, treating her wispy silk underwear with a similar lack of care. He came down over her, all sleek dark predatory male, primed for action, and her mouth ran dry. 'Believe it,' he urged thickly. 'I am *never* letting you go. I'm not a changeable person, *piccola volpe*. I never wanted to keep one particular woman before and the emotions involved are much stronger than I realised they'd be.'

'Are they?' As he slowly lowered his big body down on hers, every skin cell in her body was flaring alive with sensual energy and with the connection she had only ever felt with him. He loves me, she thought in awe and intense relief. He had deserved to be loved. Trusting him and giving him that chance to prove himself worthy had been the biggest emotional risk she had ever taken but had also brought her the most magnificent reward.

'Yes, you've noticed that I'm not always reasonable where you're concerned. I'm possessive, territorial. I would be jealous if you so much as looked at another man.'

'No chance of that,' Rosy scoffed tenderly as he looked down at her with burning adoration in his jewelled gaze, her fingers skimming appreciatively across the smooth hot skin of his wide shoulders. 'You're it for me. I'm here for the long haul.'

'I was worried that you would think it would be too soon to tell you how I felt but I didn't want to keep it a secret.'

'And you got a dog-sitter lined up for Clover so that she doesn't come whining and scratching at our bedroom door and you ordered champagne and strawberries.'

'I wanted to make more of an occasion of it but you get embarrassed if I make extravagant gestures.'

'You can't buy a vet a new clinic just because she looked after Clover for a week and a bit—other people just pay the bill,' she pointed out gently.

'It was for you. You were so impressed with all the rescue work she did for free. Some people deserve that you go that extra mile…and I may not have mentioned it, but she *is* getting that new clinic. It's not extravagant. She runs a charity and it's a tax write-off,' Alessio informed her with just a hint of one-upmanship.

'I love you so much I could burst sometimes!' she gasped chokily.

He wiped the tears from her cheeks with his thumbs and bent down to kiss her. 'I love you so much,' he husked.

'Me too,' she said with an inelegant sniff.

And then that seething passion they generated together wholly claimed them, bonding hearts and bodies in a wild scorching rush of emotion, sensual pleasure and satisfaction.

EPILOGUE

Five years later

'I MISS DADDY!' wailed Isabella, Crown Princess and future Queen, with a quivering lower lip. 'He's s'posed to be here for my tea party!'

Rosy comforted her daughter, explaining as best she could to a four-year-old about a flight being delayed, and quietly reminded her that it was bedtime. Isabella, however, was very much her volatile father's daughter. With her favourite doll, her favourite teddy, her favourite bunny and even her favourite snake all set up at the little table for the toy tea party, Isabella was inconsolable at her father's failure to appear. Clover, who often functioned as a large, moving, breathing soft toy for the children, sat calmly nearby, her gentle eyes firmly fixed, not to Isabella, whom she adored, but to the real biscuits on the tea plate.

Rosy hadn't planned to produce an heir to the throne quite as quickly as she had. In fact, she had intended to wait six months before even trying to conceive. Her cautious schedule, however, had failed owing to a forgetful moment in the shower one morning. Alessio had been over the moon while Rosy had been shaken out of her usual composure. There had been parties across Sedovia after Isabella's birth, the heir destined to be the first queen in several generations.

And once they had settled into parenting Isabella, it hadn't seemed a major deal to consider a second pregnancy, only Rosy had unexpectedly conceived twin boys, Enzo and Armando, who were now adventurous two-year-old toddlers, presently fighting over a toy in the far corner of the room. Francesca, the baby currently crawling across the floor and threatening her big sister's tea party, was definitely, Rosy had assured her husband, their fourth and *final* child.

The respectable size of the royal family had surprised Sedovia, accustomed to previous rulers who had mostly had only one child. Rosy had never expected to find herself the mother of four children under five but with nannies and staff to help out she had seen no good reason to restrict Alessio's deep, driving desire for a proper family of his own.

Rosy had also seen that Alessio was never happier than when he was with them. He spent a lot of time with his children. Indeed, Patrick complained that he was being held to an impossible standard with Alessio by his wife, Vittoria. Their little girl, Ginevra, was only several months older than Isabella and family gatherings were lively now. As for Rosy, she had learned that she received a deep inner contentment from being a mother and she cherished the huge amount of love surrounding her.

Certainly, she was not in a position to be as full-time a parent as she once would have liked. On the other hand, she enjoyed her multi-layered life with all its many shades. She had a royal role as Alessio's consort, which entailed ceremonial appearances, and she attended events for several favourite charities.

Even so, she very much appreciated her freedom to continue working as an art restorer of growing repute. Mostly she restored paintings within their own household in rooms set aside for that purpose. Lucy, now retired while still working as a consultant for the palace restoration team, was a frequent visitor and adviser. Rosy had been suggested as Lucia's replacement, but Rosy hadn't wanted the role, knowing that she wouldn't have sufficient time to devote to the job. It was enough for her to still have the ability to work in the career of her choice.

Alessio's enquiries in respect of her long-lost mother had, following a two-year search, finally given her answers...*sad* answers. Medical records had revealed that her late mother, Heather, had been a drug addict, a fact that Vittoria, a student at the time, had not been aware of but which they both knew that their father must've known even though he had chosen to keep it a secret. Most probably, Rosy's mother had left her baby immediately after her birth because she was desperate for a fix. Heather's life had gone downhill fast and, within a few years of her daughter's birth, she had died of an overdose. She had had no other relatives alive and no more children. Tragic though that backstory had been to learn, Rosy had adjusted to it, even more grateful now that Vittoria and Patrick had stepped up for her in that vacant parental spot and still continued to fill it.

In fact, just at that moment, even though Alessio was late and the kids were stroppy over the fact, Rosy acknowledged that she was remarkably happy in her life. Alessio might be the exciting centre of his children's world but he was at the heart of Rosy's too. They often spent family weekends at El Palacio in Spain and, in the summer, at the much improved and extended cabin in the mountains, where the kids could run a little wild and skip through the surf and where, occasionally, Rosy and Alessio got a little frisky in the cave behind the rocks. They always spent their wedding anniversaries at the cabin and she cooked and often that was where they got together with her sister and husband and kids because it was a perfect place where everyone could be themselves and not worry about prying eyes.

It occurred to her that she was downright grateful that Graziana had run out on that wedding that should have taken place with Alessio. Having been deported from Sedovia, Graziana had settled back to life on the island of Eboltz and as soon as she had been granted her annulment from the unfortunate bodyguard she had wed in such haste, she had married a wealthy businessman, who had swept her off to live in France. There, from occasional glimpses of her face in glossy magazines, Graziana was living the highly visible, glossy life she had obviously craved. But that kind of life would *never* have suited Alessio, Rosy reflected fondly.

'Daddy!' Isabella shrieked so loudly that Rosy jumped, sprung from her reverie with a vengeance.

A crowd of children engulfed him in the doorway. Clover stole a biscuit and ran off with it. Francesca commenced her very slow crawl in her father's general direction. Rosy smiled as Alessio succumbed to the challenge of the tea party.

Alessio's heart lit up in lights the instant Rosy smiled at him, that warm, welcoming smile that enveloped him. She was still his *piccola volpe*, impossibly pretty and delicate in the snazzy blue cocktail frock she wore. It was her birthday but she still wouldn't put herself forward and would insist that he took his time with their children.

An hour later, the royal couple dined in private with candles and all the little touches their staff had included to enhance the occasion. Rosy sipped wine, the light reflecting off the stunning diamond crescent necklace she wore, her latest gift. Her attention, though, was all for Alessio, who had been absent for a week. Now he was describing someone he had met while he was overseas, lean, darkly handsome features with those classic cheekbones animated, stunning green eyes alight, shapely sculpted mouth compressed with amusement while his hands sketched vivid word pictures in the air between them. Still drop-dead gorgeous, still *hers* in every sense of the word and the pleasure induced by that acceptance flamed through her like a wildfire.

Slowly, gracefully, she slid upright and settled entranced blue eyes on him. 'Early night?'

'It's your birthday,' he protested.

Rosy grinned. 'So, it's my choice what we do next...'

'You're a wicked woman but I love you for it,' Alessio groaned, closing his hands over hers to pull her close, tugging her into stirring contact with his lean, hard body. 'It's been a very long week without you, *piccola volpe.*'

She smiled below the circling caress of his erotic lips, reacting to the physical urgency of his hips rocking against her. 'For me too...'

And they careened into the bedroom, Alessio knocking a shoulder off the door, disconcerting the dog, who looked up and then went back to sleep again, having seen it all before.

A while later, they lay luxuriating in a hot, limp pool of fulfilment.

'I love you so much,' Alessio said huskily, winding one of her curls round a long forefinger as he gazed down at her dreamily. 'And you look absolutely fantastic in diamonds.'

'Clearly, I was tailor-made for you,' Rosy murmured drowsily. 'Yes, I love you too, more than I even did five years ago.'

'Love sort of grows, doesn't it? I've never been this happy in my life...'

* * * * *

A WEDDING
BETWEEN
ENEMIES

LORRAINE HALL

MILLS & BOON

For all the animal lovers

CHAPTER ONE

SERENA VALLI KNEW two things with full certainty.

First, and most importantly, she hated Luciano Ascione with the fire of at least four generations of fury behind her.

Second, and quite unfortunately, she needed him.

Luckily, he needed her as well. If he cared at all. Which was certainly up for debate.

They were both failing, drowning, and about to implode if they did not reach out and save each other.

She supposed it was the kind of poetic justice born of their fathers—sworn enemies from birth—dying in the same automobile crash. As if they'd both been racing toward something but, so focused on each other, they hadn't been able to reach that end goal.

Serena was determined to learn this lesson her father hadn't. If it meant proposing a deal with her sworn enemy, she would swallow that sword.

Because neither Serena Valli nor Valli Shipping would give in without a fight, no matter how brutal. How demoralizing. How *embarrassing*. Her feelings didn't matter—only the fate of her legacy did.

If there was any way to honor her father's memory—and more importantly, her grandfather's— it was this.

She'd grieved, she supposed. In her way. In the Valli way. There was, after all, no great affection between father and daughter. There had been respect—hers given out of duty, while she'd had to earn his with perfection, and so she had. Serena believed in duty.

And she would continue to do her duty for the Valli name and business, for her legacy. And with that as her mantra, she stepped into the lion's den.

Luciano had never bothered himself with his father's company, Ascione International—the biggest issue they both faced right there in the company's name. Valli had Italian shipping under lock. Ascione fared better in global waters.

Both were being encroached on by an upstart American company, slithering through the cracks left in Valli since her father's death last year. She knew Ascione also suffered cracks, though she doubted Luciano knew.

It was well known he was a thoughtless, careless, reprobate. The one and only thing he'd *ever* accomplished on his own was this club she ventured into now.

He'd inherited everything else and was likely to run that inheritance into the ground. She could let him, but she was afraid if she did, their new rival would win. But if she could manage this, Ascione and Valli working together, they would take down their *mutual* enemy, instead of each other.

Serena would swoop in. She would save everything. And if there was the opportunity, she would do what her father had never been capable of.

Take Ascione down for good.

But for now, she needed them. Or Luciano anyway.

Serena did not spend her time in *clubs*. The dim lights, the pulsing music, the crowds of bodies appealed to her not at all. The only thing she could say in a positive nature about Luciano's Cattiva Idea was that it did not smell of smoke and alcohol, and the bottom of her shoes did not stick to the floor as she'd expected from reading about places people went to at night to drink and frolic.

Instead, Cattiva Idea was…elegant—too loud, certainly,

but with a sophistication underneath all the nonsense of gyrating heirs and heiresses trying to outshine each other.

She *supposed*.

Now she made her way through the tables full of the young and sparkling, wincing only a little at the noise level. She was only twenty-six, young yet, but she felt ancient to all their blatant posturing. Her grandfather had once told her she'd been born an old soul, and she could not deny that she felt like one in the audience of her peers.

She changed her focus from the revelers to the corner of the main floor, where on a raised kind of platform, Luciano sat, his arm draped over the bare shoulders of a beautiful woman Serena thought she recognized from one of her favorite television shows. There was a handful of other people at the table and his section seemed to be roped off. *A VIP section*, she supposed and rolled her eyes.

There was no doubt Luciano was a wealthy man. He was dressed in the best of the best, even if he left a few buttons of his shirt undone, as if the glimpse of olive skin was some kind of temptation, some kind of power move.

Serena did not allow herself delusion. He was a handsome man. All jet-black hair and dark eyes. High cheekbones and a Grecian nose. Full mouth, chiseled jaw. Then there was the height, the broad shoulders. There could be no argument. He was stunningly, classically attractive.

He knew it. He used it. She could disdain him for it, but she could not blame him for it.

She too used whatever tools were at her disposal. It was why she'd donned four-inch heels this evening—so she could be closer in height to him. It was why she hadn't worn a *business* suit, though as she didn't lend herself to the frivolous, her dress *was* black. And probably a little more suited for a work cocktail hour than a youthful club. But she'd uncharacteristically left her hair down, allowed it to curl in all the ways it would instead of taming it into a braid or twist as she preferred. She'd worn makeup more in keeping with a night out than a corporate meeting, and added a few pieces of jewelry, on loan from her mother, a far more ostentatious creature than Serena herself.

Serena took after her father, as her mother so often liked to tell her. A deadly dull vulture in the presence of far more interesting peacocks. It was why after the divorce, Serena had spent more time in her father's home than her mother's.

But deadly dull vultures were *successful*, her father had always liked to say. All peacocks did was strut about.

Luciano was most assuredly a peacock. All feathers and color and no substance. *How* was she going to get through to him when all of her motivations would fall on deaf ears?

You'll figure it out, she told herself sternly.

As she got closer, his dark gaze drifted over to her and sharpened in recognition. She didn't stop walking, but she braced herself for the fight ahead. She held his gaze and walked straight to him. She didn't even look at one of the men she supposed acted as some kind of security for him when the suited hulk held out an arm to stop her.

She held Luciano's gaze. "He'll see me," she said.

And Luciano must have waved his little bodyguard off, because the arm dropped, then the rope, and Serena was allowed to move forward.

Once she got close enough to hear him over the pumping music, he smiled. Like a shark. "Ah, if it isn't Satan herself."

Serena smiled in return. Like a wolf. Because a wolf could swim, but a shark couldn't do a damn thing on land. "Do you really suppose the devil would be a woman, when we all know men are the crux of all our problems? Two men in particular."

This got a laugh out of Luciano's companion.

"*Two* men," he scoffed. His gaze dropped to his glass. "The investigators thought differently."

"*Your* investigators thought differently. The ones not on your payroll blamed both men for foolish, unreasonable speeds. A fact that, knowing our fathers, is undeniable."

"Did you know your father?" he asked, tilting his head, as if to consider such a thing. "It is rather difficult to know a snake."

"Perhaps just as difficult as it might be to know an Ascione scorpion."

"As much as I love our little *tête-à-têtes*, I am busy." He gestured to the woman under his arm.

"I think we both know you are not." She gestured to the club around them. "Per usual. But we do have a problem, and I'd like to discuss a solution with you." She offered a polite smile to the actress who was watching them curiously. "In private."

"I shall pass."

"Do you think I came all this way with something that can simply be *passed* on, Luciano? I know you do not understand how anything important works, what kind of threat there is against your legacy, but I would think you would understand just how dire everything is if I would deign to come to you. In *this* place."

"What's wrong with your legacy?" the actress asked him, innocently enough.

Serena had to bite back a smile when he muttered irritably but stood. "We will discuss this in my office," he said.

She glanced back at the actress, wondering if the woman had purposefully helped her along. A wink told her yes.

Serena chose to take this as a good sign for what was to come. She'd take any good sign in this nightmare.

Luciano marched ahead, and she followed him easily enough. Through throngs of people, into an elevator that a card opened. She assumed only his staff had access to the second floor. After a brief elevator ride, he moved into a hallway, and then into a well-appointed office.

He flipped on the lights, closed the door behind her when she entered, then faced off with her, arms across his chest.

"I do not care for accusations about my *legacy* in front of my companions for the evening."

Serena nodded. "I do apologize," she said, without any sincerity. "Are you unaware then? Perhaps this may come as a surprise to you, perhaps the men actually running Ascione have not filled you in. Or perhaps you simply do not understand—"

"I understand just what Ascione is up against," he all but growled, looking fierce and dangerous.

She would not feel intimidated by that. She had been facing down wealthy, ego-driven men since she'd been a teenager. And she had learned how to come out on top. She had won over her father, which had been no small feat. It had required absolute perfection in everything she did.

And she had achieved that perfection. Still did, even with him gone. She used it as ballast and assurance that she could win over *anyone*.

"Then you know that if you do not do *something* in the next six months, Ascione will have to declare bankruptcy."

His expression shuttered. "I know nothing of the sort."

"Well, *I* do. Valli has more time, because I have been at the reins." She would not admit that her father left her a mess *almost* as big as the one Luciano's had left him. She would not admit that for a very brief period of time, she had been struck by the injustice of him being an imperfect mess while requiring perfection from her. "But there is a simple solution to our problems. A cure for both of us. Like with any cure, it is distasteful and might just kill us both first. Such is the nature of a last resort."

"I am all aflutter, Serena. Do tell me your brilliant plan."

Brilliant? She wished. She was down to desperate.

So, she didn't pretty it up. She didn't start with a lot of excuses or foolish words she didn't mean. She went straight for it.

"Marry me."

Luciano Ascione did not believe in hate. It was a wasted emotion. One that had eaten his father alive. Though he would never admit it to the woman standing before him, it had killed the great Gianluca Ascione just as much as the head on collision with a mountain had.

Luciano had always allowed himself one exception when it came to his relationship with hate. The dastardly Vallis. Most specifically the icy, perfect and damnable Serena Valli.

He hated her and enjoyed that hate almost as much as he enjoyed a salacious woman and an expensive whiskey.

It was a shame Serena was beautiful—that she wielded herself in a way he could not help but respect, if he was a fair man.

Luckily, he was not.

Marry me, she had said.

Chin raised, hazel eyes a sparkling challenge. Shoulders back, wearing the highest of heels that *almost* put her on equal footing with him.

Almost.

What he was really having a hard time getting over was the state of her hair. He wasn't sure he'd ever seen it…like this. A halo of dark curls around her face, untamed and… He'd be tempted to call it wild if he thought Serena Valli was capable of wild.

She was not. She was a cold, calculated *verme*. Like her father before her. But worse, she seemed to have no vices. She did not gamble, as her father had. She did not seem to ever drink to excess, as his had. There were no trails of men, gossip or scandal. She was a robot.

And she was suggesting they *marry*. He knew it was a trick, but he couldn't begin to reason out what the trick might be.

"Perhaps I've had a stroke," he offered, to buy himself some time. Because Luciano did not ever find himself *shocked* or at a loss. Except on the news of his father's demise.

And Serena Valli's marriage proposal.

"You have not. Nor have I, though I can understand the confusion. Instead, it is an extreme solution to an extreme problem. I do not relish it, but do you know the kind of attention we can garner if we marry? Do you know the kind of money we could save if we merged our companies? The absolute stone wall to keep this upstart American out of *our* customers' accounts? I don't expect you to, of course, but I have the spreadsheets for whoever handles actually understanding your legacy for you. I shall e-mail them and answer any questions, if you'd give me the appropriate contact information."

"There's just one little problem," Luciano said, smiling at her. Or perhaps he was only *trying* to smile. Her perfume was poisoning his office with a subtle, romantic floral scent that did not suit the woman at all. Perhaps that left him scowling.

"I hate you?" she supplied brightly.

"Not as much as I hate you."

"This, we can debate later," she said, waving it off like an annoying fly, not the center of both their beings. "This marriage, this merger, has nothing to do with emotions, and everything to do with saving our companies."

"Why should you care about saving Ascione? You don't. So, you are thinking only of saving yourself."

"Yes. Lucky for you, the only way I can save myself is to

save you as well. I do not expect your thanks, though will gallantly accept it should you ever be wise enough to extend it."

Thanks. She was always such an incredibly arrogant harridan.

"The attention certainly wouldn't hurt your little club either," she continued, as if he had already agreed. As if he *needed* to agree.

"My club needs no extra attention."

"What billionaire *needs* more, Luciano? They simply take it as their due. Or so I thought."

He hated that he agreed with her. Hated that she was right about Ascione—any of his own money that he infused now would simply draw out the inevitable. He needed more of a plan than just plugging holes with money.

She claimed to have one, but…he did not for the life of him understand what she was attempting to do.

"If you give me the contact information of whoever handles Ascione business for you, I will e-mail them my spreadsheets immediately. I am prepared to give you forty-eight hours to consider my proposal once your staff have explained the situation to you."

It was all so condescending. *She* was condescending. As if he needed *staff* to explain his own legacy to him.

But that was the image he had created. While his father had been alive, Luciano had lived and embodied that role when it came to Ascione—having nothing to do with the company, making sure he lived down to every one of his father's low expectations, while quietly and privately focusing his talents on his club.

But after the accident, Luciano had been forced to catch up. Though he did not allow anyone to know just how much work he'd done there, how much he knew and understood. He'd invented a character, instead, and this was the contact information he gave Serena now.

Alan Emidio was Luciano's "man of business". He answered e-mails, took phone calls, studied P&L statements and all the deadly dull business things Luciano's father had long ago given up on Luciano understanding.

Alan did not attend meetings, take phone calls or interact with anyone but Luciano because he did not exist.

Because Luciano understood just fine, now that he did not have to contend with the weight of his father's impossible moving standards.

"I will expect to hear from you soon," Serena said, with a politeness only *she* wielded like an accusation and a weapon. As if every time she chose the high road, she was sneering at whatever lower road she considered him on.

It was infuriating. "I would not wait up, Serena," he returned, smiling at her with as much charm as he could manage. Because it annoyed her. "I have many...companions lined up for my evening."

He saw the annoyance he'd wanted and an added dose of disgust chase over her face, even as she smiled in return, offered a nod and then turned and left his office.

Marry me, she had said.

Not a question. Not a beg. Not a *joke*. A statement of fact, as if that was the only possible answer to this problem they found themselves in.

Except they were not a *they*. They were enemies. Generations of Ascione and Vallis had fought to take over the shipping world in Genoa. And generation after generation, they had been more obsessed with hurting each other than changing with the times and building a sustainable business that would last.

Luciano had always considered that a waste, and pointless to try to talk his father out of. So he'd found something better to do with his time. He had convinced himself he did not care about his father, or Ascione or legacies.

It was funny what death could do to the things you convinced yourself of.

Still scowling at the door, he moved around his desk and then sat down at his computer. He booted up the profile for Alan Emidio.

She had, of course, already e-mailed him. So Luciano read the missive—businesslike, polite and to the point. There were a handful of attachments, and Luciano ignored everything—his guards, the club manager, his phone buzzing in his pocket—until he'd gone through every last one.

Then he sat back in his chair and cursed, scowling at the screen. She should not have known so much about Ascione. She must have implemented some spy—or more likely, her father had before he'd died.

When his father had been alive, Luciano had not been involved in the business. He had not been deemed worthy. He would not *fight* his father's low opinion of him.

But with the man gone, Luciano had not been able to let Ascione crumble into the sea. He had thought he would, but something ate at him. A surprising need to show a dead man he'd been dead wrong.

He'd been bailing water out of a sinking boat without a lifeline. And still he had not given up, even though Serena was right. Six months, unless he did something drastic, was the most he could eke out of Ascione before failing.

He didn't *need* Ascione, but he wanted it. Alive and whole. Perhaps one last *I told you so* to his father.

He could hardly marry Serena Valli, *merge* their companies. It was ludicrous on many a level. It was beyond drastic. It was insanity.

He could ignore it, but she had information and insights she shouldn't.

And that could not stand.

CHAPTER TWO

SERENA HAD DRIVEN HERSELF, as she liked to do when she wanted to feel most in charge, and she took the long, scenic way home, enjoying the play of light and dark as she drove from Genoa up to her estate.

Serena loved her home. Her privacy. The one place she could go and not worry about being Serena Valli. Even before her father had died, the old Valli castle atop a hill looking out over the Ligurian Sea had been her safe place. Her hideaway and sanctuary.

She had moved there permanently in her early twenties to aid in caring for her ailing grandfather. He'd been ninety-one to her twenty-one, and still she thought he was the one person in the world who'd understood her, and vice versa.

When he'd died two years ago, she'd decided to stay. If there was no one left on earth who understood her, at least this place did.

She drove up the winding pathway to the castle now. It was dark up here—very little artificial light at night. Her headlights led the way, and she could see only the shadow of the old house on the jagged peak of hill.

Her mother called it a morgue. Her father had called it a crumbling atrocity.

Serena had begun to call it *home* and meant it. Because neither her father's ostentatious estate in the city, nor her mother's unending array of apartments, houses, villas—all usually funded by the next man down the line—had ever been home.

She parked in the garage, then moved inside, unlocking and then re-engaging the security system. As was so often her habit, she went straight to her room and began the process of taking Serena Valli off.

The heels went first, then the expensive dress and jewelry, making sure to put her mother's belongings in a little case to be returned as soon as possible. She scrubbed her face clean of makeup, took out her contacts and replaced them with her glasses. Neatly, she put everything back where it belonged.

The house could get drafty at night, so she grabbed a shawl before she went down to her sitting room, where a hot mug of tea, a book and her cats would be waiting for her while a fire crackled cozily in the hearth.

She'd need a good hour to decompress before she could even begin to consider sleep. Leopold immediately meowed at her as she entered the luxurious room she'd done little to change since her grandfather's death.

She knew to anyone else it would appear fussy and out-dated. *Elderly* even with its dark woods, floral wallpapers and heaps of shawls and throws, but she loved it, and now that some of the sharp grief of losing her grandfather had softened into a subtle missing him, the room comforted her as her grandfather once had with just his presence.

What she had done was add another kitten—this one after her father's death. She was also considering a bird, though Pierro, her house manager, had threatened to quit over that. Her trio of dogs had been trained as guard dogs and they had their own little outbuilding for the evenings, but she was considering getting a puppy that was *just* a dog. *Just* a companion. To be allowed inside to cuddle up in bed with her and the cats. Something tiny and yappy and wonderful.

Serena loved animals. They were so simple. They could be so loving, and interesting with their own little personalities. They could be pleased easily with daily meals and attention.

She settled into her chair now and took a sip of tea as Leopold hopped onto her lap, and Kate watched with jealous eyes but did not move from her perch at the window. On a sigh of pleasure, Serena smoothed her hand down Leopold's spine, closed her eyes and finally relaxed.

In the quiet, only the sound of the fire crackling, she sipped her tea, but she did not pick up her book. She was exhausted, but she would not be able to sleep.

The solution she had suggested to her sworn enemy was not one she relished, not one she *wanted*. It was simply the only one available to her. And now she'd have to wait—for days, no doubt—to see if Luciano would be smart enough to take such an unfortunate deal.

She worried there. It had always been clear he had no real loyalty to Ascione. She had been surprised, in fact, that he hadn't sold it upon his father's death. It was well known in their world that he would not take over any role in his father's company.

But apparently he'd inherited it all the same.

Now she just had to wait.

"I am good at waiting," she told Leopold as he hopped off her lap, no doubt to go harass Kate.

She let her eyes drift closed for a minute. Maybe if she fell asleep here, she would actually sleep for more than an hour or two, before another worry woke her up.

Then she heard someone enter. Reluctantly, she opened her eyes to see Pierro standing in the doorway. He looked... perplexed, which was unlike him.

"Ms. Valli. I apologize for interrupting, but you have a rather...insistent visitor."

"I am not seeing any visitors at this hour, Pierro. You of all people should be able to see to that." She was in her *pajamas*, with a shawl wrapped around her. Honestly, what would possess Pierro...?

She heard it then. A familiar dark, ill-boding voice somewhere in the house. Getting closer by the moment.

"We could call the *polizia*," Pierro offered.

But he knew, as well as she did, that this would be a tactical error and bring all the wrong kind of attention to a problem they were trying to hide. That was why he posed it as a question, rather than going ahead and doing it.

Serena sighed, tried to find some inner center of strength here as she got to her feet.

She'd taken off all of her armor, but she could *hear* him.

"Please, show him in," Serena said between clenched teeth, hoping Pierro could take *some* control of the situation.

"You must be on your best behavior, Leopold," she murmured to her younger cat, who had a habit of getting a little rambunctious at night. Sweet Kate was placid in her old age and blinked from her perch in the window.

When Luciano strode into her cozy living room, she was not dressed to be Serena Valli, but she would not let that deter her. She stood, chin up, hazel eyes defiant. The fire that crackled in the hearth and the shawl around her shoulders might give the aura of cozy, but she would not.

He swept in, dressed as he had been in the club. Though his hair looked a little mussed, like he'd raked his fingers through it not all that long ago.

Or, more likely, someone else had.

He stopped on a half-stride, something in his expression

moving toward surprise before he managed to hide it away. "You need better security," he said by way of greeting.

"You need to take no for an answer." She clutched the shawl a little tighter at her throat, pretending as though she was dressed in her boardroom best. "What on earth are you doing here at this time of night?"

His gaze perused her then. Took in the thick socks, the pajamas, the glasses, the shawl. His mouth curved ever so slightly in pure amusement, but only for a moment.

He scowled. "Explain to me how you have this information."

"What information?"

"The numbers about my company. The projections. You should not have this information, and I want to know what dastardly things you've done to obtain it."

She was shocked someone had already distilled the information for him. She figured he'd wait forty-eight hours out of spite at the very least. "Surely you did not wake up some poor employee to explain it to you when it could have waited until morning."

"No one should have this information," he said, ignoring her.

She supposed she should have seen this accusation coming. Not *everyone* was as thorough and good with numbers as she was. Certainly, Luciano wasn't. But she'd assumed his man of business would explain *this* to him—how easy it was to know your job if you tried.

"It was easy enough to use what I know of the industry, what public information there is, and then extrapolate accordingly." She shrugged. "I am brilliant, Luciano. Trust me, my father would not have allowed me near his company if I was not. If my choices, my decisions, my outcomes weren't perfect. He had rather outmoded ideas about women in the workplace."

"Perhaps we should have switched fathers, then. Mine often lamented that if I was a woman, at least I'd be good for *something*."

For a moment, the silence around them was awkward instead of hostile. This sort of admission that they might have been better off in each other's shoes.

Then his scowl intensified, and he stepped forward. "There is no way you simply *surmised* this information."

She supposed his proximity was meant to be intimidating, so she refused to be intimidated. Even as her heart rattled around her chest in an unfamiliar rhythm. Without her heels, she had to look up at him, and she did so now, letting none of her nerves show. She clutched her shawl tight and refused to let herself sound winded by the strange sensations twisting through her. "There is, because I did."

"You will tell me the truth."

"I *am* telling you the truth."

"Do you think I will go along with this ridiculous plan because of some pathetic lie? You will tell me how you got this information, or I will destroy you."

She rolled her eyes, lifted an arm. "Destroy away, Luciano." Because she was already almost there.

Luciano realized he was not handling this well, but that only spurred him on.

She had *rolled her eyes* at him. When he was actually being serious instead of his usual insouciance.

Something brushed up against his legs and he only just stopped himself from jumping back. It looked like a stuffed little ball of fur, but it moved, and then looked up, its cat eyes blinking at him.

"*Che cazzo*, is that *real*?"

The ball of fluff offered a pitiful *meow*. Luciano stared

down at it for a full minute until his mind could accept it was another cat to go along with the one perched in the window.

Who *was* this woman sitting in a room better suited to an octogenarian cat lady? He knew she was stuffy, stiff, *annoying*, but he'd still assumed she'd live in something sleek and modern and befitting the CEO of a generationally successful shipping company.

He had not expected her to wear *glasses*. To look somehow...innocent and vulnerable standing there in her pajamas, even as she scowled at him, ever the picture of control.

"I think it would be best if you leave, Mr. Ascione," she said primly, no doubt using the *mister* to remind him of his father. "Your assistant may call mine and set up a meeting whenever you would like to discuss my proposal, at an appropriate time and place, but I will not tolerate accusations against me in my own home, at this hour. Call Mr. Emidio and have him explain to you just how I would have gotten my information *without* whatever nonsense corporate espionage you are accusing me of."

"I do not need to call Mr. Emidio," he ground out.

"Surely he is smart enough to see that anyone with a deep understanding of the industry, and your father's shortcomings, would know how to extrapolate that information. Call Mr.—"

"*I* am Mr. Emidio," he exploded.

Regret was a sharp pain, but he'd never allowed himself to let regret sink its teeth in. When he made a mistake, he embraced it, rolled with it, then made it a success.

Serena stopped short, studied him. "I beg your pardon."

He would not explain to her. He would not compound one mistake with another. She was right. They needed a meeting. A business meeting.

"My assistant will be in touch," he ground out, then turned

on a heel and let himself out of the sprawling, *ancient* building. Into the dark, with a shining moon and dazzling stars and the sounds of the sea all around him.

He paused there in the drive, having driven himself over. He took a deep breath, then turned around and stared at the looming shadows of the old castle. A ridiculous place to live. Up here alone with the wind whipping and the sound of waves lapping all around him. There were a few lights on in different windows.

In one, he saw the clear shadowed outline of a cat.

Who the hell was Serena Valli?

Well, he intended to find out.

CHAPTER THREE

SERENA STUDIED THE grainy picture in the video. She listened to the local gossip content creator make wild suppositions about what had happened between two rivals last night at Cattiva Idea. Serena appreciated that the photographer had made sure to circulate a picture from an angle that hid the fact Luciano had his arm around another woman, just as Serena had paid her to do.

If Serena managed to get Luciano to agree to this plan, she had no expectations he'd be faithful to a fake marriage. But she wanted it to look—for the first year at least—as if there *had* been something of a fairy-tale element, a *romance* to their union. Something to get people talking about Valli and Ascione. To get their name out there and interest in both the companies up.

At least while she sorted out all their business problems.

I am Mr. Emidio…

Could he really be that ridiculous to pose as his own man of affairs? Could he actually be that…devious? Yes, of course. Could he be that knowledgeable of Ascione? This she had a harder time believing.

She drummed her fingers against her desk, looking back at the picture that made it look as though Luciano Ascione was giving her a great deal of attention in his very own club.

Only she could tell that the smile he'd angled her way was full of venom.

She supposed they all played their roles. Maybe he'd been playing the role of flaky playboy while being anything but.

Except he was most definitely a playboy. There was no faking the array of models, actresses, influencers and the like that he always had on his arm.

This was her biggest battle, besides Luciano agreeing to marry her. While, with enough work, she could look elegant enough, whatever beauty she could create was not over the top. She was all-around average. She could not compete with his usual fare.

She had considered the shared grief angle. It had some positives, and it was believable. Grief made people do all sorts of things. But…and Serena knew this was pride over sense talking, she did not want to spend the next few years pretending losing her father was some great loss. She wasn't sure Luciano *could* pretend that losing his was.

So she had to play up the star-crossed lovers angle. Make everyone believe that for years they had been kept apart by their evil fathers. That their union was preceded by years of denial. Not sudden and out of the blue.

"Ms. Valli?"

Serena looked up from her phone to where her assistant stood in the doorway. She beckoned her inside. "Andrea. Is Mr. Ascione here?"

"I'm afraid not. He's…changed plans."

Serena didn't sneer or growl like she wanted to. She waited patiently for Andrea to continue, a placid smile on her face.

While inside, she pictured herself putting her hands around Luciano Ascione's neck and squeezing as hard as she could.

"He has sent a car. It will take you to Le Marin, where Mr. Ascione is waiting for your appointment."

Underneath her desk, Serena balled her hands into fists, letting her nails dig into her palms. She kept her voice pleasant. "How kind of him to think of having a meal together. You may tell his driver I will be down momentarily."

Andrea looked at her speculatively but nodded and disappeared. Serena jerked out of her chair and allowed herself approximately one minute of pacing and muttering curses before she went to her office bathroom, touched up her makeup and did her deep breathing exercises.

She hated a change of venue, hated petty games of control, but if she wanted her staff to believe in this marriage as much as she wanted the public to, the acting had to start now. She had to move forward with every step, believing that she would get him to agree with her plan.

And *she* would be in control.

She tried to come up with a simple excuse for driving herself, but in the end it just seemed the easiest and less suspicious thing to take the ride offered by Luciano.

She told Andrea that her meeting with Luciano was most important and that she was not to be interrupted, then left her father's—no, *her*—office building and slid into the car waiting for her.

The drive would not take long, so Serena did not get out her phone or try to do business. She closed her eyes and went over her mantra.

I am strong. I am sure. I am in charge.

The car pulled to a stop at a private entrance in the back of Le Marin, where a staff member, if the crisp black suit was anything to go by, waited.

Even with this backdoor entrance, people would see her. See them. She did not care for the fact they would have an audience of businesspeople and socialites. People who knew them or of them. People who would *talk*. She did not trust that this was a move made in her best interest.

Or maybe those were the excuses she made for herself so she didn't have to admit she was just mad he'd changed the venue on her, because she'd had a battle plan drawn for a meeting on *her* turf, in *her* office.

And now, she had to adjust.

"You will sway it your own way if need be," she reminded herself. Just as she'd done with the club. She was good on her feet when the situation demanded it.

Now it did.

She got out of the car, was greeted by the staff member, then led through a small, narrow hallway and into a room with a beautiful view of the marina. Not everyone's version of beauty, she knew, but symbolic. Because Ascione and Valli boats, shipping containers and the like were all out there.

And in front of the window was Luciano himself. Dressed on the side of *casual* that normally she would have criticized, but he somehow made it look sophisticated and regal, even without a suit jacket or tie.

He made a striking picture there, with such a background, and his own undeniable beauty. What a shame he should be such a cad.

He stood as she approached. She held out her hand as she would in any business meeting. "Mr. Ascione."

"Serena," he greeted, taking her hand, and then instead of shaking it, turning it to be brought to his mouth. He brushed a kiss over her knuckles, his gaze meeting hers as he did so.

The use of her name, and his mouth, was unwelcome. That was all the strange pressure in her chest was. Irritation and frustration with the situation. Even if that had never made her feel breathless and overwarm, like her heart had decided to run a marathon there in her chest.

"I have gotten us a private table, so we may talk without worry of being overheard," he said, gesturing at it now as he dropped her hand. "Please. Sit."

Serena did not allow herself to move stiffly to the table, even though that is what she felt. She did not allow herself to wipe her hand on her skirt, even though it felt as though that would be the only way to rid the strange warmth from her palm.

She all but had to pry her other hand off her purse once seated, but she did not allow him to read anything uncomfortable in her demeanor.

He might have chosen the venue, but she would remain relaxed and in control. At least on the outside.

A waiter appeared, presenting a bottle of wine. When Luciano approved, he began to pour.

Serena put her hand in front of her glass. "None for me. I will stick with water. Thank you."

"Leave the bottle," Luciano told the waiter, who nodded, then melted away. "Come, *cara*. We might be celebrating by the end of this conversation."

She smiled sweetly at him but spoke between her teeth. "And we might end up tossing the wine at each other."

His mouth quirked at one side, and something in her chest seemed to mimic the movement. A quick, upturned flutter.

"I would almost like to see it, Serena," he said, his gaze moving over her face. "The ice princess losing her temper."

She held his gaze, but something was tying itself in knots in her stomach. Because losing her temper was never an issue, never much of a challenge. She was excellent at control, but the man across from her was the only man who ever tested that.

She hated that it was *him*, but what could be done? She could not control her insides, but she could control her outsides. Even when it was hard. To lose sight of her control *now* would destroy everything.

She refused to be destroyed. By a foolish car accident or a supposedly charming rival. "I hope you shall hold your breath," she offered. Because sparring with him was not a loss of control, it was a gaining of it. It was a duel. A business negotiation. The careful, planned steps of a fencing match.

Luciano sipped his wine, unbothered, leaning back in his chair so that he was perfectly framed by the beautiful lake outside the windows. If someone had taken his picture, it could have been an advertisement for any number of things, and women would sigh over that lazy smile.

She *hated* that her traitorous insides wanted to do just that. Because if she allowed herself to divorce his personality from the external look of him, she would have some *serious* problems with focus.

Luckily, she knew exactly who he was.

A waiter reappeared with the *primi*. He set a dish down in front of both of them, then disappeared again. Luciano made a big production out of discussing the weather, and Serena was well versed in stalling business tactics, so she played along.

Mainly because she didn't think he expected her to.

When the *secondi* was served, he moved the conversation along to her home. She tried not to stiffen, but it was impossible. She did not want his take on the place that meant so much to her. On the place he never should have been. Part of how she'd gotten by was to develop that inner world, that sanctuary, and keep everyone else out. So that it was safe there.

He'd invaded her safety. Gotten a peek under the curtain,

so to speak. She had spent the day telling herself it didn't *really* matter. So he knew she wore glasses and had cats? Maybe it gave him glimpses into private things, but it didn't *change* anything.

But she could tell he understood that it bothered her far more than she wanted it to.

Still, to show her discomfort was to lose, so she sipped her water carefully as he spoke.

"So…unique," he said, almost thoughtfully. "And your sitting room. Quite colorful, when you are, if you'll forgive me for saying so, rarely that."

"I do not wish to be colorful," Serena replied, trying to keep the bite out of her tone. "This does not mean I do not enjoy color."

He made a considering noise. She had no doubt he would draw this out. Make her wait for his answer. So she enjoyed her food. A delicious *tortelli* and *ratatuia*. She had never had a dessert quite like the one served next, so she savored it, only half listening to Luciano prattle on about his club.

If it was to be like this, she could handle a potential marriage. She could pretend to listen to him chattering on while she enjoyed a meal. She could be photographed on occasion with his hand in hers. All of this, she was sure she could handle.

But him being in her space last night had introduced a new doubt, and Serena *hated* doubts. She hated to address them. But the way it had felt to have him in her space, seeing who she was underneath her mask. Having to deal with the unique physical reaction she had to him—one she did not want to parse, but might have to. Because a fake marriage would require, at least on occasion, living together.

Maybe once they'd gotten some of the old clients back, once there were enough stories about them to have *everyone* taking a meeting with Valli, they could move to a marriage that didn't need to look...*real*.

But she had to get there first. Which required this dinner, his agreement and a merger of lives and businesses. It required managing the strange sensations he brought out in her, that tangled with the more familiar and perhaps more welcome irritation.

Valli-Ascione, she reminded herself, unable to stop a frown. The merger was the best thing, she knew, but she hadn't fully swallowed how much credit she was going to have to give the man across from her.

After all the work she'd done, after all the perfection she'd achieved—first to gain her father's trust, then to clean up the mess he'd left her—and for the rest of their lives, no doubt, Luciano would get more credit for saving their companies than she would. Because this was still a man's world, no matter how much better she was at it.

She reminded herself she didn't *need* credit. Never had. As long as *she* knew she was the mastermind behind this. As long as *she* knew she'd saved Valli, like her father couldn't. As long as she was perfection to all her father's imperfection. *That* was what mattered.

When the waiter put a *caffe* in front of her, she smiled up at him in thanks. How many more minutes would this go on? Usually, her patience was endless, but the mere existence of Luciano reminded her that there were variables in this whole plan that she would not be able to control.

Mainly him.

She flicked a glance at Luciano who was watching her with surprisingly shrewd dark eyes, like he could see through her. When no one did.

Her chest felt oddly tight. The idea of being seen settled in her in tangled ways. Because she did not want *him* to see her, but she missed the easy understanding her grandfather had once given her. So it was both uncomfortable and wistful.

She was glad when he leaned carefully forward, made no attempt to hide the shrewdness in his gaze. He did not signal a change in conversation in any other way. But she knew they would now discuss what she'd actually come here for.

"I am still not wholly convinced that you came to this information on your own," he said, more idly than accusatory.

She sighed, but before she could say anything, he held up a hand.

"However, whether you have a spy, or are as brilliant as you claim, the result is the same. Our companies are failing."

"Thanks to our fathers."

"Indeed. And I have no long-lost love for mine, may he rot in hell along with the rest of the Asciones, but I will not let his failure stain *my* reputation."

She was surprised at the fervent note in his voice. Like he cared. About his reputation, though she was quite sure he didn't. About Ascione, though she hadn't been sure there was any loyalty there considering he'd had very little to do with it all these years.

But she'd banked on the probability that somewhere deep down, all the talk of legacies she'd grown up with would have been instilled in him as well.

"You'll marry me then." She managed to sound calm, but inside she was a nervous wreck. Inside, she was *praying* he said yes. And somehow dreading that yes at the same time. It was what she knew needed to happen, but it was not what she *wanted*.

And that really was the story of her life, so she couldn't fathom why it unsettled her as much as it did.

"Marry you? I thought you were brilliant, *cara*. Why

would I have met you in public, for many to see, if not to plant the romantic seeds of our engagement?"

She could not stop herself from pulling a face at the word *romantic*.

Luciano chuckled. "You will need to work on your acting skills."

"Indeed." She cleared her throat. "But, if you did not notice the papers this morning, I have already planted my own seeds."

He did not frown exactly, but she could tell he had not gotten wind of the stories yet. She pulled her phone out of her purse and brought up one of the gossip channels that had the picture she'd arranged. Then she slid the phone across the table to him.

He picked it up. "Look at you, Serena," he murmured, studying the picture. He handed her phone back, then smiled, his gaze sharp and on her.

A flutter centered in her chest. Like nerves, but warmer. She felt…compelled to hold his gaze, even as something shifted low in her stomach. She didn't understand it.

Or like it.

Because as much as she'd like to pretend it was some kind of victorious feeling from having him agree to her plan, she knew it had nothing to do with agreement, and everything to do with that smile and his eyes on hers.

He lifted his glass of wine. "Then I suppose we have a deal. Let the games begin, *compagna*."

Partner.

She thought about how he'd said his father should be rotting in hell and hoped for a brief moment her father was doing the same for leaving her to deal with *this*.

They had agreed their first public appearance would be the dinner party put on by one of the CEOs of the major American conglomerate that had been swooping in and stealing their clients away.

As Luciano prepared himself for the dinner, he thought back to their parting shots to one another at lunch.

"I should like to see you in a color. Perhaps a hint of skin," he had said, to see if he could watch closely enough for her mask to slip.

It hadn't.

"I cannot fathom why you would care at all what I wear," she had replied as they'd walked back to his car.

"There should be some sense that we are rubbing off on one another, should there not?"

"Then what will you do?" she'd asked, sounding sincere. She'd delivered the blow with that same tone. *"Learn to read?"*

He had been torn between shocked affront and a laugh. She was indeed a worthy adversary. Except, no longer an enemy. Now, they were partners.

He wondered how long it would last before one of them would plan a betrayal.

Not until both companies were back on even footing. Serena would not risk Valli, and while he wasn't quite so taken with Ascione, he wanted none of his father's failures associated with his own name.

Because I am better.

So for a few months yet, they would have to be full-on partners. No behind doors backstabbing just yet.

What a shame.

In the days between their lunch and the dinner, he sent her flowers to her office. An outrageously large and overly bright combination that he knew would embarrass her.

And that would be the talk of the Valli offices.

It amused him to imagine it. Just as it amused him to recall their lunch. And the different Serena's he'd come across in such a short time, after only ever seeing the perfect ice princess for so long.

But it was clear, she was not perfect. There was a strange hidden woman underneath the surface. There was something sharper there too, that he brought out when he irritated her enough. It poked at something deep within him, something he hadn't figured out quite how to articulate to himself. So he kept poking, waiting for clarity.

He could not recall a time he'd ever been so fascinated to see what made a woman tick, but then again, when women shared his company, they generally *wanted* to, with little reason to hide themselves away.

It was a marvel, and while the idea of being connected to her in any way, especially beyond business, was of course an atrocity, he was certain her plan would work.

She was that good at embodying a lie. How else had he spent all this time thinking her perfect, only to find her in thick-lensed glasses and octogenarian shawls surrounded by *cats*?

So when his driver stopped in front of Serena's home, Luciano did not hold on to any worries. The dinner party would be beyond mundane, and pretending to care about Serena's needs would be an odd experience, but he had no doubts they'd be successful.

He stepped out and studied the castle—it could only be called a castle—in the falling light of dusk. It was not elegant. There was no sense that this was an abode of luxury, though the inside *was* luxurious. But the outside gave more the aura of centuries long gone, when life was weary, bloody battle after weary, bloody battle.

This was a battle—though hopefully not bloody—so maybe the mood of it fit. He strode up the heavy set of concrete stairs that wound around, not romantically, but practically, and up to the main doors. He noticed what he could not have last night in the dark. There were hints of color here and there. A pot the color of the sea full to brimming with red and orange blooms to one side. A colorful stained glass trinket hanging from a hook that tinkled in the breeze along with the sounds of waves in the distance. A full awning of weeping wisteria shaded the entry.

He knew now that these were all glimpses into the *real* Serena, and he wondered…would he catch a glimpse of her now? That owlish little creature trying to pretend to be a lioness.

No, she'd be ready this time. He had no doubt. And he had the oddest sense of disappointment at that.

The door opened before he'd even stepped forward, and the man who'd argued with him that Serena was not to be seen the last time he'd been here answered.

His expression was grave. His eyes were wary. He gestured Luciano inside.

Luciano smiled charmingly at him when he said nothing. *"Buonasera."*

"Ms. Valli will be down momentarily, Mr. Ascione. You may wait here."

Luciano looked around the entry way. It was grand, indeed, but hardly the place to sit and wait. Luciano doubted very much that the typical visitor was asked to stand in the bright white room and *wait.*

But before he could suggest that, Serena appeared. She was walking at a quick clip, checking the contents of her purse as her high heels clicked against the stone foyer floors.

There was no denying Serena was beautiful. Even in her ridiculous pajamas and alarmingly large glasses the other night, one could not deny that there was something *within* her that glowed, that enticed.

The business version of Serena was always sleek, elegant and…demure, he supposed, was the best descriptor.

But there was something…altogether different this evening.

She wore color. A vibrant, gleaming green. She…sparkled. He didn't think that would have caught him off guard all on its own. He was used to glittering, brightly dressed women. It was the brevity of that skirt, and the surprisingly long, lean legs now viewable because of it, made all the longer by the gold heels she wore.

Worse than the surprise was the awkwardly potent bolt of lust that fisted inside him. Unexpected and unwanted. Because lust was usually quite welcome, easily dealt with. He did not find himself attracted to women he had no intention of having.

And there was certainly no appeal to having Serena Valli.

She looked up absently. *"Buonasera,"* she offered, but her gaze was moving to her butler. "Pierro, you'll make certain Kate gets her medicine with her food this evening?"

"Of course."

She nodded, as if that settled that, and Pierro drifted out of the room with one last disapproving look in Luciano's direction.

Luciano would have asked her who the hell Kate was, but her hair was pulled up, and wisps sprang free in lazy curls. Her hazel eyes were painted dark, which somehow brought out the flecks of green and gold in them. Her lips were bright, which showed off just how full they were.

It wasn't that she looked any different than she usually did in the grand scheme of things, particularly considering the neckline of the dress was high, the sleeves long. It was just that she was portraying herself in a style that made her look like anyone he might have on his arm.

It twisted some signals inside of his brain. Because he could admit she was attractive, but he could not admit he was *attracted to* her. She'd put on a costume of sorts, but he could not allow it to trick him.

She was a snake.

"Is everything all right?" she asked, cocking her head slightly, making the gold earrings dangling from her ears catch the light and refract it.

"Of course," he said, sounding so stiff he barely recognized his own voice. Unacceptable. "You look different."

She glanced down at herself. "I suppose I do. You were right, an admission I don't make lightly. But wearing color, looking more like someone you would usually have on your arm, will be far more gossipworthy than if I dressed as I usually do. Just as the hideous flowers you sent me did."

It was disorienting, to mix business with fake pleasure. That was all. He just had to get his wits about him. He put on his usual smile—always so easy—offered his arm and felt somewhat reassured when she hesitated.

It was still the same Serena underneath this costume, and he'd need to remember that to make it through the evening.

CHAPTER FOUR

SERENA WAS A bundle of nerves on the inside. On the outside, she was a fortress of sophistication. But taking Luciano's arm was like one final step into a madness she did not want, but had no choice about.

So she wasn't *eager* to start this farce.

She did not care for the dress. It left her feeling exposed, when usually her wardrobe, hair and makeup felt like armor. Today, it was simply a costume. A role she was playing.

A woman foolish enough to be caught up in the charming smile of Luciano Ascione. Because this was the element she *was* nervous about. How did one pretend to be in love with a man they hated?

And yet *hate* wasn't quite accurate as she put her arm in his. Something *else* was happening inside her body. It wasn't disdain. It wasn't revulsion. She had been in a male-dominated business enough to know what *disinterest* felt like.

This wasn't that, and she could not make sense of it since she did not like Luciano Ascione and never would.

Never.

He led her outside, and the cool air felt good against her overwarm skin. The act of *walking* helped take her out of her tumble of thoughts and focus. Because everything in business was focus. One step and then another.

And any inner feelings—good or bad—did not matter.

He led her to his car and opened the door for her, and she did not make eye contact. She had been haunted for too many nights about what it felt like in that restaurant to meet his gaze.

She wanted nothing to do with it.

Once seated in the back of his car, she closed her eyes for a moment. Just to center herself. Just to remind herself what this was for.

"Nervous?"

"Of course not," she said, reacting too quickly, too forcefully. She knew it the minute she nearly jumped a foot out of her seat when Luciano put his large hand over her clasped ones in her lap.

She wanted to scoot farther away from him, but he was hardly crowding her. Even his hand came off hers quickly. There was absolutely no reason to find the spacious backseat too small. Too enclosed. And smelling far too much of his expensive cologne, something woodsy and enticing. Subtle, when the man was anything but.

"I suppose I am nervous," she said to him, because claiming the emotion she felt was the first step in defeating it. In maybe eradicating this winded feeling. "You are the experienced actor in this little play."

"Then let me do the talking."

"Talking, I am good at. I am not good at..." She trailed off, because she didn't know how to articulate it. She was always playing a role, so it wasn't that. It was simply that she usually played a role she chose, or maybe it was less of a role, less of a fiction, and more of a mask over her real self. One that suited her. Businesswoman. Whether it required a little flirting and ridiculous compliments, or shrewd no-nonsense facts. She could do it all.

But she did not know how to attend an event and pretend that it was simply to enjoy the company of her date. The goal was not business—it was gossip and drumming up interest in *her*.

She had always preferred to be in the background, to let the business do the speaking. No one needed to know about her cats or what she liked to read or the name she had planned for the miniature dachshund she was *this* close to adopting.

Now, she was pretending to let everyone know something. Something she didn't actually want anyone to know, because being fake in love with Luciano was embarrassing. He was a notorious playboy, flirted with anything that moved. Everyone would look at her and feel *pity* for thinking she of all people would have won his loyalty.

"I'm waiting for you to confess something you don't think you're good at, Serena. Frankly, I did not think hubris one of your main qualities."

She scowled at him. "One does not need hubris when one is self-aware," she returned with a primness that steadied her. Because she was *prim*, and organized, and controlling and therefore *in control*. She knew her flaws. Understood them and tried to keep them under that same control.

But she hated to hand her own shortcomings to *him* on a silver platter. Even if they were partners, short term, they were long-term adversaries. And she knew, from having to deal with her parents her entire life, that letting adversaries into your inner thoughts, inner worlds, only lead to hurt.

She would not let this man hurt her. And maybe that was why his smile, his touch, upended her, the strange sensations they elicited. These were not the actions of adversaries. There was some warmth under it all, and she only knew how to fight her parents' frigidness.

"It is not so much that I think I am not good at something,

but I do have some concerns that, even with this wardrobe choice, some people will question the likelihood of…an *us*. We do not have anything in common, except hating one another."

"I suppose you have not heard the concept of *opposites attracting.*"

She sighed. Heavily. "Except a woman as smart as I am would not be foolish enough to be attracted to the opposite of everything she valued—truth, intelligence, loyalty. And so on."

"You would be surprised at the amount of *intelligent* women I have had in my bed, *cara.*"

She hated that her cheeks heated, because she had no doubt he had said it for that very reason. So that she would have to fight any *imagining* of such a thing from happening in her head.

But it was far too easy to imagine. Perhaps she had never been in *anyone's bed*, but she enjoyed love stories. Reading them, watching them. She liked believing that for some, that kind of companionship, dedication, romance and, yes, enjoyable sex, was possible.

Even if *she* wasn't made for it. There had been no physicality in her life to make her believe she was. Even her grandfather, for all his kind points, had not been a hugger. Her parents somehow less so. She had grown up with such a lack of physical touch, she did not know how to be comfortable with the *idea* of it in her romantic life.

So the fact he was mentioning it, the fact she was even… *thinking* about it, jumbled up all her certainties and plans, and *that* could not be born.

"I would never be surprised by the amount of people in your bed, Luciano," she managed to say, hoping she sounded sophisticated and casual about the whole matter. "But I feel it imperative to remind you that for our purposes, in public you must refrain from behaving your usual way. Flirting with anyone in a skirt. Touching other women. The crowd must believe that you care for *me*, and that will require the great lothario of Italy to keep his eyes and hands to himself."

There was a beat of silence where she thought maybe she'd shocked him, or offended him or scored some kind of point. She would have felt triumphant and celebrated that, but he seemed to purr out his response.

"Ah, but not to *himself*. I will have to keep my eyes and hands on you. No?"

He asked this like a kind of dare, so she kept her placid smile in place and refused to blush as his dark eyes held hers. It felt like his hands were on her all the same.

Her heartbeat seemed to *tremble* there in her chest and, for a breathless moment, she could almost *imagine* just that. His hands on her. Skin to skin. Warmth to warmth. A physicality that only existed in her imagination.

But, good lord, not with *him*. That was ridiculous. They would only ever have to pretend physical intimacy in public, like a hand hold. Perhaps a dance.

A brushing of bodies, of lips.

But no more. No *more*. Because this was a ruse, and she could not allow him to think he had some upper hand, like he no doubt wanted. Maybe he thought he was charming. Maybe he wanted her off balance and thought this was the way to do it—no doubt, he used his charm and innuendo as a weapon as easily as breathing. So that was it.

So she did not wilt. She would *not* look away. She would not allow him the upper hand, no matter how her heart seemed to riot there in her chest. So she didn't just *act* unaffected, she made sure to put him promptly in his place.

"I suppose you are right. *Me*. I know it will be a great

challenge, testing your wherewithal deeply—something you are not accustomed to. But I will endeavor to have faith in you, Luciano. Sometimes the most challenging people only need someone to believe they are capable of them being better than they behave."

She kept his gaze the entire time. Watched as a chill moved through his expression, a sharp-edged anger he did not unleash. She had insulted him.

Good.

Luciano had agreed to this party assuming that Serena might be *annoying*, insulting and her usual bland self, but he had not expected her to challenge him in quite such a way.

He wasn't certain how to combat it just yet. He knew what *he* wanted to do. Seduce every woman in the room simply out of spite. She seemed to expect it of him anyway, and he had no doubts he could do it, more or less.

As if he needed her *belief* in his ability to be *better*.

Oh, he'd be better. His usual approach to any problem was to live down to whatever low expectations he could muster, then dig even lower. It suited him well. People underestimated him, and he succeeded around that. Then, if they had to come face to face with his successes, they'd easily brush it off as a consequence of his name.

But Serena's expectations were *so* low, he found himself challenged to rise above them. Because as much as they couldn't stand each other, they had the same goal. So why not beat her at her own game? Why not, for once, be the victor in plain sight?

He liked that idea quite a bit.

He had never had reason to play the besotted lover. In fact, he tended to discourage such…connection. He made certain the women he dated understood that he was not looking for a Mrs. Ascione. That there would be no *future*. That he was interested in fun and fun alone.

The women who agreed enjoyed his brand of fun. The women who did not agree were shut out. It was a simple approach that had not caused him any trouble yet.

This was far more complicated. But if Serena wanted a besotted fool, dedicated to her and her alone, for the press and the stories and the good of their companies, why not deliver?

Why not show her just how *good* he was? So all her barbs no longer had any heft. So *she* had to adjust *her* plans that no doubt included being completely in charge, because he was too dim, or too busy seducing women, to handle what needed to be handled.

No, he would be the fifty-fifty partner she did not want, and he would make everyone in this silly room believe he was in love with her, so this plan went off without a hitch. And any hitches would be *her* fault.

They walked into the charming villa, brimming with flowers and people, all important and rich. Some clients. Some enemies. He smiled, greeted, a hand lightly placed on Serena's back to make it clear they had arrived together.

She was right about one thing. He was an experienced actor. He'd been playing a role all his life, he liked to think. At first, he'd stepped into roles to garner his parents' attention— so they'd stop gearing their slings and arrows at each other.

He'd worked to be the perfect student to show his father he was an intelligent and worthy heir. He'd worried over his mother and done everything to show her he could be the protector his father had not been for her.

Both had rejected him and his earnest tries, so then he'd done the opposite. It had suited him much better when it came to his father, to see disappointment and regret in the old man's eyes. To live down to low expectations.

It had been more…complicated with his mother. She had shut him out, rejected him. So that there could be no *living down*. He could only stop trying, and with that came a guilt he had never fully been able to untangle.

Something he did not wish to nor need to contend with when it came to business, so he shoved that thought aside and focused on Serena. There would be no living down, no guilt, because she meant nothing to him, no matter how interesting she'd turned out to be.

It didn't matter. Only playing his role mattered.

His hand slid lower, and it was strange to have to even pretend to see Serena in the light of a *woman*. Because she was indeed. In fact, if there weren't any history between them, and she weren't so stuffy, he might have been tempted. She did make a pretty sparkling package.

When his hand drifted lower, pulling her closer, she went still and stiff. He had to bite back a grin. But then he just aimed it down at her. "Relax, *cara*," he murmured cheerfully. "All eyes are on us."

Her mouth curved in a pretty approximation of a smile, even if he could tell she'd like to shoot daggers from her eyes at him. "Then we are getting exactly what we wanted," she replied, nodding at someone who called out a greeting.

They moved through the room, greeting people they knew, getting sucked into conversations where avid eyes watched Luciano's hand on her back, her shoulder or clasping her own. Serena didn't *relax* into it exactly, but it was clear she was playing it up as best she could. He thought she was good enough to fool just about everyone else.

Eventually, they got hailed in different directions and were separated for a bit. Luciano talked to a very disapproving member of his father's staff at Ascione, who didn't want to come out and *ask* what Luciano was doing holding hands with the devil's daughter but came close enough.

Luciano had just laughed it off, irritating the man and entertaining himself.

When a pretty woman he'd usually flirt with sidled up to him, he was polite. He smiled. But he did not lay on his usual charm. In fact, he should pretend to look for Serena. Pretend to be distracted by her. *That* would get this group talking.

But when he found Serena with his gaze, he did not have to pretend. She stood with Tomasso Bonetti—who had once been a very important customer at Valli but had lately taken up with the American conglomerate—their heads bowed together.

They laughed and Luciano frowned.

She was the one who'd come up with this ridiculous plan. She was the one who'd warned him off flirting with other women. And now she stood *laughing* with another man. Tomasso was a good decade older than Serena, but Luciano did not trust that sly smile of his.

He didn't even bother to excuse himself from his current conversation companion, because he'd forgotten about her entirely. He strode across the room and approached Serena, sliding his arm around her waist in an easy movement that had her stiffening.

"I shall have to steal Serena away," he said to Tomasso, a feral smile in place. "They're playing our song."

Serena didn't frown. Not with her expression. But it was fascinating to be able to read the frown underneath the pleasant smile. Especially when no one else seemed to. She made her excuses to the man she'd all but been drooling over and then allowed Luciano to pull her onto the dance floor, and no one even looked twice at her. No one acted concerned that *clearly* the little dent between her eyebrows meant she was a little frustrated.

Did anyone ever watch her face like this, see it smooth out, and know that she'd thought through the issue, decided to make it a positive?

Something threaded through him at the idea that he did, *only* he did. A kind of weight. He was a man who liked to avoid weights and complications, but he found himself wanting to hoard this one. To have it only ever be his.

"Very clever," she said to him as the music began and he pulled her into his arms. She sounded surprised and vaguely indulgent, like a nursery schoolteacher, and that poked his frustration with her flirting with that *stronzo* even higher. "Make it look as if there is jealousy. Excellent touch."

He made a noncommittal noise. "Perhaps, but I feel I must remind you of the little warning you gave me earlier this evening. It is a two-way street, you know. You can't be draping yourself all over another man."

Serena laughed, and the sound was surprisingly light, *frothy*. A sparkle that had a few heads turning. The women immediately turned to whoever they were with and whispered behind hands adorned with jewels.

The men lingered too much on the length of Serena's legs as they moved to the slow, string notes that filled the air.

Luciano had to remind himself not to scowl.

"Draping? That's rich." She shook her head, the earrings at her ears winking in the light. "No one expects *me* to flirt, and even if they suspected that's what I was doing, which I can assure you no one did, they would consider it harmless. I do not have an endless array of famous, public lovers, Luciano."

"No, indeed you do not." And since he was feeling inexplicably frustrated, something he might call *jealousy* if he didn't know better, he leaned into a scathing reaction. Into her and figuring her out so he stopped feeling this...unsettled thing. "In fact, you don't seem to have a whisper of *any*."

She stiffened in his arms, and he knew he'd made a direct and interesting hit. She didn't like that pointed out to her.

"I am discreet," she said, with a little sniff and that prim, pompous tone she trotted out like a weapon.

"Discreet or a virgin?" he asked casually.

She tripped over his foot, but before he could maneuver them back into the simple dance, the sharp heel of her shoe found the top of his. She put her full weight on it, causing a shock of pain to erupt in his foot.

"Oops," she offered with mock contrition. "I *do* apologize. Would you like to end our dance early? Perhaps you want to put some ice on it?" She asked all of this with a sweetness that was fake as the day was long. "I am just so terribly clumsy sometimes."

He gritted his teeth as he glared at her. "I will somehow survive your clumsiness, *cara*." Survive it. Survive her. Use this farce as the start of a new direction for himself. He would win this battle of the wills, rather than withdraw, rather than obscure, rather than *hide*. He had uncovered little hints at something softer under the icy demeanor, and he wouldn't rest until he'd found them all.

So he smiled down at her and brought a hand up to tuck a curling strand of hair behind her ear, making sure his finger grazed her cheekbone.

He kept moving her on the dance floor even as her posture went rigid, her cheeks a fascinating shade of pink, and she could not hold his gaze.

Oh, she'd like to be immune to him, and there was something about that realization, that *determination*, that she wasn't that gave him a thrill. A sense of purpose and satisfaction that he hadn't allowed himself in some time.

A challenge, because while he would no doubt win her over, charm her, get under that cold demeanor, it would not be *easy*. Serena *was* brilliant, and different. He did not know anyone like her, and there would likely be surprises in store.

There was a strange little alarm bell in the back of his mind, a warning about getting in too deep, too involved, too *interested*.

But this was Serena Valli he was contending with. No matter the challenge, he would win.

He had no doubt.

CHAPTER FIVE

SERENA WAS EXHAUSTED. Pretending was a chore and she did not care for it at all, but it was necessary. She wasn't convinced all his *touching* was necessary, but she supposed it put forth the appearances she wanted, so she couldn't complain.

But her muscles would be sore tomorrow from all the tensing against the strange reactions his touch elicited inside of her.

She had been on a few dates, because it was expected of her to carry on *some* social life—and to prove to her father that she was not "defective," as he liked to say, and that she might potentially marry. But the men she'd chosen had been just like her. Contained. Careful. Obsessed with work, usually.

And her work had been everything, just like proving herself in school had been everything before that. Her father required perfection, and she met it. Over and over again. She liked clear goals, and she liked keeping people relegated to business because it made it easy.

So the *dates* never became *relationships*, and there hadn't been any since her father's death.

Still, even without much experience, she had been confident she could pretend to be in a romantic relationship because she read novels and watched movies.

But the reality of pretending was…exhausting. She hadn't expected that.

She wanted to lean into the seat, close her eyes, and sleep the whole way home, but Luciano was still right next to her, and she didn't dare sleep in the presence of a scorpion.

Once home, she would take the longest, hottest bath imaginable. She would sleep in tomorrow—something she only allowed herself once a week anyway. She had earned her lazy day tomorrow.

Thankfully, Luciano did not speak the entire drive back to her house. Nor did he put his hand over hers again. He sat in the other seat, and his quiet and stillness made her nervous. Like he was *plotting* something.

But she wasn't about to ask *what*. Maybe she'd think about it tomorrow, try to suss out what he thought he was up to. But not tonight.

The car pulled to a stop and Serena made a move to get out herself, but Luciano *tsk*ed. "Come, Serena. You know better."

"We do not need to pretend in my front drive in the dark."

"Doesn't your staff need to believe our little farce?"

She opened her mouth to argue with that, but she had decided before this that of course they did. She wasn't sure she could pull one over on Pierro. He'd been the caretaker of this castle and its inhabitant since her father had been a child. He knew her too well.

But if everyone else fell for it, he would pretend he did not know it was fake. He would go along with it.

But she hadn't thought about how that would…*look*. In her private life. She'd been focused on how to make the public believe they were a couple.

He was opening her car door for her now, offering his hand to help her out. She didn't want to take it, pretend or no, but she had to. Just another curse to lay on her father's memory, she supposed.

Luciano kept her hand in his as he closed the car door behind her. Then he walked with her. Toward the castle. His large hand enveloping hers. Warm and strangely rough, when she would have expected his hands to be as smooth as the rest of him.

They walked up the stairs to the main doorway. Her heart tripped over itself in something like nerves. She wasn't *nervous*. She was just…uncomfortable. He was only walking her to her door. Like a good date would. She would turn, offer her cheek perhaps? She didn't *want* to feel his mouth on her, her hand, her cheek, her…

No, she didn't want to know what that felt like. Just the thought made her jittery and sick to her stomach. Maybe that jittery feeling was more like a free fall on a roller coaster than any kind of revulsion, but she was certain it came from not wanting to do it. Excitement wouldn't feel like this, so untenable and shaky. Besides, any *excitement*, would be a betrayal of her own self.

So it couldn't be that.

But some sort of physical good-bye was *necessary*, she told herself firmly as they reached her door. She turned to him, pulled her hand away, almost having to resort to tugging for it to be free. Once it was, she knew she had to give a little more. Pretend for the staff, as he'd said. She tilted her head, offering her cheek. A chaste kiss on the cheek was something she was going to have to get used to. So why not start now with only the audience of his driver and possibly someone looking on from inside?

But as he leaned forward, closer and closer, those dark eyes intense and on *hers* so that it felt like a touch in itself, her breath seemed to catch there in her throat. She couldn't inhale or exhale as his mouth brushed against her cheek.

Lightly, almost friendly. Certainly not *romantic*. But his breath on her skin was an intimacy she hadn't considered, and she didn't like the way it shivered through her. How it elicited wants that clearly had not originated in her *brain*.

She needed this to be over. She needed to be alone. To regroup. To… To… *Something* away from him.

"Good night, Luciano," she said, sounding polite and warm, she hoped, but it was hard to tell with the buzzing in her ears.

That intensified when she opened the door and he did not turn around and walk back to his car. He followed her into the warmly lit entryway.

"What are you doing?" she demanded, rounding on him as if she could protect her space from him physically.

"Coming inside," Luciano replied breezily.

"I did not invite you inside." She knew she sounded shrill. She could *hear* it, but she couldn't stop it.

"Quite the failure on your part. You *should* invite me in for a drink. And then we *should* retire to your room."

She could only gape at him. He wasn't actually suggesting…

"We are to make a splash, are we not?"

A splash?

He was mad. "I don't see what that has to do with you following me inside against my wishes. With you…" She couldn't say the rest. A drink was one thing. Her *room*?

"What better splash than a tabloid photo of my car leaving your home early in the morning? The speculation will run rampant."

The thought of him in her *home* overnight was…horrible. Absolutely terrifying. Maybe the fear she'd felt before had been heavy with claws, and this was light and fizzy. Maybe this felt more like a drink of champagne than any threat. The idea of him in her room, the idea of him…

She could not let her mind traverse down that road. It felt imperative to shut the door on any imagination there, before it…changed something.

A smart woman did not walk roads or have sleepovers—no matter how fake—with creatures who could sting. "You cannot spend the night here."

"Admittedly your crumbling castle is not my first choice in accommodations. Perhaps next time you can spend the night at my estate. With running water."

"I have running water. I have every amenity—" She stopped herself from continuing to defend her *home*, particularly in that horrible screech that made her want to wince. He was no doubt just trying to get a rise out of her. She inhaled, put all her armor back in place and smiled sweetly at him. "And I wouldn't stay at your estate if held at gunpoint, *carissimo*."

"Then I guess you are not as serious about this endeavor as I'd thought you were." He *tsked* lightly.

She finally understood the meaning behind the saying "seeing red." "I am more serious than you can *imagine*, Luciano."

"Perhaps you are. Perhaps you are just that out of touch with reality. You do realize a modern couple shares a bed before the wedding? Or does your choice of accommodations allow you to believe it is the year 1500?"

She hated that he could make her blush. That he should keep talking about *beds* and that whole thing about her being a virgin.

How could he *tell*?

It didn't matter.

"*We* will not be sharing a bed. Ever."

"No," he agreed so easily it made her want to stomp her foot like a child. "But people must think we are."

"So you intend to spend the night in my room?"

He shrugged. "Unfortunately, I do not see any way around it."

"You're *mad*," she shot at him as her heart rattled around in her chest, and a heat she couldn't seem to control crept into her cheeks. Because it was embarrassing to even consider. Embarrassing that people would think they were...

Embarrassment was the only explanation for this heat, for this skittering pulse inside of her. She didn't know what else it could be. Refused to consider anything but humiliation.

Everything about this was a disaster.

"I seem to recall this being your idea," Luciano said blandly. "In fact, I seem to recall you coming to my office and proposing to me."

"Yes, but—"

"Then, take me to your bedroom, *cara*."

Luciano hadn't really planned on enjoying himself. But it took no effort at all to have her spluttering and red-faced. When for as long as he'd known her, she'd been an icy, impenetrable wall. He'd gotten a little peek behind it that first night he'd come here, but only the polish. Now, he was seeing an actual unraveling, not just a pair of glasses.

Who knew all it would take was a fake relationship, a kiss on the cheek and some suggestion of *beds* to break through her perfect mask?

But she would not be Serena Valli if she did not know how to rein herself in and carefully put that mask back in place. Her chin lifted, her eyes flashed, but other than that her expression was perfectly bland.

He found himself completely fascinated by this change. By the way she could wield such strength of character. It made him want to unwind it, again and again, perhaps even in unwise ways.

"Follow me," she said briskly, then stalked out of the entry and deeper into her strange house. There were narrow, dark hallways, tiny windows that hinted at little light, and only when they reached the third floor did he realize she must have taken him through the back of the castle that was no doubt originally built for an array of medieval servants. Because the part he had been shown through the other night had been bright, opulent and cozy.

He wondered if it was a purposeful attempt at a slight— no doubt, really, when it was Serena doing the slighting. It amused him, in spite of himself. The little swipes she could take at him that she would no doubt deny.

Like stomping on his foot during their dance.

It did not fully make sense to him that he was enjoying her sparks of defiance. Perhaps because he'd once thought her blandly above such emotion.

Once at the top of the staircase, she led him down what would be a brighter hallway in the light of day since one wall was dotted with windows. The hallway was short, and only led to one door.

With the slightest of hesitations no one would have noticed if not looking for it, Serena pushed the door open. She flipped on a light, and he followed her into the room.

It was big and bright. One wall seemed to be made entirely of glass, and he could not make out the entire view it gave since it was dark outside, but there was water below. Right now, all he could see was a brightly shining moon and pretty starlight.

There was a truly spectacular ornate bed against one wall.

Four posters, an array of comfortable looking and colorful blankets and pillows. He found himself transfixed by the idea of cold, uptight Serena cozying into that warm, cuddly bed.

But Serena did not look at the bed. She marched over to a door, jerked it open and stepped inside what appeared to be a very large closet. She reappeared, a little stack of folded clothes in one hand, before she crossed over to yet another door. The bathroom, he imagined.

She said nothing, just disappeared behind this door and firmly shut it behind her. He heard the *snick* of the lock being engaged and laughed.

He took in the rest of the room. It was an interesting combination of softly romantic art, brightly colored and patterned textiles, a bold view of the world outside her castle and…animal paraphernalia. There was a row of portraits— cat and dog faces, all painted up to look like kings and queens and military generals of a sort.

What on earth…?

He recalled the little fluff of a cat that had been in her sitting room the other night as something streaked out from underneath the bed and took a swipe at his shoelaces, then disappeared again. For a moment, he could only stare at the space where a cat's paw had just been. Before it crept out once more.

Luciano took a step away and then another. He could not quite get a read on Serena's private, interior life. Cats. Books. A homey kind of…grandmotherliness when the woman wasn't a day over twenty-eight, perhaps even younger, if he remembered correctly. A direct contrast to the sharp, modern businesswoman she presented herself as.

And he wondered what caused such a dichotomy. Perhaps he pretended to be less determined and hardheaded than he was, but he did not hide key elements of his personality away.

What would make a person do such a thing? What did it mean? Why did it all come together like a story he was desperate to know the ending to?

The door reopened and Serena stepped out. She was dressed casually now, but he didn't think there was anything casual about the way she was covered from head to toe. A soft sweatshirt that had a mock turtleneck. Pants that were utterly shapeless and looked equally soft. And thick socks. The only skin he could see was her face and her hands.

"There is a cat under your bed," he told her.

"There are likely two cats under my bed," she replied. "It's one of their favorite places." She looked up at him then. "I don't suppose you're allergic?" she asked.

Hopefully.

"Not to my knowledge."

For the first time since he'd stepped inside her house, she smiled at him. "You could rub your face in one and find out."

"I shall abstain, I think."

She shrugged, but the smile stayed in place. "Let me know if you change your mind." She said nothing else and didn't move from her spot all the way across the room from him. She just stood there, offering nothing into the silence.

Except what he could only define as a nervous energy. She held herself perfectly still, her expression placid. But there was a tension *wafting* off of her, and Luciano could not lie. He enjoyed having that effect on her.

Any affect, really, that chipped through what he'd once thought was impenetrable ice.

So he took a few steps in her direction, grinning when she took the same amount of steps in the opposite one.

He stopped, regarded her across the room with a raised eyebrow. "What exactly are you afraid of, Serena?"

The look of outrage chased across her face. "I am not *afraid*."

"You locked the bathroom door like I'm the big bad wolf. You stand across the room like I might bite."

"I locked the bathroom door because that's what you do when you go into a private area that you wish to remain private."

"Do you think I'm going to burst in and pounce upon you?"

"Of course not. Don't be ridiculous." But her face was getting redder and redder, like now that he'd introduced the words *bite* and *pounce* she could picture it all too well.

Which had him considering what that picture would look like. What it might be like to cross the room and—

Before he remembered himself. Who he was. Who she was. What *this* was. A farce.

But that did not mean he could not enjoy a farce. As long as he remembered himself. Which had never been a problem before.

Why should it be a problem now?

"This is a large bed. I suppose it shall do for our purposes." He moved over to it now, eyed the bed skirt for any evidence of paws, then decided to leave his shoes on. He settled himself on the bed in a sitting position, crossing his ankles over a bright purple coverlet of some kind and lacing his fingers behind his head against the padded headboard decorated with images of tiny...pigs?

For a moment, he wondered if he'd given her a kind of stroke. She stood utterly still, her mouth hanging open ever so slightly, no noise coming from it.

Eventually, she blinked, as if coming back into herself. "I am hungry," she declared, reaching for the door.

"As am I. Have a tray brought up. I'm not picky about

food. If you have any good liquor, I wouldn't mind a drink as well."

"You are not... We are not..." She spluttered on some more without actually articulating a word. It was fascinating. He had never seen her struggle to undercut a man—any man, including himself—with an icy smile and perfectly sharp words.

She didn't stutter. She didn't falter. She was the kind of woman who showed up at a man's club and suggested they *marry* to save businesses and legacies.

But slowly, she brought it all back. She took a deep breath. She closed her eyes for a moment. There was a whole process of resetting herself, and he watched it happen in front of him.

Fascinating. What must it be like to have that inside a person?

"I have considered your point," she said, in that prim, controlled voice of hers. "You are somewhat correct that any engaged couple should be considered to be...cohabitating at times. If we arrange someone to photograph and leak said photograph of you leaving here early in the morning, we'll get a lot of traction from that."

"That might even be why I suggested it," he returned dryly, still lounging on her bed that smelled crisp and reminded him of spring.

She ignored his sarcasm. "That being said, we must consider our own comfort while we engage in this little facade."

"I am quite comfortable."

She inhaled through her nose this time.

"I am not. I am used to having my space to myself. I am used to a certain level of..." She paused, searching for a word, though she was back to her normal self, not faltering. Just being careful. Precise. "Solitude. It is my preferred state of being. So, perhaps we should use this time together to fully iron out an agreement."

"An agreement?"

"Yes. We don't want to go the route of full legal contract just yet, as that could be leaked. But an agreement between the two of us. How we will proceed, behave. Lay out expectations."

"Expectations."

"Are you struggling with the meaning of the words themselves or something else?" she asked, smiling sweetly. But no amount of masks could hide the annoyed snap in her tone.

"I find myself baffled by the way you speak."

"I will try to dumb down my vocabulary to meet you where you are."

She said this almost kindly. Luciano smiled mildly at her. He did not defend himself to anyone. He'd learned from a young age there was no point, and it usually worked in his favor to be underestimated.

But her comments grated all the same, and he had to remind himself that there was a larger game at play then this inconsequential conversation in her bedroom.

"Well, by all means. Let us iron out an agreement. But have some food and drink sent up first. God knows I'll need one to get through this."

CHAPTER SIX

SHE HAD INDEED had food brought up, and a bottle of scotch. Though Serena had moved to take the tray herself, Luciano had swept in and smiled charmingly at Pierro, who had uncharacteristically delivered the tray himself.

It had been clear he hadn't wanted to relinquish the tray to Luciano and that he was…checking on her, she supposed. But she'd smiled and inclined her head, a nonverbal *Give him the damn tray.*

Just so this could all be over with.

Luciano had taken it, closed the door rather pointedly, then taken it over to the bed. He'd poured himself a glass, made himself up a plate of the elegant snacks, then settled himself back into her bed.

Her *bed*. She knew he did it to annoy her. Perhaps even to shock her. So she was working very hard to pretend like it didn't matter.

But it grated. The way his long body made her large, soft bed look small. The way that it was now too easy to picture him there, where she *slept*. It brought to mind the books she loved to read where a couple who hated each other were stuck at some inn somewhere with one bed. And the end result was always…

Well, she was *not* going to think about that right now. Not with *him* in *her* bed.

Since he'd taken the bed, and she had no intention of being anywhere near him, even if she *was* hungry, she settled herself at her desk. She opened the drawer that held her notebooks. For this endeavor, she'd chosen one decorated in scorpions. An apt reminder. While she liked to use a variety of colorful pens in her note-taking, for the Valli-Ascione merger she used a scathing black. She'd drawn a little cover page with her own rendition of scorpions, snakes and rats with red eyes. It made her chuckle every time she opened it.

A necessary levity in this otherwise nightmare endeavor, that only seemed to become more nightmarish as time went on.

She began to flip the pages until she found the first blank one. She smoothed out the paper, letting the act soothe her. Any difficult problem could be solved if she put pen to paper. This had always been true, and she refused to acknowledge this problem might be too complex and fraught.

She would find a way. She labeled one side of the page *Expectations* and the other *Rules*. She was so intent on writing each letter precisely so it would be aesthetically pleasing, a physical representation of the perfection she sought, that she did not notice Luciano had gotten up and come to stand behind her.

Until he spoke, making her jump and accidentally draw a harsh line across the corner of the page.

"What is this?" he asked.

"My notes," she replied, staring at the ugly line. Ruining her perfection. Just like *him*. Because of course Luciano Ascione had never had to be perfect.

"On paper?"

"I find I think best when I can write everything longhand," she replied loftily. Later, when she was blissfully alone, she would rip out this ruined sheet and rewrite all her notes quite carefully. But for now, she would have to make do.

"You are a far stranger creature than I could have ever given you credit for, Serena."

She did not like the way he said her name. He seemed to linger on the consonants, drawing it out. Unnecessarily, in her estimation.

She was tempted to write under rules, *Do not say my name*. But that was ridiculous and petty.

Perhaps in the back, when he wasn't here, she'd make a ridiculous and petty list. Just for her own amusement.

For now, she would focus on building the scaffolding she needed to survive this without resorting to violence.

"I feel it should go without saying, and I'm sure you were just *jesting* before, but obviously we will not share a bed."

"Metaphorically or literally?"

She gritted her teeth at the silky way he spoke. No doubt it worked on whatever targets he actually wanted to talk into bed, but when it was aimed at her, it just felt like… Something sharp and confusing. He was jumbling her up purposefully, but she felt out of her depth because she did not understand this kind of…jumble.

"Both." Then, in her precise, careful script, she wrote it down.

Will not share a bed—literal/figurative.

When he snorted, she did not *glare* at him. She moved down to the next line and wrote the number two.

"Number two, I should think, would be to not flirt with a CEO in the camp of our enemies."

She could not understand why he kept harping on that. "There is professional flirting and then there is private flirting. One is necessary, and no one will think twice about it. Particularly coming from me." She'd never considered it flirting so much as…stroking the male ego. And none of the businessmen she'd encountered had ever taken it as more than that.

Perhaps Luciano did not understand this because he was so handsome and charismatic, because he wanted that kind of attention. Men simply did not look at her that way and she knew it was a combination of how she handled herself and how little…*spark* she had. Her mother had been explaining that to her since she'd been a child.

"Is this so? You will have to explain to me the difference between professional flirting and personal flirting."

She sighed. No doubt all the flirting *he* did was meant to lead to the bedroom, so he could not understand the fine art of *actually* doing business. Wooing clients. Soothing concerns. "Professional flirting is like manners. No one thinks it's leading anywhere. It's…friendly. A little ego boost for the party who needs it."

"And how is this magically construed as different than *private* flirting?"

"It's simply part of the *professional* interaction. No direct invitations made." She looked down at the paper rather than him *looming* over her. "Private flirting is probably anything *you* do," she muttered irritably. She'd seen him do it. Maybe he'd dialed it down at the event, *pretended* to aim all that charm at her instead of the kind of woman he usually had on his arm.

And thinking of that frustrated her, because she understood just how potent and effective it could be if you believed in an Ascione scorpion.

Luckily *she* would not. She was too smart to think a little flutter, a little eye contact that had her pulse scrambling, mattered. Even if she could still feel all those things right now.

"Perhaps you could be more specific?" He was closer

then, somehow, and he lifted her to her feet by the elbow, then turned her so that they stood face to face. Then he smiled. And it didn't look like *malice*. It looked like intent, which even she knew was different.

Not that she trusted it.

"Show me," he said, his hand still cupped there on her elbow, and even though she was wearing a sweatshirt she could *feel* the heat of his palm through the fabric.

She found herself having to swallow in order to speak. He was toying with her, and she had prepared herself for all the ways he might test her, but she hadn't counted on…this, she supposed. She knew she was smarter, more determined, far more professional than this man, but he knew how to zero in on the things she was not confident in.

Mainly…this strange magnetic pull. She could not call it *charm*, because she was not *charmed* by him. It was something darker, more illicit. Seduction…but at least she knew it was only meant to embarrass her. She had no *interest* in him, nor he her, so it wasn't as though she was afraid something untoward might happen. More…

She simply did not know how to box it up, control it, undercut it. She could not seem to control her body's odd, unfamiliar responses. Frustrating, but not the end of the world. She would learn.

Serena *always* learned.

"It is not anything that requires a demonstration," she told him, using her best haughty managerial voice. She did not jerk her arm away, no matter how much she wanted to. In a test of wills, she would always, *always* win. But she did not dare look directly into his dark, amused eyes. She fixed on a strand of dark hair that swept across his forehead. "Laughing at a terrible joke, complimenting someone. These are all harmless flirtations. Business flirtations. Private flirting involves touch. The brush of a hand. Knees touching under a table. It is *physical* and promises something physical in return."

"So, what you are saying is, for our audience to believe in our little fiction, we must engage in the promise of something physical?" He let that sit there between them. A silence that settled in her throat like some kind of blockage, as his mouth curved ever so slightly, the look in his dark gaze downright piratic. "In public, that is," he added, with a feigned innocence that did not suit the *scorpion* tail in his smile at all.

Or the way his hand moved from elbow to waist. Curled there, in a strangely possessive touch. And for a moment, that touch—not at all different from when they'd danced tonight and she'd been wearing much *less*—seemed to do something to drain all the thoughts from her brain.

Which, she thought, was the *point*. And if she could focus on the fact he was playing some kind of... *Luciano Ascione* game with her, she would not be felled by...whatever this was.

"I suppose, if you think it necessary." It irritated her that her voice sounded *lower*, but she did not let it show. "But you know what else would suffice?" she replied, pleased with her cool tone this time, even if she could feel the heat on her cheeks betraying her.

"What?"

"A ring. Expensive. Gaudy." She held up her left hand, wriggled the ring finger. "For all to see." She carefully dislodged herself from his grasp, because she didn't know how much longer she could hold on to that *detachment* when the feel of him seemed to brand himself there on her skin.

No one could accuse her of scrambling away. For that she would be proud. She fixed him with an indulgent smile, meant to grate. "No public groping necessary."

"I have never been accused of *groping, cara.*"

She made a considering sound, making it clear she didn't believe him without coming out and saying it. Then she settled herself back in her desk chair. "Now, what other rules should we commit to paper?"

She'd come up with ten more. Luciano couldn't even remember them. She yammered on like the most boring of school lecturers, and he'd settled himself on her bed where he'd determined he would sleep. If only to watch her splutter like an offended nun.

After she took what seemed like a million years to meticulously put away everything in her desk, she turned to him with that cool look, a small smile in place. "Now, we must discuss sleeping arrangements."

He didn't discuss it. He slept in her bed. He had offered to share it and enjoyed doing so. She had so icily declined, it had delighted him. Particularly when she'd stalked over to the closet, pulled out some linens, then made herself a little bed on the window seat. Her tiny demon cats had hopped up and made themselves comfortable on her blankets, blinking at him in ways that felt…threatening.

Which was ridiculous, of course. Neither of them were much bigger than his *hand*.

In the morning, he'd woken in her surprisingly comfortable bed to find her gone from the window seat. Any bedding she'd used had clearly been put away.

The man who seemed to run the staff had met Luciano in the kitchen when he'd found his way there and told him coolly that Ms. Valli was indisposed and that he was welcome to leave whenever he saw fit.

Reading between the lines, Luciano read that as *now*, but he'd taken the offered coffee instead, overstayed his welcome to all and sundry before waltzing out of the place and to his car.

In the midmorning light, Luciano drove back to his apartment in the city. He noted the photographer hiding in a curve of the drive up to Serena's home, but pretended he did not.

The stories would be abuzz in their circles by lunchtime. He would no doubt start hearing from his father's stalwart advisors who would love to oust him if they could figure out how.

This would certainly ignite their ire, but no one would be able to fault him for what this would do for the company. The attention would put their name in circles where the Americans had been dominating. It would have their on-the-fence customers interested enough to take meetings again.

Two wealthy people from families long known to be in a feud would indeed be gossip fodder. Not new to him, considering the company he tended to like to keep was very interested in press and any kind of publicity they could drum up, but it would be new to Serena.

In some ways, she had a far better plan than he could have come up with. And in other ways, he didn't think she had the slightest clue what she was getting herself into.

He supposed that dichotomy was why he had such a difficult time pushing thoughts of *her* away as he went about his day. It was the only possible reason, really.

Besides, what modern woman in their twenties kept a drawer full of colorful notebooks and markers and used them? What kind of young woman lived in a castle decorated with the strangest animal themes?

Pigs on her headboard. It was insanity.

He couldn't seem to stop thinking about it. About how the oddness suited her, interested him, *charmed* him. For all her attempts to be average and customary on the surface, she was anything but underneath.

As he arrived at Ascione, he told his assistant he would be indisposed until after lunch. To hold his calls, allow no one in. Then he'd let himself into his father's office.

His office.

He'd redecorated, finding it necessary to not spend his time in his father's oppressive style. Luciano didn't *mind* the heavy handed opulence his father employed like a power move, he simply didn't think it was necessary.

He much preferred everyone to underestimate him. So everything was simple. Expensive, of course, but sleek lines and minimalism as a direct contrast to his father's maximalism. It suited his purposes here and, even better, Luciano knew his father would have hated it. So there was satisfaction in that.

"I hope there is a view from hell," he murmured to the line of portraits on the wall. The one thing he hadn't been able to get rid of. The line of Asciones who had built this company, built the wealth he'd used as a jumping off point for his own. This row of bastards who'd treated everyone around them like a pawn or an enemy.

Because Luciano might have disdain for them all, but he knew he was one of them. He had tried to be good, noble. Tried to be a protector.

And never managed.

This was his legacy, his blood. Might as well remember it.

He moved for his desk, pushed away all thoughts that weren't next steps. He went over all the information Serena had sent his pretend man of affairs again. Her plan was thorough, but not complete. She was looking for stability. Shoring up foundations. The attention their union, their merger, would draw would be huge and it would no doubt win some of their lost customers back. But that was all she'd planned for. Getting the old back.

Per usual, he thought bigger. Not just setting themselves

up for what they'd *had*, but destroying the American inter-
lopers in the process and giving themselves the opportunity for more.

As she'd said the other night: billionaires never needed
an excuse for wanting more.

So, in his own document, he used the foundation of her
plan to make a bigger one. No doubt hers stopped short of
bigger, because she had plans for what would happen *after*.

Once they vanquished their common foe, they would become enemies once again, even if they were legally wed.
He would need to have a plan in place to come out on top
then. She clearly did.

So, he would. But he would need some…subterfuge. A
distraction. Last night had started the seeds of that plan,
and going over all this, adding to it, made it clear—the only
thing that would work against Serena was the one thing she
was so sure wouldn't.

He would simply have to seduce her.

He ignored the troubling wriggle of doubt in the back of
his mind, because it did not stem from *doubt*, but rather how
little the prospect bothered him. It would be no hardship,
because there was a bloom of *something* under all that ice.
A fire he seemed well adept at bringing out.

That concerned him. His own physical reaction to it. A
shade too eager for his liking. But that only required control, and he knew how to wield it when it was necessary.

Besides, if he felt it, so did she. He had never seen her
falter, except the few times he'd managed to have his hands,
no matter how chastely, on her.

She was innocent, clearly, but not immune. His biggest
hurdle would be convincing her that one didn't need to *like*
the other person for the physical match to be enjoyable.

So perhaps she was due a lesson.

CHAPTER SEVEN

SERENA DID THE laundry herself once he was gone. It was cathartic to strip the bed he'd *defiled* with his long, rangy body, to heft the entire basket of bedding down to the washer and dryer and handle it with her own two hands.

An exorcism of sorts. She would wash away the memory of waking up to him in her bed, sprawled out in *her* sheets, *her* duvet, *her*s. He had looked fierce, even in sleep, like some ancient conqueror. And she had sat there in her window seat, staring for far longer than she'd like to admit, wondering what it would have been like to have woken up *next* to him. To feel his body heat, his skin and all the ways her body reacted to those things.

She'd had to leave her own room, just to find her usually firmly in place common sense. She'd avoided any good-bye because she *knew* embarrassment would swamp her.

But now she'd washed him away and all would be well. She'd make sure of it.

Because the sheets had put her behind schedule, she'd decided to work from home. She had a few calls, lots of e-mails to respond to, but no meetings that required her in the office today, thank goodness.

During her lunch, she'd gone ahead and written out her ridiculous and petty list as a fun little break. Maybe it was pointless as they were not rules she would enforce, or even show him, but it felt therapeutic to put all her wishes into the written word. Complete with stickers depicting donkeys in flower crowns.

Do not utter my name.

Do not touch me.

Do not look at me.

Do not enter my room, let alone even look *at my bed.*

It frustrated her that just writing down these things brought images to her mind. Remembered bodily reactions. A jump in her stomach, a throb too low to have a great excuse for. The way her skin seemed to flush at certain looks he gave her.

It frustrated her that even knowing what an absolute reprobate he was, he was handsome as a devil and knew how to use it against her. She liked to think herself better than such *base* reactions, but she supposed she could not fully fault her brain for what was simply a *physical* reaction.

Besides, he was a man who knew how to use the physical, and she was just not…used to that. She did not engage in such behaviors and gave a wide berth to anyone who did. The few men she'd gone on dates with had not made physical overtures. The last one had even asked permission before kissing her cheek good night.

She'd hated it. And hated herself for hating it. Because it had simply made it clear that she would have to settle for a future where she was truly and utterly alone. That even someone who might be *like* her didn't…match. Didn't allow herself any comfort.

Or worse, any excitement. Which she didn't *think* she was looking for. Didn't *want* to be looking for.

For the best, she often assured herself. Perhaps the castle could get a little lonely, particularly during long winter months when even work couldn't distract her from the fact there was not one person in the whole world who cared about her beyond what she could do for a company.

But it was better to be alone, to do exactly as she pleased without having to don all the masks required of trying to make someone like her. Or pretending to be swept away by someone who asked permission to *kiss a cheek*.

Luckily, she did not need to make Luciano like her. This wasn't a business deal that required dancing to the tune of the male ego. In public, perhaps she would have to pretend more than she'd ever pretended before, but at least behind closed doors she could let loose with what she really thought of him. It was…refreshing, actually. To just say what she thought. To just be herself and not *worry*.

She could be herself in every way, at least in private. So long as she did not let the strange *physical* reaction somehow win. So long as she found a way to stop him from playing these power games that left her feeling unsettled. So long as she did not engage in that so much that she forgot to keep an eye on whatever his counterplay would turn out to be. Because if *she* was thinking about what happened after they vanquished their common enemy, no doubt so was he.

She considered, yet again, the fact that he was allegedly posing as his own man of business. She was not *shocked* he might hide a keener mind than she'd like to give him credit for, but she did not understand why he'd hide it away. She'd refused to ask or even acknowledge it, because she thought that's what he expected of her.

Still, it sat there in her mind like an unsolvable puzzle. It made her wonder what else he might be hiding away. She had to be careful. Even if she'd underestimated him in the beginning, *maybe*, she'd known that she had to be careful.

That this would not be straightforward or easy, and the upper hand would require constant vigilance.

Still, she worried she wasn't seeing the whole picture. She flipped pages back to the front of the notebook and went over her plan. Considered what she now knew about him and how he worked.

How had he built that club to the height of popularity?

Money, of course. No doubt using some of his father's contacts. But there had to be some business sense there. She'd watched him engage with people at the dinner party last night. He used *charm*. Compliments and smiles and easy jokes. He used the way he looked to dazzle.

But with her, he'd taken an opposite approach. He tried to make her uncomfortable. Innuendos about her bed. The way he'd said the word *bite*, when saying she acted afraid he might.

He wanted her flustered. Blushing and uncomfortable. And he undoubtedly thought it some special power he had, not just the fact that she was uncomfortable with the idea of...intimacy. He thought she was flustered by his handsomeness and insinuations.

He was most certainly wrong. Her discomfort last night had nothing to do with *him* personally. Nothing at all. She just wasn't used to a man in her space. That was all.

Confident with that interpretation of last night's events, Serena gave herself a little nod and carefully put her notebook away. The plan that was taking shape was not one she could commit to paper now that he knew she liked to write things out.

No, this would have to stay in her head. Because she knew he'd proceed with her as he had last night. Charming smiles, feigned innocence in his touches and threaded innuendo in everything.

This was how he would attempt to get some upper hand, no doubt. Continue to push her boundaries. Not just in the personal space of her home, but farther. Into her *actual* personal space.

Yes, he would certainly try to seduce her, and going into this, she hadn't really considered he might seriously. It was such a bizarre way to handle business, and she knew she was not the type he usually lent himself to. But it wasn't about what he *liked*. It would be about what he wanted.

Her knee-jerk reaction to this was obvious denial. If he so much as tried it, she'd cut him off at the knees. She would resist. Forever.

She *could* resist, if she wanted to. Curiosity wasn't the same as being unable to resist. Her imagination *sometimes* drifting his way didn't mean she wasn't smart enough to remember who and what she was.

And what he was.

But rejection was expected. What kind of power might she wield if she didn't react the way she usually did? What if she gave him the illusion of the upper hand? What if she *let* him seduce her?

The idea was appalling of course—that was the only thing the feeling in her stomach could be, because it certainly wasn't a jump of anticipation. That pulse scramble, that woozy feeling in the pit of her stomach, like when they'd locked eyes last night. Intrigue and interest as to what all that might lead to.

Nothing, Serena.

But he would assume he had all the control if she let him believe she was dazzled by his…physical prowess. If she let him believe she was foolish enough to be swept away by him, physically and maybe even romantically, he would think he had all the upper hands.

But really *she* would. If she went in with her eyes wide open. It would leave him open for a mistake—for lots of mistakes.

If she saw this as a business move, it wasn't lowering or embarrassing. It was simply what must be done to save her legacy. If she focused on *business*, she wouldn't worry that it might feel like…more.

Besides, maybe she wouldn't have to give in completely. Would he *really* try to take her to bed when he found her dull and frumpy compared to the beautiful women he surrounded himself with? That was a line even he wouldn't cross.

Besides, that was a problem for later. A cross-that-bridge-if-they-come-to-it situation. For now, she had to set up the first steps. The fake-falling-for-his-charm steps.

She pulled out her phone. Brought up a text to him and typed it out.

Dinner at seven, here at my castle.

She would couch it as a business dinner. She'd made some progress with the D'Angelo account, and she would apprise him of this. Along with a plan for him to dazzle the Franco team next week.

When her phone dinged, his response was obnoxious. Of course.

Where is the "please", amore mio?

She didn't bother to respond to that.

He would show up. And they would have a romantic dinner, discuss business and then she would let him flirt and push the boundaries and this time, she might respond. At least a little.

So the trap would be laid.

And if there was a little flutter of anticipation—no, not that. *Nerves*—well, she would master those as well.

Luciano was full of good humor as he drove up the twisting road to Serena's castle once again.

His assistant had dutifully collected all the stories about him and Serena this afternoon, and Luciano planned to go over them with her and discuss next steps in their "relationship" department.

He did not know what *she* had planned, but he had plans of his own beyond business. No doubt that would be the story of their strange partnership. A constant battle. Skirmishes lost and won. It was oddly…exciting. The prospect of clashing with a worthy adversary.

As long as he came out on top more than she did, he had a positive feeling about how this could end up.

She had definitely brought him a brilliant idea. He would enact it even better than she could possibly imagine. Though whether she gave him any credit was doubtful.

Most of his challenges were done in private, where no one ever knew. It was best, always, for no one to truly know him. It allowed him to always accomplish what he set out to do. And while everyone attributed his success to *luck*, he knew the truth. How hard he'd worked. How much he'd overcome. And that no obstacle was too big for Luciano Ascione.

The knowledge had him whistling on his way up her staircase. He was let inside by the disapproving butler Luciano had yet to charm. He'd get there though. He always did.

"Ms. Valli has dinner waiting on the sea balcony," the man said stiffly, and then led him through the house. The back of the house, as Serena had last night. It amused him, these silly little slights.

Up a winding staircase and into a different hallway than last night, Luciano was led out a door and into the warm, breezy evening on a large balcony. Vibrant plants spilled from colorful pots. More strangely fanciful decoration popped out here. Wind chimes and all sorts of sculptures of animals in different mediums.

What *was* her obsession with animals? She made no sense. That feeling did not diminish when his gaze finally found her where she was standing at the curve of the railing, surveying him with those cool eyes.

Her expression was guarded, but the way she stood at the edge of the balcony was relaxed. And still… There was something about the way she held herself that made him wary. Was this the same woman who'd been frustrated to let him into her home last night? Smiling at him welcomingly now?

"Good evening, Luciano," she greeted.

He did not like the way she said his name. Something about it scraped along the back of his neck like a terrible portent melding with goose bumps. He had to fight off a scowl. What man got *goose bumps*? Certainly not *him*.

"Good evening," he offered, forcing himself to smile at her in the way that usually had her frowning.

She didn't frown today, though he did see the way her hand tightened briefly on the railing she rested it on before she relaxed it again. She gestured at the table. "I know this isn't visible like a restaurant might be, but the press was eating up your car leaving the hill this morning."

"Are you inviting me for another sleepover?"

Her mouth flattened, but she didn't scowl. She seemed to be making a great effort not to. She inhaled, then the corners of her mouth turned ever so slightly upward. "Whatever furthers our purpose," she said, with a kind of knowing that was almost…sultry.

Except this was Serena, so he was imagining things, surely. Still, it was clear something was off. He couldn't quite put his finger on the difference. She was dressed casually enough. The pants she wore looked soft and gave little hint at shape. She was not covered to the chin, he supposed, instead wearing a tank top the color of the sky at dawn, a pearly kind of blue. It was formfitting, but hardly skimpy. Still, he could see the shape of her arms, the freckles that dotted her shoulders as if she spent considerable time in the sun, which didn't seem true to the woman she was at all.

And now he knew that these details, like the long, lovely shape of her legs, would be lodged uncomfortably in his brain.

He tried to look at it as a positive. Being attracted to her might be a bit of an affront considering she had always been his enemy, but it would make seduction enjoyable. Still, there was an uncomfortable tug of war going on inside of him, like there was a complication threading through all of this. It wasn't just business. It wasn't just seduction. It was layers— who they were because of their fathers, what they'd built themselves into, all the strange ways she fascinated him.

He did not care for *layers*. He preferred things to be… straightforward.

So he looked at the table between them, set for dinner. A bottle of wine in a bucket of ice, bruschetta displayed prettily on a colorful serving platter. It had every detail of a romantic, private dinner for two.

"I thought we should eat outside, then we can take a walk down to the beach. It's private, but an intrepid photographer with an excellent zoom lens should be able to catch sight of us from there."

"Smart."

"Besides, being outdoors means the stench of rat doesn't infect my dining room." She offered that sweet smile meant to slice a man to ribbons.

Ah, *there* was the Serena he expected. With a fiery orange sunset lighting her from behind, she looked a bit like a painting...

Vengeful Goddess at Sunset.

She only needed a bow and arrow or spear of some kind. Instead, she moved forward and lowered herself into a chair at the table. She lifted the bottle of wine and began to pour. When he did not immediately take a seat, she raised her gaze and an eyebrow at him.

He wasn't sure what was causing him pause, so he moved forward and took the seat across from her.

"Have you seen the stories?" she asked.

"Yes. They have bought into *us* hook, line and sinker."

Serena nodded, a wine glass in her hand as she gazed out at the water beyond the balcony. Her expression was thoughtful, and she did not sip from her glass. "I think we'll want to move quickly. No long, drawn out courtships. We don't want the excitement to ebb. Just one story after the next."

He agreed with her, which shouldn't frustrate him as much as it did. He should be happy when they agreed. It would no doubt be rare, even with a common goal. But he hated the idea of her congratulating herself for her good ideas when he had them as well.

So he said nothing—not agreement or disagreement— as they ate in strangely peaceful silence. Like people who'd known each other long enough not to need to fill in those spaces.

When dessert was served, darkness had fallen except for

fairy lights hung expertly, illuminating the balcony in something that felt like candlelight.

The *millefoglie* was delicious, the night lovely, the company…oddly comfortable. But realizing how thoroughly he'd enjoyed an essentially silent dinner bothered him on a cellular level.

He stood. "Shall we take that walk?" he offered.

She sighed heavily. "Yes, of course." Reluctantly, she got to her feet. "I suppose we should talk about something."

She sounded genuinely and amusingly disappointed that they might actually have to have a conversation.

"I don't mind a silence now and again."

She snorted. "Come, Luciano. You have built a life in which you never have to live in the silence of your own thoughts. It is much talked about how much time you spend at that club of yours."

She was not completely wrong. Up until his father's death, he had always sought to drown out the thoughts, the feelings by throwing himself headlong into his club, into the women there.

But something happened when his father died. He supposed it was a kind of natural understanding that he himself would not live forever. He too could do something stupid tomorrow and end up a mangled mess on a cliffside.

Luciano wanted to be something more than his father had ever allowed him to be. So, in an effort to reacquaint himself with Ascione and deal with the fallout of everything, he'd begun to insulate himself. Against his club, his old, loud friends. The women, the music, the booze.

Oh, he still went out. He could not let his reputation suffer completely. But he also spent a lot of time alone and in silence, rewriting the prophecy his father had left for him.

The balcony led to a staircase down to the gardens below,

and Luciano met Serena at the top. He held up his palm—an invitation to link hands.

The slight sneer she failed at hiding amused him. So much about her amused him. Perhaps because while she kept that perfect icy mask impeccable in public, when they were alone together she could not seem to help resorting to her true self. Even if that true self hated him, it was amusing.

But she also did what needed doing, and as much as he'd like to hate that about her, he could only respect it.

He felt that she had to respect *something* about him as well to be here. To be doing this. For all her little barbs, she *did* treat him like an equal partner in this. She did not ridicule his ideas. She had not once treated him as his father often had, as if everything he did was the wrong step.

Besides, he had no doubt there was at least some small part of her that *wanted* him. Maybe she didn't like it any better than he did, but it was there. Vibrating underneath the surface. They could both ignore it, they could both use it. It didn't matter. It was *there*. An entity and a being he didn't think either of them knew how to fully parse.

Her hands were soft, fingers long and slender like her legs as they linked with his. For a completely incomprehensible moment, he found himself wondering if so much would be different if they had not been raised as rivals, raised to hate one another. Would there be mutual attraction and respect without all the complicated thorns of being a Valli and an Ascione?

Because if she treated him like an equal, she saw him as one, and that was very rare in his life indeed. He made sure of it.

And why the hell should that matter? It didn't.

There was the faint scent of lavender that seemed to cling

to her or the air. He wanted it to be the air, but he'd been in her bed and knew what her sheets smelled of.

He had to fight off a scowl as they descended the staircase. She led him through a pathway through the unlit garden. He only had the general feeling of lots of growth, but the darkness did not give away any detail.

She opened a gate, and out they stepped onto the beach. It was a small slice of sand, mostly barricaded by big rocks. But not too far down the waterline there were lights. Some resorts, along with other houses and estates along the water.

"Do you really think someone would be watching?" Luciano asked.

"What I know is at least two cars followed you up to my gate. My security team will be determining their identity, but I would imagine it was press of some kind. If they know you're here, they know air and sea is the only other way to get a glimpse. I'm not sure we've reached helicopter or drone levels of interest yet."

"*Yet*, being the operative word."

"One hopes. No doubt anyone in Genoa will be intrigued, and the way social media can make a story of anything might give us some global reach, but one never knows what will catch the public's imagination."

"Indeed not."

"So, do I think someone is out there watching?" She gestured out along the shoreline. "I think we have a fifty-fifty chance, so we might as well take it. It's about the only way I'd let your hand hold mine, naturally."

He smiled in spite of himself. "Naturally," he agreed. "But hand holding is so…childish, is it not?" He dropped her hand, lifted his to her back, then slid it down the curve of her spine as they walked. "There are far more intimate touches a man and woman might engage in on a moonlit walk on the beach." He ran his hand back up, curled his fingers around the nape of her neck and felt the shudder there, the soft escape of her breath.

He did not care for how much his own body seemed to shudder in response, but it was all for the end goal. All of it.

"I have some ideas on how to handle the Francos next week," she said after a moment. She did not try to dislodge his hand from her neck. She did not angle herself so that they were not essentially hip to hip as they walked. She even seemed to be trying to relax into his touch, rather than stiffen against it.

But the change of topic was clear. She was accepting the touch on the fifty-fifty chance they were being photographed, but she would not engage in innuendo.

Yet.

So, he responded to her change in topic in kind. "As do I. In fact, I think we should approach this meeting as a team. Go into it together."

"We are not officially a partnership yet," Serena said, a faint frown on her face. "We will need everything in place legally before we start muddying up those waters."

"Then, let us move forward with that."

Starlight dappled the sand. The quiet sounds of waves echoed gently as they walked. If there was any romance in the world, it was in this setting. So, it was time to get on with the show.

He pulled the box from his pocket, fingering the velvet as he watched her.

She looked remote in profile. An untouchable goddess with her hair down and her face upturned to the moon so she seemed to glint silver as she considered his suggestion. For all her strength and determination and *hate* towards him, the moonlight made her seem ethereal. Lit from within. Someone else entirely—like the perfect Serena could be soft and romantic somewhere underneath all those sharp glaciers.

And maybe she could. To someone else. Not to *him*.

The strange pang in his chest at that thought was...nonsensical. Ridiculous.

The tightness in his chest wasn't nerves, because he'd long since vanquished those from his life. It wasn't lust—he knew what that felt like, and while he could not deny the strange appeal Serena had, here in this moment it wasn't a bolt, a sharp need that wound through him.

It was something else altogether. Something he wasn't familiar with. He didn't like it or trust it, so he shoved it away and focused on the plan. He released her neck, stepped back and then dropped to one knee.

And waited for her to turn to him.

CHAPTER EIGHT

SERENA BRACED HERSELF to deal with whatever Luciano had stopped for. Probably a kiss for the cameras. A romantic embrace. It was the smart thing to do, but something about the environment added dread to something she'd already decided.

Because it was romantic—the starlight, the soft lap of waves, the darkness. And when she turned, she would be faced with a far too attractive man, whose simple touch made her shudder and sigh even when she didn't *want* to. When she had worked so hard all her life to make all her reactions just what she wanted them to be.

No matter how hard she tried, she could not make her reactions what she wanted them to be when it came to him. She could not find a safe place in her icy perfection.

She *would* let him touch her. She *would* have to let him kiss her. Perhaps she could continue to protest a *little*, but she needed to start showing a weakening, so she lulled him into complacency.

And she desperately needed to think of it that way, so she did not think about what a kiss might actually feel like. Business over shivers and pulses.

She had already had her lawyers involved in drawing up papers that would solidify their business partnership once they were married. He would no doubt need his lawyers to go over them and counteroffer different things. It was likely to be drawn out, so yes, they should move forward.

But that meant moving forward with the marriage.

She had been so ready to do that, and then they had walked hand in hand, and her body had felt…foreign.

Then he had skimmed his hand along her spine. She understood why cats purred now. How the gentle caress of a hand could make a body feel content and pleasurable. Then he'd put his hand at her neck, and it had been like…little explosions in her bloodstream. No longer just *content*, something more…wanting.

She wanted to focus on business, on what needed to be done, and still her body pulsed even though he'd released her. She squeezed her eyes shut, tried to find some of her always available control.

Upper hand, remember? she told herself. *Not for pleasure…for the upper hand.*

Trying to find a smile, something flirtatious inside of her instead of concern over her body's reactions, she turned to look at him. Except he wasn't standing. He was kneeling in the sand and—

Serena's breath caught. Not at the scene itself—romantic and movie-like as it might be. It was the ring. It glittered there under the celestial lights above, a beacon of pretty… perfection in its cozy little box that Luciano held out to her.

"I considered your style and mine," Luciano said, his voice low and as lulling as the sea waves. "I could have had something designed, but I think we should strike while the iron is hot. It is expensive, indeed, but not quite gaudy as you had indicated you wished for last night. Still, this should do, shouldn't it?"

It was gorgeous. Absolutely, thrillingly beautiful. She was not a flashy person, and the ring bordered on flashy, but not so far that she didn't like it. It was a pink diamond, settled among other winking diamonds on a slim band that made the center stone look that much bigger.

It reminded her of being a child, going through her mother's jewelry boxes. Enjoying the feel of cool precious metals on her fingers and wrists and neck.

But that was a reminder of her mother always telling her that she was too plain for such things. And she was, fair enough. She was plain and unassuming. Dull. This ring didn't match *her*.

But it matched the image of someone who'd caught Luciano Ascione's attention, the fake fiancée for the fake marriage. So she had to go with it. Didn't she?

He gripped her hand and held it still as he slid the ring onto her finger. She wanted to keep her gaze on the ring, but it seemed to move, of its own accord, up to meet his gaze. Dark and intense. Potent, looking up at her. Like a shot of liquor.

Why? She didn't know. Maybe some men were just given that kind of power. So incredibly unfair, but impossible to deny in this moment. She had to lick her lips and swallow in order to speak. "This was a smart move," she managed to say.

He got to his feet and looked down at her, his dark eyes alight with amusement, his mouth curved into something cutting and intriguing at once.

"Why, thank you, *cara*. I so appreciate your approval." His tone was wry. "I suppose that is your way of saying *yes*."

She was afraid to speak. There were too many emotions battering around inside of her, making her throat feel tight. The way her body felt. The way this felt real, when she knew it wasn't, and didn't want it to be. And still, that pulsing *need* throbbing deep inside of her that she had to get a hold of to come out on top. "I suppose it is," she managed.

"Do you think your photographers caught any of that?"

Photographers. The *play* they were essentially acting out. She had to remember that even if the ring was real, even if whatever papers they signed to be married and combine Valli and Ascione were *real*, the whole...personal side of things wasn't.

She wanted to rub at the odd pain in her chest, but couldn't seem to find control of her own body.

"If they don't, I shall be sure to make an appearance somewhere notable with this on my hand. That should start the talk." She frowned down at the ring. "However, I shall have to break the news to my mother first." Something she did not relish. It left a worse taste in her mouth than actually marrying Luciano.

"Ah." His arm came around her, and she could give him credit here—he knew the act. Relished it. She still felt shell-shocked. "Shall I expect pistols at dawn then?" he asked, guiding her back toward her gardens.

Serena shook her head. She felt strangely...afloat. Like she was in a dream where she was a fairy-tale princess, and the handsome man in front of her represented some kind of love and future. She could remember a time when she'd had silly little dreams like that. But she'd been small, naive. It was before she'd realized that she would never achieve that *sparkle* her mother had. Back when her parents had divorced and split their lives forever, shuttling Serena back and forth like an unwanted gift they could not get rid of without offending someone. That was when she realized all she had to offer was perfection, and maybe that would never earn love, but it would get her *somewhere*. It would earn her a place.

She needed to get a hold of herself. It was just a ring. "No, my mother never cared about Valli business. She won't have any compunction on you being an Ascione. She will insist on a dinner and she will…" Serena trailed off. She didn't know exactly how to warn Luciano how her mother would be.

Serena had learned how to be perfect in her father's eyes. How to be what he wanted, more or less. She had been able to work and *prove* to him that she had some worth.

She had never been able to make that kind of dent with her mother. Serena didn't allow that to put them at odds, but she did keep a certain kind of distance from her mother. But a life event like this would require dealing with her, lest she make a scene.

No doubt, Luciano wouldn't even notice. Mother's barbs tended to be for Serena and Serena alone.

But it had to be done. Mother was the only family she had left. And the whole point was everything needed to seem real to outsiders. Her mother would have to be…somewhat involved going forward.

Serena contemplated the sea for a moment. Maybe she could just run into it and swim until she found a deserted island or simply perished instead. But before she could give any serious consideration to running away, Luciano stopped their forward progress toward her home.

"I'm afraid, there is one thing we will have to do before we head back inside and break the happy news to your mother."

"What is that?"

He turned her to face him. When she glanced up at him, she saw that his expression was oddly grave. But then his mouth curved. An attempt at a smile. She thought it might have even been an attempt to be roguishly irritating, but it didn't meet his eyes.

Not as he pulled her body close, so they were pressed

together. His heat surrounding them. The smell of the sea, the sounds of the waves, the strange lull of a darkened evening and his hands on her hips. It was like something out of a book or movie. Romantic and...something darker. A strange, twisting need that she might have words for if she wanted to find them.

She didn't.

"We should seal this deal with a kiss, Serena," he said, angling his head down so that his mouth was close to hers. So she could feel his breath along with his body. "Just in case those photographers *are* watching."

She swallowed, trying to think of something smart to say. He was right, of course. This was all an act so they had to act, but...

He did not ask permission. He did not brush his lips across her cheek. He pressed his mouth to hers, pulled her body to his.

And devoured.

It couldn't be chaste. He'd known that going in. A long lens in the darkness would need a prolonged embrace. They would still likely just be grainy shadows, but a grainy shadow could be used with the right story.

It would need to take its time. It would need...

He lost the thread of his thoughts at the first shudder of her body against his. Something like heat scorched through him. A longing for things he didn't fully recognize and knew better than to try.

So he focused on what he did recognize. The contours of a kiss. The delicate press of her body, surprisingly soft and small. She held herself in such a way, he'd expected something...stronger, he supposed. A leanness with sharp angles ready to cut him to pieces.

He'd also expected her to be more stiff, to push him away, to resist…even if she eventually gave in.

But there was no resistance in her. Innocence maybe, but she allowed his mouth the enticing tour of hers. When he splayed his fingers wide, swept them up her side and settled just short of her breasts, she shuddered out a sigh that had a newly appointed hunger digging its way deep inside of him.

And because it was there—her parted mouth, a mystery too close to walk away from—he tasted. A stunning combination of the wine from dinner and something unique to this kiss and this moment alone.

He supposed her innocence allowed him to set the tone, and there was a delirium in that. He was in charge. Of this moment. Of tough, icy Serena who was none of those things in this moment. She was soft, sweet and a million other words he'd never once used to describe Serena Valli.

Serena Valli.

It was her name that reminded him of who he was and what this was meant to be. He didn't jerk back, though he wanted to. But no, this was an act.

No matter what strange detours his brain, or body, had gone down, this was still just an act. So he carefully eased away. First his mouth, then his body. Until cool air swept between them.

His own body was too hot, too hard. Too prepared for something that had grown more and more tempting as the kiss went on. Oh, he'd planned on seducing her. He'd told himself their chemistry, as it was, might allow him to enjoy it.

Now, he could admit that he was a little concerned it might end in a mistake. Committed by *him*.

Impossible. Unthinkable.

They regarded each other in the short distance they'd created, wary and aroused. A dangerous tightrope. One Luciano realized in a strange way he was as new to as she was. He doubted very much that Serena had ever been buffeted by something as base as physical spontaneous combustion as he had, but he'd never dabbled in *unwanted* desire before. He rarely drew lines like that. If a woman was willing, and they usually were, he slaked whatever desires they both had.

To hold back was new, and he didn't like it. That lust and concern fused with irritation at himself, at their fathers, at the entire damn world for throwing him into a gray area he had never wanted.

"I think that should suffice for tonight," she said coolly. And he might have believed she was cool inside and out, but her hand shook as she reached up to smooth it over her hair.

He wished she were the ice princess he'd once believed her to be. It would be so much easier to set aside that kiss as a one off. But there was something underneath all her veneer, and he'd gotten another intriguing peek at it.

Damn her.

"Indeed," he managed to grit out.

"And you will take the window seat tonight," she said firmly, an order, then marched into the gardens, leaving him behind in the dark.

Hard and aching for a woman he wanted nothing to do with.

CHAPTER NINE

SERENA FOUND THAT having her own bed back had done nothing to help her sleep, with Luciano stretched out on her window seat. She had tossed and turned and...throbbed and ached for half the night.

She hated to think what she might have done with herself if she'd been alone. The thought *haunted* her, no matter how she tried to set it away. She had not known that pretending could be...

Well, it didn't matter what it could be. What mattered was how she was going to deal with it. In reality, it was a *good thing*, part of the plan. He'd kissed her for the cameras, and ideally, she'd fooled him enough that he'd gone to sleep thinking she'd enjoyed it.

You did enjoy it.

And that was the disturbing fact she kept coming back to. She had wanted more. Giving into any kind of seduction last night would not have been part of any *plan*.

Not that he'd tried to seduce her. He'd eased away from that kiss, stepped away from her as if he'd...tasted something bad. But for a while, for the majority of that kiss, he had not.

She had nothing to compare it to, but it had *seemed* like he'd had a physical reaction somewhat on par with hers.

An act. Of course it was an act. Everything they did except hate each other was an act. And the act was important.

Which was why she slipped out of bed, shrugged on her robe and grabbed her phone. She had an order of business to get over with.

She stepped quietly out of the room and took the door out onto the balcony that overlooked the sea, the colorful buildings crowded along the shoreline. And her, alone and isolated on her castle on the hill.

Just where she wanted to be. What she did not want was to do what must be done, but she could hardly put it off if pictures of last night started to circulate. She took in steadying breaths of air, let it wash through her and fill her with calm.

She would need it.

She dialed her mother's number, watched the morning sunlight dapple across the water. Part of her hoped her mother wouldn't answer, and she couldn't help feeling ashamed of that hope. Even if her mother didn't deserve her devotion, she was not an *evil* woman. Just a self-centered one, who didn't realize how words could hurt.

"Serena." The greeting was tinged with disappointment. "Haven't we discussed how busy I am in the mornings and how little I like to have conversations before lunchtime?"

Serena didn't sigh. "I apologize, Mother."

Angelica Valli—she'd kept her ex-husband's last name despite many romantic partners since because she liked the cache it gave her and the opportunity to discuss what a terrible husband he'd been—sighed heavily.

In her youth, she'd been an actress, and she still missed the stage so played whatever role she could whenever life gave her the opportunity. She liked attention in whatever ways she could get it, and she was very good at getting it.

The one role she'd never played well, from Serena's point of view, was mother.

But that was neither here nor there.

"I have some news, and as it will likely be made public soon, I wanted to tell you first," Serena said, being careful to keep her voice neutral. "It won't require any conversation at all. I am engaged. To be married." She stared at the beautiful ring on her finger. If nothing else, her mother would certainly be impressed with that.

Her mother laughed, and Serena winced in spite of herself. The caustic sound reminded her too much of how uncomfortable she'd been in her mother's care. Neither of her parents had quite known what to do with her, and as much as her father had not been a loving or devoted man, he'd mostly ignored her.

Angelica preferred to *poke*. It had been there before the divorce but had only gotten worse after.

You'll always be as dull and uninspiring as your father. Nothing I could do could change it.

Yes, Angelica had always made it clear there was nothing to be done, so Serena had leaned into the *dull*—which was where she felt most comfortable. And in the dull, in the *as your father*, she had found her mark.

She had made herself into a businesswoman to *rival* her father. So perfect, so smart, so cunning that even he who had no interest in her at all had been forced to admit she was an asset to Valli.

"Well, that *is* interesting," Angelica said after a while. "I hope you'll be smart enough to protect your own assets, while getting access to as many of his as possible. Don't let romantic notions fool you."

"Of course not."

No congratulations. Not even excitement over the prospect of a wedding. Just: *make sure to protect your assets.*

Which was fine, because this was entirely about her assets, even if her mother didn't know that.

"Is that all?" Mother asked. No questions about a wedding, or even about the man in question. Just *is that all*. Serena did not understand why she thought there might be more, except her mother had always told her to focus on tricking a man into marrying her, rather than do something so boring as go into the Valli *business*.

And here she was, doing both. And Mother didn't care. *Why did you think she would?*

Serena had to clear her throat to speak. To finish the conversation with all the pertinent information, no matter how much she preferred to just hang up. "I believe you know of my fiancée." As if mentioning him conjured him, Luciano stepped out onto the balcony wearing black trousers and a button-down shirt.

Unbuttoned. With sleep-tousled hair. And still too unfairly beautiful in spite of it. He looked like an ad for cologne or expensive watches.

"I cannot imagine I'd know anyone who would find themselves engaged to you, darling. We move in *much* different circles socially."

Socially, maybe, but the men she did business with tended to be in the monetary echelon that her mother preferred to socialize with. She did not know if Mother and Luciano had ever been properly introduced, but no doubt Mother had been to his club. No doubt Mother knew just who he was and what his financial portfolio looked like.

Something about that made her hesitate, but any hesitation about giving her mother this information and dreading what she'd do about it had to be moved past. This needed to be done. "Luciano Ascione."

He did a little mock bow, as if she'd introduced him to a crowd of people who were thrilled and applauding. It had a foreign feeling settling in her chest. Almost like amusement, when a conversation with her mother never had any of that.

There was a beat of silence, and Serena would blame Luciano distracting her on the fact that she was not prepared and braced for her mother's reaction.

"Serena. You cannot be this stupid."

Serena blinked, stiffened even though she'd taught herself long ago not to let her mother's barbs land. "I beg your pardon?"

"What would a man like Luciano Ascione want with *you*?"

The question was an honest one, even if it twisted in Serena like old insecurities she'd forced herself to leave behind. Mother didn't *mean* anything by it. She simply and honestly did not understand.

And Serena knew she'd never be able to convince her mother, but she supposed she had to at least pretend to try. "I'm sure it does not seem like it on paper, but Luciano and I actually have quite a bit in common."

Luciano raised an eyebrow, and the strangest sensation of wanting to laugh overtook the dull ache of dealing with her mother. Perhaps she should always have him around when handling this kind of undertaking.

Luciano held out his hand, a kind of sign that he wanted the phone.

She nearly did laugh out loud then. She shook her head, tried to remember what she'd been about to tell her mother. They had things in common and…

He made the gesture again. Serena turned away from him so he couldn't distract her anymore. "Mother—"

The phone was plucked from her fingers and she whirled around to try to retrieve it, but Luciano held her phone to his ear and his arm out like he was warding her off.

"Mrs. Valli, so good to talk to you," he greeted cheerfully.

"Luciano Ascione here. I'm not sure we've ever spoken, but of course Serena has told me much about you, and I believe you were friendly with my uncle for a time."

Serena advanced on him, trying to reach for the phone, but his free hand clasped her wrist and held her out of reach. An easy display of his height and strength.

"Serena accepted my proposal just last night. I like to believe I've won over her suspicious nature, but I won't be able to believe it for sure until she introduces me to you."

Serena considered kicking him in the shin, but she must have telegraphed the thought because he quickly dropped her hand and took two steps away. Humor danced in his eyes while she hoped murder danced in hers.

She tried to advance again, quickly this time. A quick grab out and she'd have the phone and—

Instead, she found her back plastered to his chest, one muscular arm of his banded around her midsection, holding her arms down at their sides. Effectively immobilizing her. She was so shocked that for a moment, she only stood there, fully still. Fully…something.

If anyone came upon them, it would look a bit like a lover's embrace with his chin tucked over the top of her head. Rage warred with the unfamiliar feeling of being so close to someone, held so tight. It wasn't *threatening*. She didn't feel the desperate need to escape.

No, she felt…held. And the foreign feeling of wanting to sink into something so…strong. So warm. A direct antithesis to the morning.

But it was annoying, she reminded herself. He should not be talking to her mother. He should not be…any of this.

She lifted one leg, trying to determine if she could bend it at the right angle to come into hard, painful contact with a vulnerable part of his body.

He chuckled and the rumble of his chest against her back reminded her, so unfortunately, of last night. Of the way it had rippled through her when she'd felt his heart thud against hers, body to body, mouth to mouth. So that security meshed with that unfamiliar *pulse*, and she didn't know what to make of any of it.

"We would like to invite you to dinner," Luciano was saying in a voice full of cheerful vivacity. "If your schedule would allow it, of course. To celebrate our most happy news."

Oh...no, was all Serena could think and she began to squirm in earnest. She had to stop this. Luciano's grip was tight, but she could move the lower half of her body. If she twisted back and forth...

"I'll work out the details and send a formal invitation once it is set. Let me give you back to Serena."

So quickly that she nearly stumbled forward, he released her. He held out the phone to her, his mouth curved into an amused smile. But there was something about the look in his eye, the way he'd angled the lower half of his body away from her that left her feeling suddenly...winded. Like they had narrowly missed...something.

But she could hear her mother's voice coming from the receiver and had to lift the phone to her ear.

"I suppose I will come to dinner," Mother was saying, sounding so affronted and exhausted by such a simple request. "But I can't promise I will be able to pretend this is anything but an embarrassment."

"Mother, you don't have—"

But before she could finish, Mother was saying good-bye and hanging up.

Serena whirled on Luciano. She felt too many things to parse, and she knew better than to let loose with temper when she was churned up in ways she didn't understand. But she hated him.

Hated.

"You shouldn't have done that."

"Why not?" he returned in that maddeningly insouciant way of his. "She will have to be at the wedding. Besides, if we have the dinner somewhere public, there's another opportunity to be seen. If I am not mistaken, your mother loves to be seen."

"Yes, she does. In any way she can. She also enjoys to *cause* a scene, and since she thinks this is an *embarrassment* and I am stupid for thinking you could want to marry me, this can only end in disaster."

For a moment, Luciano said nothing. He studied her with a kind of seriousness she did not recall ever seeing in him before. It made her...nervous. Like he could...understand all the twisted pieces inside of her that Mother managed to work up no matter how hard Serena tried to remain unmoved.

She knew very little about his upbringing, except that Gianluca Ascione had been a hard and exacting man to everyone in his life—including his son.

This realization poked holes in her growing balloon of rage and had her deflating into something...tired. She just felt *exhausted*. Like no matter how hard she tried, all her perfection was an impossible wall to keep building, because *he* would always slip through the cracks.

"Then we shall have a dinner at my penthouse," he finally said.

It would be easier. Mother hated the castle. But... "Why?"

Luciano shrugged. "If she is going to make a scene, I prefer handling scenes on my home battlefield." His smile was sharp. "Besides, it gives us an opportunity to have people see you and your mother go into my building, without anyone seeing the scene itself. This is our goal, is it not?"

She closed her eyes, pinched the bridge of her nose and turned away from him and toward the balcony. She rested her elbows on the rail and took a deep breath of sea air in.

She felt him come behind her and she tensed, for too many reasons, really. But somehow she knew he would touch her. She thought she didn't want him to. She wanted it to be because she didn't want to be touched by *him*, but she did. And that's what she didn't want. This constant proof that she wanted more of his hands on her, and all her denials were just that. *Denial.*

Then he pushed his thumb against the tight muscle in her neck, and she could be embarrassed later at the happy sigh that escaped her mouth. *God* that felt good.

"Did you not sleep well, *cara*?" he asked in a soft, sultry murmur.

She was tempted to melt into the touch, into the quiet lull of his voice. His thumb rubbed circles against her neck and it was truly a glorious relaxation. It hit the exact right spot that had tensed and tensed and tensed. She wanted him to do that forever.

Until she remembered she hated him. And the fact his question was just him being a jerk, not actually expressing concern.

"I slept beautifully," she replied, stepping away from his hands. They were a problem. And while she was planning on giving in to the seduction route, sometimes, a girl had to know when to retreat. "And now, I need to get to work."

"*We*, darling," he said, holding out his elbow like he expected her to loop her arm with his. "We will head into work together this morning."

Serena had not fought him as much as he'd anticipated. She'd surveyed him with that regal disdain as he'd explained that they should take turns going into each other's offices, begin to lay the groundwork for a merger while the lawyers drew up contracts and what not.

And show off her ring. The stories should start weaving their way through their mutual acquaintances, so giving everyone something even more concrete to talk about would be good. He had no doubt that both he and Serena would have all sorts of meetings lined up—customers who had left crawling back and begging for a moment just to get a sniff of gossip.

Then, together, they would offer a new deal that the Americans would not be able to match. Serena's homegrown connections. Luciano's ironclad global partnerships. Together, they would offer their customers *everything*.

It was such a good plan, he sometimes forgot it was hers.

They walked into the Valli office building, arm in arm yet again. Serena ensured it was her left hand in his, so the diamond was what anyone would come face to face with as they approached.

She greeted anyone they came across by name—something the Vallis were famous for. A personal approach. Family to family. Ironic considering how little of a family man Serena's father had been, but in the confines of these walls, Mr. Valli had built his own family. And made a lot of money from it.

His own father had considered it beneath him. He'd gone for the glitz, the glamour. A royal kind of viewpoint, handed down from generation to generation. A counterpoint to the allegedly humble Vallis—which of course had only infuriated his father, because they'd amassed as big a fortune as he had.

Honestly, both methods were just smoke and mirrors to hide the fact that both men were ill-equipped to manage the legacies handed down to them.

Ironic that their children should seek to save said legacies. Together.

When they stepped out of the elevator on a higher floor, Luciano realized that this would be *her* floor. The woman behind a desk that guarded the hallway of doors immediately jumped to her feet.

"Good morning, Andrea," Serena greeted, moving in a straight shot toward whatever target she sought. But as she passed the desk of who Luciano assumed was Serena's assistant, Serena paused and turned to look at this Andrea.

Luciano watched as Serena carefully composed herself, put on that fake smile she was so good at. Meanwhile, the assistant couldn't seem to stop herself from staring, openmouthed, at the diamond on Serena's hand.

"Andrea, I'd like to introduce you to my fiancée, Mr. Luciano Ascione. You will likely be seeing quite a bit of him in the coming months. I hope I can count on you to help him feel welcome and at home here at Valli."

"O-of course. Welcome, Mr. Ascione." The woman hesitated, like she wasn't quite sure how to greet him. A handshake. A curtsy. A spitted oath.

"Thank you, Andrea." He offered her a warm smile, trying to balance his usual charm with something more… homey. He did not think he succeeded when Andrea's cheeks turned a faint shade of pink.

"We will be in my office. You can send any phone calls through, but please no visitors."

"Yes, ma'am. Ms. Valli—"

But before she could say whatever she was going to say, a group of men appeared in the hallway it appeared Serena had been meaning to go down. Luciano didn't think *they* noticed the change in Serena's demeanor. It was very subtle.

But clearly a kind of putting on armor.

"Serena," one of the men said. He had a thick mustache and heavy middle. Luciano thought he recognized him as one of the Valli high-level managers his father had once tried to woo away from Valli.

"We've called an emergency meeting," the man said firmly. Like a father might tell a child they were grounded.

Every single man blocking their way stared at Luciano with disapproving eyes. Honestly, it wasn't all that different than being in his own office. Disapproval was comfortable and easy. Especially in these circumstances, he liked that they felt like a challenge.

"You'll need to discuss an appropriate time in my schedule with Andrea," Serena replied dismissively.

"We already have."

Serena looked back at Andrea, who nodded nervously. "You had space at ten-thirty and they were very…determined."

"Very well. I will see you then. If you'll excuse us." She gave them an imperious glare, gestured for them to move out of her way.

With her left hand. Luciano watched as every single one of them zeroed their gaze to the ring on it. There was not surprise, but there was consternation. But they shuffled out of the way so Serena could march through.

She led Luciano to what he assumed was the door of her office. She opened it and gestured him inside.

"Serena, this is very perplexing," one of the men said, making a move as if he'd follow her into her office.

"For you," she said cheerfully. Then she shut the door on his face, without so much of a hint of regret. She moved to her desk and placed her briefcase on it. Every move was precise and economical, as if she didn't care one bit about the grumpy old men in the hall.

"Did your father really trust those dimwits?" Luciano

asked casually, wondering if she'd leap to their defense when it came to him.

She did not. "I am afraid so. They agreed with whatever he said, and that is how my father preferred to run a business."

"But not you?"

"Why would I surround myself with people who agree with me when I could surround myself with intelligence and tact and ensure that I have the best operations by nature of the fact I'm bringing sharp minds together for a common goal?" She moved about her desk with impatient movements—a woman on a mission.

It surprised him a little to hear her say this. She seemed so determined and sure of herself, he was surprised she gave any time to anyone else's intelligence or sharp mind. Also, it sounded too close to how he managed his business. "I quite agree with you," he said, settling himself into a cushy armchair in the corner.

The office itself was sparse, minimalist and not at all like her or her home. But this chair was cozy and comfortable, and no doubt something she'd chosen for herself.

"Yes," she surprised him by saying, instead of trying to eviscerate him with some politely delivered stab at his intelligence, or lack thereof. "I looked into your club."

He watched her face, especially when she expressly did not meet his gaze. "Did you?" he murmured, intrigued that she might look into anything that had to do with him. But maybe he shouldn't have, and maybe he shouldn't be pleased. If she'd looked into it, it was no doubt to get her hands on it later.

He'd blow it up himself first.

"I expected, like so many trust fund babies, you would have filled the books with paying off school cronies and others riding the coattails of their family's wealth," she said, settling down to her laptop. "Instead, you've hired some heavy hitters."

"Your acting is improving. You don't even sound shocked."

"I wouldn't say your ability to make a decent business decision *shocks* me," she said thoughtfully. "Not at this point. You are not quite as dim as I would have liked to have given you credit for."

"Why, Serena, I must be rubbing off on you. Has our kiss or my ring robbed you of your senses?"

Then she did meet his gaze. She even smiled. "It must be both."

It was a joke, bordering on flirtatious, and Luciano could not account for the way that made his chest tight. Made him think of said kiss, of her body pressed to his—on the beach last night, on the balcony this morning. How different and intriguing she was. How completely, uniquely *her*.

He did not know anyone like her. Except, just maybe, himself. Though he did not share her strange obsession with animals and floral.

Their gazes held a few beats too long, just like at the beach last night. When she finally looked away, he'd hoped it'd feel like he won a challenge.

It didn't. It felt like a loss.

"You'll attend the meeting with me. We'll outline our plan—the parts they need to know anyway. Then we'll meet with the lawyers. We'll need to move that along so no one can attempt to throw a wrench in it."

"Which means we'll also need to move the wedding along, don't you think?"

She sighed, but she didn't argue with him. "Yes. The sooner the better."

CHAPTER TEN

SERENA LED LUCIANO to the meeting room. She didn't feel nervous. Even if Luciano was his obnoxious self, she knew how to handle these men.

And, at the end of the day, they had no power over her. They'd try to find some. They'd try to stop her. But they hadn't been able to yet. And, much as she hated to admit it, in a war like this, Luciano would no doubt be an asset. She tended to focus too much on the *should be* and not enough on the underhanded ways people could behave when their power was threatened.

She hadn't threatened this group's power, except by the fact she was a woman and younger. She couldn't help but wonder how different this would all be if she'd been her father's only *son*.

But that was neither here nor there.

She could fire them all, but she knew that would lead to revenge plots. That too she could handle, but she didn't want to. Not yet. So she kept them on. Pretended to listen to their manly tutting. Then did however she pleased.

"Serena." Riccardo Esposito was her least favorite of this group. He always talked to her as if she was perennially twelve. The only reason she hadn't fired him was because she was afraid the other three would get so worked up about it, they'd cause problems she couldn't yet afford.

Someday. Someday, they'd all be gone in one fell swoop. But for today, she had to deal with them as she always had. Endlessly polite. Carefully cool. Unbothered by their complaints and criticisms.

And sure of what she was doing.

"This is a business meeting," Riccardo said, as if this was news.

Serena settled herself at the head of the meeting table, and Luciano gracefully slid into the seat Riccardo had no doubt been about to sit in. Serena had to bite the inside of her cheek to keep from laughing at the mottled red of Riccardo's cheeks.

"It *is* a business meeting. On company time and everything," Serena agreed as the rest of the men took seats. "So, let's move this along."

"*He* is not part of our business."

"I'm afraid that won't be the case for much longer." Serena smiled placidly. "The lawyers are already working on a Valli-Ascione merger. We're still working out the details, but all your jobs will be safe, of course."

"For a period of time anyway," Luciano murmured.

Serena supposed she should have found his input irritating, but it hit just the right note. A bad cop, good cop kind of approach.

She met disdainful and disapproving gazes of the four men who'd been her father's top advisors. Serena had let them maintain their positions, and she listened to their suggestions still, out of respect for what they'd done for Valli previously.

But she rarely listened to their outdated and insipid ideas. Her father had hired and trusted *yes men*, not brilliant minds.

Since Riccardo had never found a seat, he stood there vibrating. "A merger would violate everything your father stood for."

"My father apparently valued drinking, driving and kill-ing himself. So, this is not quite the censure I think it was meant to be."

"Your grandfather—"

"You did not work for my grandfather," Serena cut off coolly. She did not let the simmering anger that they would *dare* mention her grandfather to her permeate her tone or her expression. "You did not know my grandfather. You will not invoke his name if you wish to remain employed, and let me take it a step further." She met Riccardo's furious gaze, cool as a cucumber. "I am in control. Full control. If Valli fails, that will be on my shoulders. Not yours. So I will make the decisions. And this decision? It saves us."

"Serena." It was Mattia Adamo's turn to try to reason with her. She could tell from the way he said her name. "This is a huge decision and an incredibly large undertaking. You cannot expect us to approve simply because you..." His gaze slid to Luciano. Disdain hardened his gaze. "Because you have found yourself personally involved with our *rival*." His gaze returned to her, a paternal and patronizing smile on his face. "You must give this time."

All generous understanding, with the undercurrent of condescension that was close enough to remind her of her mother's disapproval.

Funny, that never bothered her here. It never had. Her mother still had a knack for twisting a knife Serena fully didn't understand, but these men were...nothing to her. They were forever simply obstacles in her way, and she appreci-ated that role for them. You could not stay sharp if you were not continually tested.

But if they got too far into her way now, they would have to be cut. And she would deal with the fallout, even if she didn't want to just yet.

"My dear boys," Luciano said, and the way he drawled out the word *boys* set every single man in this room's teeth on edge.

Serena relished it.

"*Rival* is such an antiquated word in this current landscape." Luciano gave every impression of the relaxed, borderline bored, playboy. But his words were absolutely true. "The American company has swooped in and hurt us both. Because they can offer *both* global and local services. Because they can throw a few minnows our way and have us fighting for the scraps of it all like starving sharks. Let us not be desperate. Let us be smart."

"And merging companies would be smart because…?" Riccardo asked this with malice, and yet, Serena could not help but note he waited for an answer. He might *hate* Luciano, but he did not try to treat him like a child speaking out of turn.

"I'm sure once Serena shares her plan company-wide you'll have all the answers you need." He gestured at her, and she had to hold herself carefully still lest she give away her surprise.

All of this was an act, but she hadn't counted on him to act like anything was all *her* plan, or particularly smart.

"Now, is that all, gentlemen?" Serena asked, making a production out of standing. "I have an afternoon full of meetings. The work of wooing customers back my father lost from his own stubborn refusal to move on with the times awaits. For all of us," she added pointedly.

"You cannot announce an engagement, a merger, as though you are a dictator," Riccardo said, overloud and as close to losing his temper in a business meeting as Serena had ever seen.

"Mr. Esposito, please. Calm down." Luciano clucked his

tongue and glanced at Serena. "Surely Valli employees are reprimanded in some way if they should throw a little tantrum?" He phrased it like a question.

The splutter that came from all four men was truly a thing of beauty. Serena might have clapped if it wouldn't ruin her illusion of cool, controlled leader. "I think that will be all for now, gentlemen. Should you want to discuss this more… calmly…after you've read through my plan, which will be sent out once the lawyers are satisfied, we can call another meeting." She began to move for the door.

Luciano stepped outside the meeting room first, but Riccardo all but leaped in front of the door before Serena could follow.

"You can't do this."

"On that, you are wrong. If you recall, that is exactly how my father set up his version of Valli. One fully in control leader. No checks. No balances. No *cannots*. I hope to change that eventually, but for now, all decision making goes through me and only me. Now, if you'll excuse me."

She pushed past him, only to be stopped by Vincenzo Conte. "Serena. Please, reconsider. You know that I'm only looking out for you."

She had thought that in the beginning. Of the four of them, she had considered Vincenzo something of a mentor. But in the aftermath of her father's death, she had quickly realized that just because he didn't argue with her, it didn't mean he *supported* her. He was more chameleon than businessman. Out to maintain and amass more power, not save Valli.

She did not trust him, but she pretended. So she smiled. "I appreciate the concern, but I have given this as much thought as anything. It is the right pathway forward."

Vincenzo sighed, clearly meaning to convey concerned

disapproval. "What could you possibly see in that man?" he asked her gently.

She looked at Luciano, standing there in the hallway, an amused, satisfied smile on his face. He'd handled the room beautifully. He had a goal, much like she did. They would become enemies again, no doubt, but right now...?

Right now, they were on the same team. And she did see something in him. Something she didn't particularly care to.

"A kindred spirit," she muttered, detesting the fact that it wasn't altogether untrue.

They went through the next few days like this. He went to Valli. She went to Ascione. They met with lawyers. They drew up papers. They planned a wedding.

Serena suggested they could stand a few days not staying in the same place since the papers were abuzz with engagement news, and since that wasn't completely wrong, Luciano had agreed.

Taking space here and there would be essential in keeping his guard up. And it allowed him to think, to plan, to reassess.

Most importantly, he was collecting pieces of her soft spots. By watching her every day. In her own territory. In his. And so he began to notice the things that didn't just irritate her—him, mostly—but the things that offended her. A use of her grandfather's name against her. Anyone at Valli telling her she *couldn't*. Her easy camaraderie with animals and the way she required concentration to appear easy with people.

The way she appeared at ease and peaceful every day in Ascione, but he could see her gaze taking in everything. Without fail, she went home every night, went through the elaborate process of getting one of her notebooks and fancy pens out and then wrote every last thing down.

Meticulous. Determined. Controlled. A fascinating woman, all in all. He could not say he'd ever known someone quite like her. Underneath all that ice was something far more complicated. And a little odd, truly.

But there *were* those soft spots. All of them noted—mentally because he did not require *notebooks*—to be used later when they would suit him, help him. When *he* would have to come out on top.

He told himself this, because it was a much more palatable reason for his interest. Self-preservation over...

Over being fascinated by her.

He scowled a bit because as good as he was at denial, he was having a hard time believing his own lies when it came to *her*.

The *her* who swept into his penthouse early in the afternoon wearing a cheerful summer dress that he wouldn't have thought suited her at all. She carried a large bouquet of flowers tucked into one arm and a large bag hanging off the other.

But she stopped short, because he was no fool. Flowers had already been taken care of, and the caterer was hard at work in the kitchen, filling the penthouse with delicious smells.

"Oh," was all she said by way of greeting, frowning at the colorful floral centerpieces that had been delivered that morning.

"What's in the bag?" he asked, curious what else she thought he wouldn't have planned for.

"Simply some of my things. It's been a few nights, so I thought it best if I spend the night here tonight. We haven't done that yet."

"No, we have not." Fascinating that she'd be the one to instigate it. "I seem to recall something about gunpoint needing to be involved if that were to happen?"

She got very prim looking, that haughty chin of hers going up. "I was referring to your estate when I said that. An apartment in the city is little different than a hotel, all things considered."

It was semantics, of course, but he could admit he appreciated her ability to twist semantics to suit herself.

She moved forward, shoved the bag at him. "If you have an extra room, put this in there. If not, we'll deal with it after dinner, but you should put it away. I shall see about adding these flowers to the bouquet."

She was a woman so used to giving orders and expecting them to be followed, that there seemed to be no question in her mind whether he'd follow through. He, however, was not a man used to taking orders, so while he took the shoved bag, he did not immediately move to *stow it away.*

She, however, moved for the table—already elaborately set—and unwrapped the flowers. She didn't even *look* at him as she fussed with the centerpiece.

Though she hid it well, he could read the nerves under the surface. He was learning to see under that careful, icy facade. He wanted to believe that was just good business sense, but he knew part of it was pure fascination.

He didn't *revel* in understanding her, but he couldn't seem to stop himself from trying to.

Her mother was coming over for dinner tonight, and if there was one soft spot he still didn't fully understand it was the one that involved her mother. He aimed to figure it out tonight.

So, with that thought in mind, he decided to fully embrace his acted role of doting fiancée. He went and stowed her bag in his bedroom, then returned to the dining room that featured a curved wall of floor-to-ceiling windows to show off the beautiful cityscape and the sea.

He realized, somewhat abruptly, that there at the edge of the far window, if he angled himself just so, he could just make out the jut of rock her little castle settled itself upon.

He wished he had not realized this. It felt strangely...intimate to know he could look out, look across, and see the place he knew represented her true self better than anything she ever let people see.

"It's a beautiful view," Serena said, without ever looking up from her flowers. She was just about done with them, but she took her time with the last stems and arranging them into the centerpiece that already existed.

Luciano made a noncommittal noise as Serena finished what she was doing. He had never once felt uncomfortable in his own home, but suddenly he didn't know quite what to do with himself.

It felt dangerous to think of her *true self* when her mother would not be here for some time yet. When it was just the two of them. Waiting.

"Perhaps I should give you a tour, so it appears to your mother as if you've been here before."

"Good idea," she agreed, but did not immediately move away from the centerpiece.

Luciano tried to find something to say that might irritate her, get that stiff back and cool look of hers geared toward him. But he couldn't seem to think of anything.

Maybe he was ill.

Eventually she let the flowers be and moved closer to where he stood in the living room. She straightened her shoulders, much like she'd done before going into that meeting with her coworkers the other day.

He half expected some dressing down.

"Before we begin, I feel it necessary to explain that…
Well, it's just that my mother will be…" She trailed off. The
nerves never showed on her face. They were in the way she
gripped her hands together, then seemed to realize it and
dropped her hands at her sides. She had done this at least
five times since arriving. "I do not know how to articulate
how my mother will be, but it will not be comfortable or…
normal."

He found her nerves strange, but he didn't like it. "Luckily I am an Ascione. Well versed in uncomfortable and ab-
normal."

Her mouth curved at that, and a strange warmth settled
in his chest. Because it was a real smile. He'd amused her,
settled some of those nerves.

And he liked being able to do so.

He could not for the life of him fathom what that *meant*,
so he pushed it away as he pushed away so many confusing
things when it came to her.

He showed her around the rest of the place feeling a new
sort of tension creep into him. It reminded him of a time long
gone that he'd gone through great efforts to ignore. That part
of his youth when he'd still endeavored to impress his father.

The idea he wanted to impress *her* was a personal affront,
and he rejected it. He had to reject it.

Luckily the announcement of Serena's mother's arrival
interrupted his thoughts on the matter, and he lead Serena
to her mother, plastering on a broad smile fit for the host
of the evening.

At first glance, Serena didn't look anything like her
mother. The woman was blonde, perhaps a little too thin,
but knew how to perfectly accentuate her assets. A beautiful woman. The kind Luciano tended to gravitate toward.

There was a sharpness to her that was the complete opposite of Serena's sharpness.

Mrs. Valli clearly knew how to move around the world as an important businessman's ex-wife. She knew how to dress and flatter and what parties to go to in order to be seen. She had the *socialite* part of her role down while Serena channeled all her energy into understanding the business. As long as she had that crutch, she did very well for herself. But left to her own devices, well, she'd no doubt be home with her cats.

No, he could not see any similarities between the two women, and when Serena did not immediately step in as she often did, Luciano knew it would be his role to take the lead tonight. Between two opposing, though related, forces.

Luciano moved forward, all gallantry. "Welcome to my home, Mrs. Valli. I hope you'll allow Eduardo here to take your things."

She gave a little nod and handed off her wrap and purse.

"May we get you a drink?"

Mrs. Valli studied the butler, Luciano and the room around them with quick, cunning eyes. "Surprise me."

The butler nodded his head and then disappeared. Before Luciano could guide Serena's mother deeper into the apartment, she reached out and grabbed Serena's left hand. She drew the engagement ring into the light, moved Serena's hand this way and then that. Luciano could not account for how *stiff* Serena seemed as her mother studied the ring on her finger.

"It's positively exquisite," Mrs. Valli said, with very little inflection. Then she trilled out a little laugh as she finally dropped Serena's hand. "Honestly, it looks more suited to me than it could ever be to you, darling."

"I quite like it," Serena said, and Luciano could not ignore the note of hurt in her voice that she tried to hide.

"Of course you do," Mrs. Valli tutted. "It's *gorgeous*. It's simply that a gorgeous piece like this tends to require a…" The woman sighed and pouted a little as she studied her daughter. Then her gaze turned to Luciano. "You know what I mean."

He did not, but as his goal was to charm Serena's mother, he smiled broadly and gestured her inside. "Come. Sit. Let us drink to a happy future together."

Mrs. Valli made a noncommittal noise, but she stepped ahead with Serena toward the dining room and the well-appointed table just as the waitstaff appeared with the drinks and the *primi*.

"You have a quaint little place here," Mrs. Valli said as Luciano held out a chair for her. She seated herself grandly while Luciano tried to deal with the strange slight of his expensive and luxurious penthouse being called *quaint* and *little*.

"Grazie," Luciano managed to mutter before moving to the next seat and holding it out for Serena. "I thought having a nice, private celebration of our families joining would allow us a better opportunity to get to know one another."

Mrs. Valli made that same odd humming sound, that was somehow both polite and a disagreement at the same time. Luciano looked at Serena. Her gaze was out the windows, as though, inside her mind, she was anywhere but here.

Luciano found he hated that too. Because he had never once seen Serena remove herself like this. She was always the first to handle things, putting on that armor and brave face to handle whatever needed to be dealt with.

What would cause her to shrink in on herself instead? His gaze turned to the mother, and he wondered if his *charm* tactics were all wrong. He took his own seat at the head of the table and lifted his glass. "A toast?"

Serena blinked, as if awoken from some spell, but then held up her glass as well. Mrs. Valli, however, only looked from the glass set in front of her, to the ring on Serena's hand, to him. Her lips were pressed together as if in deep thought. Then, after a great drawn-out moment, she raised her glass and smiled.

"Let me congratulate you both. It's an inspired decision, truly."

Luciano thought the choice of words odd, but there was no point dwelling on it. *"Salute."*

Serena echoed the word with little inflection. There was no fierce determination. No ice. No fire. She seemed a ghost in her own skin.

As they ate, Luciano shared the details of the wedding planning he and Serena had agreed upon. If he managed to lure her into conversation, she gave one-word responses. Everything about her was muted, dull.

Mrs. Valli, on the other hand, was vibrant and talkative. And *vocal* about what she approved of. What she didn't. In some ways, he could see Serena in the woman. The way she noticed everything, filed it away.

But there was an *unnecessary* cruelty to her that Serena didn't have. When they'd discussed the procession and forgoing the tradition of having someone walk Serena down the aisle, Mrs. Valli had rolled her eyes.

"I'm surprised there's no animal parade walking her down the aisle."

"What a lovely idea, Mother," was the only thing Serena said the whole dinner that reminded Luciano of the *actual* Serena.

She was clearly being sarcastic, but Mrs. Valli used it

as an opportunity to complain about Serena's cats and the crumbling castle she haunted, and then reached over to touch Serena's styled hair. "How many times have I told you to leave it loose? You look like an ill Victorian child with it all scraped back from your face."

"Perhaps it was the look I was going for."

"*I* quite like it," Luciano added. "For whatever that says about me." He chuckled genially.

Mrs. Valli did not join in, but Serena *almost* smiled.

By the time they got to dessert, Luciano got the impression that Mrs. Valli had drank more than her fill. She spoke a bit overloud and enthusiastically, which only seemed to make Serena shrink in on herself even more. That hint of her old self was a fleeting thing he wished he could find a way to tease out again.

Mrs. Valli let out a loud sigh that had Serena flinching— her first outward reaction since the beginning of the evening.

"Let us drop these niceties," she said, leaning forward so that she met his gaze. "I know you are no doubt a skilled actor, Luciano, but do you really think you can get the public to believe you're interested in Serena?"

For a moment, the words didn't fully penetrate. They were so different than anything he'd expected to hear that he did not know how to absorb her meaning. "I beg your pardon."

"It seems very obvious this is some sort of business ploy. And while I commend you for having that kind of…spirit about you, you don't honestly think people will fall for it? Aside from Serena, of course."

There were so many insults in those few words, Luciano could scarcely understand them all. Especially with Serena sitting right *there* and not offering any kind of fiery or icy rebuttal like she would have if he'd said these things.

But she did not say anything. She was nothing but blood-less ice. No, not even ice. Just…dull, gray rock.

He, on the other hand, felt like all the blood had rushed to his head. In anger and outrage. Some of it misplaced, he knew. Some of Mrs. Valli's behavior felt far too familiar. It was just usually aimed at him, not someone else.

Still, this was about Serena. And her mother. So he cleared his throat and attempted to speak carefully. Not letting his own issues bleed into this. "Mrs. Valli, I think it is very obvious to *me*, you misunderstand much. There is no…trick I'm trying to pull over on Serena. Surely you know your daughter better than that."

But it was clear from this evening that she did not. And it was so odd, because he saw so many echoes of how his father had treated him in the ways Serena's mother treated her—and even more shockingly, so many similarities in how Serena got through it. For every insult against her looks, her animals, her house, she seemed to latch on to them all the harder. Just as he had to every barb that he was stupid, useless and lazy.

While he was happy to play down to any negative inter-pretations of *him*, he found he could not with determined, brilliant, beautiful Serena. And so he decided to play Mrs. Valli's game for this round. Rudeness wrapped in fake con-cern.

"You must have loved your ex-husband very much."

She blinked, reared back almost as if she'd been struck. "What?"

"I know the marriage ended before his demise, but it is the only way I can fathom misrepresenting your daughter in such a way. She followed his business footsteps and this hurts you in some way because you loved him and it did not work out, so you do not allow yourself to see past it." He went so far as to tut compassionately. "Losing him twice must have been quite the blow."

"Blow?" Her eyes narrowed icily. He should have seen Serena in them. They were the same shape, the same color, but there was a lack of warmth in the layers of brown and green. "I celebrated the day that useless failure of a man left this earth. I only wished he'd done it earlier."

"Mrs. Valli. That is no way to speak of the dead, or your daughter's father." And so Luciano got to his feet. "I'm afraid I cannot allow this evening to continue. I do not care for the whole of how you've treated my soon-to-be wife this evening. There will be no more invitations until you can assure me that you will be pleasant and positive toward your *only child.*"

He looked briefly at Serena, who was staring at him wide-eyed and stunned. Luciano gestured to the butler. "Eduardo? Would you see Mrs. Valli out? I'm afraid Serena and I are indisposed and cannot walk her to her car ourselves."

"Serena!"

"I'm afraid this is Luciano's place, Mother," Serena said quietly. Her eyes were oddly shiny. "As polite guests, we must abide by what he says." She did not rise from her seat, so Mrs. Valli whirled on Luciano even as Eduardo came forward.

"Are you…? Do you think you're kicking me out? Do you really think—"

"I *think* it is in all of our best interests to take a pause." Luciano commended himself for his calm demeanor. Working in a club for so long had certainly taught him how to deal with the ridiculously entitled. "When you've taken a break, I hope you will come to the conclusion that you have behaved poorly, and you owe your daughter an apology. Once that is issued, I hope we can move forward more pleasantly." He managed a patient smile.

Mrs. Valli made a noise of fury. "Perhaps you both deserve each other," she ground out before jerking away from Eduardo's proffered arm and marching toward the exit herself.

Luciano tried to calm himself with a deep breath. Bullies were a dime a dozen and no doubt both he and Serena had seen their fair share. Their business was rife with them, and her father had been one just as his father had.

But something about the way her own mother had spoken of her. Like a childish adolescent trying to tear down someone who got even a scrap of attention. It was infuriating, but moreover, it was like holding up a mirror to his own adolescence and forcing him to see it through an adult lens.

Had his father really thought all those terrible things about him? Or had Luciano simply existed, soaking up attention and interest that his father preferred only on him.

He did not wish to consider it, so he turned to deal with Serena.

She stood, still as a statue and perhaps just as remote, bracketed by one floor-to-ceiling window. She watched the world outside—a soft, pastel sunset. "You did not need to stand up for me," she said after a few beats of quiet.

She sounded very…tired. Her expression was blank. A careful mask. She did not *act* as though her mother's behavior hurt her, and yet Luciano could not shake the idea that this was how Serena would react to hurt. Cold and stony.

"It is what a fiancée would do."

"I suppose it is," she agreed. Her hazel gaze remained on the darkening world outside the large windows.

Luciano had the rare experience of not knowing what to say. So he stood next to her and said nothing. He stiffly told

Eduardo he was dismissed with the kitchen staff, and that Luciano would handle everything at the apartment for the rest of the night.

Which left just Luciano and Serena and her silence.

When Serena finally broke it, it was with that careful, detached tone he knew so well. This was the one she'd always used on him in the rare occurrences their paths had overlapped over the years before she'd approached him with this plan of hers.

"Even with you standing up to her, she will never believe this is genuine, and I worry…" She swallowed, then carefully turned to face him, her gaze meeting his. He saw courage hiding something in the brown and green depths. Something like vulnerability. "I worry she won't be the only one."

Something reared inside of him. And much like the entirety of the dinner had whirled up familiar feelings in an unfamiliar setting, this did the same. Because the hint of vulnerability incited a long-buried need to fix, to *save*. When he'd been a child, he'd wanted to protect. When he'd become a teen, he'd given it up.

You could not protect those who did not wish to be protected.

No doubt Serena fell into that category. And he'd be damned if he twisted himself in all those old knots to make the same mistake twice.

That was one thing Luciano refused to do. So, he took her words at face value, and ignored the hurt underneath.

"We don't need people to believe. In fact, doubts might help. People will be watching us. They will be intrigued. We need attention. Our names out in the ether."

"Perhaps," she agreed on a sigh. She turned her attention back to the window. "But we also need to appear like a united business front if we're hoping to woo any of our lost customers back. We want them to take the meetings because they're intrigued, but we need to close the deals because we're the best."

"Then let us be the best."

She nodded at that. No doubt a foregone conclusion for the both of them. Another heavy silence settled, though her expression was less detached and more...intense. Her lips pressed together and her eyebrows furrowed.

"Everything she said is true, you know. Or not said, but hinted at. I am dull. I like animals better than people. This ring would better suit someone like her." Serena said all these things with a certainty that irritated him. "She is not *wrong*."

Luciano could only stare at her. He didn't even fully disagree with what she was saying. But it still *grated*. Because yes, she liked animals perhaps too much. She had quirks the size of the entire country, and yes, that ring was maybe not suited to Serena's personality, but...

But Angelica Valli *was* wrong. About everything. It was clear as day to him, and it was shocking and just...wrong for that not to be clear to Serena.

It wasn't his business. None of this was an area he should insert himself into. He did not need to protect her. Serena Valli protected herself.

But she was *wrong*, and something that had broken free during that dinner whirled around inside of him, ruining his good sense to keep his mouth shut.

"*I* think she is wrong," Luciano said, too intently, no doubt. "Because in the long space of time I have known you, Serena Valli, I have never once considered you *dull*."

CHAPTER ELEVEN

SERENA HATED THE feelings battering around in her chest. Hated that she couldn't seem to ice them away.

His fault. Half her mother's. Half his. Had to be, because she was better at dealing with the way her mother was when she was alone. When she was in her own space.

He added a new element and she *hated* it. She so desperately wanted to hate it and him and everything inside of her she couldn't control, organize or perfect.

I have never once considered you dull.

"You do not need to stand up for me," she insisted. It seemed imperative, even if she couldn't understand why, to get that through to him. Though she couldn't meet his gaze. Or even the gentle waves of the ocean as dark began to fall. She turned away from both.

She'd planned on staying, but maybe she could go and that would be okay. Maybe...

"I thought you understood, *cara*, I do not do what anyone else needs. I do what suits me. I say this because it is the truth."

The truth. When the truth never mattered. And something about the way he was acting, like he was some noble person, and not the reprobate she'd always known him to be. Like the facade of his was a lie, and underneath it all was this man who was not vapid or frivolous or careless.

How in this moment she *needed* him to be all those things she'd once thought him. She didn't understand why, but she absolutely needed the old Luciano to be the true Luciano. So she lashed out, pretending he hadn't upended everything she'd thought about him.

"How I would love to be like you, Luciano. So unconcerned with what anyone needs. Flippant about legacies and responsibilities." Because it felt like she had the weight of *everything* sitting on her chest, and he acted as if it was nothing.

He didn't outwardly react to her words. He stood there, a beautiful mountain made of stern jagged edges. She wanted him to flash one of those insouciant smiles. A dagger in its own right.

But he did nothing but speak very carefully. "I am here, am I not?" His voice was deep, cutting. A warning, and she should heed it. She always heeded warnings.

But something was exploding inside of her. And it was *his* fault, because she could always deal with her mother. Maybe sometimes the barbs landed, but mostly it was just the same old insults and they didn't matter. They were simply different people, and the great Angelica Valli would never understand understated, introverted Serena.

It was fine.

It had always been fine.

Then Luciano had created this experience where he insisted on being a witness to her mother's barbs and that had felt...

Terrible. Belittling. Embarrassing and shameful.

Even that she could have withstood with her usual fortitude. But for him to kick her mother out? Insist on an apology before anything else progressed? As though... As though this thing she had spent her childhood telling herself didn't matter, actually did.

He'd stood up for her, and she'd had to come to the startling revelation over dessert that no one ever had before.

She had clung to her grandfather because he'd understood her, given her space to be herself, but he'd never protected her from the slings and arrows of her parents. He'd told her to endure them. To create a shield through which they could not penetrate.

He had never offered to be her shield. It had never occurred to her that he should.

Until tonight. Until this man, her enemy, her rival, her soon-to-be fake husband had, in just one meeting, done what no one in her life who claimed to care ever had.

Tears stung her eyes. Unreasonable. Unfathomable. She didn't cry in public. She always, *always* willed any emotion away, but she was failing in the moment and it was awful.

She couldn't possibly stay here. She whirled away from him, blinded by those tears. Horrified by them. "I have to go." She thought nothing of her purse or how she would get home without her keys, her wallet, her anything. She only thought of escape.

She didn't even reach the entry. Luciano caught her by the arm and turned her around. He blocked the exit and held her there. So her only option was to look down at the floor and hope he didn't notice the teardrops fall and land on the soft carpet at their feet.

Because, God, how could she ever let him see a weakness, an imperfection such as this?

One of his hands came under her chin. Pressed up. She could have fought it. Could have jerked her chin away, pushed him, a million things she could have done. Instead, she let the pressure move her chin up, and she looked him in the eye, even with tears streaming down her cheeks.

She did not know what she saw in his expression, only that it thundered inside of her like a storm. Only that it made her shudder from head to toe. That it seemed to reach inside her and change the very chemistry of her being.

He brushed the wetness away with the sides of his thumbs as his hands cupped her neck. It was impossibly gentle. This man who'd represented, like his father and her own, everything she hated. Waste and foolish pride and carelessness.

Except in these short days, she'd come to accept he wasn't that man at all.

It was such a betrayal.

As was him being the only one to ever wipe away her tears.

"Come, *cara mia*. You must not cry. Particularly not on my shoes. That's expensive Italian leather."

She *almost* managed a bit of an amused sound at that, but there was nothing to be amused about. If dinner was embarrassing, this was a humiliation she did not know how to bear. *This* was why she preferred to be alone. This was why she preferred her cats. This was why her icy shields *were* important. She could be perfect there.

She could not be perfect when Luciano did not let her go. His hands on her neck, large and warm and like an anchor amidst all the chaos inside of her. A heated center point to the ice she could not seem to muster up.

"You must not let her get to you," he said, very earnestly. When she wasn't certain she'd thought him capable of earnest.

But he did not understand, and she could only blame this new *earnestness* of his for her wanting to explain it to him. "*She* does not get to me. *She* is not the problem. She is who she has always been. Selfish and, perhaps it's fair to say, mean. My father did not marry her for her warmth. I'm not entirely sure why they even bothered to have me." She shook her head. Hated that even all these years later the thought depressed her. "But I do not…base my worth on what my mother said. I would have given up on success a long time ago if I did."

"Then why do you cry?"

She sucked in a deep breath, but it didn't settle the need to get it out. A need bigger than her fear of exposing herself to an enemy.

"Has it ever occurred to you how alone you really are?" she demanded, feeling the tears return in earnest, though she furiously blinked them back. "You cannot imagine what it is like to have someone…stand up for you, and realize they are the only one who has." Her voice broke on the last few words.

"You do not mean *someone*," he said, his voice quiet and serious. "You mean someone like *me*."

"Someone who hates me," she returned, lifting her chin. Daring him to argue. She should have known better than to lay down a dare.

"I have never *hated* you, Serena." He said it with such deep conviction that it felt as though her heart shivered inside of her chest.

"You needn't lie," she managed to rasp out. She cleared her throat, worked on getting back her armor. "I believe you once likened me to Satan. To my face."

One side of his mouth quirked up in amusement. "Perhaps I did. But that wasn't about *you*. It was what you represented. I didn't know you were a strange little cat lady when I likened you to Satan. And while I think one of those creatures of yours *might* be an evil minion sent from hell, I do not think you are."

She choked on some strange mix of a laugh and outrage.

He made no sense. This actually making her feel somewhat better was baffling.

"Does it matter what I think?" he asked.

"Of course not." She didn't want it to. She didn't think it should. But his hands were still on her neck. His body was still far too close. And while she usually felt hollowed out and beat down for a few hours after dealing with her mother and refusing to cry—the crying, being comforted, was cathartic.

She should hate him for that. Or thank him. She relished neither and didn't know what to do with herself. What to say. Especially with the understanding that they were too close and didn't need to be.

She could feel his breath, mingled with hers. So close. So unnecessarily close. His hands were still on her face, holding her just there. While his gaze, dark and intent, searched hers for something. She didn't know what. She couldn't fathom what.

She shouldn't want him to find it. She shouldn't *want* this, but her heart was beating overtime as a heat seeped into her bloodstream, spreading through her like alcohol. A drug-like softening. Until she found herself nearly melted against him, and a new, alarming pulse beat deep within. Wanting something…something only he could give.

And she knew it was wrong, this yearning. Letting him be this close. All the lines they were crossing instead of carefully adhering to. And she had always, *always* done the right thing.

But never in her life had the wrong thing been quite so tempting.

Luciano did not know what he was doing. He did not recognize himself. The violent ricochets of need rattling around inside of him. A gentleness that was either foreign or something so long lost he'd fully forgotten what it felt like inside of his body.

But there was a need wriggling through, one that was all too familiar. He tried to remember that this was all part of his plan. Seduction. Want. Need. To lull her into a false sense of security.

But it was supposed to be *her* wants and needs more than his. And he did not know how whatever was roaring through him could be matched. It was all-encompassing, consuming to the point he wasn't sure he cared about what he'd meant to do, what was important, who had the upper hand. Not if he could once again get his mouth on hers.

Which is what he did. Closed that small distance and tasted her once more. It wound like relief through him. It had only been days since that fake kiss on the beach…that hadn't been as fake as he'd like. But there was no hiding that this wasn't for potential photographers.

It was for him. *Him.*

And her, he supposed, as she sighed into him. An echo of the relief he felt inside of himself. Because thank God they both wanted this thing they shouldn't. What a disaster it would be if it were one-sided, this sizzling, warping, *thrilling* want.

She made a sound, some odd mix between a moan and distress, so he eased back.

She gripped his forearms as if to steady herself, and maybe he should have released her face. But he couldn't seem to get his brain to send out any signals to the muscles that held her still. Her mouth was swollen, her eyes wide and leaning more brown than green, her cheeks flushed.

She breathed heavily, her eyes darting from his mouth to

his eyes to his mouth again. But she seemed to come to her senses before he did.

Except there was no sense in what she said.

"There's no one to pretend for, Luciano."

Damn the way she said his name. "Who said I was pretending?" he demanded on a growl, resisting—narrowly—the desire to give her a shake until she got it through her thickest of thick skulls. He should have stopped this. Should have used that sentence against her.

But something about the vulnerability he'd seen today made him incapable of being as ruthless as he should be. Something about her tears had stripped him down, and he could only offer her the truth in return.

"I want *you*, Serena."

She looked at him, those eyes wide and wet. There was such confusion in them. Mixed with lust. "Why?" she asked on a pained whisper.

But her pain had nothing on his. That she could ask that question. That he didn't have an answer for it. "How the hell am I supposed to know?" And this time when he kissed her, he held nothing back. He let the whole war inside of him explode between them. He tasted her, deeply and selfishly. Just for him.

He half expected her to be cowed. Scared into pushing him away, into demanding he stop. Instead she met every kiss, every nip, every tightened grasp with one of her own. Dragging them both deeper into an inferno that would no doubt destroy them.

Luckily, he'd always been a fan of destruction.

He molded his hands over her shoulders, her arms, then anchored them at her waist to draw her closer. As close as she could get. A wild, desperate pressing of body against body. And her arms came around his neck, so she arched into him.

A jolt of pleasure so deep it almost mixed with pain shot through him. His body was iron hard, and she was a warm softness, begging for more.

Something incomprehensible was unfurling inside of him. None of his usual walls. There was too much emotion infiltrating that which should only be physical, light, easy.

There was nothing easy about this woman. About this kiss. He was being sucked in. Drowned. Which made no sense. *She* was the virgin. Not him.

There would come a moment where he would push her too far. Where she would want to stop. To pretend this wild loss of control had never happened. So he rushed forward to greet it. Or thought he did.

When he unzipped the back of her dress, she shrugged her shoulders to let the dress fall. She didn't even hesitate. His heart seemed to stutter in his chest, and this was what had him pulling her back, away, but whatever denials had been on the tip of his tongue died.

Her underwear was a serviceable, virginal white. It made her look like a confection. One he desperately needed a taste of. She was a goddess. Soft and enticing. No doubt luring him to his doom.

What a way to go.

They both were gasping for air. Her pupils were large and dark and a flush had crept down from her face to her chest. For a moment, he thought he saw a flicker of doubt, but before he could use it…or refute it, she stepped forward and lifted her mouth to his once more. She kissed him and her hands slid up his chest, to the buttons of his shirt. She fumbled, but she didn't give up, kissing him and unbuttoning his shirt one by one until he thought there was no sound in the world expect the sound of his own heart beating like a booming drum chorus in his ears.

His hands, without any permission from what little part of his brain he thought he still might have control over, slid down her back, over the curve of her backside. Every inch of her was soft, supple, warm.

The kiss could have gone on forever, but there was a warning bell somewhere deep down. A sense of self-preservation just barely nagging at him. Tiny, but abrasive. He wrenched his mouth from hers, alarmed at how winded he felt. This couldn't continue. This couldn't *be*.

He stared down at her, this unexpected temptress, still feeling an incomprehensible need. What would he do if she walked away?

What would he do if she did not?

Devour.

Which was wrong. It had been one thing to think of seducing her in vague terms, but the reality of wanting her was something far different. Far more alarming. Far more complex.

He was not a man who allowed for complex. He was not suited to it. He could not stand for it or dive into it like this.

"Tell me to stop," he demanded. It was the only thing that could save him. Her good sense was all that stood between them and the ruin of giving in to this. Because it wasn't seduction games.

It was something more. Something he wasn't sure either of them would survive.

"Tell me you don't want this," he demanded of her. She didn't say a thing and he wanted to yell it again until she *reacted*. Instead, he issued the order again, quietly and sternly with all the strength and control left in him. "Tell me."

She inhaled sharply, then shook her head, chin lifted. "No," she said firmly. Then she jerked his head down by the hair and crushed her mouth to his.

CHAPTER TWELVE

SERENA HAD NEVER been reckless. Never thought she would be compelled to behave in such a way. Danger was for people like Luciano, who would suffer no consequences, no qualms. People who could afford to make mistakes.

Or so she'd believed.

But everything changed tonight. She did not know how, and perhaps at some later date, when her body wasn't throbbing with a need she did not fully recognize even if she knew what it meant, she would dissect it all. Understand it all.

Despair of herself.

But for this moment, the only thing she could possibly think to do was dive down the reckless, fiery disaster of it all. Disaster felt like a revelation. Giving in felt like something she *owed* herself for once.

And what would it matter if she crashed and burned on the glorious mountain of him? Tomorrow she would wake up, still Serena Valli. Still in charge of Valli and marching her way toward a merger—marital and business—with this man. And her mistake might be there, but what would it change?

Nothing. Except she would know where all this led and how much her body could feel.

So for tonight, none of what they *were* mattered. All that mattered was his mouth, his tongue, his teeth. The way his hands streaked over her, stoking fires she had never once thought possible within herself.

She'd preferred ice to deal with her weakest emotions until this moment. Fire seemed everything now. At the end of all this, she would not be a hollowed out shell like she usually was. She would be something rising from the ashes.

Powerful.

And that's exactly what she felt. Though she was in nothing but her underwear, and he was fully dressed except for the fact his shirt was unbuttoned, it felt like *she* had brought this moment on.

This wasn't about her vague plans of letting him seduce her. Because she had not been seduced. She had not been lulled into something. She had *chosen*.

This kiss, his searing touch and wherever this led was about...whatever stirred between them that neither of them particularly wanted, clearly. Neither knew what to do with it.

So they were diving into the unknown together.

Except it wasn't fully unknown. He clearly knew what he was doing. The way his mouth dragged down her neck, causing her head to fall back. The way his hand moved over the front of her thigh, huge and hot, and she thought aiming for the most intimate part of her, only to bypass it entirely.

A game. Meant to stir, to tease, to frustrate. And if there was anything she knew how to do, it was how to match wits with her rival. She lowered her hands down the length of his torso, reveling in the impossibly defined muscle. Though she'd never even seen this man break a sweat...

He would now.

She unbuttoned his pants and grinned into his shoulder when he tensed. She took her time with the zipper but lost her train of thought when she felt her bra loosen because he'd unclasped it. He pulled it off her arms, dropped it onto the ground.

Serena's breath caught. She'd never been naked in front

of a man before, and she did not know quite what to feel about being exposed this way. Except there was no hiding that the man liked what he saw. And there was really nothing her quivering muscles could have done except work exceptionally hard to keep her upright as he reached forward and cupped her breasts. A move both possessive and thrilling, sending an intoxicating jolt through her. When his thumbs brushed the taut nipples, Serena's legs nearly buckled. Would have, maybe, if he had not smoothed his hands down to her rib cage and pressed her to the wall.

All so that he could taste. His mouth, hot and foreign, feasted on her. Everything inside of her began to wind like a taut string. She wanted so many things, she did not know how to find them, how to demand them.

"Luciano." She sounded breathless and desperate and that might have bothered her if it did not prompt a rumbling sound deep in his throat, like a predatory, primal growl. The sound shot sparks through her, like she was nothing but fire and heat and wonder.

Then his finger traced the seam of her underwear. Then it wasn't tracing, it was dipping underneath the fabric and exploring a new part of her. Her head thunked back against the wall, and his laughter was dark against her neck.

"Serena," he murmured, his mouth tucked against the sensitive skin under her jaw. "I can feel how much you want me."

"Yes." With what little control she had, she reached out, placed the palm of her hand against the hard jut of his arousal against his pants. "And I can feel how much you want me."

"I suppose we are evenly matched then."

She wanted to say something—something cunning and sophisticated—but the only sound that escaped her mouth was a wordless noise, some mix of a gasp and moan. Because his finger was inside of her, sparking to life fires she had not known could exist. An all-encompassing, heady climb that had her forgetting about everything except that center point of her body.

Until something imploded within her and she shattered into crumbling rubble. It was a blooming, arcing explosion that messed with her equilibrium, because somehow the pleasure another person could bring her was better than anything she'd ever done herself.

Still shuddering, she tried to catch her breath. Still standing, pressed against a wall in the living room of his apartment. In front of huge windows.

She had lost herself, and that could be terrifying if they stopped here. If that's all that happened. He'd touched her and she'd fallen apart. How would she live with that?

She couldn't. There was no turning back. Not now. Not so close. She needed to know how it ended. She gripped his face, met his gaze. "More. Luciano. All."

Though he hesitated, he did not pretend to misunderstand her. After a halting moment, he swept her into his arms. In an impressive feat, he carried her through the penthouse and into a bedroom. The light had faded, so it was all dusk.

He laid her out on the bed, surveying her like some hulking conqueror, and she supposed later she might consider what it said about her that it sent a thrill through her. That she wanted to be conquered in every way by this man she would no doubt regret wanting.

"There will be no going back. When you think of your first, it will always be me."

It was meant to be a warning. She should take it as one. The stark way he looked at her. The planes of muscle and sinew that made up his powerful body. What could possibly come after this and compare?

Which was enough of an answer. Perhaps she would curse him, her weakness, this moment, forever.

But it might be worth it.

So she held his serious gaze. She could not to be afraid of mistakes now, not when she'd already made so many. It would be worse to hide and stand still. "Then it will always be you."

Something flared in his gaze. She wasn't sure she'd understand that emotion even if she was experienced. But he shrugged out of his shirt, revealing the impressive musculature of his arms. She had known he was strong. An impressive form of man, but she had not realized how deep that went.

He divested himself of his pants, all while she watched. And while she had read about all sorts of romantic encounters, she had no real-life scenario to compare this to. Nerves fluttered, but they weren't the kind made from worry. It was something else. Something akin to hope.

And then he pushed his boxers down, revealing the impressive hard length of him. She hated to be a cliché, but she simply did not know how that was truly meant to fit inside of her. She nearly laughed at the foolishness of the thought, but she was breathing too hard to laugh. Heated and pulsing too much to do anything but *watch*.

He pulled something out of the drawer, and she realized dimly that he must have more brain cells left than she did. He opened the condom package and rolled it on, watching her the entire time. She did not know if this was really considered an intimate act, or part of it, but she supposed it only mattered what they wanted it to be. And she could scarcely look away. It was all so new, so enticing.

To have a man move atop her, glare down at her. Hard

and surely aching as much as she was. He wouldn't be doing this otherwise. Not like this.

"It may hurt," he said, his voice sounding like it was being scraped out of a closed throat.

"What a shocking revelation. I have no concept of how sex works despite my twenty-six years on this planet. Please explain it to me, Luciano." She felt him tense every time she uttered his name, so she drew it out syllable by syllable, hoping she might hear him growl again.

He made a low sound of amusement instead, but it rumbled through her all the same. Because the hard, dangerous length of him was positioned at her entrance.

Nerves fluttered around her heart, but they were the anticipatory kind. That breathless feeling before jumping into the unknown. It felt like power. A choice. *Her* choice. Everything *she* wanted.

It didn't so much *hurt* as feel impossible as he moved into her, slow and determined. A deep, uncomfortable stretching, but it was buffeted by so many wonderful sensations it was impossible to focus on that discomfort. Especially when she moved and he growled.

He liked it, she realized. Pleasure gave pleasure, and the more she relaxed into that, the less she felt as if it simply wasn't physically possible to enjoy the feel of being so stretched, so invaded.

But it wasn't just possible, it was elemental. Echoing through her, with every slow, controlled thrust. She wriggled beneath him, desperate for that climax he'd given her with his hand out in the other room. She wanted it now. So she began to meet his thrusts. Knew it was what he wanted as the muscles in his neck strained for control.

It felt wild and free. Nothing she'd ever been. Nothing

she'd ever wanted. But that reckless fury in his eyes felt like everything she'd been missing. For maybe her whole life.

She came apart in panted sighs and his name on her lips. It was earthshaking. Rearranging everything she'd ever thought…if she could ever reasonably *think* again.

He held her still, there under him, as the orgasm rattled through her, eased. But he was still deep inside her. He was still here, looking down at her like she was something he could not bear to look away from.

Because he could see her. *Her.* He had gotten under her armor, her mask, and he saw her and wanted to.

She felt oddly emotional. Wanted to reach out. Wanted something she did not know how to express. A connection, somehow. Because she'd seen underneath his armor too. The way he'd talked of his father. Not the careless throwaway lines about how they didn't get along.

The cord of truth as to *why.*

She put her palm to his cheek, needing some kind of guidance for this huge thing expanding inside of her. "Luciano."

"Hush," he ordered. And then he was pulling her up. Into his lap. Sliding into her from this new angle. She nearly burst apart again in one simple thrust, everything whirling in her mind forgotten in lieu of feeling. His mouth found her breast, one hand holding her hip as the other slid up her back, then gripped her hair.

It was not pain exactly. Instead, it vibrated through her like rapture.

"You will come apart for me again, *cara mia,*" he muttered in a dark, commanding voice. "Now."

The order thrilled her, and yet she couldn't resist *some* reluctance to be ordered about. "You cannot tell me what to do, *carissimo.*" But she panted it, at the end of some race she couldn't fully understand, and couldn't imagine not wanting to do again. Moving against him, building that climb again. Again and again, she wanted this and him.

His laugh was dark and thrilling. He was deep inside of her. He was everything.

And she was lost.

She had stripped him of everything. Every mask he'd worn, every piece of armor he'd lovingly crafted for himself. He felt soft and weak and utterly...lost with need. Not a need for that final push, the rush off the cliff. As much as he wanted that, he did not *need* it as much as he needed her in his arms.

It was inexplicable and problematic and horrible, and still she was so warm and pliant against him. And still she had breathed his name like a prayer. And *still* all he wanted was this, knowing all the ways it could not, would not, work in his favor. It wasn't even a tactical error at this point, it was simply catastrophe.

Understanding that did nothing to stop his enjoyment of her. The lavender smell that had infiltrated his bed. The soft, sweet give of her skin. She was perfect from head to toe. The pleasured sleepiness in her hazel eyes a kind of drug he could not imagine finding elsewhere.

"Now it is your turn," she murmured. "You will come apart for me."

"Will I?"

She made a sound low in her throat, then she moved against him, clearly testing. When he sucked in a breath through his teeth, her grin was self-satisfied and gorgeous. What an unexpected siren she was.

And since she was, he let her take over, with her teasing moves, her careful strokes, her breath fluttering against his sweat-slicked skin. Her breasts brushed against his chest, and every time she sighed, it was in pleasure. Because she was building herself up again. Finding what she liked along with him.

He let her. He tried to let her. Until he could not control it because she was tightening around him yet again, breaking that last grip on his command. He moved her onto her back and thrust home one last obliterating time. The climax exploded in a preternatural burst of pleasure that made very little sense to him. That something he had done many a time could feel different and unique and *important*.

He would deal with that later. When he could breathe. When he could see. When he came down from whatever high he was on. When he could find the sense to roll off her.

It should have come when she stroked a hand down his back, then up again, as if to comfort. It should have come when she gently raked her fingers through his hair.

It was such a soft, gentle gesture that everything inside of him tensed. Iced. A strange niggle of something that felt like *fear* chased through him.

Her hand slipped from his hair. Her expression grew grim. But she did not look away.

"Well," she said. "I suppose that is done."

But everything in him, no matter the fear or the ice, rejected that sentiment. Because *no*. No. It wasn't *done*.

"Not yet."

CHAPTER THIRTEEN

SERENA AWOKE IN a strange bed, in a strange room dimly lit by the faint glow of daylight coming through a corner of the window.

Alone. In a room that smelled like Luciano's expensive cologne.

She took a slow, careful inhale, trying not to catalogue the way her body felt. If she could be still in her mind, *feelings* wouldn't start infiltrating her decision making.

And *boy* did she have some decisions to make.

It was good to be alone. It gave her a moment to come to terms with all that had changed. Because as much as she'd like to be cosmopolitan enough to pretend as though this had just been a fun one-off, all that lingered in their future was not *fun*.

And she had to know how to proceed before she faced him.

Maybe she wouldn't have to face him at all. Maybe he was so embarrassed he'd left fully. She half wanted it to be true, half felt bereft at the thought.

Surely if he was *that* embarrassed, he wouldn't have turned to her in the night. He wouldn't have gruffly told her she wasn't going anywhere when she had suggested she return home, late into the evening.

Surely.

But maybe it was the heat of the moment talking. And now that the heat had cooled into the morning after, he felt… Oh, she didn't know.

She squeezed her eyes shut, focusing on breathing. She was not and had never been a catastrophizer. She dealt with problems coolly, rationally. She wasn't going to sit here and panic over uncertainty. Over what a man might feel or not feel here in the aftermath of what they'd done to each other.

Because it didn't matter what *he* felt. It mattered what she did. And here in this moment alone, she needed to decide what that was and how to go forward. Only once she was sure of herself would it matter what was on *his* mind.

Sex had been revelatory. She didn't *relish* that realization, but it was true so there was no use denying it. Would it feel that way with anyone else? She had concerns it would not. There was something too…elemental about Luciano. About who he was and how he saw her.

It did not fully make sense, but in so many ways, the past week of working together had begun to show how much they were alike. There were still many differences, but there was so much core similarity, it was almost as if they *complemented* each other when they wanted to, rather than opposed each other.

Of course, that was neither here nor there either. The question was, how would this move forward with Luciano? He was the crux of her business plan moving forward. Which also involved him becoming her husband. So perhaps sex was simply…part of that. Perhaps, no matter how it had felt, it didn't *need* to be a big deal. It could be something they indulged in when they felt like it. Like an overly rich dessert.

She considered that for a few moments. Was it sensible? Or did she just want to feel him inside her again and that was clouding her judgement? She wasn't sure, because her judgement had never truly been clouded before.

She really wished she had one of her notebooks. She could create a pro and con list. She could remind herself of her goals, center herself on the mission statement she'd created for this little plot.

Never lose sight of what's best for Serena Valli.

Before she could make any decisions about what last night meant for that, the door to the bedroom opened. Serena tucked the sheet under her chin and watched as Luciano appeared carrying a tray full of food. She hadn't realized until this moment just how hungry she was. Hadn't thought to concern herself with how late in the morning it might be.

"You're awake. Wonderful. Here is breakfast," he offered, keeping his gaze on the tray as he settled it into the middle of the large bed. It was full of breakfast pastries, a selection of fruits, yogurt and a carafe of coffee.

"Help yourself to whatever suits," he said with a sweeping gesture, standing there at the side of the bed.

She studied the offerings and selected a decadent *bomboloni*. Not her usual choice for breakfast, but today seemed to call for decadent and sweet. Maybe come Monday she would reset herself. Get back to reason and good choices.

"Coffee?" Luciano asked.

"Please," she agreed, then watched him as he poured two mugs of coffee and handed her one.

He didn't sit on the bed, or any of the other seating in the room. Instead he stood and sipped. He was acting…a little odd. Awkward wasn't the right word. She wasn't sure Luciano could ever be awkward. But there was a strange stiffness to him, as though this was as new a territory for him as it was for her.

She might not have thought that possible, and she did not

know about his romantic history, but she knew he hadn't been fake-engaged to any of his previous lovers. So there were strange, new and complicated elements this morning that they both found themselves in.

She mulled this over as she ate and drank her coffee. Last night, she had felt powerful. Equal to whatever Luciano gave. She had not *expected* that to be the case, but it was. And now, it was the same. Because, no matter how many *mornings after* he'd encountered, *this* was something else.

She did not *smile* at the thought, but she wanted to. Still, she doubted he saw this in the exact same way.

So, she needed to approach this as she approached anything else. With a carefully thought out plan. If nothing else, they *did* work well together—in and out of the bedroom— no matter what a surprise that was.

"I suppose we must discuss the events of last night," she ventured, wondering how he would take that since he wasn't the one introducing the topic.

"I suppose we must," he agreed neutrally.

She wanted to frown at him, but she focused on the pastry and tried to decide where to start. But perhaps *start* was the key, because for as much as she'd enjoyed it, she wasn't sure she understood it. "Why did it happen?"

"Well, if you recall, I gave you many outs and you did not take them."

She sighed heavily. He was being purposefully obtuse, and she did not care for it. Except she thought it meant that it must matter to him in *some* way, or he would be more… dismissive or superficial. He would be leading this discussion. He would be blustering and telling her what's what.

But it was her leading the charge, which meant he was just as much in the dark about how to move forward as she was. It was comforting and allowed her to settle back into the pillows and enjoy finishing off her pastry as she tried to consider the facts of the matter over the feelings from last night *and* this morning.

"You did not have to kiss me," she said carefully. "While I don't care to cry in front of others and avoid it as much as possible, I have never been kissed in response to tears."

His grunt was irritable, and it always—even now—felt like a bit of a personal victory when she could be the one irritating him.

He offered no response to her, so she kept talking. "Perhaps this all makes sense to you, but it makes none to me, and I am trying to…understand it so we can decide where to go from here. But you will have to be more forthcoming."

"It is not complex, Serena. You are a beautiful woman." He smiled at her, and she knew she was meant to see that arrogant charm, but there was something darker underneath it, the edges of that deep frown still flickering in his expression. Even as he delivered the rest. "And I am a handsome man."

She could leave it at that. Perhaps she would be smart to. But he was here. He could walk out of this room, end this conversation. Maybe he wanted to be difficult, but he didn't seem eager to end it.

"It's more than simple attraction."

His expression was grim. His entire body rigid. "I did not expect you of all people to romanticize things, Serena. No one said you have to like a person to have good sex, *cara*. Surely even you know this."

That was the trouble. She was starting to like him. Or respect him. Or *something* more than the easy disdain she'd once had for him. That was when he'd been nothing more than a caricature to her. Now he was a man. Not perfect by any means, but far more complicated than she'd ever have given him credit for without spending time with him.

For instance, she could see he was *trying* to be insulting. Which was simply a distancing mechanism, not an actual belief he had. Because he was so far off base, she couldn't find offense. Romanticize? Romanticizing the situation would be dreaming about real *I do*s and *happily-ever-after*s.

She was simply trying to figure out how to ensure that sex—or this *like* and *respect* for him that was creeping up on her against her will—didn't affect their bottom line.

"Perhaps this is true," she said carefully. Arguing with him wouldn't change what he thought. "But I think we recognize something in each other. That is not romantic. It is a reasonable observation based on the events of the past week. And I think it's imperative we understand it, lest we…make mistakes moving forward. Mistakes that hurt what's most important."

He stared at her then. His gaze hard. Not even a flicker of warmth or kindness in their dark depths.

"And to you, what's most important is a business." He said this with some disdain, which was rich, coming from him.

"A legacy, Luciano," she corrected. "Mine. And yours. The whole reason we spent more than five minutes in a room together, in fact."

"I see. So you want to analyze it. Perhaps make some data points in one of your little notebooks. How did it come to be that you were swept away by a cad like Luciano Ascione?"

She considered the snap in his tone. The way he called himself a cad, when she hadn't been thinking that at all. He gave himself away when he let his temper rule, so she could not deny that she continued to poke at that temper in a way she knew would annoy him the most.

Remain calm and controlled and focused on the facts alone. "I would not call you a cad in this instance."

He snorted with disgust. "In this instance," he said, in

a mocking tone. "I would think you a robot if not for last night," he muttered.

"I truly don't understand why you're angry, Luciano. We had a pleasurable evening. It is a complication, but one I think we can reasonably maneuver if we discuss it like adults."

She thought she was being the *most* reasonable and adult, but clearly he did not agree. *He* looked like he was about to throw a temper tantrum.

So she settled into the pillows even deeper and tried not to smile.

She was infuriating. He'd woken up, tied in knots he didn't understand. He could not untangle them, even in the time he'd taken away from her sleeping soundly in *his* bed, *his* room, *his* life.

And she was sitting there eating a pastry in his bed trying to *understand*. Wanting to have a calm discussion. *Smiling* at him, like she was the queen of the world in control of everything, and he was a foolish serf, stomping his foot in defiance.

What was calm about what had occurred? What was *reasonable* about anything? He could not make sense of the way she'd tangled inside of him like a poisonous vine.

She wanted to discuss *sex* like adults. She wanted reasons. She wanted truths.

Well, fine. He'd give them to her. All the hard truths she wouldn't want to hear. All the truths that, if she were as smart as she allegedly was, would send her running.

"Do you know, last night as I watched your mother play her little games, I had the most startling realization that I'd seen it all before?"

She studied him silently, clearly not following but not willing to say that. Her smile had dimmed though. She definitely hadn't expected him to bring up her mother.

"You see, I recognized something in the way your mother treated you," he continued. "Because she was wrong, and I could not fathom what would be the reason for a mother to lie about their child."

She blinked, gathered that sheet a little closer to her chest, all traces of that smile gone.

"It reminded me of my own childhood dinners. At the time, I was not old enough to realize that every night, my father was playing his favorite game. He would insist my mother dine with us, then treat her terribly until she ran off in tears, then insist we do the same thing the next night. He enjoyed that—something I understood even as a small child, even if I did not understand why."

He had begged his mother to refuse to show. He had tried to chase after her, only to be rejected by her. He had tried, as he'd gotten older, to convince her to leave. He had tried so many things, but his father had been the center of everything in that house.

And Gianluca Ascione had known it.

"Once he'd finally gotten her to break, he would turn to me. Just as your mother turned to you last night. Different insults, naturally, but the same tactic. He thought me stupid, or claimed he did. He characterized me as the character I would then become. I knew he was wrong. For a while, I thought it was a mistake. I would simply prove it to him. Then I realized I could not. But I never understood why, when I *knew* I was not what he claimed I was, most days. Until I saw your mother. Doing the same thing. And it was wrong, but I have no doubts about you, so I *knew* it was wrong on a deeper level."

Serena's expression was growing icy. He told himself that's what he wanted, even as it settled in him like pain.

"She was not fully wrong," she said in that careful, horrible way.

"That's rubbish," he spat. "She wants you to be those things—dull and foolish—because admitting you are all the things you *actually* are—beautiful and certainly quirky, but not foolish—would be intimidating to her. She wants all the attention, all the good for herself. You are a…threat, I suppose."

She wasn't so icy now. She was breathing a little heavily, color in her cheeks, the sheet clutched so tight in one hand her knuckles were white. "My mother is far more beautiful and worldly than I am. Which is fine, because I do not need to be those things."

"Even if I agreed, it doesn't matter. At the heart of her, what I witnessed last night was blatant insecurity. And instead of looking at you as your own person, or someone to be proud of, she sees you as a symbol of what she isn't. Young and brilliant and successful."

She looked completely and fully arrested by this very true description of herself, and he wanted to crawl into that bed and cover her body with his and think of nothing but the pleasure they could give each other.

That would be easy and, by God, that was what he wanted. What he'd always wanted. So why he stood here and kept talking, he'd never fully understand.

"And in the middle of that dinner, I realized that my entire childhood was simply that. Enduring the insults of an insecure man who was afraid I might be better, or more interesting, or more worthy of the attention he might someday get. Trying to save a woman who would rather be the victim of that than stand up for herself."

Stand up for me.

And he had not saved his mother. He had never gotten through to her, never protected her, never turned himself into something more powerful than his father. "She did not wish to be saved by the likes of me, and perhaps that was her right. It is your right."

She looked up at him then, and something there in her hazel eyes sent a bolt of fear through him. That everything would change now that she knew him. Saw him.

Now that she had showed him this softer side of herself. Not just the heat behind the ice, but the warmth, the soft spots he'd once been so sure he'd expose and use...

Now she had some twisting power over him instead. He had been drunk on actually saving her and now he was drunk on that look in her eyes. Soft. Vulnerable. *Mine.*

"No one has ever stood up for me before. Not like that."

He did not want to hear that. It was a power that was too big. Too much. She would come to realize, as everyone did, that he was no one's savior. And then where would they be?

But he had stepped in and saved Serena last night from some small piece of hurt. Clearly, it had caused him to lose his damn head. Because she now knew more about his inner workings than anyone else in his entire life. It left him feeling exposed and vulnerable and disgusted with himself.

Perhaps his father hadn't been jealous, but right. Because if Luciano was *smart*, he would have unveiled none of that to her. His enemy. His rival. The woman who he would someday certainly betray.

She sighed and finally looked away. At the windows, even though the drapes hid any view out of them. He could not begin to imagine what she was thinking about, but he found himself bracing for it all the same. Because somehow he knew... He knew it would be too close to a truth he did not wish to acknowledge.

"We are alike, it seems," she said quietly, her gaze still on the drapes. "More alike than different when all is said and done."

He refused to respond, but it didn't seem to matter. She kept talking.

"I knew... I do not think my mother is fully wrong about me, per se. In her world, I *am* dull and not as beautiful. This is not an...insult to me. It is simply a fact. I... I like what I like. I am who I am. It is hard sometimes to harden myself against the way she wants to belittle me in front of others, but I might be able to weather it better with your interpretation of her behavior, because I think you are right. She is insecure." She gave a little nod, as if it would solidify the truth of the statement.

But he could see the tears starting to collect in her eyes. Particularly as she continued to speak.

"It seems... That we both did the same thing in response to these people in our lives. We created characters." Her gaze moved back to him, shiny but direct. "But we did not fully believe them to be true because we knew ourselves well enough not to."

A revelation he did not want thundered through him. He certainly didn't want to share it with *her*, when everything about her was already too damn confronting. So he did not touch that truth with a ten-foot pole.

"For the love of all that is holy, you will not cry again."

She lifted her chin. "I shall cry whenever I like."

But she didn't. She blinked the tears away, sitting in the middle of his bed, looking like a queen—royal and in charge.

"Perhaps there are more similarities than we first conceived of, but that changes nothing." He said this firmly, wishing he believed it.

She nodded, which felt like a dagger to the heart. A heart he didn't want. Wouldn't accept. A heart got a man nowhere.

"I suppose we should avoid complications then."

He agreed, wholeheartedly, but couldn't get his mouth to work. She moved her hazel gaze back to him again, studied him in that way of hers. It spoke of that brilliance she had, but there was warmth under it.

An understanding that he didn't want under it.

She moved to the side of the bed, the sheet moving off of her. He should not watch the smooth silk of her skin come into view, but he could not help himself. She walked toward him, completely naked, her hair a compelling mass of waves around her shoulders. There was nothing but confidence in her stride, and she never once let her gaze dip from his.

A challenge. Not just to him. But to his words. Even though she'd agreed.

He refused to clear his throat, so his words were rasped. "My thoughts exactly. This is complicated enough, after all."

She gestured behind him, to a chair where he'd settled her discarded dress from last night. "I believe that's my dress. If you'll move or hand it to me."

She was only inches away from him. Naked and perfect. Not an inch of embarrassment or carefulness in her gaze.

She was doing it on purpose. Testing him. Teasing him. *Something.* When he'd seen plenty of naked women in his life. He had had amazing sex. He had been there and done that and she wasn't special.

He didn't want her to be special. He didn't want her to tempt him. Why should she tempt him? He should be stronger than that.

But he wasn't.

CHAPTER FOURTEEN

THEY DID NOT avoid complication. They reveled in it. They did not have another serious conversation about what they were doing. They went forward with business plans and wedding plans in full force.

They spent too much time together. Every night. Mostly at her place, but sometimes at his if their business meetings went late.

Serena recognized this was too much—especially without a serious, adult conversation on what it meant. She always told herself, when she was alone, that she would do something about it. That they would sit down and discuss what they were really doing. She'd never been in a relationship before, but she knew a conversation was needed, and she would need to be the one to instigate it.

But she never did.

She kept waiting for *him* to do something about it. To reject her. To distance himself. Surely he'd get bored.

But he never did.

Being around him was…she hesitated to use the word *addicting*, but it was certainly something similar. Because she had never realized just how lonely she'd been. Even when her grandfather had been alive. He had been so much to her, but he had been an old man. In some ways, his wisdom and his acceptance of her quirks served as almost everything good in the foundation of her life.

But that didn't mean she hadn't been starved for companionship her own age. Her own stage in life. Someone to grow…with. And that's what this felt like. As she and Luciano tackled business problems together. As they went out to business dinners or just to be seen. As they spent every night together. To the point where she had begun ruminating on her choice of whether or not to get a house dog out loud to him.

She didn't think he actually *listened*, and she didn't think she needed him to. It was just nice to have a living and breathing sounding board, even when it was silent.

But he didn't remain silent.

"Why do you not just buy the damn dog then?" he demanded one sunny weekend afternoon as they drank lemonade on her balcony. She was on her computer, looking at pictures on the breeder's website. She'd though he was taking a nap.

But his gaze was on her now. Frustration mixed with amusement in his gaze. And since there was some amusement, she posed her concern.

"What if he doesn't get along with Kate and Leopold?"

"*Mio Dio*, Serena. This is madness. Buy the dog or do not. You must make a decision and *move on*."

Somewhat stung, she sniffed. "I only started considering the dog because Pierro said no to the bird."

"The man has sense. You? I am not so sure about. Can't you go…meet the furry creature with your demon spawn in tow to find out if they get along?"

"I suppose I could ask," she murmured thoughtfully. Both because it was a good idea and because for all his bristle, he didn't seem *opposed* to another *demon spawn* traipsing about.

She made the appointment for the next day and was shocked when he insisted on driving her out to the breeder's estate. He grumbled the entire way, warily eyeing the cats in their carrier in the back of his car. But he went.

And he was kind and charming to the breeder. He even let the puppy chew on his laces without any complaint. And when he knelt down and stroked the puppy's soft, silky ears, and a small smile appeared on his face, she couldn't help but tease him a little.

"It's official," she'd said as the dog tried to climb up Luciano's leg.

He lifted his gaze, sobered his expression and raised an eyebrow at her. "What is?"

"You don't hate animals. You're just a dog person more than a cat person."

His mouth turned downward, though not into an all-out frown. He looked down at the dog. Then he simply grunted.

When she put down a deposit to bring home the puppy when he was old enough in a few weeks, he offered no approval or disapproval, but Serena couldn't help but believe he was pleased. That he would *enjoy* having a dog around.

When they returned to the castle, he hefted the cat carrier himself, all the way upstairs, and even undid the door to let Kate and Leopold free.

Something strange battered her chest then, but she did not fully realize what it was. Or maybe she didn't let herself put a name to it then and there. Perhaps it was too big or too scary and her brain needed time to wake up.

Because one morning she woke, tangled up in him as she usually was, and realized it was the week of their wedding.

Joy spurred through her. Anticipation and excitement.

Not for the event itself, but for the fact they would be husband and wife.

And she finally realized she'd made a serious mistake.

Because she had been humming over the last-minute alterations to her dress the week before. She'd been dreaming of the way he'd look at her when she walked down the aisle of the historic church they'd picked out together. She was thinking about giving him a small say in the naming of her puppy when she was able to bring him home.

She was not daydreaming about mergers or ways she would push him out once she had some sway in Ascione. She was dreaming about *romantic* things, just as he'd once accused her of.

So it dawned on her, as he slept soundly with his arms wrapped tight around her, that she'd fallen in love with him. His humor. The way he buried all his caretaker tendencies under a sharp edge. Like he was protecting himself from something, and it made her desperate to find out what.

She would need to find out what, she supposed, but for right now she was so startled by how foolish she could be—and how wonderful it felt—that she spent a few days weighing this feeling. She continued watching him and tried to determine if he might feel the same.

They had not discussed anything of weight since their first morning after, but they still spent time together. They still worked on business together. He supported her, in small ways, at work. She tried her hand at homemaking for someone and thought…maybe, just maybe, he enjoyed it.

They all but lived together. In every single way, they behaved as a real couple. In public. In private.

Except one very important thing. They did not discuss what was happening. Where it could lead. They did not acknowledge the *truth* of what was happening between them.

In some ways, they both pretended like it was still a fiction, even though it was the most real relationship she'd ever had.

Still, it was missing something important. She did not know his feelings on love. Futures. Real futures—the kind with commitment and children. She was not opposed to asking him, but she supposed there was a selfish part of her that wanted to be sure they were married first.

So Valli-Ascione wouldn't suffer.

So he couldn't run away that easily.

If she felt any guilt over this, she refused to give it the time of day. A woman had to protect herself and her legacy in whatever ways she could. Loving him did not mean she should put herself at risk.

She had to remind herself of this too often. Their wedding was in three days. She would keep it to herself for three more days.

"What do you suppose I should name the puppy when we get him?" Serena asked one night, curled up on the couch together. She dropped the casual *we* and wondered if he would stiffen.

He didn't.

He acted as though the casual intimacy was nothing, but to her it was…everything. Everything she never considered she might have. Her head in his lap, his fingers trailing through her hair as he read e-mails on his phone.

"Perhaps another name from that terrible movie you made me watch," he said, surprising her with any suggestion at all, let alone one so…perfect. "Keep it all on theme."

The movie was not terrible. It was her favorite. But he had watched it last night and put together that the cats were named after the main characters. It was the silliest thing to want to cry over him understanding that *themed* names would appeal to her. Tears pricked her eyes anyway.

"I…" The words were ready to erupt, but they stuck there in her throat before she could utter them. She couldn't say it once his gaze moved from his phone to her.

She saw the wariness creep into his eyes, clear as day, like he could see the love in her eyes clear as day as well. So she didn't say it. She swallowed the words down. Where they belonged. At least until they were married and the businesses were fully merged.

Once she was protected, maybe…just maybe, she could let it all out. But she couldn't do it now. Still, it didn't mean she wanted to shut him out. No, she wanted him any way she could get him, and she didn't really care if it was pathetic.

"Take me to bed," she murmured.

And he did. No wariness involved.

Luciano felt nothing but unsettled the closer it got to their wedding day. Because what had once felt like it could be nothing but a farce now felt…too real. He had been avoiding that reality for days now, but the closer the actual ceremony became, the less he could seem to hold it at bay.

They seemed to spend every second together, and when they weren't together, he wanted to be with her. He found himself *obsessed*, and not just with her body, but also with her mind, with her strange quirks.

The joy she'd exuded the day she'd put money down on that ridiculous dog. How she had almost cried when he'd created a silly little countdown to Stuart the dog's pickup day. How she teased him for being as excited as she was.

He could not quite understand the appeal of *cats* with their slinky eyes and snooty attitudes, but when he'd told Serena that, she'd said that it was simply because he was too much *like* them to like them. He'd wanted to be affronted.

He hadn't quite managed, because he knew in Serena's

world, any comparison to an animal she loved was a great compliment. He lived for a compliment from her. They were never lies, never superficial.

She did not have either in her.

And the horrible truth was that he *did* feel some excitement about bringing a puppy home. He had never been able to have animals before. His parents did not enjoy them, and then he'd assumed himself too adult, too busy to keep them.

Serena had showed him otherwise, and there was something…just *something* about the idea of walking an animal around, enjoying its exuberance in their home—*her* home— as he'd enjoyed it on their visit.

But it wasn't just her softness he was obsessed with. The *real* Serena she let out only at home. He also appreciated the business side of her. The icy, curt way she'd cut one of her managers down to size the very next morning when he dared suggest the merger was a mistake.

She was alarmingly amazing, and he recognized this feeling growing inside of him as an old, dangerous one he'd put away. He'd stopped yearning for his parents' affection and learned to do without. Because he was strong. Because he was purposeful. Because he did not *need* those people who had refused to see him.

Love him.

But the need winding its way around his heart when it came to Serena was too much. He couldn't seem to cut it off.

And he didn't know which prospect was worse. That the soft light in her hazel eyes—the way she sighed his name, the way she looked at him sometimes, seriously and intently— might mean she felt the same.

Or that he was delusional. That it was an act. That he was desperate for any affection and reading into things. That everything his father had once said about his intelligence about business *and* people was true. That one day Serena would look at him with tears in her eyes and turn him away, because there was nothing he could *do* right.

He didn't stop this though. Because they were getting married tomorrow. Because this was business. Because this *wasn't real*.

Not real, no matter how soft her gaze seemed to be. No matter how much taking her to bed each and every night was a glorious and never ending source of enjoyment. No matter how much the past few weeks had begun to feel like a *life* he'd never known he'd wanted.

Calm. Cozy. Serene. *Real.*

Because the want was insidious and deep inside him— the want to make it real. To be her husband. To love her. To build a life.

The knowledge he could not. Because he did not know what a real marriage looked like. What a real husband did. He wouldn't be good enough. It was *impossible*.

He remembered all too well what it was like to want something out of his control. His father's approval, his mother's love. Other people's feelings were not concrete, and they could change with the whims of time. He had no control over them.

And so he'd gone along these last few weeks, waiting for his own whim. Waiting for something to change. To feel suffocated. To find some flaw in her.

For her to finally, *finally* realize that all of the many flaws in him were not charming or acceptable at all.

But nothing changed. She simply got her hooks deeper and deeper into him. She simply settled into a life in which they were in each other's space constantly. Drowning in each other. With neither of them sensible enough to escape to shore.

Maybe she had even convinced herself that she was in

love with him. He saw the way she looked at him sometimes. The way she opened her mouth to say something, then closed it as if she was afraid to say the words.

When she was never afraid. Which meant it was all wrong. Wrong. How could he exist in a place where Serena Valli was afraid? It had to be his fault somehow.

He glanced over at where she stood over the stove, humming as she cooked them dinner. Something she apparently liked to do. She was more than adept at it, and he enjoyed watching the pleasure in her expression when he enjoyed what she'd made.

Her hair was piled up on her head, and she wore casual sweats he knew would be almost as soft as she was under his hands.

The desire to touch her—to lose himself in *her* rather than the way the anxious, horrible dread kept drifting over him and pulling him under this strange wave of…fear—was overpowering.

He never considered himself afraid, but she made him so. She made everything *so*. But if he lost himself in her now, they would be married tomorrow.

Married.

He wanted to believe it could be like this. The past few weeks. The *ease* of it. But didn't he know better?

He had watched what his parents had done to one another. He had heard Serena's own mother berate a dead man. What were they doing? What made them think they could do this?

It isn't real.

But it was. It was real, and there was no more time to pretend it hadn't become so. So, he had two choices.

He could forget every lesson he'd ever learned and try to make something work. He could believe and be crushed. He could let this destroy them both, as it no doubt would.

Or he could find his wits, his smarts, and do the right thing.

The thing that would save them both.

She was the only person he'd ever successfully saved. He could not continue on this path without saving her one last time.

And suddenly, watching her hum as she cooked them dinner, he realized what must be done. It was reckless. Shortsighted.

Necessary.

He stood from the chair he'd been sitting in abruptly. "I'm going to my club tonight," he announced, perhaps a bit overloud and out of the blue. "I have business to attend to."

"Would you like me to join you?" she asked, still focusing on whatever she was making in the skillet in front of her.

For a moment, he stared at her back. *Join you.* Yes, that was what he *would like.* Her. By his side. In his bed. Forever and ever. Smiling at him, cooking for him, crooning over her animals and making her incessant lists. He wanted her lavender scent surrounding him for all his days.

A want so bone deep he knew he would never have it. Something would change. Something would break. He would turn her away, or she would turn him away.

They would destroy each other, just as their fathers once had.

He could not live under the fear of it. Maybe fear made him a coward, but he saw it differently. He was saving her. He would *save her.* Once and for all.

So, he would not be touching her. Not tonight. Not again. If she would not be the one to call it, he had to be.

"No." The refusal was harsh and sharp. Enough that he saw the way she subtly flinched at his blunt response. "It would be a distraction," he said, though he should have left it at sharp and harsh. "I have some things that must be done before the wedding and honeymoon."

Her shoulders were stiff, and he waited for some argument. Something cutting. He waited, perhaps even hoped for, some kind of *fight*. A fight would be clear cut. A fight would be easy.

But all she said was, "All right."

It stabbed like a knife all the same. Her easy acceptance. The understanding in her eyes that she refused to acknowledge there between them.

Then again, so did he.

So they stood staring at each other, both afraid to say the things that needed to be said. Because they were alike, and maybe too much so.

"Are you going to eat before you go?" she asked blandly, some of that old ice he hadn't seen in weeks now seeping into her tone.

Guilt tried to take root inside his chest, but he refused to let it. "No. Thank you." He moved away from the kitchen, toward the exit. He had to get out. He had to change the trajectory of all of this.

And he knew… He knew just how he could do it. What would be best for all of them. He would save her.

"Luciano." Her voice was firm, chilly and it brooked no argument.

He stopped at the exit. He didn't want to look at her, but when she said nothing, he felt like he had to.

Her gaze was direct, but not icy. There was that softness he hadn't imagined Serena Valli capable of *before*, though now he realized that was the real core of her. Under all that frigid perfection was this gloriously sweet and caring woman. How she could be both the harsh businesswoman and the softhearted animal lover, completely unafraid to be herself in private, made zero sense to him.

It twisted him into a million knots, and a man could not live with these knots choking him. He could not live with the expectation of a woman like her upon him.

He would never, ever meet it.

So he would save her. He would save her from this. It became a mantra in his head, repeating. If he ran. If he broke it all, she would be free and saved.

"We're getting married tomorrow," she said, very seriously.

He looked at her. She was beautiful. Wonderful. Soft and lovely. So damn smart it hurt. He wanted her. Every night. Every day.

And he could not think of a single positive thing that could come from this. She would betray him, and he would be a fool. He would fail her, and she would be destroyed.

He would drive her from that dinner table in tears someday, like his father had done to his mother.

She would send him away someday, like his mother had done to him.

She would see him for what he really was, because it was certainly not worthy of *her*, whatever he was, whoever he was.

It wasn't good enough for *this*.

Besides, there were no forevers in this world, and he would rather ensure *now* that he did not believe in any, rather than make this worse.

For the both of them.

Still, he managed to respond. "Yes, we are getting married tomorrow," he said hoarsely. "Perhaps I will stay at the club tonight. Is it not bad luck to spend the night together before a wedding?"

She was very still and quiet for a long few moments. Her eyes were steady on his but he saw…too many things in their dark depths. "I suppose I've heard that. Then I will just… see you at the wedding tomorrow? Our wedding."

He didn't miss the way she clarified that, the way she watched him, as if she could see inside his tangled brain and make sense of what he couldn't.

It made him desperate to run, but he didn't. Because she did not call him on it. If he was a coward, so was she.

Still, he answered her. "Yes."

Then he walked away. *Walked.* Purposefully, and perhaps with some speed, but it was not a run. He did not run away.

When it's important, you do.

He shoved that thought away, the disturbing fact it sounded like Serena's voice in his head. An accusation that buried deep and sharp but proved to him he was doing this right.

I will save you.

He called his lawyer on the way. He arrived at his club, but ignored all greetings and went straight to his office. When his lawyer arrived, he said it plain. "I would like to change our arrangement."

"I knew the marriage part of this was ridiculous," the man muttered unwisely. "I can meet with the Valli lawyers tomorrow and—"

"No. I want everything signed over to Serena Valli now. No marriage necessary."

"Mr. Ascione, you can't just…"

"I can. I will. Whatever it costs, it must be done by to-morrow."

"Mr. Ascione…"

"Is there a problem? Should I call someone else who can handle the task?" he demanded.

The lawyer shook his head, began to back out of the room. "O-of course not. You will need Ms. Valli to sign off on it as well."

"She will."

The lawyer swallowed and nodded. "All right. It shouldn't require overmuch. Would you like me to deliver the papers to her when they are done?"

It was tempting. So damn tempting. She could sign the papers with this man, and no doubt her team of lawyers, and he would not need to be involved. He would never have to see her again. He would not have to deal with the fallout.

He could fly off to London tomorrow. Tokyo. New York. Anywhere but in the same country as *her*.

But he was too much of a businessman to think that would work. To end this, to truly stop what had spiraled out of control, he could not let someone else do his dirty work.

"No. I will deliver them."

And then he would say good-bye to whatever strange interlude this had been and go back to the man he had to be.

The caricature only Serena had ever seen behind.

But she would be saved, and that was all that could matter.

CHAPTER FIFTEEN

SERENA GOT READY for her wedding day essentially alone. Oh, there was the woman who did her hair, her makeup. The wedding planner helped her into her dress, buttoning up the back and babbling nervously.

Luciano had not arrived yet.

The wedding planner assured Serena that it was okay. That they were in touch with him and other such nonsense.

But Serena knew. She'd known last night. There had just been something about the way he'd behaved. Fidgety and strange. The spell of the past few weeks broken.

She did not know why. If she looked too deeply at it, she thought she might crumble, and if there was one thing she could not do it was that. She had never crumbled. Not once. She could not let Luciano Ascione be the reason she did so now.

Perhaps that was why she could not seem to stop the motion forward. It would be less embarrassing to call it all off now, before she put the dress on, before someone—some *stranger* had to come break the news to her.

He wasn't coming. She felt it in her bones. She *knew* it.

And yet she couldn't seem to call it off. Couldn't seem to save herself the upcoming embarrassment. It was like she had to go through it, in the absolute worst way, or she might be tempted to forgive him.

Not that he'd ask for her forgiveness or want it.

She did not know what had changed. She wanted to believe it had been a bit of cold feet he'd get over. Drink it away and he'd come back in the morning with declarations of love.

That had been the romantic inside of her, and she'd known better than to believe in it. But she'd hoped in spite of herself.

Because she loved him. Loved their life.

She did not know what spooked him about that. What had changed his mind? What had *scared* him? Because she knew he *was* scared. Someday, she would think about it. Someday, she would make sense of it.

Today, she couldn't seem to. There was too much stupid, pointless yearning that she only had herself to blame for. Her mother had always told her she was dull. Never enough.

Serena should have believed her.

So she settled into the old ice. The old frigid detachment. Move one step at a time, calmly and rationally, so that when he didn't show, this horrible love inside of her would crack into dust and die.

So she'd be so embarrassed and angry that the only thing left would be to turn it around to hurt him. She'd find the fire within…eventually.

But she could only do that if she made it through whatever this was.

The wedding planner bustled out of the room to "check on things." No doubt to try to track down Luciano. Serena let her. She wanted to be alone anyway. Blissfully alone in this little room.

Just her and a full-length mirror and a beautiful white gown, simple if not for the intricate lace details. Serena studied herself in said mirror. If she pretended to smile, a picture would show a beautiful, glowing bride, eager to start her new life.

But her face in the mirror right now showed the truth. The makeup could hide that she was pale. The white lace could give her an ethereal look. But her expression was all brittle ice because that was what she was made out of.

If she moved the wrong way, she would shatter. All because she'd fallen in love with the last man she should have.

That was on her. And she always took responsibility for her own mistakes.

So she stood, leaning into every last protective instinct. Detach, detach, detach. Don't let the pain through. It doesn't matter anyway.

You were always meant to be alone. It was stupid to be fooled into thinking otherwise.

It was something her mother would say if she was here. But, because of Luciano, Angelica was not here. She'd never apologized, and so she'd never been invited.

Tears pricked Serena's eyes at that thought, but she gripped her hands into fists and blinked them back. She would not cry. She'd rather *die*.

Before she could decide her next steps, the door creaked open. She looked at it in the mirror, still too fragile to move, then nearly fumbled right there at the sight of Luciano entering the room. But she didn't whirl. She didn't sob. She stood completely and utterly still and regarded his reflection in the mirror.

Their eyes met, held there.

He was *here*, and she knew better than to let her hopes soar. There was that grim set to his mouth, that haunted look in his eyes and the fact he wore now what he'd worn last night leaving her.

And carried a folder full of papers.

Serena inhaled carefully, bracing herself for all that was

to come, then turned to face him. Every muscle in her was tense. But she kept her chin up and her eyes cool.

"The wedding planner is looking for you, I believe," she offered when he said nothing. Just stared at her. "And the wedding is due to start soon. Yet you are not dressed. You do not appear ready at all."

He blinked once, then twice, before looking down at the folder in his hand. Serena took this moment of him not looking at her to lower herself into a chair. Maybe if he couldn't see how gently she moved, he wouldn't see through her.

He took a step forward, held out the folder. "I have come to some new conclusions."

"I just bet," she murmured, and she absolutely refused to reach out and take those damn papers, whatever the hell they were.

"I do not need Ascione. You can have it."

He dropped the file of papers into her lap. She didn't want to touch it, so she hesitated, trying to work through his words. What he was saying.

What he wasn't saying.

I do not need Ascione might have been the words he said, but what she heard was *I do not need you.*

So she firmed her mouth, pulled the papers out of the folder. She took her time and made sure her voice would be clipped ice before she spoke.

"While it's good to come to this conclusion before we married under these false pretenses," she said, skimming the document and feeling a strange twist of emotions that she couldn't make sense of. Success. Failure. Love. Hate. And because there was so much inside of her, she treated him to ice when she looked up at him. "I do wish you'd done it before we'd planned everything. Before I'd gotten dressed."

His eyes roamed over her. "You look beautiful."

That just about broke whatever kept her temper firmly frozen, but she was too tired to start a fight. Too tired to do anything but survive.

She pressed a finger to her throbbing temple. "Why are you here, Luciano?"

"It is our wedding."

She snorted inelegantly, eyes still closed against the assault of all this. "I have the sneaking suspicion you weren't planning on attending."

For a moment, he said nothing. "I will not take the coward's way out," he said loftily. "I have given you Ascione outright. It would not do to have someone else deliver this news."

She laughed. It was a little bitter, maybe tinged with hysteria, but she laughed all the same. "What about the news that you don't plan to marry me?"

"You get Ascione."

She opened her eyes and looked up at him, staring for perhaps a full minute. He said it like it was a trade. She got his company. He got to not marry her. It shamed her and made her feel small, and she would have settled there. She would have accepted that.

Before.

Before he'd spent evenings with her watching the movies she liked. Before he'd gone with her to meet their—*her* future puppy. Before he had stood up for her and treated her like she mattered. Not because of how smart she was, or what she could do or represent, but simply because of her.

Because of how he had recognized his own experiences in hers. And everything from that moment had felt real. The unfurling of something...wonderful and lasting.

The ice was melting, and she wanted—needed—to hold

on to it, except she remembered what he'd said about his mother. About trying to save her.

That night had been the changing point. For both of them. She had realized someone might stand up for her, and she had thought he'd realized someone would allow him to.

But he hadn't. Whatever resolve he'd had faded, and that made her anger win. She stood, violently enough that the chair nearly toppled behind her. She stepped toward him, fury propelling her.

"Not take the coward's way out? You are nothing but a coward! But I do not for the life of me understand what you are afraid of." She shook the papers. "Success? Hope? Happiness? Commitment?" Despair wound through her, but it had nothing on fury. "A fake one at that."

"This is not fake, and you know it," he said starkly. "It has become…something else."

Oh, that should not make her heart soar, especially the despairing way he said it. And still… "A coward too afraid to say what is true. But I am not. You're afraid of love?"

"I am not *afraid*. I have chosen a course of action that will keep us both…" She watched him struggle for the word, when he never struggled for words.

"You have chosen to be an absolute idiot."

His mouth firmed. His eyes narrowed. There was anger there in his strained shoulders. "I have given you what you want. I have given you Ascione."

"I don't want—well, no, I still want Ascione." She could not lie about that. Holding the papers was like holding a golden goose. But it was still just a *thing*. She didn't only want a thing. "But I don't *only* want Ascione. I want *you* along with it. I want this—what we've built these past few weeks." She realized in this moment, that she had also been a coward. Because she had been waiting, putting off the inevitable, afraid to tell him what might drive him away.

And he'd driven himself away anyway, so why not drop the bomb he didn't want?

"Luciano, I love you. I think you might know that, but maybe you cannot fathom it. I love you. And I want to marry you. For you. With no worries or concerns about Ascione *or* Valli. I want there to be an us."

Luciano had prepared himself for many responses. Tears. Accusations. Violence, even. That is what he was used to when going into spaces he wasn't wanted.

He should have prepared himself for her ice, and maybe he had tried, but it had still hurt. Gotten under his skin in ways he'd convinced himself it wouldn't. But he'd been holding his own.

Until this.

He had not prepared himself for love. Even knowing she might have convinced herself she had some soft feelings for him, he had not assumed she would use it like...

"Why?" He had not meant to question this out loud. Hated the look of soft concern, too close to pity, that chased over her face.

"Luciano—"

"No." He slashed a hand through the air to get his point across. "No. I have made my choice, my decision. I have given you all that you wanted when you came into my club that night. From here on out, I will focus on my club, which is what *I* built. And you may focus on this." He gestured at the folder. "If your lawyers have qualms on the paperwork, my lawyer will be happy to discuss it with them. This..." He gestured between them. "This cannot be."

She did not have a quick retort to that. So he should leave. Take this silence for what it was and retreat.

His legs would not move. She was the most beautiful thing he'd ever seen. The dress was simple, but it made her look like an angel. She wore the ring he'd picked out for her and little pink diamonds on her ears that matched. He needed to leave because everything in him screamed to move forward, touch, grab.

Beg. For things he still did not fully understand.

Success? Hope? Happiness? Commitment?

She accused him of being afraid of those things. And love. Maybe he was, but it wasn't fear of having them that kept him rooted to the spot.

It was the fear of failing to hold on to these things that mattered. He could fail anyone and everyone. He had, to some extent. But he could not bear the thought of failing her.

"Cannot be," she finally murmured. "Why? What is it that would be so awful about getting married and loving one another? So awful that you would sign away your legacy, retreat to the caricature of yourself you created and pretend that you do not want all the things I know you do?"

It was everything he'd thought, and he did not understand. She couldn't… She couldn't possibly see him for who he was, no matter how right she was in this moment. "You do not know me. What I want."

"I do. Better than anyone," she replied in that clipped, calm way of hers. "Because I believe I am the only one you have ever actually been yourself around."

Yourself.

He shook his head—because he didn't know what being himself even was anymore, but he knew it couldn't be anything she wanted.

"Then you should have the good sense to take this deal

and run, Serena. If you claim to know me, then you would know…" That no one ever loved him. That nothing he did or did not do could change how another person felt.

"I know that you are Luciano Ascione," she said, very firmly. "And I would never call you perfect, but I would certainly call you a good man. One whom I love."

Disgusted, he turned away from her. He wished he could turn away from himself. He did not know how this terrible swath of loathing that he had kept at bay for so many years had somehow grown instead of dying away. "You are the only one."

"Then so be it. I will gladly be the only one." There was fire in her now, blazing from within. "Do you think that matters to me?" she demanded, grabbing his arm and jerking him back to face her. "Me of all people? What anyone else thinks? When I know you? No one else matters."

"How could you know me, Serena?" he demanded, finding his own anger in this whole mess that she would not let him handle appropriately. "I am not certain, after all this, that I know myself."

"Then let me save you this time, Luciano," she said, softer this time. "Let me stand between you and the things others have said about you. You are clever and kind. You are an arrogant bastard when you want to be, but it is not mean. And I think, perhaps, what you are most afraid of is not your own shortcomings so much as the fact you do not know what to do with this."

"With what?"

"You love me, Luciano. This scares you, but it doesn't make you less."

There was an anvil on his chest. Something lodged in his throat. Love. *Love.* This useless emotion that was never, ever reciprocated.

Except she'd already said she loved him. How she could, he did not know, but Serena did not lie. She did not exaggerate. And still...

"Loving me doesn't scare you?" he demanded in a rasp.

"Of course it does," she said, in that same confident and unbothered way she confessed any of her odd little idiosyncrasies. "But being scared is no reason to run away in business, so why should it be in life?"

"You cannot run life like a business." He thought he sounded very sure and worldly then, but she only rolled her eyes. There in her *wedding dress*. Arguing with him about love instead of taking this deal and running.

Like she should.

Like he'd expected her to.

Like he'd *needed* her to in order to survive this rising tide of hope that he knew would end in pain.

Pain.

"I do not see why not," she replied haughtily. "It's all the same. Keep something alive and thriving for as long as you can. Show up every day, work through problems without giving up. It *is* the same. Except for one thing. One matters, Luciano. I..." She inhaled deeply, took a moment, and her eyes were shining now. Which always undid him. It was unfair. To be undone by this woman.

"I had my grandfather when he was alive," she said, her voice quiet now. "And he was also not perfect, but I know he cared for me in his way. And that has meant more than all the successes I ever found at Valli. Because love and care are more important than profits and clients. I have no one now. No one to love and care for—except my animals. And you."

She said it softly, but it landed like a vise around his lungs.

"I could run a Valli-Ascione merger without you. It would be hard, meticulous work. I could do it. I *will* do it if you insist on ruining everything, but you will not walk out of this room under the very wrong conclusion that you have saved us from anything. If you walk, you ruin it. What could be. The future we've both been a little too afraid to admit is possible, but I won't be afraid any longer. What about you?"

She did not understand. Could not. Except every word she said made it feel like she did. But how could he sentence them to this…this…certain disappointment? "Serena."

"You have two choices. You may stay. Get dressed for the wedding and marry me, knowing that we have work ahead of us. A business merger and a life merger. That includes a wide variety of animals, now and in the future. That includes love and difficulties and joy. And children. I think I would like to have children with you."

Children. Just the idea of it sent opposing feelings through him. An icy, paralyzing fear. And a warmth of hope and joy that threatened to melt it.

Children with her brains, her eyes. Children. Theirs. A family. One that would not look like theirs had growing up.

It was impossible. She was saying it was possible, but how could it be? How could it be with him?

"Or you may walk out that door," she continued, when he stood there paralyzed by her words. "But you will not walk back in it." She said this fiercely, and he could see she meant it. She needed to mean it. "Ascione will be gone from you forever." She clutched the papers. "And so will I be. I suggest you make that decision wisely."

Gone forever. Even though that's what he'd planned, the idea of it—with her standing there in white, looking like a beautiful angel, looking like everything that had filled his life with warmth and worth for the past few weeks—cleaved through him like a blade.

She represented everything that had changed him.

Brought him back to life after lying dormant under that caricature. Or perhaps she'd simply taken a moment to see behind the mask, because she held up one of her own.

And because it was her, and because she was annoyingly always so right, he realized that it was more than what she'd done for *him*. He wasn't saving her from *him*, because... This was not one-sided. It was not parent to child.

It was partners.

He had melted her ice. He had stood up for her when she had been fighting alone for so long.

Was that why she loved him? How she could? He had...offered the same thing to her as she had to him. Just like under all their surface differences, they were so much the same.

He supposed it made as much sense as anything. And maybe it was selfish. Maybe that horrible disappointment was waiting for both of them. The fear of it nearly had him walking out.

But he was more afraid of walking out that door and being refused reentry. Because he believed her. She would not give him a second chance. He would not deserve one.

So maybe...like she said, they could show up every day and work on it. If there was anyone in this world he trusted to do that, it was Serena.

Serena. The woman he loved.

"It sounds like blackmail, Serena," he managed to say, though his throat was still tight. "Is that any way to start a life?"

She didn't smile like he wanted her to, but there was *something* in her eyes. Something warm. "All in all? It sounds very on brand for any Valli-Ascione interaction."

He could not help himself. He laughed. He did not know how he could when it felt as if all his safe foundations were crumbling, except that she made everything...better. Right.

Just by being her. And if she could be brave, if she could love him, did he not owe it to her to do the same?

She moved forward, reached out and gripped his arms. She even gave him a little shake, her expression earnest. "Stay. Love me," she said, and it was a demand, but he was not one to be demanded into doing anything.

Unless he already did. "I do," he replied, as seriously as the vows he would soon say. "Love you."

"I know. I'd just take the business if you didn't," she replied haughtily, making him smile.

He pushed a strand of hair behind her ear, studied her beautiful face. "I will make mistakes."

"Horrible ones," she agreed.

"And you will ice me out."

"Most assuredly."

"And we will…show up every day and try in spite of ourselves."

"Every day," she agreed, reaching up to cup his face.

His hands shook as he reached out, as he placed them on her hips, held on to her. His match. His mate. His everything. "Marry me, then, Serena. For real. For love."

Her eyes were full, but she did not cry. "For us," she agreed, and then put her mouth to his.

EPILOGUE

THEY MARRIED IN a splashy society wedding that was the talk of the town, but they said their true vows before—in that little room. When they thought of their wedding, they thought of that.

Because they were happy to give the public that which would suit Valli-Ascione, but it was not the *truth* of them.

Together, they slowly rebuilt their father's destroyed legacies. Until, as the years past, they built their own legacy. Not in any boardrooms or shipping containers, but in their home. The castle on the hill. Full to the brim of animals, and then a handful of children.

And through both, they learned how to love, and how to show it. How to believe and hope, even in spite of the challenges and griefs of life.

They encouraged their children to be their truest selves, and accepted each of them exactly as they were, no matter what challenges arose. They protected and stood up for each other. And when they fought—ice and fire—they always made up on the foundation of love they spent their entire lives building. Showing up, day after day.

It was the *new* Valli-Ascione legacy, rising from the ashes of the old.

Made with love. The kind that lasted lifetimes.

* * * * *

MILLS & BOON®

Coming next month

HER ACCIDENTAL SPANISH HEIR
Caitlin Crews

Something else occurs to me. Like a concrete block falling on me.

Something that should have occurred to me a long time ago.

I count back, one month, another. All the way back to that night in Cap Ferrat.

I stand up abruptly, gather my things and stride toward the front office.

My mind is whirling on the elevator down and I practically sprint out the front of the building then down a few blocks until I find a drugstore. I give thanks for the total disinterest of cashiers in New York City, purchase the test and then make myself walk all the way home to see if that calms me.

It does not.

I throw my bag on the counter in my kitchen and tear open the box, scowling at the instructions.

Then I wait through the longest few minutes of my entire life.

Then I stare down at the two blue lines that blaze there on my test.

Unmistakably.

I simply stand there. Maybe breathing, maybe not.

The truth is as unmistakable as those two blue lines.

I'm pregnant.

With *his* child.

With the *Marquess of Patrias's* baby.

Continue reading

HER ACCIDENTAL SPANISH HEIR
Caitlin Crews

Available next month
millsandboon.co.uk

COMING SOON!

We really hope you enjoyed reading this book.
If you're looking for more romance
be sure to head to the shops when
new books are available on

Thursday 19th
June

To see which titles are coming soon, please visit

millsandboon.co.uk/nextmonth

FOUR BRAND NEW BOOKS FROM
MILLS & BOON MODERN

The same great stories you love, a stylish new look!

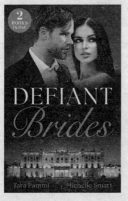

OUT NOW

Eight Modern stories published every month, find them all at:

millsandboon.co.uk

Afterglow Books is a trend-led, trope-filled list of books with diverse, authentic and relatable characters, a wide array of voices and representations, plus real world trials and tribulations. Featuring all the tropes you could possibly want (think small-town settings, fake relationships, grumpy vs sunshine, enemies to lovers) and all with a generous dose of spice in every story.

♪ @millsandboonuk
◎ @millsandboonuk
afterglowbooks.co.uk

#AfterglowBooks

For all the latest book news, exclusive content and giveaways scan the QR code below to sign up to the Afterglow newsletter:

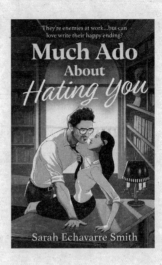

LET'S TALK

Romance

For exclusive extracts, competitions and special offers, find us online:

f MillsandBoon

X @MillsandBoon

◎ @MillsandBoonUK

♪ @MillsandBoonUK

Get in touch on 01413 063 232

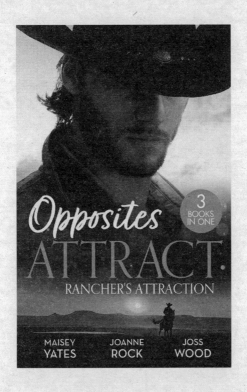

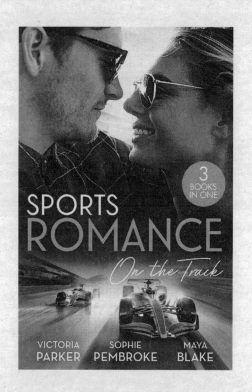